The Mercenary's Daughter

By

JoAnn Cummings

PREFACE

Retired General Theodore Gregory looked up when the door to his office opened. He expected his secretary and hoped she was bringing him some kind of distraction. Immediately, he felt guilty. Deadly situations shouldn't be preferred over paperwork and the only kind of distraction he would get would be a potentially fatal situation—someone else's death. Truth be told, Gregory would rather stare down the barrel of a rifle than stare at a stack of files; war wasn't nearly the hell that paperwork was. When he had a command, he'd had people to do the paperwork for him. The Division of Anti-Terrorism Activities, or "The Division", didn't like a lot of paperwork. Leading an organization opposed to a paper trail had been one of the biggest draws about this job. However, when the paperwork came, it came dumped in a colossal steaming pile on his desk.

The man standing in the doorway looked nothing like his secretary. He didn't look like someone who particularly cared about how organized the general's days were either. He looked like a man delivering exactly what Gregory had accidentally wished for—and to top it off he carried a huge file. Gregory indulged himself a brief moment of irritation about Richard Powell getting around his secretary, Peggy. The irritation drowned in a wave of sour stomach acid. He'd rather do paperwork than hear what had brought the CIA handler across town. Any other CIA rep would have been okay; any other one than this particular man. This man brought only one kind of news.

Normally, Richard Powell was Gregory's opposite: tall, slim, tailored, clean-shaven and pretty. His Italian leather dress shoes made soft whispering noises on the industrial-grade linoleum floor as he closed the door behind him and walked across the office to Gregory's desk. Gregory wouldn't be surprised if the man got those manicure and pedicure things too. He saw this guy at all the society parties Mrs. Gregory insisted on attending. Powell had a different beautiful woman on his arm at each shindig. While Powell seemed to enjoy himself at those expensively adorned gatherings of high society liars and cheaters, Gregory had to listen to his wife complain that he didn't look as "put together" as Powell and other men like Powell—mostly politicians. He wondered if other men heard the same thing from their wives—the wondering kept him from focusing on the one thing which could have brought Powell out of his Manhattan office and down to the basement in Queens. He didn't want to face that. He'd rather do paperwork.

Today, Powell didn't look so "metrosexual" and Gregory found a certain amount of joy in that, a silver lining to a very dark cloud. The man's tie was loose and the buttons at the top of his untucked shirt were open. He had dark rings under his eyes and his face was drawn and pale as if he hadn't slept in days. His hair was uncombed; his beard had grown out in splotchy patches in the way of all men who should never attempt to grow beards. Without a word, Powell sat down in one of the two leather arm chairs in front of Gregory's desk. He barely looked like himself. He certainly didn't look "put together." Gregory wished his wife could see the guy now.

3

The general reached for the unlit cigar lying in a clean ashtray at the corner of his desk. He'd stopped smoking years ago; now Glenda, his wife, nagged him about mouth cancer from chomping on unlit cigars. That woman wasn't happy if she wasn't nagging or complaining; which is why he'd taken this job when he'd retired from the Marine Corps Special Forces. Anything was better than being at home and attending the endless luncheons and cotillions; he loved his wife, but she drove him crazy. Still, his gut knew this was one of those times his job would be as uncomfortable and ugly as one of those functions.

The Division was stuck somewhere between officially sanctioned activities and the really dirty stuff. He wondered if Powell had to do paperwork. Powell represented the really dirty stuff most of the time. The coiffed CIA controller ventured out of his dark hidden hole when one specific topic came up, a topic where Powell and the Division had a mutual interest. The ties that bind, as they say, were strong and hard and personal to both men.

Powell laid a thick folder on the general's desk. The words "MOST SECRET" were stamped on the face of the folder. With the words "do not copy" printed in smaller but equally bright red text below it. He turned the folder to face the general then leaned back in the chair and ran a hand over his mouth and unshaven jaw. He watched Gregory but didn't say anything.

Gregory shoved the cigar in his mouth. He stared at the folder, afraid to touch it, afraid to open it, afraid to see what was inside. But of course, there was only one thing that could be inside. Powell didn't need to say anything. "You found her," Gregory said, the words nearly catching in his throat.

Powell pressed his lips together. He took a deep breath. His haunted eyes seemed to get a faraway look before they returned to the office. It'd been a little more than three months since Gregory had spoken with Richard Powell—since just before Christmas—but the man seemed to have aged. Gray feathered through his temples, lines etched around his eyes and the corners of his mouth. "She is the sole subject which would bring me here, unannounced and in person, with a folder which looks like that, General." His diction was so perfect you could practically see his Ivy League education hovering in the air around him.

Gregory nodded. "Glenda and I will claim the body and take care of the burial."

"General—"

"Don't try to argue with me or fight me on this, Powell." He glared at the man and pointed a thick finger at him. "She was family to us. You know we tried to adopt that girl when she was a toddler? Joe McBrady was one of my boys. Even though I had him discharged for being under age, the man was still one of the best Marines I ever commanded. If I could have looked the other way, he never would have become a mercenary. But he was, and that's not exactly a job for a teenager or a single parent. I had to agree with the wife on that one. We tried to adopt her. She would have been different. She would have been safe."

"I know everything about her, General. Maybe more than anyone. I never stopped looking for her," Powell confessed. "And Alexandria Rae McBrady would never have been safe. Safety was never encoded into her DNA."

Gregory ignored the tinge of irritation in the man's Ivy League voice. He continued on with his tale. "Joe wouldn't have it; and, we thought he was crazy for thinking he could be a mercenary and a single parent. But, we loved her. Glenda still has a closet filled with little girl's dresses for parties which never happened; Glenda thinks she should have been that girl's mother. But Alex was Joe's; she was always his. To you, she was a tool, a stepping stone for your career."

"General—"

"I'd bury her next to her father, but she was so pissed off about her father being buried at that veterans' home in Ohio. I think I'll just have her cremated and take the ashes to Southeast Asia. Joe told me that her home was in the jungle." He pushed his chair back and stood up. He walked to the four drawer file cabinet and picked up a framed photo from the top. Glenda refused to allow the photo in the house because she said it wasn't natural for people to not dress up for photos.

The photo reminded him of a lot of things: that anything was possible, that love didn't change a man but made him a better man, to never let things get too serious, and to never underestimate someone based on appearances. "Jesus, Joe," he said to the man in the photo. "How did it come to this?"

"General—"

Gregory thrust the picture at Powell. "These two people were more alive than any single person I've ever met. How the fuck can they both be dead within a year of each other? If you know who is responsible for this, I want to know."

"General, I—"

Gregory shook his head. He straightened up again and took his cigar out of his mouth, jabbing it in the air as he spoke. "If I'd listened to Joe and fired her, she would have been forced to quit. She wasn't a killer. I should have listened to Joe. If I had, she might still be alive."

"General—"

"What, Powell?! I need to figure out how to tell my wife that the girl she thought of as a daughter died some horrible death in an alley and it took me three months to tell her about it," Gregory barked. "Right after I explain that she died of injuries from being tortured for six months, which I also neglected to mention." He chomped down on the cigar again.

Powell leaned forward and opened the folder.

On top was a surveillance photo of a group of homeless people under some bridge amid boxes and ratty tents covered with patches of snow and dirty slush. At the edge of the group, but in the center of the picture, was a smaller figure dressed in sweats and an oversized Army jacket. Underneath the jacket the person wore a hoodie with the hood pulled up. But the face was turned and a gloved right hand was lifting a silver flask to lips partially hidden by a curtain of tangled dark red hair; the right arm seemed awkwardly bent. The left shoulder of the person hung low, the left arm dangled, hidden by the over-long sleeve. The right foot was turned in.

Gregory stared at the photo, his heart started pounding hard. He lifted his eyes to Powell. He caught the cigar when it fell from his gaping mouth.

"Is it her, General?" Powell asked, his voice tight and demanding and somehow pleading at the same.

Gregory narrowed his eyes. "How the fuck is that possible, Powell?"

"Is it her?" he asked again, speaking slowly and emphasizing each word like a

Gregory shook his head. "She's got to be dead. Hell, it was a miracle we were keeping her alive as it was. But then when she escaped..." His voice trailed off and he stared at the picture.

Powell moved the first photo aside to reveal an enhanced close up of the central figure in the first photo. "Is it her?"

Gregory stared at the grainy face. Despite the problems with the blow up of the photo, despite the gauntness of the face, Gregory felt the impact of recognition in his gut. "When and where was this taken?"

"Two days ago in Cleveland, Ohio."

Gregory shook his head again as if to clear it off cobwebs and the screaming intuition that said what he saw could not be fact. "Her mind was shattered, her body in pieces, she was suffering from heroin withdrawal. How in the hell could a dead woman get from New York City to Cleveland?"

Powell sighed. "So you think it's her too."

"How?"

"She's been frequenting a soup kitchen. They noticed a hospital bracelet on her arm and called the number—our hospital. We sent a drone."

"Why didn't you just go in and get her?"

Powell took a deep breath. He glanced down at the photo Gregory had shoved into his hands.

The photo backdrop was jungle and ruins which could have been Angkor Wat if not for the closeness of the jungle and the clear indication that the place was not tourist friendly. A man sat on a huge toppled stone with a rifle lying casually across his lap. Lean sinewy muscle stung the man together and a weathered tan painted skin shiny with sweat and dirt. The sun had bleached dark hair; sweat curled the shaggy ends. He wore a faded blue shirt with a superman "S" on the front. His cargo pants were khaki colored with loops and pockets; a grenade and several magazines for the rifle were being held in those loops. There was a survival knife strapped to his calf just above black jungle boots. Standing beside him, balancing on the thin edge of a crumbling wall, stood a young girl maybe ten years old. She had red hair in a braid down her back and a dusting of freckles over her cheekbones and the bridge of her nose giving her a little girl look, but it was clear she would be more than a little girl very soon. She wore hiking boots and cut off jean shorts; in between were long legs which seemed to go on forever. Her green tank top had a *Star Trek* logo on it. She was laughing, her head tossed back slightly. Her eyes sparkled with an intensity greater than the man's; however, their familial relationship was clear. The man smirked; but, he was looking at the cameraman too. His eyes held a warning; somehow that look drew one's eye to the calloused, tanned hand resting casually on the rifle with a finger draped over the trigger guard. Joe McBrady had been the guardian of the girl's laughter and her innocence. Joe would have destroyed anyone who tried to destroy her world.

Powell sighed. He looked back up at the gruff retired General. "Before Joe McBrady was murdered—"

"Murdered?" Gregory asked, his voice getting quieter.

"He was gunned down in a warehouse in Honduras, not in the jungles like the official report says."

Gregory stared at the man. Joe McBrady had been one of his men; and later, after Joe'd been kicked out of the Marines, one of his best friends. "Did Alex know that? Jesus shit, Powell, did you send that girl out on a mission of vengeance so you could make her into a killer? Who? Who killed him?"

"The same person who kidnapped and tortured her."

Ted Gregory looked down at the photo. After getting out of the Corps, Joe McBrady joined a mercenary group rather than return to the States. Gregory didn't blame him; Joe McBrady had been a hell of a soldier. The only time Gregory disagreed with Joe was the day Glenda Gregory went behind both their backs and tried to take Joe's baby girl, Alexandria Rae. Alex had spent two days in foster care; well, a lot less than that since she escaped from every place they put her and spent most of her time in a car with a case worker driving to a new place after being caught. She'd been four. He remembered her looking tiny as she sat on the witness stand and told the judge that she didn't care much what they did or where they put her because she'd go back to her dad. She'd said: "He's my daddy and I know he's the best daddy, but you can't have him because he's mine. You're going to have to keep your own daddy." Gregory felt his mouth tug in a grin at the memory. The social workers had made her wear a blue frilly dress. She'd taken the stand barefoot telling everyone she'd given her new pretty shoes to some other child who actually liked them. She wanted her own clothes back, she'd told the judge. When Glenda's attorney asked why she didn't cry when they took her away from her father, she'd told the man she didn't have to cry because she'd find her father, or her father would find her. "No one will ever take my daddy from me," she told the attorney. "But you can keep trying if you want to be stupid." Joe had managed to cough over a laugh; he'd managed not to rub the loss in Glenda's face too. In truth, Ted figured Joe might have killed Glenda if not for his own fatherly relationship with the young soldier.

He remembered Alex at Joe's funeral too, standing stiff and stunned beside the casket. Her father's righthand man at her shoulder as if to give her strength and support. Everyone waiting around for her to break down and collapse. So many hard men with anger in their eyes. Alex back to being that little girl who'd been stunned that someone had apparently managed to take her daddy from her.

Powell cleared his throat, drawing Gregory out of his memories. "It appears that Joe made sure his enemies believed Alex was the weak link. He did everything he could to make sure they would torture him to get the information out of Alex rather than the other way around."

Gregory frowned. "He died."

"I think they figured they could break Alex without using her father."

"Who are they? What did they want?"

"They are the mercs who worked for McBrady. Specifically, Peter Van de Moeter, the man who was Joe's protégé. They are hunting for Alex and have been since her escape. They don't think she's dead."

"How do you know this?"

Powell leaned forward and shoved the satellite picture aside. "Report from the SEAL team that recovered Alex from the mountains in Pakistan." He shoved it aside. "Medical report from the Navy doctors who first treated her." He shoved that report aside which was several pages. "Medical report from the Division doctors."

Gregory grunted.

Powell shrugged. "Your order to have her right arm crippled was redacted. I didn't think it was in anyone's best interest for Alex to find out her right arm was crippled on purpose. Especially if she is alive and unstable."

Gregory clenched a thick fist. "I wanted to make sure--if she lived she wouldn't be a threat to herself or anyone else. She had all that martial arts training, you know. I didn't think she would live anyway. Why did you suspect she wasn't dead; how could you even imagine?"

Powell hesitated. When he spoke again, he spoke choosing his words carefully. "General, you and I both know Alexandria Rae McBrady's CIA training ratings are inaccurate."

Gregory snorted. "As I recall she managed to finish exactly above every cut off. She could shoot like her father and was twice the athlete he was. Glenda kept telling Joe that if he'd let her stay with us, she would have been an Olympian." Hell, she

10

would have been a gold medalist. Too tall to be a gymnast, but she could have made any college team in the country. Amazing and stubborn. Too stubborn to give up and die."

Powell cleared his throat. "The traditional CIA black ops training isn't all she had. We didn't train her to be a thief and a ghost. We trained her to be an assassin. A single asset to take out targets around the world with little backup."

Gregory grunted. On missions he'd sent Alex on, she'd gone out of her way to avoid killing people. Often at the expense of her own safety. "How did that work out for you?"

Powell laughed. "Oh, she failed miserably. She made sure everyone knew she didn't have the stomach to pull a trigger or slash a throat. It was an Oscar worthy performance. I might even have bought it if I didn't have proof that Alex had killed before."

Gregory blinked. He arched a bushy gray eyebrow.

"After her martial arts teacher died, she went to visit her father in the Amazon. He was trapped down and surrounded by heavily armed forces. Alex slipped in through the enemy lines."

"That's what she did. You know that. She was a ghost. You and I both saw her walk around a prison yard filled with murderers and rapists who hadn't seen a woman in years without being bothered. She broke into and out of our best prisons and top secret facilities. Hell, didn't she steal something from the Oval Office?"

Powell grimaced. "Yes, she was a master thief. The Oval Office thing saved me from getting my ass handed to me for recruiting her when it became clear she would not kill or carry a firearm into action. She could have gotten out of her father's camp, unseen. Joe and his mercenaries couldn't though. Those guys were going to have to shoot themselves out and they expected to take heavy casualties. But when the mercenaries launched their attack to escape the jungle, half the enemy camp didn't wake up. Thirteen men dead in their bunks, post mortem exams suggested all thirteen of them had been stabbed or had their throats cut."

"You don't know that was Alex."

"Her training wasn't limited to killing people. She also learned how to resist torture and interrogation." Powell took a deep breath. "Van de Moeter sent us a digital recording of—" his perfect, prep school diction faltered. He swallowed hard. "He recorded her torture and edited it down to three hours which he delivered to us after she escaped from the hospital. That's how we know he was behind Joe's murder and how we know what he wanted from Alex."

Gregory paled. He glanced at the thick medical report— hell, he'd seen Alex in the hospital and was certain she was going to die. He didn't think someone could live through what she had, but there she'd been. "Why would he do that?"

Powell sighed. "To make sure we were afraid to let Joe McBrady's daughter loose. To make sure we would want to hunt Alex down just as much as he does. To make sure we wouldn't assume she was dead because we'd see how strong her will to live actually was." He swallowed and closed his eyes. "And he accomplished all those things."

Gregory saw the man compose himself. Powell wasn't military, but he should be accustomed to violence.

"You are going to need to watch that recording, General. So will the team you send after her."

"Send after her?"

"Alex McBrady knows the location of seven dirty bombs hidden around the United States. Her father found a ledger which he refused to give up. Peter thinks that ledger went to Alex. The only person Joe would have trusted with something like that is Alex. These are bombs planted by a KGB agent during the height of the Cold War; the agent died of radiation poisoning and never gave up the locations of the bombs."

"Joe had seven nuclear bombs?!"

"Alex has them or knows the locations where they are hidden. Alex is trained by CIA covert ops for wet work. She's a woman who has, in all probability, lost her mind. Avenging her father's death may be the only thing keeping her alive. Joe would kill anyone who hurt his daughter and he died making sure his daughter would be the one to deliver the punishment to the person who betrayed him."

"You're saying Joe McBrady set up his own daughter as a weapon," Gregory said. "Joe wouldn't do that." But even as he said the words, he wasn't so sure. Joe McBrady knew the price of war and he was better than anyone Gregory had ever met at making sure the price for winning was paid. If he'd been able to deal with authority and able to wait until he was of age, Joe McBrady could have won the fight with Middle Eastern terrorists. Gregory believed Joe McBrady's name would have been spoken in the same breath as MacArthur, Grant, Washington, and Patton. "So, let's go get her and just ask her where they are."

"She might tell someone she trusts where those bombs are. But who does she trust? She killed three people in the hospital while escaping."

Gregory's eyes widened. "What? I thought she could barely walk."

"Yeah, we buried those murders too. The report of her escape is in there as well, General. We couldn't really let the world know that a killer we trained is on the loose and probably completely insane. We need to find the bombs before Peter finds them and sells them off to our enemies. Or before she uses them to kill Peter Van de Moeter."

"She wouldn't."

"Get her to talk. Or stop her."

"That's cold."

Powell narrowed his eyes at the man. "You won't appreciate how cold until you watch that video. Then you'll know I'm a fucking bastard. Use that team you always sent in to do the killing when you pulled her out of a mission. Those four guys were her friends. She'll be vulnerable and, with her father gone, she'll need someone to lean on emotionally. Use that to get the bombs."

Gregory took his cigar out of his mouth. He ran a thick, calloused hand over his short gray hair.

13

Powell rose from his chair and met the general's scowl with one of his own. "Whatever you think of me, I would have done anything to spare her what's on that recording." He sighed. "Don't underestimate her, General. I need you to get those bombs before someone detonates them. I need you to convince her to tell you where they are. I need you to use whatever means necessary."

"What then?"

Powell's face went blank. "We'll cross that bridge—"

"Bullshit, I won't let you kill her."

Powell gave a hollow laugh. "I'm not sure I can, General."

General rolled his eyes and laughed. "She's not immortal."

Powell shook his head. "Find her, General. Get those fucking bombs before we have a disaster." He turned and walked out of the office without another word.

A second later, Peggy came in. "General, I'm so sorry. I don't know how he got in—" She stared at him for a minute. "Are you okay?"

Gregory looked up from the photo. "She's not dead."

Peggy furrowed her brow. "How is that possible? How can she be alive?"

"Call up the extraction team. They have two hours to get here. Until then I don't want to be disturbed."

"Of course," Peggy said. She hesitated as she turned back to her own desk. "I'm glad she's alive, but after what she suffered…well, I almost hoped."

Gregory nodded. "Close the door behind you, okay?"

She nodded, frowned and stepped back out, pulling the door closed behind her.

Gregory took a deep breath. He pushed the thumb drive into the computer. There was a slight whirring sound, then the screen went black.

As the scene lightened and started to clear, he could make out the image of a woman tied to a metal chair. She was barefoot. She wore jeans which were stained with something dark that might have been blood. She wore a white shirt, but the left shoulder was bloody and clearly sported a bullet wound. The stone floor was wet.

"Wake her up," a digitally altered voice ordered.

That was how it began.

It took nearly ten minutes of edited tape—probably a couple of weeks in real time—for Alex to scream. The scream filled his office. He jerked in surprise. He fumbled for the sound button.

Peggy rushed in, her eyes wide behind her thick glasses. A lock of gray hair falling from her bun.

Another scream filled the office.

Peggy paled.

Gregory found the pause button. Then he found the bottle of Jack Daniels in the bottom drawer of his desk. He also had a glass there. His hand shook as he poured a finger of whiskey. When he remembered that the bottle had been a gift from Joe McBrady, he threw the entire drink back in one big swig so he could fill it to the rim. "Peggy, shut the door," he said, his voice shaky. He took a deep swig from the second glass. "Do you know where I put my lighters?"

"In the back top drawer."

"Thanks. It'll be quieter from now on, Peggy. I'm sorry I disturbed everyone."

When the door was shut again, Gregory fumbled for a lighter and lit the cigar. He inhaled deeply and steeled himself for more.

The recording ended with Alexandria Rae McBrady screaming and writhing on the floor. Even as she screamed she laughed at the people hurting her.

Gregory turned his attention back to the grainy photo and the enhancement of the homeless woman with dark red hair. What he saw was a smaller, female version of the kid who'd lied about his age to get into the Marine Corps. Joe McBrady had been the victim of horrific child abuse. Joe had a wild, I-don't-care-if-I-die look in his eyes when he first showed up in the desert. People mistook suicidal thoughts for bravery out there. He'd debated whether to reveal Joe's age and get him thrown out, in the end, he'd chosen to follow the rules. Instead of leaving, Joe joined up with some mercenaries. Less than a year later, someone apparently delivered a baby to him, in the middle of a firefight. Joe's story was that he'd had an affair with a slave of some Arab sheik and she'd sent the child.

Joe'd already been a hard ass when that baby got delivered. He was barely twenty years old, but in many ways older than men twice his age. He could have refused the baby. However, something about the baby changed him, it saved him. According to Joe, the mother had left a single note with the child: "The baby is yours. Make sure she grows up to never be the victim I was. Make her strong and independent. Make her grow into a woman who is never afraid." Joe'd relayed that information at the custody hearing.

Alex had saved Joe.

Gregory wondered what kind of luck he would have trying to save the daughter.

He pulled the zip drive from his computer and stood up. He didn't feel drunk; and he half suspected his wife had replaced the whiskey with water and food coloring. He walked out into the outer office.

Peggy looked up from her computer screen. "Sir?"

"We had Alex test the security of the holding cells here, right?"

Peggy nodded. "Of course, General."

Alex's job description had been pretty simple: test security systems for the federal government, act as a courier between covert agents and handlers in hot zones, and steal things the government wanted. Gregory frowned. "Have someone else test one and keep it empty. Did we ever revoke Alex's computer password?"

"When she went missing, we hoped she would give up the code and we could track someone breaking into our computers," she said.

"Revoke all access. Mark her as rogue. Throw her face into the system."

Peggy's eyes widened.

Gregory didn't make sure Peggy did her job, neither did he repeat his order. She would do what she needed to. Gregory carried the zip drive and the file to the conference room.

The Division's extraction team was already waiting for him. Four men. Alex's only friends. He was going to ask them to use that friendship and to betray it if necessary. But they were Marines and their country came first. He took a deep breath and ordered them to sit.

CHAPTER ONE

I am drunk, Alexandria Rae McBrady thought to herself as she limped into the soup kitchen. *Perhaps I have overplayed this part.* If someone on the outside were to describe her state of mind, "drunk" would have come far down the list. The list would have been topped with the word "homicidal." People all over the globe were concerned about her state of mind at the moment. Alex put drunk in the top five and left homicidal further down.

Outside the soup kitchen, three members of the Division's rescue team hid on the street, oblivious to her observation. Their leader skulked in the shadows behind the soup kitchen's steam table. It'd taken two months; but, the assholes at the Division and the CIA were predictable. Alex knew they'd come and she knew they'd send the four man rescue team who'd worked with her at the Division Against Terrorist Activities. These were four of her six candidates for her next premeditated murder.

The ground beneath her feet moved like waves of an ocean. She had an uncanny sense of balance; but, staying upright took concentration. Concentration which slipped through her grip when she tried to hold tighter; she would have appreciated this irony if she'd been sober. Sucking in a deep breath of cold air, Alex stepped across the threshold as if she were entering from stage right. *The curtain lifts. Act One begins.* She moved with the deliberate purpose of the outrageously inebriated. She concentrated on the injuries inherent in the role she'd chosen.

In many ways, her father had scripted this play. If not actors, these people she played were chess pieces making their predictable moves. Her father had known the game. She couldn't explain how she still lived, like a character in a play you thought died in *Act One*, but returned for the final curtain. She couldn't explain things that defied the very physics she'd spent her life depending on. Her father had been the man always telling her to believe in miracles and magic. She depended on her balance to keep her upright when she was drunk; she depended on the sun to set and to rise the next day. These things should be set facts like her injuries, set facts. One could not regrow lost parts or recuperate from obliterating injuries. On should not regrow or recuperate.

She resisted the urge to sigh against the anxiety her role inflicted on her.

Today, her costume consisted of untied boots, gray sweatpants darkened in most places from the March rain, and an oversized Army jacket with the insignia and rank patches pulled off. Underneath the jacket, she wore an extra-large black hoodie with the hood pulled up over her head. She hid her face inside the hood. Beneath the hoodie she wore two more layers: a t-shirt and a thermal long-sleeved shirt. Her long hair hung in wet strands like a curtain to further hide her face from the light. If there'd been a script, she wanted to be listed under the label "crippled, drunk homeless person."

Three months ago, Division doctors had shaved her head and removed a chunk of her skull to relieve swelling. There had never been a surgery to return the block of skull; the long strands of hair were connected to an intact skull, not a wig. She shouldn't be alive. *But you are*, said the voice in her head. *You are alive to fulfill your destiny. Pull your weapon and be what you promised to be.* This voice had offered her a choice as she lay dying: die or sell your soul into slavery and get the revenge you desire. It talked to her a lot these days, cajoling her to violence and mocking her choices to avoid it. Perhaps she really was crazy. Perhaps it had been more than three months ago. Time confused her. *Pull the weapon and it will all go away. Spill blood and let me drink up souls and I will set you free.*

Some spaced out mad killer would fall into the grip of this voice; a power hungry egotist would slip into the insanity it offered. It wasn't a hallucination; the voice was real. Opposing this constant voice in her head, Alex's best friend urged her to become a pacifist who spoke softly, clearly, and without hidden agendas. Still others, an organization called the Offspring and the CIA, wanted her to be a pawn for their political agendas. She would not become what the voice wanted, what her best friend wanted, or what the politicians desired. She would be what she wanted to be. Her insanity would be her own, not the insanity of some director—not even her father.

She had made a promise in exchange for an impossible return. She would fulfill her promise and get what she wanted at the same time. She would not succumb to the temptations of the voice or the promises of the monk who was her best friend, or the controls of people who thought they knew what they were speaking about. The weapon whose voice she heard could drink to sooth its bloodlust when she gave it permission, not when it demanded. She would watch the guilty ones die. Then, she could die like she should have months ago. Death didn't scare her. Death felt like a familiar friend with a welcoming warm embrace.

Her father taught her that a plan was only as good as the first five seconds, then the rest of all those tedious hours of strategy would probably be shot to hell. Adaptability won the war. When your target is clearly in your crosshairs, strike quick and strike hard, her father would advise. Do not let them walk away. She should have listened sooner; but she'd had to learn things the hard way. She hadn't learned soon enough to save her father or herself. But now, she understood. People would pay for the things they'd accomplished by spilling her father's blood.

She swayed in the doorway and her right shoulder leaned against the door frame. It was hard to remember being crippled with a foggy brain. She forced herself to remember where all the body parts should be and how they should react. Her right leg dragged and her foot was turned in at an awkward angle. Her right arm was bent, stiff, and held close to her body. Her left arm hung low and dangled uselessly at her side. A normal person would be cursed with chronic pain. *A normal person would have died within the first month of that torture. You have never been normal.* Alex ignored the voice and focused on remembering all of those injuries, of trying to be a product of the medical reports rather than a miracle they would want to dissect.

She dragged her dead right foot over the raised threshold into the soup kitchen. The humid heat of the soup kitchen suffocated her front while the cold from outside chilled the back of her thighs. She paused, swaying.

Kathy, the manager of the place, closed the outside door. The retired trauma nurse had been trying to engage Alex for months. It'd been Kathy who'd picked up the dropped hospital wristband and made the connections. Alex had been practically dropping hints all around them, hoping the CIA would pick up on them and come looking. They hadn't; so, she'd used Kathy. Two months of winter in Cleveland, Ohio, made her a little desperate. The real homeless were more dedicated to their state of discomfort than she was.

Alex refused to allow a panic attack. The claustrophobia was real, like the voice in her head, like the missing time, like the fact that her hair was too long, like the fact that she should have permanent damage from everything she'd been through. Despite the cold outside, Alex would have chosen outside over the walls. However, there were some positives. Usually filled with a few diners, the small dining area was empty of patrons

21

this afternoon. The steam table was completely unmanned. The pastor hid in the shadows of the hall between the steam table and the kitchen area. With the pastor stood the leader of the extraction team, Marine Corps Captain Sinjin Doucet. Then there were Kathy and Carol, the woman who signed everyone into the soup kitchen. Four hearts: racing, beating. One drunken heart beating hard and slow and calm. The tension felt like another occupant in the room, dense and heavy in the heated air, like a predator hiding in the brush of a dense tropical jungle. She squinted against the overhead lights. She preferred to hide during most days and roam at night. See, she silently told the voice in her head, you've made me into a fucking vampire. *You want to spill blood, not drink it. Subtle difference, but an important one, my friend.*

Alex grimaced. She wasn't that thing's friend; she was its hostage. She heard it chuckle inside her head, the incessant mocking laughter. She took a deep breath and shuffled to the sign-in table.

Carol, the sign-in lady, watched her drunken shuffle with far too much interest. The wide woman wore a cotton shirt with oversized flower prints and polyester pastel pants; her shirts was stained with whatever she'd eaten, something yellow, maybe mustard. During the last two months, Carol had proven to be arrogant, treating all the people who came in to the soup kitchen like mange-infected puppies who deserved, at best, nothing more than to live under a porch. She talked too much. She thought she was an authority on too many things.

The sound of smacking gums as Carol prepped herself to talk made Alex shudder. If she closed her eyes, she could sometimes feel the punches that had struck her face and cracked her jaw. She should have lost teeth. Part of her remembered them cracked and flying out of her mouth or choking her. She opened her eyes quickly and shook her head, to stop the memory from taking over.

Drunk and pretending to be crippled, the shudder came off more like a violent twitch that almost toppled her unsteady balance. She ran her tongue over her teeth, checking all of them.

Carol leaned forward and tried to get a look at Alex's face.

Alex's mouth twitched in the shadows behind the curtain of stringy wet hair. This woman had never paid attention to her; Alex was just another cipher in a world of strays. If she didn't already know the Division Marines were here, she would have known from Carol's curiosity to see the face of the person who'd attracted so much attention. She swayed in front of the table. The lights caught highlights of red in her dark, wet hair. When dry, Alex's hair was a deep dark red, like garnets or Merlot poured by candlelight. Or like her blood drying on a cave floor in Pakistan. Her blood. Drying. On a cave floor.

She twitched again.

The woman pushed the sign-in book towards her and held up a pen.

Alex flinched at the aggressive move. She heard Kathy make a disapproving sound behind her.

She reached for the pen with her right hand and pretended to misjudge the distance three times before her fingers finally found it. When she did, her dirty fingers appearing out of the too long sleeves, she fumbled and dropped it. She pretended not to notice and brought her hand to the book.

Then she stared at her hand as if the pen had vanished into thin air.

"Grace," Kathy said. Her voice filled the room's silence.

Alex flinched again, faked this time. Her entire body turned as a unit instead of a twist.

Kathy stood behind her, but not too close. "Honey, go on and sit down. I will get you something to eat. You need to eat."

Alex hesitated and hunched her right shoulder only as if she were trying to crawl into the oversized, army surplus jacket. She hoped she could pull off timid; it wasn't an easy act. Drunk and insane came easier.

Kathy's voice changed to a touch more authoritative. "Grace, you aren't the first one to have a bad couple of days. We all have them and you're entitled to yours. Go on. Sit."

Alex turned to the door; her back to the four people in the room. She wanted to make sure Captain Sinjin Doucet could see how her left shoulder hung a lot lower than her right one. For a long minute, she stared at the door to the outside. The room grew quiet; the only noise was the hum of the water cooler and the clicking of one of the trays on the steam table. Master teachers in the monasteries around the Far East used silence like a bubble around themselves. For the masters, silence became a living thing like a billboard hanging above their heads identifying their skill set. The silence controlled the students—for the most part, Alex had been a challenge to every teacher she'd ever studied with. Alex could not be controlled.

Until now, the voice taunted. Shaking the moment of stillness.

She let go of the silence so it could filter away. Most martial arts masters reveled in that silence and that calm; Alex did not. She didn't want anyone to sense the power of the monster which lived inside her. Sometimes she envied the peace others found; but, she never envied the boredom which came with peace. She dragged her right foot across the aged white and black squares of the floor: faux tiles nicked and scratched and damaged, drunk and crippled with their attachment to this place. She kept her body stiff and her left arm low and dead. Scarred into a statue barely able to move, homeless and dirty, lost and unstable; she thrust this image through the silence in order to bring it to life through force of will alone. Until further notice, that image would be her identity.

Eight red and white checkered tables filled the front of the soup kitchen. When she'd first started showing up here, the red and white checkers on top of the black and white squares on the floor hurt her head. Now, the Formica tops seemed to mock Alex with their silence and their scars. Behind her, she felt Carol's eyes on her back. Behind Carol, a podium and a crucifix stood ready for the preacher to bring it sound. Posted on the wall above a table covered with dirty trays and a trashcan, a sign announced: "Though I walk through the valley of death, I shall fear no evil; for thou art with me. Thy rod and thy staff comfort me." Alex preferred the comfort of sharp blades; but each to their own. She had a doctorate in the philosophy of theology and could have argued with the things she'd heard from that podium during the last two months. She'd silently cursed her decision to play mute more than once.

A steam table where the food was kept warm and served cafeteria style filled the back of the room. Today's meal looked like meatloaf, mashed potatoes, gravy and green beans floating in water. The smell of the beans and the meat mingled in the moist heat and rolled in her liquid-filled stomach. On the wall with the front door, a dry erase board listed the rules: no cursing, no smoking, no weapons, no inappropriate behavior, no alcohol, no illegal drugs, and respect other patrons and staff. The chairs at the tables, four chairs per table, did not match and many sported holes in latex cushions.

Alex swayed slightly as she moved, not completely faked. It was mid-afternoon, and she'd been drinking whiskey since before dawn. She'd been awake for more than 36 straight hours. She collided with two chairs before falling into one at the table in the far corner of the room, the darkest corner. With her stiff right arm, she made a production of pulling her right leg in so that it was straight under the table. She slouched in the chair. Her right hand shook as she pulled the hood forward to hide her face more; she did this awkwardly as if her arm wouldn't bend completely to reach her head. Her back was to the room; but, she could feel the focus of attention. The frosted windows reflected the motion of bodies behind her. If not for the reflection, she wasn't entirely certain she could have dealt with the turning her back on them all.

She rocked slightly as she watched Kathy grab a red tray from the pile at the end of the steam table, then move to the hallway which connected the eating area with the kitchen. Kathy stopped just inside the hallway. Her voice was a harsh whisper. Alex had trained herself to listen to whispers, the

25

product of an overly curious mind. For years, she'd used her excellent hearing as a way of making people think she was psychic. *That's your game, not mine,* the voice chided. *But, it also keeps you alive.*

"Let her eat first," Kathy pleaded.

"I would, if there was time, ma'am," replied a deep Cajun voice which rolled slowly like the bayous where he'd grown up. Alex knew him well, a tall man with thick dark hair and a perpetual tan that spoke of his Native American heritage. His accent charmed women. She'd watched women practically swoon just to hear him talk. He had the chiseled body to pull it off.

Kathy wasn't moved by the smooth show of masculinity or the southern charm. One of the reasons Alex liked the woman was for her practicality. "You've waited two days for her to show up, what's another twenty minutes? She probably hasn't eaten in those two days. Alcoholics go on benders where they don't eat anything. She smells like a brewery."

Alex thought that was a kind description of how she smelled. She had been living on the streets since January. She showered at the dojo where she trained, but she always put the same clothes back on to return to the streets. She could sometimes practically feel the fleas. Just the thought made her twitch—it was good for effect anyway.

The Cajun voice replied: "I will make sure she eats as soon as I know she's safe, ma'am."

Kathy sighed. "She's suffering, Captain. Surely you can see that."

The pastor's voice came next, louder than the other two voices. Alex disliked the sniveling pastor almost as much as she disliked Carol. "These men are her friends, Kathy. They will take care of her. You asked for someone to come and help her. That's why they're here. Captain Doucet promises to get her the treatment she needs." The pastor had been charmed by the smooth-talking, pretty boy captain, but then Alex expected nothing less from him and Carol.

"They've done such a fine job of helping her so far. His three friends are standing outside with guns ready to shoot her if she runs," Kathy replied.

Alex stifled a smirk. She liked Kathy. She almost felt guilty for lying to the woman.

"No one is armed," the Cajun told her with his smooth charm cranked to full blast. "We aren't her enemies." Alex had watched them stow their weapons in a dark SUV several hours ago while they were staging up to wait. She'd been on a roof, chugging Cutty Sark from a bottle. She'd been watching for the people who were following the Marines, the ones who'd been alerted by the traitor in her group of "friends." Putting away their guns had been a mistake. *Playing this game is a mistake,* the voice said. Alex ignored the voice.

The pastor put his two cents in again. "Now Kathy, you've been trying for months to get Grace to open up to you and trust you enough to get her the help she needs."

"If she's my friend, her name isn't Grace," the Cajun told them. "My friend's name is Alex. Maybe it isn't her." But Alex heard from his tone that he'd already decided on her identity. And why shouldn't he? They'd played a game of circling each other for years. Alex wondered if that game, that circling, had led Doucet to turn her over to Peter Van de Moeter. Who'd decided to stow the weapons? Who'd opened the door for Peter's men to win any confrontation here?

Peter had been her father's righthand man. He was also her father's murderer. He'd kidnapped her and tortured her. Someone had set her father up. Someone had set her up. That someone would die. She wondered if Doucet fit the bill. Of course, Peter and his traitorous aide weren't the only ones who would die by her hand. She'd made a deal to kill the one who pulled Peter's strings. The person who claimed to want some dirty bombs from Peter actually wanted another weapon. Alex had bought her own life with the promise to kill the person behind Peter—kill him with a sword—with THE sword. One death for her father. One death for herself. One death for whatever had managed to give life back to her. Three deaths and then she could surrender a last breath.

"I've been looking for her for a long time," Doucet said, his low voice rolling out all the charm.

Kathy snapped, "I can imagine how difficult it is to keep track of a crippled girl who can't walk and can't speak, Captain."

Her harsh, sarcastic voice made Alex jerk in surprise.

Doucet continued to be steady, strong and unflappable. "Less than a year ago, Alex was a beautiful woman and an amazing athlete. It hurts to see her like this." His voice came out from the hallway.

Alex watched him in the reflection, moving around Kathy, coming out into the open. Shadows moved in front of the frosted windows. A fight. The mercenaries were moving in, taking down the three Division men outside. Her heart seemed to slow down. Adrenalin leached into her muscles. She held on to the drunk even as it began to retreat.

Kathy put her hands on her thick hips. "She's still those things. It takes an athlete to push through the kind of chronic pain she must endure. I assumed she'd been in some kind of car accident or something. Someone did this to her; didn't they?"

"Ma'am, I'm not allowed to say."

"She never says a word or makes a sound."

"She can't. She screamed so loud and so hard that her vocal cords shredded. That's why she doesn't talk," Captain Sinjin Doucet replied. He cleared his throat as if the thought bothered him, as if he'd been there.

Alex felt a wave of unfocused anger. Peter and his cameras. Humiliation broadcast to make them think she was insane. She could use that though; she could use it to fuel her dedication to this game.

Doucet continued on. "I promise you, Kathy, I will get her help; but, I can't let someone hurt her again. And they *are* after her, ma'am."

In the windows, Alex watched the reflection of the big Cajun step into the dining area of the soup kitchen from behind the steam table. The shadows on the other side of the window had marched off. Probably around back so they could come in through the empty kitchen. Bringing the unarmed and over-powered Division men with them, no doubt. It was bad strategy and the Division men should not have let it happen. Granted, these four specialized in rescue missions not abduction missions; but, they still had some of the best training in the world. Their leader had left his backup in the line of fire. Not good strategy. Unless he had no fear of being shot.

Alex listened to Doucet approach; the nearly silent rub of rubber soles on old linoleum marked his progress. His reflection in the glass grew as she watched it through a curtain of hair. She braced herself. All her instincts told her to turn and face him; but, she held them all in check and waited.

"Alex?" he said, his Cajun accent thick. "It's me. Sinjin." He reached out and touched her right shoulder.

She jolted out of the chair, toppled another chair, and shoved the table over the linoleum. She hit the floor hard and shoved herself away from the towering Marine Corps captain using only her left leg, dragging her right leg as if it were dead weight. One of the chairs hit her head; her back hit the wall below the window. She kept shoving herself against the wall with her left leg and brought her right arm up to protect her head. It happened better than she'd envisioned it would.

The towering man jerked back in shock, then stepped towards her as if to help. Alex couldn't see his face because of her hood and her own act. *Concern or indifference on his face? Would that really tell you if he was dirty or not?* Alex knew figuring out the traitor wouldn't be as easy as seeing a look on a face; she was going to have to force the traitor to betray her again. She wasn't sure how she was going to make that happen yet.

Sinjin leaned down to her with a hand outstretched.

"Don't," Kathy ordered. The retired nurse pulled the Marine back and crouched down where the table had been. She made no attempt to get any closer to the cowering woman on the floor. She waited. After a minute, after Alex stopped trying to push away with her leg, Kathy spoke. "It's okay. No one is going to hurt you, Grace. I promise."

Alex's harsh rapid breath was the only reply.

"Grace, can you hear me?" Kathy asked, not expecting an answer. "You are okay. Listen to my voice."

Alex's forced her breath to sound harsh without whimpering or moaning. She made her right arm shake violently as if she were terrified.

Kathy pressed her lips together. Empathy passed like pain over her face.

Alex felt guilty for that pain. She thought Kathy was a genuinely good person.

"Grace. You're okay. You're in the soup kitchen here in Cleveland," she said in a calm voice.

"Her name is Alex," Doucet said.

Alex turned to hide in the corner as a dry heave shuddered through her body, visible even through the layers of clothing. She'd been drinking enough that the faked dry heave almost became a real heave.

Kathy rose, pulling herself up to her full five feet two inches. She glared into the captain's dark eyes. "She's having a flashback. You don't know what that's like."

Doucet held a hand up. "I have been in the military a long time. I know what PTSD does. And I know what happened to her. It's probably not PTSD; it's probably flat out insanity."

Kathy put her fists on her soft hips and glowered at the big man.

Alex admired the woman's bravery; however, she wondered if it was particularly smart. The woman didn't look like she could back up her spunk. Doucet would have a problem hitting a woman; maybe Kathy assumed that was true of all men. Some women did assume that; Alex had witnessed that naiveté many times and the shock on the face of the woman after the first blow.

Kathy didn't back down from the towering mountain of Cajun muscle. "I missed the part where you showed me your degree in psychiatry, Captain," she snapped.

"Ma'am," Doucet said, laying on his Cajun charm thick, "this woman is dangerous."

Kathy sighed. "Captain, I'm too old to be snookered in by a cute accent and a pretty face."

Alex would have snickered if she hadn't been playing the mute.

Kathy continued. "This woman has trouble walking when she's sober. One arm is paralyzed and one arm barely works. The only person she can hurt is herself. She's not capable of hurting anyone."

"If there's any hurting to be done, I'll take care of that," a dry, hard voice announced.

Alex had been too busy with her crazy drunk act to notice the man who had entered the soup kitchen from the back prep area. Her heart started racing, the alcohol fled from the sudden adrenalin dump.

Bring in Peter's mercenaries stage left.

Somehow, despite the fact that there were only six people in the universe who knew where to look for her, Peter's people had found her too. *Go figure*, the voice in her head said with dripping sarcasm.

The Cajun's hand reached for a weapon he didn't have. Whoever sold her out had now crossed the line of selling out his teammates as well; desperation was good for the soul and it was better for making mistakes. Behind her curtain of hair, she smirked.

Now, you will be forced to fight, the voice in her head whispered, like a serial killer's whispering seduction in the ear of his next victim. *Pull the sword and join me.* She had promised her best friend, the man she'd known her entire life and who'd grown up to be a monk, that she would try to kill the three people she'd set a target on without collateral damage. She promised she would not kill unless she had to survive. She lifted her head just slightly so she could see the room from under her hood. She wondered when she could cross the line without breaking her promise. The voice in her head chuckled softly. She felt its hunger. It hadn't really been a promise.

But she wouldn't fight, she wanted to be abducted again. *Stupid*, the voice whispered.

The mercenary who'd spoken had a familiar face. He'd worked for her father. She couldn't remember his name, but then she'd never gotten cozy with her father's men— mercenaries were hard, dangerous people and her father only let her talk to the few he trusted. Even then, he'd kept a close watch. This one entered with another man directly behind him, a man with a rifle.

This second mercenary pushed the pastor towards Carol and her sign-in table.

Carol was sucking in breath and letting out a high pitched keening sound. Red splotches dotted her soft, loose face.

The procession started. Four more mercenaries led in three beat-up Marines who should never have allowed themselves to get caught. The mercenaries had weapons and were dressed in black—clearly someone had watched too many movies. *And not the right kind of movies,* the voice said with a chuckle. *Skip the war movies, go straight to the martial arts movies.* Each of the three men of the Division team had their hands duct taped behind their backs and a weapon pressed against their spines. The Division men were dressed in various civilian outfits designed to make them look like they fit in on the streets.

All of the three exchanged embarrassed looks with Doucet as they marched into the dining area and were forced to their knees in front of the steam table. All three of them glanced around the room until their attention landed on her, huddled on the floor in the furthest, darkest corner, behind a toppled chair. Their faces were studies on stoicism.

Alex had six suspects for Peter's inside man. Four of them were in this room. The other two were in New York City: General Theodore Gregory and Richard Powell. These four made up the Division team specializing in extraction, rescue, and recover. They came to get her out of the various countries when she managed to get into trouble in while working for the Division. She had called for help the day Peter and his mercenaries ambushed her. Someone had hung up the phone.

This team had become her friends; not friends who knew all the secrets of her soul like Guang, the monk who'd run the Himalayas with her as a toddler. However, she had considered them more than acquaintances. Captain Sinjin Doucet was the leader of the rescue team. His NCO was Staff Sergeant Frank Dyer, her father's best friend who'd fought with him in the Middle East and a man she'd called "Uncle" while growing up. Lieutenant Mitchell Ong, a medical doctor and a computer expert, was the grandson of Chinese immigrants; his father still ran a martial arts school in San Francisco and his grandfather had run from Chinese communists. The last member of the team did all the driving and flying: Sergeant Trevor Prince; she'd spent a lot of her time off with him in his native Hawaii where he'd taught her how to surf and introduced her to the joys of Spam. All of that a lifetime ago. *It was a different life*, the voice mocked her.

Gregory and Powell had more power than these four, but less opportunity. Richard Powell, her CIA handler, had tied his career to her and had been disappointed when she refused to kill for him. General Gregory had commanded her father and he'd once tried to rip her away from her father. Both of these men had access to her training records—her father warned her those would come back and bite her in the ass one day. The four Marines of this team were more likely suspects. Every one of them had seen her in action—and damn it hadn't been easy to go through the shit the Division sent her through without killing anyone and at the same time make it look like she'd just been lucky. None of them had seen all she was capable of.

Doucet was a student of the *tenshin shoden katori shinto-ryu*, a fairly exclusive martial art school which only had one teacher outside of Japan. The school focused on eight separate art forms: sword art, the art of drawing the sword, the art of using both a long sword and short sword simultaneously, staff art, glaive art, spear art, spike throwing art, and unarmed grappling. Doucet was one of the senior American students and he believed it was his favor with his master which had allowed Alex to spar with him in the *dojo* when both of them had been in the city. While she'd always made sure to let Doucet win any sparring match they had with each other, his wins were never easily obtained. His teacher, his *sensei*, didn't allow her to spar because of Doucet; he allowed her to spar in his *dojo* because it honored him to have her there.

Dyer had vacationed with her and her father when she was a kid. If anything had happened to her father while she was still a minor, Alex suspected Dyer would have been her father's chosen guardian. Surely, Joe would not have sent her to the horrors that awaited her at the Gregorys' household with their servants and lacy dresses. Dyer was all about the Marine Corps. He'd served with her father under Gregory in the Middle East and had been there when her father got thrown out.

Ong was a nerd who understood the culture where she'd grown up but also the American culture. They
shared a love of movies and science fiction television. Of the entire team, he was probably the only one who knew she was smarter than she pretended. He didn't know about the doctorate she'd earned, but he knew she'd taken classes beyond a bachelor's degree.

Prince and she had once spent an entire afternoon racing wave runners on Lake Erie around her father's island, pushing them to their limits; they were both major adrenalin junkies. Of the entire team, Prince was the one she'd expect to follow her out on any limb.

She couldn't see any of them betraying her, but one of them had. One of the six. *And when you find out who, you can fillet them into bits and pieces,* the voice said.

The leader of the mercenaries pointed a shiny Beretta at Doucet. "Go join your buddies over there. The lady can join the other civilians. The nut case can stay where she is."

Doucet stood almost 6 feet 5 inches tall. His long jet black hair was pulled back in a ponytail. He studied the man for a long minute, then slowly raised his hands. He glanced down at Kathy. "Go over there," he said, pointing his chin at Carol and the pastor; the Cajun accent had disappeared. Turn off the charm, turn on the Marine. Alex had watched it happen before.

Kathy glanced back at Alex.

Alex ignored all of them as she struggled to get at the flask in her coat, with a shaking and nearly paralyzed right hand. Her left arm was dead like some flesh and bone stapled to what remained of her shoulder. At least that's how Alex wanted it to look. At the same time, she tried to will Kathy to join the others. Defending the civilians would mean breaking her homeless, helpless act.

The leader of the mercenaries pushed Doucet over to the steam table.

Another mercenary held a rifle on Doucet while still another duct taped his hands behind his back as they'd done with the other three. All of the mercenaries ignored Alex. If she hadn't wanted to get caught today, she would have crawled away and disappeared, but she'd waited months for them to find her. She didn't have that kind of patience—dropping the hospital wristband had been an act of desperation. She'd been using the name Grace West, which was the name of a missionary who'd died in the very first mission Alex did for the Division.

She managed to get the flask out of her jacket. She lifted it to her mouth and took a deep swig. She was so drunk, the stuff didn't even burn on the way down. They might kill everyone else in the room, but they weren't going to kill her. All she had to do to honor her promise to Guang was to let herself be manhandled out of here. *It isn't so much a promise as an agreement to attempt other methods first,* the voice whispered.

The mercenaries wanted the dirty bombs and the money they'd get for selling them; her father always told her that mercenaries were 90% money and 50% psychopath. As she took another gulp, she palmed three razor sharp throwing stars. Just in case, she told herself. *Just in case*, the voice mocked.

"What's going on?" Kathy demanded, overcoming her fear. "What do you want? We don't have any money here."

Alex winced at the defiance in her tone. The cold of the metal stars pressed against her palm.

"We've come for the nut job," the mercenary with the rifle on the three civilians said with a thick German accent. "Why don't you shut up like your blubbering, fat, old lady friend and the guy who thinks his Bible will stop a bullet."

Kathy stiffened and jutted out her jaw.

"He will kill you," Doucet told the woman as she inhaled to speak again. "He's just looking for an excuse. You need to shut up."

The leader smiled. "Not as dumb as you sound; are you, Chief? Not your first day off the reservation."

The pastor paled. "We don't tolerate racism here. This is a place of peace—"

The mercenary leader laughed out loud. He spat on the floor. "Peace is a fucking illusion, Pastor, and my soul has been in hell for a very long time."

CHAPTER TWO

"She can't talk," Doucet told the mercenary leader. "What does Peter think he's going to get from her? She can't tell him where the bombs are. She can't write where they are. She's not your golden ticket. Peter is lying to you; let her go and the US government won't hunt you down."

The mercenary laughed. "You think your precious government bothers me? You've got a President that hasn't got the stones for doing what needs getting done. You got a population of hippies who'd rather be stoned then learn how to read. You, my friend, are living in a delusion. You are defending a third world nation; you're all just too stupid to realize it." He ran a hand over his buzz cut hair and shook his head at the four Marines his men held at gun point. "Look at you four. You call yourselves soldiers? You come to negotiate with someone who you admit is a walking vegetable. What you're doing is fucking embarrassing to real soldiers. Fuck you, Chief Dumbass."

"Peter wants—" Doucet began.

The leader of the mercenaries waved an impatient hand and made a face of disgust. "I don't care what Peter wants. I just want paid. For all I know, he wants one final fuck before he shoves a grenade up her pussy and pulls the pin. If you ask me, that's too good for this bitch. Her fucking father killed my brother."

Alex remembered who he was. He looked like his older brother in some ways—except he wasn't chasing her through the jungle and then claiming to her irate father that she'd come on to him. She'd been eleven and between schools of training. She'd been staying in the mercenary camp with her father while he lined up getting her situated at the next martial arts school. Peter must be desperate if he was sending someone with a clear reason to kill her or maybe Peter was just that stupid. Maybe this guy had with Peter stayed because he was so worthless he couldn't get hired in with any other band of mercs. *He lacks discipline*, the voice said. *You should have no trouble defeating him.* Alex sighed. Six mercenaries with weapons. Four Division Marines duct-taped and without weapons. Three out of shape, non-violent civilians. She could take all of them and barely work up a sweat. *Even drunk*, the voice whispered. Perhaps it wouldn't have been true if they hadn't bought into her play; but, any attck she launched would take all of the people in the room by surprise.

The mercenary slid his shiny weapon into its holster, oblivious to the eyes that watched him from behind a curtain of stringy, dirty hair and in the shadows of a hood.

What kind of moron soldier carries a weapon which reflects light? the voice whispered to the owner of the eyes which watched from behind stringy red hair. Alex shivered at its seething lust for blood. She reminded herself that she wanted to be captured. Being captured was still the quickest and easiest route to Peter, the unknown traitor, and whoever had hired Peter.

"Leave her alone! I won't let you take her," Kathy said as if reading Alex's thoughts.

The merc leader rolled his eyes at the retired nurse. "Shut up, I don't want to kill you. I don't want to clean up the mess, lady. But, I will."

Doucet shook his head. "You're not going to get away with this. This isn't a mess you can clean up."

The mercenary leader chuckled. "Because you're such a great rescuer? I mean we had her for six months and you people didn't even look." He sighed. "Well, we better check to make sure it's her first; don't you think?"

Alex sat in the corner, drinking to refill her drunk. Whiskey spilled over her chin and on to her jacket. Her right hand shook violently. She was ready to give herself an Oscar for her performance.

The mercenary grabbed Alex's jacket and yanked her to her feet.

She didn't make a noise, but the flask flew from her hand. It skittered across the linoleum. Whiskey gurgled out of it over the floor. She watched it spread over the linoleum. She could keep up the wounded act until they dragged her out of here, she reminded herself. With a claw-like right hand, she tried to pry his hand off her jacket; but, she didn't bend her arm far enough to actually reach his hand. Somewhere in the back of her mind, something feral was taking note that it would be getting slippery there with the whiskey and the bad linoleum. The feral lust for violence and revenge.

The mercenary leader grabbed the hood with his free hand and yanked it back.

Strands of dirty, tangled red hair spilled out.

The mercenary leader grabbed her jaw shook her head so the hair fell away from her face.

The room spun. Alex swallowed sour whiskey; it burned on the way back up but didn't make it all the way.

The mercenary forced her face to tilt up. "Ah, yes. Daddy's spoiled brat, the bad ass ninja, has become a vegetable," he snickered.

The other mercenaries laughed. Six mercenaries total, her feral brain counted. Six men dressed all in black. Was their wardrobe inspired by having watched too many movies or by a secret lust for beatnik poetry, she wondered.

The guy let go of her filthy army jacket and shoved more hair away from her face, holding her by the chin. His fingers pressed hard into her thin face. His calloused hand scraped hard against her face.

She could do insane. She could even do unfocussed terror. She put on a great show. A few whimpers would have made it better, but she was stuck with silence. She'd put herself there with her initial act. She looked into his eyes and she knew this wouldn't be a simple snatch and grab. You can take some punishment, she told herself. Eyes on the prize. You know you can take some punishment. *But you don't want to take punishment. You don't want to take it ever again*, the cold voice reminded her. The voice seemed to almost relish what was going to happen.

A cold grin stretched the man's thin mouth. "Hard to believe this is the same bitch who walked around camp like she was the greatest thing on the planet; fucking karma got something right. Always acting like she fucking knew what it was like to fight—when all the time Daddy is standing behind her with his gun waiting to shoot anyone who thought about teaching her a fucking lesson."

"Leave her alone," Kathy ordered.

The man let go of Alex's face, shoving it hard. He caught her jacket again before she could fall. Alex felt the room spin. Drunk. So damn drunk. It'll make it easier to take the hits, she told herself. *It'll make it harder to resist your instincts*, the voice chuckled.

"Daddy isn't around anymore and you aren't enough to protect her, Lady." His fist jabbed out and connected hard with Alex's jaw.

This time, Alex did fall. It took just about every ounce of drunken control she had to take the punch without flinching away from it. She didn't make a sound at all. She tasted blood in her mouth as she lay on the floor.

Carol started blubbering. "Please, please, just take her. She's nobody. Don't hurt us. We're trying to do good work here. Don't rape us!"

Some of the mercenaries chuckled.

The mercenary watching the four Marines leered. "I think we'd all rather fuck the vegetable than you, Shamu." He turned to Doucet and leered. "Maybe you'd like to watch that, Captain. I'll bet you already tapped that, huh? Pretty boy like you, bet she just fell on her back and spread her legs for you."

On the floor, in front of the door, Alex struggled to get back up using only one hand and one leg. She tried to make it look really pathetic, along the lines of a turtle on its back. Her boot slid in the spilled whiskey, spreading it further and testing its effect on the floor. The voice in her head chuckled softly, knowingly.

"Just like your father, too stupid to stay down," the mercenary said. His boot connected with her ribs.

Alex collided with the closed door, cracking the glass with her head. She still made no sound and immediately attempted to get up again, this time swaying unsteadily.

"You really think your boss wants her brains scrambled any more than they already are?" Dyer yelled. His deep voice rumbled like distant thunder in the small, crowded space. The veins in his thick neck bulged. He grunted when one of the mercenaries hit him.

The leader laughed. "I think I probably only cracked two or three ribs with that one." He pulled his foot back to kick again.

Kathy grabbed his arm. "Stop."

Doucet twitched as he prepared to move to protect her; but, he froze when an AK-47 got shoved in his face.

The leader smirked at Doucet, and sent waves of cold amusement to Kathy. "You're right. I shouldn't hurt her any more than she's already been hurt."

Alex already anticipated the kick. When it came at her, she reacted to it enough to take most of the power out of the blow. He meant to do some serious internal damage with that one. She'd caught him pulling the kick on the first try; but, he didn't do that this time.

Despite reacting to the blow, Alex's head bounced off the glass door, cracking it further. Her vision tunneled; the room spun. She actually almost hurled up the last bottle of Cutty Sark. She curled into as much of a fetal ball as she thought her act would allow. Her twitching pain wasn't altogether faked.

Kathy, the older woman, and the pastor all cried out in shock.

The four Marines just pressed their lips together tight and waited for an opening, but their wrists were held behind their back and they had no weapons.

The mercenary leader laughed. "That's how your father ended up when I finished with him too, bitch." He spat.

The wad of spit hit her shoulder where the jacket looked baggy from her dangling arm. Alex stayed on the ground this time. Her temper flared at the mention of her father. Struggling to keep it down proved more difficult than swallowing the bile of burning whiskey. She'd broken enough ribs in martial arts training over the years to know that she didn't have any broken ribs now—part of the benefits of starting training while a toddler was the development of stronger bones. Still, Alex was grateful for the layers of clothing she wore to fight the Ohio winter while waiting for the Division to find her.

At least the arrival of the mercenaries and their easy takeover of the Marines confirmed that the Division had a traitor. It also confirmed that she shouldn't be making any promises to a monk; this wasn't going to end well. She eyed the four men who were on their knees in front of the steam table. She didn't move, just wheezed over her bruised side and hoped another blow would not arrive. Her boiling anger wasn't going to tolerate much more.

The leader of the mercenaries pointed a finger at Kathy's face and yelled.

Alex couldn't quiet comprehend the words. He seemed to be talking too slow.

Alex liked Kathy. Kathy was the only one here who never invaded her space or told her to pray so that God would cure her. The Bible thumpers were thick in this place. Some days, during the last three months, Alex felt like slapping them all upside the head with a copy of her PhD. She took a deep breath to control her anger. As she did, she noticed the dark eyes of Captain Sinjin Doucet watching her. He'd been so proud of himself for convincing his teacher to allow her admittance for practicing in the *dojo*. He'd been so cocky about beating her. All she wanted to do right now was scream at him that it had all been a lie. Everything had been a lie; just like her drunk, crippled act now, her life had been a different act, a different role.

Instead, silently, Alex met his eyes from behind her curtain of stringy, tangled hair.

His dark eyes narrowed. A muscle at his jaw twitched.

Yes, she thought, so much for the little act of helplessness. The Marines weren't going to save her for fear of civilian fall out. *Good,* said the voice in her head, *three months of this crap has been enough. Sure, the crippled harmless act would have been easier. But the crazy murderer act is going to be more fun.*

The leader of the mercenaries laughed and sneered at Kathy. His voice seemed to pop back up into full speed as if some invisible hand had hit a button on a remote. "You're so fucking righteous. Her father murdered my brother; shot him right between the eyes after she came on to him. She murdered five of the best soldiers around while escaping. She's a fucking bitch, a tease, and a whore."

Kathy, all five feet and fifty years of her, slapped the man hard across the face.

A stunned silence fell over the room.

Alex's hand tightened around the three throwing stars she'd gotten out of her pocket when she'd retrieved the flask filled with Cutty Sark. The razor-sharp edges pressed against the calluses of a lifetime of fighting. The CIA thought she was a thief; they'd wanted to train her to be a killer but she'd stopped that; she'd told them when they recruited her that she would never be a killer for them.

Kathy lifted her chin in defiance. "Beating up cripples and old women; that sure makes you a big man," she told the mercenary leader.

43

The leader smiled, but the expression on his lips didn't reach his eyes. He was every bit the killer that the CIA hoped they would find inside her. "Would you like to see up close how big of an asshole I am?"

Alex relaxed a touch. She didn't have to come to Kathy's defense just yet. She could just wait for him to push her over the edge. It seemed inevitable now. At least she could tell her best friend that she'd tried up until the moment she snapped.

The mercenary leader, the brother of the dickhead would-be pedophile who her father killed, pushed Kathy into the arms of one of the other mercenaries.

Kathy started to struggle, but the guy put a gun to her head.

Alex took account of all the mercenaries: the leader, the guy with the gun to Kathy's head, the two flanking the four Marines, the one with a rifle pointed at Carol and the pastor, and the sixth one who scanned the room waiting to back up any of the others. Six mercenaries in the room. Six men who were smirking in amusement or indifferent to beating a woman and a crippled one. Not a one of them sick or horrified about what was about to happen.

The Division's rescue team knew what was coming. Alex saw it written across all their faces. If one of them was the traitor, he was a fucking hypocrite who didn't want to face what he'd subjected her to. They looked sick and helpless and horrified. She drunkenly tried to get up off the floor again, all the time anticipating the pummeling the merc leader planned.

The mercenary leader grabbed a fist full of her jacket and pulled her to her feet. He threw her up against the door. He punched her in the face. Alex threw her head back for effect and a spider web of cracks appeared in the top part of the glass. She let blood drip down her lip. While training in various schools of martial arts around Asia, she'd been too fast to learn how to take a blow. Training in the East was brutal compared to all the middle class martial arts schools around the United States. They'd forced her to stand still and take a punch. All that training to control her natural reactions came in handy now as the leader landed a heavy punch to her side.

44

She made no effort to defend herself and had no room to pull back. Swallowed as much of the grunt as she could and thanked years of training for hard ribs. Her long hair hung over her face like a tangled curtain; her head hung low. The guy hit her again and she felt the crack in the rib; air grunted out of her lungs. *Well, now the doctor over there on his knees suspects you aren't completely mute,* said the voice in her head. *Nice job, Einstein, maybe you'll need surgery for a ruptured spleen.* Alex coughed and let spit and blood drip over her lip onto the linoleum. She let the guy hold her up as he punched her side again.

"Stop it!" Kathy cried. "Stop it! She can't even defend herself."

The leader ignored her. He wrapped his hand around Alex's throat and started to squeeze.

You're not really going to let him choke you out; are you? the voice asked. Alex didn't try to breathe; she could hold her breath for a long time. She could fake blacking out and then maybe it would stop and still go the easy way.

Alex slid one of the razor-sharp throwing stars into her hand. Before she could cut the guy's femoral artery or fake passing out—she was surprised to find she was considering both options—Kathy wrangled free.

The short, pudgy woman punched the mercenary in the back and tried to pry his hand off Alex's throat.

Alex admired her bravery.

Darkness fell over the mercenary leader's face. He bunched up his free hand into a big fist and pulled his elbow back. His upper body started to pivot.

He was a strong man. Alex had felt the effects of his strength. Alex figured a punch like that on the temple of a woman who'd never taken a punch in her life, a woman who didn't expect it: that was the kind of punch that would kill that woman. Alex's body moved without thought, before she even really told it to. She imagined the voice in her head sitting back and clapping its hands in glee.

45

She moved one step, grabbing the mercenary's jacket and forcing him to turn with her. His punch was well on its way, too much behind it to stop the momentum despite the fact he no longer faced Kathy. He'd been spun too quickly to adjust. His punch flew through the glass door just below where Alex's shoulder had been a moment before– Kathy was shorter than Alex.

He pulled his bloody fist out of the door. It sparkled with pieces of glass.

In her head, Alex heard the roar of a thousand ancient warriors; Mongols charging across the Gobi, Huns charging Roman ranks, Spartans facing down the Persians, blue faced Celts pillaging the Brits. A calm enveloped her whole body. She stared into the leader's cold eyes with a coldness of her own.

If the mercenary hadn't been blinded by anger, he would have recognized the danger he was in.

Alex's left arm hung at her side. Her body was completely relaxed, but her head no longer sagged to her chest. *Bet you can take him with one arm tied behind your back*, the voice challenged.

He stared at her over his bloody fist. Behind his shoulder Kathy stared in shock, her jaw hanging open.

Alex smirked at him with mocking humor knowing he would never be able to resist.

He swung.

He missed.

Because he moved so fricking slow.

Alex's right elbow connected with his nose, smashing it flat against his face.

Blood poured from his nose.

No mercy, whispered the voice in her head.

He swung again.

Alex didn't even have to move her feet, she just leaned back with a quick fluidity which had seemed impossible for her broken body just moments earlier. She smashed her heavy steel-shanked boot against the side of his knee. It made a pop like a chicken wing being dislocated by a chef and the man went down to his knees.

Before Alex could finish him off, she had a gun in her face.

She looked over the barrel at the mercenary behind it. At the same time, her brain was analyzing the gun. Glock 21, one in the chamber, no safety.

"You're coming with us," said mercenary number six, the backup guy.

Alex had a habit of numbering people she was going to fight so she could keep track of them. Numbers were easier to remember then names. One, the leader, was on his knee in front of her, gagging over his destroyed knee and babying a bloody hand. Six was the floater who'd been positioned to back up anyone who might be having some trouble.

"That ship just sailed," she told him, her voice hoarse like she'd just recovered from a bad cold or laryngitis.

"It's six against one," he said. "And you only have one arm that works."

Alex arched an eyebrow at the leader.

"Okay," he said. "Five against one. Because those guys can't help you. You and I both know they're the only ones in the room who care about civilian casualties."

"If this guy was your best, I'm not going to need the other arm."

"You think you can beat five armed and trained men with one arm?" he growled.

"Two."

"What?"

"Two armed and trained men," she said.

"Brain damage mess with your ability to count?"

"No," she said in a level voice void of emotion. "I'm too drunk to figure out how I can finish off the last two of you without getting myself shot."

"Arrogant as ever."

"Three of you are already dead, you just haven't started to bleed."

"Shoot the fat one," he told the man Alex had dubbed Mercenary Five, the one guarding the preacher and Carol.

Carol gasped. She ripped open her blouse. "Just take me, don't kill me."

"What the—" the man, Five, said. He reached his hand up to his neck as blood started to poor out of his mouth instead of the words he'd meant to say. He cut his hand on the throwing star sticking out of his neck. When it pulled it out, his carotid spat blood over the leader who'd been dubbed One.

Carol screamed and passed out. Kathy cried out as hot blood sprayed over her.

The guy with the gun on Kathy, Mercenary 2, and one of the men guarding the military prisoners, Mercenary 3, sank to the floor. Both had throwing stars planted deep in their eyes. That left Mercenary One groaning on the floor with a busted knee, Six pointing a Glock at her head, and Four pointing an AK47 at the Division Marines.

Alex took the weapon out of Mercenary Six's hand with a quick twisting move. The magazine dropped to the floor. She used the wall to push back the slide slightly, slid her hand down the gun and pulled down the take down levers. Years of sword training gave her strong hands. She pulled the gun away from the wall and the slide fell off the gun. The spring bounced over the floor in front of Mercenary One.

When the leader reached for the frame of the weapon that she dropped immediately after taking it apart, she kicked him hard in the groin. Unlike him, she didn't pull her kick in an attempt to save anyone or anything. She'd learned that lesson quickly when she first became the student of Chen Sakai, master of the discipline which cannot be named; mercy survives to hunt you down another day. She hadn't taken it to heart until recently. Too much fucking around in the CIA where she'd refused to kill people.

The two youngest Marines cringed and groaned in sympathy.

Mercenary One puked over the floor.

Merc Six dove for her.

She spun, stepping gracefully over the leader who twitched in the pool of his own vomit. The man flew by her. His boot hit the linoleum covered with whiskey and he slid out of control into a few tables.

Mercenary Four tried a roundhouse kick to her head.

She spun to show her back and the kick hit something hard and metallic under her jacket instead of flesh. She hit him hard in the throat as Six recovered enough to come after her again.

She used his momentum to flip him over the Marines and into the steam table.

He screamed as steam and boiling water burned him.

Four tackled her.

She hit the ground hard in front of the four black ops Division Marines who were trying to free themselves from duct tape manacles. The mercenary was on top of her.

From her back, Alex glared at Sinjin Doucet. "How about some help?" she growled at him. If he didn't, she was going to have to use her left arm to compensate for Four's superior strength.

Doucet head-butted the guy.

Four grabbed his forehead and stumbled backwards.

Six tackled her before she could recover. They slid over the wet floor away from the steam table and her Marine Corps rescuers. The mercenary pulled a survival knife out of a sheath on his belt.

Alex hooked his ankle and twisted around.

He forgot about stabbing her so he could save his leg from being broken.

They grappled for a position, but Alex's training won out along with a healthy dose of meanness. She hit him and wrapped her legs around his neck. She squeezed.

His eyes bulged.

She took the knife from his hand, breaking his fingers to get it.

Four grabbed a Sig Sauer from his still incapacitated boss. He pointed it at Alex, who was lined up with the extraction team at her back.

"Fuck!" cried Sergeant Frank Dyer, the man who'd been her father's best friend. He and the others scattered.

The gun fired with a flash.

Alex felt the bullet whiz by and felt the tug as it whipped through her oversized jacket. She felt an icy cold flow into the marrow of her bones as she spun away from the bullet, already too late if it would have been aimed better. The scenario in her head had played out with him being a better shot. In her head she'd taken the bullet in the shoulder. One of the few times in her life that her battle anticipation ended up in her favor. She was uninjured and the steam table got death.

The steam table exploded with a bright flash. The smell of an electrical fire and smoke filled the air, then boiling water whooshed out across the floor like a wave coming ashore.

In the flash of light, Alex dove in the opposite direction of the civilians, knowing the bullets would follow her and not the others. Doucet and the others moved to protect the civilians. *Pathetically predictable*, the voice said with a yawn.

A fire started to burn inside the steam table. The lights flickered out and plunged the soup kitchen into darkness, with only the muted light from the gray March day filtered through the frosted windows and the orange glow of a dying electrical fire.

In the darkness, Alex abandoned her act of being at least marginally crippled.

Doucet yelled for people to get down.

The civilians screamed.

A rifle barked flashed and barked. The flashes like a strobe light with Alex moving like a creature even the grim reaper would run from. With her left hand, Alex grabbed the mercenary leader's jacket and lifted him up like a shield.

He screamed, high-pitched and then gurgling as his body jerked with the impact of bullets. The rifle wasn't the AK, if it had been, the bullets probably would have gone through One and into her. She shoved him at the gunman, Four, and followed the body. She buried the knife deep into Four's chest.

At the same time, she got hit in the back by the last mercenary alive. She staggered, but managed to keep her footing despite the water, the blood, the bodies, and the broken furniture. She blocked his next punch as he fell into his own martial arts training. Unfortunately for him, Alex could have taught his teacher a thing or two and she was twice as fast. She blocked his jab, twisted his arm. His shoulder popped as it dislocated.

He screamed.

The lights flickered as the backup generator tried to get the lights back up. The room was filled with smoke from the smoldering steam table. It gave their fight an almost surreal feel, like some old time silent film.

Alex flipped backwards to avoid a kick, landed low and slid on her knees through the water and blood. She went through his wide stance and, in a single smooth move, stood up behind him. She grabbed his jaw with her right hand, put her left hand on his shoulder and twisted in opposite directions. Fast. Before the muscles in his neck were prepared to fight her.

The sound of his neck cracking came at the same time as generators brought the lights back on, dimly.

Alex stood in the middle of the room with her back to all the survivors. Smoke swirled around her. There was an inch of water and blood and whiskey and puke on the floor. Her left shoulder hung low, her left arm hung limp. She released the man's jaw with her right hand. Steam rose from the hot water around her boots and merged into the smoke. She was breathing hard.

Mercenary Six's limp body slid down hers in slow motion.

CHAPTER THREE

Alex's heart beat slowly. The sound of her breath, slightly elevated, filled her head.

Six's body crumbled into a pile of oddly bent limbs, then toppled forward. His head lolled loosely on his neck.

The world snapped back into full speed. With it came the drunkenness and the broken rib. Alex swayed. She fell down to one knee, catching herself with a hand between the arm and body of the guy lying on his back with a knife sticking out of his heart. She groaned and lifted her hand to her broken rib, sitting back on her ankles so she didn't have to use her left arm.

"Alex!" Frank Dyer cried out, running forward.

Alex felt the rush towards her, the adrenalin had been dying, but it wasn't gone. Without conscious thought, Alex's right hand grabbed the handle of the knife stuck in the mercenary's chest. Her hand flexed over the handle even as a sucking sound announced its retrieval. She held it with the blade pointed up and slightly out. She managed to stop her instincts from slashing at whoever was behind her.

Her hand trembled with the effort. Blood dripped from the blade into the water.

"Alex, drop the knife," Doucet's deep Cajun voice ordered. He had positioned himself in Dyer's path, blocking and slowing the big NCO's rush towards her.

Alex eyed both Marines. Doucet had probably saved the life of the man she called an uncle. Instead of dropping the knife, she pulled her arm in to her side again, still clutching the blade. She winced.

"Let me go, she's hurt," Dyer growled at his commanding officer.

Alex sucked in a breath and released it with a slight moan. She rolled to her feet and turned to face the men in one smooth move. Not utilizing her left hand at all. The smooth rise to her feet came from years of rising from a lotus position to engage an attacking teacher; she'd gotten to the point where it almost looked magical. In truth, it took a lot of inner core strength to pull off. A true master would have instantly recognized the danger she presented; but, Alex felt pretty confident that present company wasn't going to fully comprehend how healed she was. Alex looked down at her jacket which was stained with blood. She suspected her face was splattered with it as well. "I'm leaving before the police get here," she told Doucet.

He narrowed his eyes. "No one is calling the police."

She lifted her head at Carol. "She did."

Doucet looked at the woman.

Carol looked indignant. "She's a psychopath! She has to answer for her crimes."

"The crime of saving your life?" Dyer growled. "Fuck."

Carol shook her head. "Are you all crazy? They weren't going to kill any of us, they just wanted her. We should have let them take her. She's a monster! I always knew she wasn't right, but Kathy kept saying she was innocent."

A cold smirk tugged at the corner of Alex's mouth.

Doucet scowled. His dark eyes were carefully masked. "I can't let you just walk out of here, Alex. I have orders to bring you in."

Alex glanced down at some of the bodies littering the floor between them. Four more bodies wouldn't make much difference, she thought, but then she would never find out which one had betrayed her. She could go to New York and kill the other two. Sure, five dead innocents; but all was fair in love and war and one bad guy would be dead. Collateral damage. The voice in her head offered only mocking silence.

"You can't kill us all before the police get here," Doucet told her as if reading her thoughts.

Alex thought she could.

Dyer spat. "That's not even an option. She wouldn't kill us; we're the good guys."

Alex tilted her head to one side and looked at him quizzically. "You want the same thing they do," Alex told him. She flexed her hand over the handle of the knife. She saw Doucet's eyes watch that knife carefully. "You can't even be certain I remember who you are. You all want the same thing from me."

Doucet shook his head in denial.

Lieutenant Mitchell Ong stepped forward before the captain could speak.

Ong had been dressed like a gang member when she'd passed him on the street. The man of Chinese descent lifted his chin in a silent greeting. "Are you hurt?" he asked, putting himself between her and everyone else.

"Do I look hurt?" she asked, hearing an edge of defiance in her voice. The adrenalin still coursed through her veins.

He kept all reaction in check. "You wouldn't let on if you were; so, I'm asking you for some honesty. I'm interested in stopping another fight. You might not care about fighting, but you don't have enough time to win before the cops get here. And if you do, you will have to eliminate the witnesses too. I need to know you're not going to pass out and die somewhere. So, I'll ask you again. Are you hurt?"

She took a deep breath and released it slowly. She did a quick self-assessment as the adrenalin leached out of her system. "I'm drunk."

A corner of his mouth twitched briefly. His eyes sparked with a glint of amusement. "How drunk?"

"I'm trying to decide if I want another drink or if I just want to puke and get it over with."

He arched his eyebrows, eyes widening slightly. "That's pretty drunk."

Alex grunted.

"You've been waiting for us," he said.

A smirk stretched her lips. She absently reached for the flask and then remembered it was on the floor. "I can afford to wait for the cops, too." This man was the smartest in the group. She wondered if she wanted to trust him on the sole basis that he was smarter, that he was Asian, that his father and grandfather had a martial arts school.

Ong glanced at the captain. "If the cops arrest her, they will arrest us as well. She's just going to turn on the crazy cripple game again and escape from a holding cell while we're waiting for the mess to get cleaned up. She used to break into and out of prisons for a living."

Alex said nothing.

Some silent communication went on between Doucet and Ong.

When it was decided, Ong turned back to Alex. "We can try to subdue you and take you back to the doctors who are going to figure out how it is that you can talk and walk."

"I wouldn't suggest that route."

His mouth twitched in a hint of a grin. "I'm a little leery."

"I have a problem with doctors. White lab coats. Needles."

His brown eyes registered a step of compassion, but he remained wary of her. "I'm going to keep that in mind. We have a couple of conditions."

"What?"

"Let me see your arms."

She stiffened.

55

"Look, I'm the only one who's willing to trust you right now. Guaranteed: the Captain wants you in cuffs and in a holding cell after this, Dyer thinks you've suffered enough and wants you out of the equation completely—safe in a holding cell in some CIA basement with a nice television and three meals a day—and, Prince would prefer you were unconscious and tied up because he knows just how far you'll take a risk. Show me your arms."

"I'm clean."

"Show me. You don't trust doctors; I don't trust junkies."

Sirens sounded in the distance.

Alex stared at Ong who just stared back. With a growl of anger, she threw the knife to the side. It buried itself in the frame of the door with a loud whap.

The civilians jumped.

She unzipped the army jacket, ripped it off and threw it to the watery, bloody floor. Underneath, she wore an oversized black hoodie. She took it off to expose a sweatshirt and clear evidence that her shoulder wasn't as damaged as they thought.

"Fuck," Dyer said. "How in the fuck does a shoulder grow back?"

She didn't have an explanation; and, if she did, it would have been forbidden for her to explain. She had rules she had to follow. Fucking stupid rules. *Rules that keep me safe,* the voice whispered. She pulled the sweatshirt up over her head.

Her bottom layer was a thermal, long-sleeved shirt. She shoved the sleeves up to her elbows and held out her arms. Scars circled her wrists. Needle tracks marked her arms, but none of them were fresh. Surgical scars tracked up the inside of her right arm like some kind of pink fossil of a prehistoric caterpillar. She heard Kathy suck in a breath.

Ong nodded. "Stopping a heroin addiction is a pretty impressive feat of control. A mentally unstable person wouldn't be able to do it."

She started to put the sweatshirt back on.

"Wait," Ong told her. "Lift your shirt."

"Fuck you, Ong," she snapped. "Go buy some chick on the curb two streets over."

Ong rolled his eyes. "You're hot for an old chick, Alex, but you scare the shit out of me."

She narrowed her eyes at him, she was only two years older than he was and she looked younger.

He chuckled at her expression. "Com'on Alex. I want to make sure your spleen isn't ruptured," he said. He winced when he realized he'd just reminded her that he was a doctor. "You let that guy hit you pretty hard and you did nothing to protect yourself. I don't want you leaving and bleeding to death in some alley."

"Twice in one year, that would suck," she mumbled in an ancient dialect that resembled modern Mandarin.

Ong jerked as if he'd been slapped across the face.

Alex's head tilted like a dog hearing something no one else could hear. "I didn't know you spoke Mandarin, Ong," she said, but the dialect wasn't quite Mandarin, and it wasn't quite decipherable in Chinese. Then with her right arm she lifted up the left side of her shirt to expose the big black bruise over her side and ribs. Her ribs were visible, but so was a flat, six pack. Scars marked her side and back. The only scar that wasn't flat was one about an inch to the right of her navel. It had a match on her back. The three-inch-long scar had healed into a strange crisscross of lines. Of course, to someone who read Chinese or Japanese, the crisscrosses weren't just random lines.

Ong started to speak as she dropped her shirt, but his voice didn't quite come out. He cleared his throat. "Uhm, broken ribs?" His voice shook.

"You don't have to pretend you didn't recognize those symbols," Alex said in Chinese. "I can see from your reaction that you know what they mean."

"My grandfather told us a fairy tale once," Ong replied, also in Chinese. "Broken ribs?" he asked again, switching back to English.

"Two maybe three," she replied. In the distance, she heard police sirens. "Make the call, Ong. Let me go or I fight my way out of here." She smirked at him, an expression that didn't reach her eyes. She spoke in Chinese. "And fairy tales being what they are, I think you need to let me go."

"Where do we meet you?" he asked in English.

"Old football stadium parking lot. Midnight. If you four aren't alone, I will find someone else to help me dispose of the bombs."

"We have a black SUV."

She smiled coldly at him. "I've been watching you try to find me for three days. You make a really crappy street thug, Lieutenant."

Ong took off his jacket and tossed it to her. "Here. There's money in the inside pocket. Find dry clothes so you don't get pneumonia."

She caught the insulated jacket he'd been wearing while walking the streets looking for her. It was big, waterproof and warm. She pulled it on.

"You can't just let her leave," Dyer protested to Doucet.

Alex bent down and grabbed something out of the pocket of her hoodie.

"What's that?" Doucet asked, stiff and on alert.

She tossed it to him. "Cell phone, I lifted it from the leader while I was getting punched. Call it collateral."

Doucet sighed. "Go," he told Alex. "Midnight."

She didn't wait for him to change his mind. She walked around them and the destroyed steam table to go out the back door. *That fight felt awfully good; didn't it?* Alex shivered and pulled the jacket tighter around her body and tried to ignore the voice in her head.

She headed straight for the monastery; she had no worries about someone following her. They wanted her to trust them and they knew they had to take a risk and trust her to earn what they wanted. Alex planned on using that as long as she could. Plus, they had to work out what they were going to tell the police about the six very dead mercenaries lying around the soup kitchen—and they had to deal with what the civilians were going to say about what they'd seen.

Guang watched Alexandria Rae McBrady jerk in her sleep. He'd been summoned the instant she'd crossed the threshold of the monastery. Three months ago, it'd been simple to figure out where she would come; her brain hadn't been working efficiently when she left Thailand. She'd left too soon, hell bent on revenge. Her condition made her predictable. However, even now, he could see that her predictability as waning. He feared what would come next.

Her face twitched and twisted in agony, reliving nightmares during her sleep. Tonight, she'd returned with a look in her eye and a refusal of the offer to spar with the monks. She'd come to the temple. Guang found her asleep on the floor in front of the large, gold-leafed statue. The others had, at first, come running to see why the woman screamed, but he'd sent them away. He stayed away and out of range himself. He'd lit incense to fill the room with the smell of jasmine and sandalwood and sage. It had helped calm her, he supposed, since the screams were replaced by whimpering and moaning. Part of him wanted to rescue her from the trauma, but another part of him recognized that even fitful sleep was better than no sleep at all.

Years ago, he'd been an orphan living in a besieged village; he'd been a toddler taken in by a monastery and destined to become a monk. That monastery and that world had been very different than this one tucked into the third floor of some downtown Cleveland building. The monks in the mountains had pooled their money and hired a mercenary to beat back Chinese rebels who wanted the village for their stronghold. The leaders and the monks had been doubtful of their safety despite the promises of the mercenary they hired. So, the mercenary had brought his daughter to prove to them that he would protect them with everything he had. Guang had only been two years old; most never have memories that go so far back. But Guang still remembered the moment he laid eyes on the mercenary's daughter, also two years old. Hair like flames and eyes filled with stars of a thousand colors; Alex's name had been as incomprehensible as her energy and insatiable curiosity. Meeting her had changed the course of his life. He would have been a simple monk, never venturing far from the walls of a monastic compound, dealing with the politics of holding the Chinese army at bay.

With the mercenary's daughter, he'd run the ridges of the Himalayas and stood on the edges of thousand-foot drops. He'd felt the power of the wind and the threat of the fall quicken his blood. In the middle of turmoil and blizzards and whirlwinds of smoke and fire and ice, Alexandria Rae McBrady never faltered. He'd stood as witness even as a toddler. As a teenager, he'd spent weeks with Alex and her father in a jungle sanctuary, allowed to be a kid instead of a monk. It'd been a magical place where everyone could let go of the walls that hid their true selves. He felt honored to be let in to see Alex's soul. And he was afraid it would disappear.

Part of Guang worried that she would not be able to find her way out of this storm. The image of her waking up in Thailand stuck in his brain. Wild, feral, covered in vomit and blood, smelling of festering wounds which were no longer there, unaware of her name, craving drugs, clutching at the Sword of Souls as if it were both a lifeline and a curse. He would never forget the look in her wild eyes which were normally so controlled. In her eyes, he'd seen so many things left bare and raw; but, mostly he'd seen fear—no, it had been terror. Terror, shame, self-hatred. It had shaken his faith in the power of the ancients.

On the sleeping mat a few feet away from him, in front of the Buddha shrine, she jerked awake. A scream caught on her lips.

From the shadows, Guang watched her hands shake. He watched her swallow the scream and the fear and control it with almost physical force. She breathed in the smoke. Her head tilted slightly. Her hands stilled instantly.

"It is a root which grows in the wilds of Tibet," he said, speaking the ancient dialect of the village where he'd been born. It was not a language many understood; but, Alex picked up languages with frightening swiftness. Almost as if she'd spoken them before and simply had to be reminded; Guang thought this a curious idea. If the legends were to be believed, then she was just remembering what her soul had forgotten.

She jumped slightly and looked at him, picking him out in the shadows immediately. The candlelight flickered in her eyes, catching the sparkle of the glitter-like flecks of metallic color. Her lips pressed together.

Guang rose to his feet and moved towards her. He lowered himself to kneeling beside her and in front of the statue. He did not look at her. "It is supposed to ward off nightmares," he told her so the silence would not swallow her up. An aura of silence hung around him like a warm blanket.

Alex shivered at how vulnerable she'd been. "Clearly, it does not work."

Guang glanced at her, amusement dancing over his features. She amused him precisely because she was not trying to be sarcastic.

"You shouldn't have let me sleep here. Someone should have woken me up." She pulled her knees up to her chest and hugged them. She looked vulnerable. A haunted look danced with the flames in her eyes.

He shrugged. "You shouldn't try to meditate while drunk off your ass."

"Did they teach you to talk like that in monk school?"

"You would know if you'd ever visited," he shot back.

"They wouldn't let me in; me being a girl and all."

He dropped some powder from his hand into the bowl. "Rules have never stopped you before." The character of the scent changed subtly to more earthy.

Alex drew in a deep breath without thinking why. "What are you doing here, Guang?"

"I have messages from your friends."

Alex made a face. "I don't have any friends. How exactly are you able to find me when no one else can?"

Guang grinned at her. Years ago, he'd sat beside her on the edge of a glacier, with their legs dangling over a thousand-foot crevasse. They'd both been about five years old. His heart had been racing with fear and the thrill; she'd seemed utterly calm; but, when one looked closer, it was clear she felt it too. Unlike himself, she thrived on the feeling. The people of the village and the monastery avoided her; they were a superstitious lot and they claimed to see something otherworldly in her eyes. Guang had been her only friend. Even then, he'd seen the lost little girl and the fear she tried to hide. These last events had torn away at the curtain she kept over those things that she perceived as weakness. She had not yet rewoven the curtain— or perhaps she had and it cloaked the reality of what she'd discovered. "Finding you would suggest that I was out looking for you. I am merely waiting for you to arrive, Alex. Plus, it annoys you and that amuses me."

Alex made a face. "I swear they have a secret class which teaches monks to speak in riddles."

He shrugged. "We have many secret classes. We hide them from the girls."

Alex blew out a soft single laugh. Her eyes dropped from his and turned on the Buddha statue. She absently rubbed the scar which circled her wrist. Her eyes focused on something far away. She sucked in a shaky breath.

Guang watched her. With someone else, he might have touched her or embraced her, but he could not do that for her. The only one who could get away with that had been her father; and, her father was gone. "Your friend Dorije Jennings says the first bomb was found and the trap sprung. You are now 40 million American dollars richer and – that man – has just under one hundred American dollars to his name."

Alex allowed a small, cold smile to land on her mouth. Her eyes refocused, she turned her attention back to him. "You can say his name."

"I won't. I'm surprised you can say it."

"I only run inside my nightmares," she told him. "That's where I die. Out here in the real world, I stand and fight."

Guang started to ask something, but he swallowed his words.

Alex sighed. "I couldn't have answered even if you asked the thing you were about to."

Guang shrugged. "There are rules you must abide by so that you do not have to abide by rules that apply to the rest of us. It is the balance of things."

Alex grunted and shook her head. "More riddles," she mused. "How long ago was the trap sprung?"

His mouth twitched in amusement at her change of subject. "A few hours ago. You have been asleep for a while. You must have needed it."

Alex winced. "Shit. What time is it?"

"After midnight."

"I'm late." Tension drifted across her shoulders. She lifted her chin from her knees.

"They will wait," Guang said.

Alex shook her head and pushed a lock of hair out of her face. "Not if I want this to play out without a blood bath, I promised you I'd try. I'm not doing so well at the moment. You said messages. Plural."

"Akiko Tanaka indicates that the Offspring have split over whether the weapon which cannot be named is yours by right or not. Your—what should I call it? A campaign? Your campaign to trap your father's murderer in the United States by strong-arming people using their power in the East has left them less than pleased."

Alex smirked. "I used my father's connections. It isn't their power; it's about time someone reminds the Offspring they are the servants and not the masters."

Guang dipped his head in agreement with her words. He'd known from the time she was 10 years old that she held back when she sparred, that she hid her talents, that she watched everything and missed little, and that she could not be controlled. That some of the Offspring were beginning to notice, pleased him. Not even her father tried to control her with force; the Offspring never would. "The Offspring expect you to do what Chen Sakai did."

"A servant to their whims? A slave to a bunch of babbling Mongols?" She waved her hand in the air without looking at him. "I would rather die. I won't be kept in some silo waiting for a bunch of arrogant politicians and businessmen to push the red button and let me out."

"When you inherited the weapon, you did not go to the burial ground and pay homage; the twenty holders of the sword which shall not be named before you visited the grave of the last True One and paid homage directly following their inheritance of the weapon. You chose not to." He left out that all of those men had reported being compelled to visit the grave.

Alex shrugged. "Not much to be gained from a pile of rocks and dust that's nearly 1000 years old except providing a location for a group of people to ambush me."

Guang arched an eyebrow, surprised that she'd known about the ambush. "You immediately positioned Akiko Tanaka to serve as your proxy inside Nyx International. They thought you were young and afraid of your responsibilities. Now, they fear they have allowed you to go unchecked for too long. They think you are dangerous."

Guang did not miss the smirk that fluttered across Alex's face.

She shrugged her shoulders. "Chen Sakai was a teacher; I am not. The holder before him was a businessman; I am not that either. They have not encountered someone like me in a long, long time."

Not in a thousand years Guang supposed, although he didn't say so out loud. "Ms. Tanaka says there is a faction within the Offspring which supports another of your teacher's students. They are speaking about invoking the Rule of Seven. Your actions have begun to swing more support for this faction."

"A lot of people are plotting to kill me. They're going to have to get in line," Alex mumbled. Something about the name of the ancient ritual stirred the monster inside of her. She nearly shivered.

"The Rule of Seven is a no-win situation; you should not take it lightly. The last True One fell in the last Rule of Seven battle."

"A thousand years ago," she countered. "The Offspring have gotten a little over-confident since then. And a little over-zealous in their attempt to make up for their mistakes. First, my father's murderer and the person who betrayed me," she said. "Then I will deal with the Offspring and their Chosen One."

Guang watched her silently. Her eyes got cold like daggers. He saw a shiver travel through her spine as if the cold were a physical thing. "Alex—"

She took a deep breath. "The Offspring invented the Rule of Sevens ritual 1000 hundred years ago. They should be careful about claiming to speak for the gods."

The candles flickered around the room.

Guang eyed the candles. "It is said that the True One was thrown from the Earth 1000 years ago when the Rule of Seven was invoked and that the weapon whose name cannot be spoken aloud has been in the hands of an imposter ever since. This faction of the Offspring believes Sakai's other student is the True One, but he is not yet of age."

Alex shook her head and lifted a hand to her temple. Alex bit her bottom lip and avoided eye contact. "It's going to take them a long time to set up an arena. And then they're actually going to have to get me there. In the meantime, I am avenging my father's murder."

"They've had more than a decade to build their arena. What happens after you avenge your father?"

"One day at a time, Guang." She rose to her feet. "I have to go meet with the Marines. One of them, Mitchell Ong…will you ask Jennings to find out all he can about him."

"Why?"

"He saw the mark. He knows what it means." She rubbed her shirt where, underneath, the scars which formed symbols were hidden. "His father owns a martial arts studio in San Francisco. His grandfather was a refugee from China." She forced a smile onto her face and looked at him again. "I have to go."

"I know."

"Seriously, Guang, how do you always find me?"

"I don't find you, Alex. You find me. I am merely patient."

Alex made a face. "That's creepy."

Guang arched an eyebrow at her.

Alex rolled her eyes at him. "Yeah, we'll avoid that conversation." She pivoted on the heel of her boot and started out of the temple room.

"Alex?"

She glanced over her shoulder.

"Do not sleep with him."

She narrowed her eyes.

"You are vulnerable, no matter how much you deny it. Perhaps you did sell your soul as you believe; but, there is no need to continue to sacrifice your body."

"I know what I'm doing."

"If this were simply about avenging your father, you would just go find Peter and kill him."

Alex sighed. "It's not just Peter. There is the one who hired him and the one he hired to sell me out. The one who hired him doesn't really want the bombs."

Guang frowned. "What then?"

Alex closed her eyes. "They threw acid in my shoulder wound—they hadn't let it heal for all those six months. It stunk with infection. They dropped acid in it. I watched it melt away. It was more pain than a human mind can take. And while I was screaming and choking on pieces of my own throat. While my heart was exploding and my brain was stroking, the torturer leaned over and whispered in to my ear."

"What did he whisper?"

"He said…" she paused and took a deep breath. "He said: Where is it? Where have you hidden the Swo—" She gasped. Her legs buckled and she dropped to the floor. She wheezed to suck in breath.

Guang jumped forward as she grabbed at her chest and all color drained from her already pale face. "Alex!"

She coughed. Spatters of blood covered the floor in front of her.

Then suddenly it was gone.

Alex sucked in breath. A cold sweat covered her skin; her arms and legs trembled with the memory of the pain. She reached for the weapon strapped to her back and pulled it to the floor with her hand on a worn spot in the scabbard.

Guang blinked. Why hadn't he seen the weapon strapped there all this time? Where had it been?

"Leave me alone, Guang," she managed.

He hesitated. He saw that her hand had left a bloody print on the floor.

"Guang, now, please," she growled with urgency.

Guang rose quickly and left her alone as her shaking hand wrapped around the handle of the weapon, preparing to draw it out.

CHAPTER FOUR

Captain Sinjin Doucet leaned against the dark SUV and scanned the empty parking lot through a cloud of frozen breath. They'd parked the vehicle at the edge of a circle of light created by parking lot lamps. His Louisiana genes were trying to convince him that it would be warmer in the light, but it wasn't working. How did people live with this weather constantly? The thought about the cold came to him in a moment of inattention, but that quickly focused again when his scan landed on Lieutenant Mitchell Ong. The youngest member of his team paced near the front of the vehicle.

Doucet trusted all the members of his team, but Ong was holding back. Ever since Alex flashed those scars that looked like someone had tried to carve something in Chinese into her abs, Ong had been unusually quiet. He'd said the Chinese exchange with Alex had been personal medical information. Doucet had no reason to disbelieve the lieutenant; but, there was something twisting in his gut. He considered Alex one of his best friends when she disappeared. He'd gotten her into Master Daisuke's exclusive *dojo*. She was good with a sword; she'd trained in Japan while growing up. It had never occurred to him that she might be sparring with Ong and his Kung Fu stuff, too. Of course, what he'd watched in the soup kitchen was more than just sword work; he wondered why his *sensei* hadn't noticed Alex held back. Perhaps the old man was so adamant about not training females that he didn't care.

In his mind's eye, Doucet analyzed Alex's moves in the soup kitchen. She'd taken punches and kicks. She'd only moved to protect the civilians. Her first move against the mercenary leader happened so fast that the man didn't have time to react. She'd gone from unsteady to cold control with precision moves. He couldn't even argue that she had lied about being drunk. He could see the unfocussed drunk in her sparkling eyes. He could see her hands tremble when she stopped. She hadn't been faking that.

Ong grunted, drawing Doucet away from his reverie again "She will be here," the young lieutenant said, but his conviction was starting to take on a defensive tone.

Frank Dyer, who'd grumbled from the beginning about their plan dove right in on the younger man's uncertainty. "She's two hours late." His deep voice rumbled through the cold darkness. He sat inside the SUV, in the front passenger seat, almost like a petulant child with his big arms crossed over his deep chest. "She's not coming. Her father would say anything to get what he wanted too. She learned from him; she's the daughter of a frickin' mercenary for Christ's sake. They live without rules or structure. Promises are fluid for them."

Doucet sighed. The big man seemed to be having issues getting around the image of Alex as a child despite all he'd seen. Doucet didn't blame the guy, it probably wasn't easy. Joe McBrady had been Dyer's best friend and Alex was like a daughter to him. He'd made a good case to just nab Alex up and take her to Division headquarters. However, Alexandria Rae McBrady was not a child. She'd trained in the CIA, it might not have been Paris Island, but it was still heavy-duty training. As leader of the team, he'd been privy to what the others were not: the CIA tried to train Alex to be a black ops assassin. She'd flunked out of training and the review on her was that she didn't have the stomach to kill. He hadn't noticed that problem at the soup kitchen; six months of torture had changed her moral code, apparently.

Only one analyst had noticed--the report was buried in the paperwork he'd read on the way to Cleveland; but, she seemed to pass every CIA test by luck, barely scraping by the cut off. Doucet thought back to his sparring matches. In his mind's eye, he could see himself battling hard; however, she managed to block his attacks as if she'd had a lucky accidental reflex. He could hear his teacher bark orders at him to push himself harder and to not hold back as if he weren't concerned at all about the woman with the lesser skills. While he'd been concerned he might make a mistake that would hurt Alex, Master Daisuke didn't share that concern. The old teacher had brutally beaten down others he didn't consider worthy of his *dojo*; the old man did not believe in coddling. But, Daisuke never showed any concern for Alex's welfare or interest in her obvious talent.

In the soup kitchen, Alex had managed to take out six armed mercenaries in about ten minutes, men who'd taken him and his team. Maybe Dyer was correct in attributing a lot of Joe's personality to Alex. He'd met the infamous mercenary a couple of times. They'd all actually spent three weeks on his private island one summer when they'd been ordered to stand down after a mission went south. Alex invited them all to her father's place. Joe McBrady had been a gracious host and his wife—girlfriend at the time—had been kind and bubbly to everyone except Alex. He didn't blame the woman; Joe doted on his daughter enough to make any woman jealous. Not to mention Alex had a way of making other women hate her without even trying.

Joe McBrady enlisted in the United States Marine Corps at 15, but got thrown out of the Corps when General Gregory, then his commanding officer, discovered that his best Marine was in fact only 16. Instead of going back to the United States, Joe'd gone AWOL. He turned up a few months later, on the battlefield, as a member of a mercenary group. According to legend, he'd been 18 years old and in the middle of a firefight when someone brought him a basket with a baby in it. Frank Dyer said Joe paid a hooker to teach him how to take care of the infant. It didn't take a psychic to see Joe's reason for breathing every day was his beautiful red-headed daughter. Alex's mother had been some concubine and slave to some Arab royal; Joe implied that the woman had died for her indiscretion with the young American mercenary.

"Her father would have said anything to get his way; she will too," Dyer repeated, pulling his commanding officer's thoughts from Joe McBrady and Alex's background and back into the cold night. "That's what he taught her. He set out to make sure she would take care of herself before anyone else. Her word makes jack shit."

"She planned for us to find her," Ong argued. "She needs us for something. We didn't even know she was alive; she dropped clues everywhere. We should have found her earlier; but, we weren't looking." He looked out into the darkness, up the street towards the city of Cleveland.

Doucet agreed with the lieutenant. There had been many, many hints and—if they'd been looking for her—they should have found her. They'd been convinced she was dead. After the first month, they hadn't even checked out the morgues with any regularity. Just like after she'd gone missing. They'd searched for a month, but she'd vanished. Eventually life moved on for the rest of the world. Not so much for Alex.

Doucet tried to quell his own irritation by reminding himself that this was not the typical mission and that Alex had earned the right to be surly and difficult. Alex wouldn't respond to a full-blown assault; as Peter Van de Moeter and his torturers had discovered. Truth was, however, no one knew Alex. Dyer had been just as surprised as anyone to see her stand up against Pater's torture. They'd all considered her a clever thief, not some bad ass fighter. Worse, no one knew who'd she'd become. As strong as she was, she could not escape without emotional scars. Her father's murder, her capture and torture, and then three months living on the streets. He'd seen it in her eyes today. Despite the fight, she was haunted by what had happened to her. Not that he blamed her, Doucet didn't think anyone could have withstood the things she had.

The old Alex would never have slaughtered those mercenaries. The old Alex would have hurt them, then gotten away. The new Alex seemed determined never to run again. He thought about his experience in the *dojo* with her. He wondered if she'd let him win and the thought made his stomach uneasy. How much had been a lie.

"If the body count increases, we're not going to be able to hide this from the General," Dyer grumbled. He sighed and leaned back in the passenger seat.

A cell phone rang inside the SUV.

Doucet looked around; he didn't recognize the ring tone.

"It's the phone we took off the mercenary," said the man sitting in the driver's seat. Sergeant Trevor Prince reached the phone out of the window between Ong and Doucet.

As Doucet stepped towards it, a shadow moved behind Ong from the darkness in front of the SUV. He stepped back, his heart skipping a beat that someone was able to get so close without being seen, his hand went to the holster on his side.

A hand grabbed Ong's arm as the lieutenant jumped as well. The hand stopped Ong from grabbing the weapon tucked in a shoulder holster inside his jacket. At the same time, a second hand snatched the ringing cell phone from Trevor Prince.

Alex stepped into the light from behind Ong. A smirk tugged over her mouth when she saw the shocked looks on the faces of the Marines. Her face was flushed from the cold, the wind blew strands of red hair over her face like bloody slashes. She glanced down at the phone and hit the green answer button.

Dyer started to say something, but stopped when she let go of Ong to hold up her hand. She put the phone on speaker.

Sinjin Doucet watched her brush the hair away from her face and look down at the phone. Something fluttered in his gut when she bit the side of her bottom lip to keep it from trembling.

"Where in the hell have you been?" demanded a voice on the other end. The voice was a higher-pitched male voice with a thick, over-the-top English accent. "You were supposed to check in hours ago. You bloody well better have her or I will skin you alive."

"Too late for that," Alex said in a soft voice. "They're all dead."

The tone made chills run down Sinjin's spine. He would have understood anger and threats of revenge.

She lifted her attention from the phone back to him. Her eyes were dark, intense, and light from the post lamp they'd parked under glittered as if it were reflecting off icicles inside that darkness.

There was a long pause. "Alexandria," said the voice on the phone, a voice trying to hide surprise and failing miserably. Doucet met Peter Van de Moeter at Joe McBrady's funeral. The thin, pale man hovered over Alex and tried to convey the impression they were a couple. No one bought the act. No one thought Van de Moeter could handle someone as full of life as Alex. But the man had chewed up that life force and spit it out. In his dreams for years to come, Sinjin Doucet knew he would hear the sounds from the tape: Alex begging and crying from the tape, begging for the pain to stop, begging for heroin, crying for her father.

The hard control of her voice echoed those moments. "Why are you chasing me, Peter? You should be looking for those bombs. You know I won't talk."

"You *can* talk. That's good. I would hate to think I'd have to fuck you in silence. I like the noises you make when you have an orgasm."

Doucet watched Alex's jaw set. He saw her take a deep breath and release it slowly. Her eyes flashed with a hint of the rage he'd expected to see burning inside her.

She lifted her jaw and turned away from the team, showing them her back. "Was finding the first bomb all you thought it would be?" she replied, mocking and cold. "Was it as good for you as it was for me, Peter? That's how you're going to be fucked from now on."

On the other end of the phone, Peter Van de Moeter hesitated before he spoke. He tried to sound calm, but the fury vibrated beneath his words. He wasn't as good with the control as Alex. "I don't know what you're talking about."

"You have six less paychecks to worry about as of this afternoon, Peter. Let's see, one hundred dollars split—wait, how many of my father's people actually stayed with you? Torturing me for six months looks like it was expensive; you pissed through half his money in less than a year."

Peter blew out a breath. "Maybe I hid some of the money so you couldn't steal it."

"Oh, I think it was probably the fancy pastel suits and all the jewelry you've been buying. You have a certain lifestyle to maintain and these last three months you've lost so many business contracts—I know I talked to a few of them and they said they just weren't happy. I know you didn't spend much money on that elaborate set up in Afghanistan; and, I'll bet your benefactor is pissed off you haven't gotten any results. Such a shame, my father's empire crumbling between your fingers and the only person still willing to hire you is making demands you can't meet. Who are you more afraid of, Peter? The guy with the money or me?"

Her voice had gone dead. The combined effect of the hoarseness and the utter lack of emotion made her words the stuff of nightmares. It reminded Doucet of an old voodoo priest he'd met in the woods once when he was a kid.

"I'm not afraid of you," Peter replied on the phone.

The corner of Alex's mouth twitched towards a smirk. "You're not smart enough to be afraid of me."

Peter either didn't hear the threat or didn't think it was worthy of note. "I don't know who you have working for you; you're too stupid to do this on your own. You never even went to school; just a bunch of monks in some pits of Southeast Asia. I'm not sure you can even read. And there is no mystery man behind my actions. You're delusional."

Alex rolled her left shoulder as if it were stiff. She sighed. "I'm going to destroy you, Peter. Just when you think it can't get any worse, I'm going to kill you. Just at that moment when you think things are starting to look up again."

Peter's breath blew out in a laugh that carried across the frigid parking lot. "You found one of the bombs. Big deal, there are still seven of them and I'm close. Plus I have the resources to go to them. How are you going to get your crippled self around the country?"

She tilted her head. Her eyes narrowed and she turned back to Sinjin, meeting his eyes. Her gaze travelled to Ong, then to Prince and finally to Dyer. Someone hadn't reported in yet; someone hadn't told Peter that she wasn't crippled. "Maybe I will sell them to your buyer myself."

Sinjin felt his gut freeze.

"You wouldn't. Your father had some kind of perverted loyalty to the United States. You wouldn't betray that."

"My father set me up to be tortured," she said. "This is his country, not mine."

He chuckled. "You know Alex, I have all the tapes of everything I did to you. I sit and watch them and yank on my cock. I especially like the video of you begging me to let you suck it in exchange for the heroin. How is that addiction of yours doing by the way?"

"One of those shadows in the corner will be me one night. Don't sleep." She disconnected.

It started to ring again.

She threw it as far as she could. It arced through the cold darkness then hit the pavement and shattered into pieces.

Doucet watched her stare at it. He waited until she turned back. She lifted her chin and stared into his eyes. The parking lot lamp caught the metallic color in her eyes and shimmered with an almost alien glow. Sinjin felt a flare of heat.

"I need your help," she said told him. "I can't get to the last bomb without help."

Sinjin studied her, tried to read her and found that he couldn't. "Where is it? We'll send someone. You have all the others?" He spoke cautiously. He didn't think it would be that easy.

Alex shook her head. "That's not how we're going to play."

Doucet sighed. He'd been afraid of that. "This isn't a game, Alex."

"Really? So you weren't planning on taking my crazy, broken self and getting me to like you again so I'd tell you where the bombs are? I mean, if that's not the case, the Division could have sent a team more accustomed to hostile acquisitions."

He felt his face flush. He was glad for the darkness and his dusky complexion. "You want paid? You want to sell them? We'll pay."

"I'm not interested in money," she replied. "I have plenty of money. I just stole all of my father's money back from Peter. I never spent a dime of all the money the Division and the CIA paid me. And they paid me well to risk my life over and over again."

"What do you want?" Dyer asked. "If it's not money. That's what motivated your father."

Her eyes tore into Dyer as if she were ripping away layers. . "I'm only interested in one thing. Revenge."

Doucet sighed. "Revenge will eat you alive," he said after a long minute.

She shrugged. "I'm already dead on the inside. We both know you can't torture the answers out of me. You have to play my way."

Doucet sighed. "I can't let you murder someone. I can't just turn him over to you."

"Think of it as a pre-judicial execution," she told him.

Dyer shook his head. "Is that what you're telling yourself to sleep at night?"

Alex chuckled without humor in her face. "I don't sleep."

Dyer frowned. "You said you would never kill anyone. I was there when your father found out that you worked for the CIA. I remember how pissed he was and how you swore you would never kill anyone."

"I swore I wouldn't kill anyone for money," she replied. "Big difference."

Sinjin Doucet took a deep breath and let it out slowly. "Get in the truck," he said. "We'll talk about it."

She shook her head. A thick dark red lock of hair fell over her face, hiding one eye. Her boots were set at shoulder width. She didn't cross her arms, it was implied.

Doucet had five older sisters and a couple of nieces. He'd seen plenty of women get that look on their face and he knew better than to try talking her out of it. He managed to swallow his groan of frustration before it came out. The general's orders were specific in that he "was to do anything to get the location of those bombs, anything except for sleeping with her." He glanced at her mouth and line that her lips made. A flare of heat rushed through him again. He wanted to protect her, cradle the vulnerability he saw in her eyes.

Her hoarse voice refused to acknowledge any of that vulnerability though. "I'm not going anywhere unless you promise you will not take me to Division headquarters. You need to promise you will not tell the General Gregory I'm with you. The CIA will whisk me away and try to brainwash me into being their assassin—after their done poking me and dissecting me to figure out how I'm okay."

Dyer shook his head. "Alex, this is crazy. These are nuclear bombs. They will kill thousands of people if they go off, at least. That's not worth revenge on one person. No one is going to brainwash you, that's ridiculous."

"Peter killed my father. He's going to die."

"Your father knew what kind of risks he took and he always knew someone would betray him in the end," Dyer told her. "You don't think that he thought about that every day? He knew one day he wouldn't come home."

"Do you want to know what Peter did to me?" she asked in a low voice.

Doucet saw some color drain out of Dyer's face. It must have shown on all their faces.

"Ah," Alex said. She hugged herself and a shadow crossed over her tightly controlled face. She shrunk back against the SUV. Her breath came out shaky. "You've seen some video."

Doucet wasn't sure anyone else had heard her speak because it came out so softly. He started to reach out for her and she jerked away. "There's nothing to be embarrassed about," he said in a low voice.

She let out a cold laugh. "I don't remember enough to be embarrassed."

Doucet watched her shrug it off. Her arms fell to her sides. Her eyes avoided his. He grunted as if he accepted her answer, then put his hands in his pockets to appear less threatening. "Where is this last bomb?"

She squared her shoulders. The wind played with that lock of hair and Doucet resisted the urge to reach out and brush it away from her face. "West of here," she said. "A couple of cities west."

"Get in the truck before we all freeze to death," Doucet told her.

Dyer sighed in resignation. He turned away and faced forward out the front windshield. "Bullshit," he mumbled.

Alex hesitated as Ong walked around the vehicle to get in the other side.

"What now?" Doucet asked. "You won."

She swallowed. "Claustrophobia."

Doucet chuckled, then stopped when he saw her face. "Seriously?"

She shrugged.

"The back seat is a bench, the cargo area is behind it. It's a big open space," he told her. "We can open the back window if we have to. You will be fine."

She nodded, took a deep breath and climbed in.

Ong got in behind Dyer.

The men turned up the heat as Travis Prince started the engine.

Doucet looked at Alex as he sat in the seat behind Travis. Her face was pale in the darkness and her strange, flashing eyes bounced with stress. Or perhaps it wasn't stress. His job with the Division was rescue and extraction and he'd picked up a lot of bad people over the years—kill teams, assassins, people who'd killed their families for a chance at survival, people who'd betrayed their countries. Alex had been the Division's thief. She'd been able to steal things from places no one had ever been able to get to. "You okay?"

She blinked at him as if she'd forgotten where she was. She nodded.

Sinjin Doucet knew a lie when he saw one.

"Where to?" Travis asked as he pulled the SUV out of the parking lot and into the streets of downtown Cleveland.

"Highway west. I-90 towards Toledo," she said, the hoarseness didn't hide the shake in her voice.

Ong frowned at Doucet in the darkness. He turned to lean his body up against the door to open up space in front of Alex. He spoke in Chinese.

She bit her bottom lip.

Doucet pressed his lips together. He'd have to speak to Ong about those secret conversations. He couldn't help but feel his lieutenant was hiding something from him. Shadows filled Alex's face. Her haunted eyes sank into shadow as she tried to force her body to relax.

"I'm not hungry," she told Ong. "Get off the highway in a town called Sandusky."

Frank Dyer's head snapped around. "That's where your father is buried. Did you hide the bombs in your father's grave?"

"No," she replied, instantly back in control and on guard.

Doucet silently cursed the older man. His overbearing attitude was making this harder.

"Then why are you going there?" he asked. "Do you want to visit your father's grave?"

"He wouldn't want to see me until I've finished the job he gave me."

Frank Dyer grunted. "Alexandria Rae, you don't need to be belligerent. I loved your father like a brother. If you want to visit your father's grave, that can happen. Peter's people are probably watching it."

Sinjin sighed. "The CIA is probably watching it as well," he admitted out loud. "They have a hard on for you." He watched her eyes dart between him and Frank Dyer. So much for not playing games. But at the moment, they were all playing different ones.

Dyer shook his head and turned into the open space left by Ong.

Sinjin watched Alex pull back deeper into the shadows. He thought if she could jump out the back of the SUV, she would have.

Dyer continued, relentlessly. "Joe wouldn't want this to happen, Alex. He'd want you safe. He wouldn't want you to destroy yourself to avenge his death. I want Peter brought to justice too."

"You want the bombs. Everyone wants the bombs. Once you have them, you'll want me locked up. And you'll hunt me like pack of wolves hunting an injured rabbit," she replied, her lip curling.

"We want you to get help," the older man told her. "We want you to be safe. That's what your father wanted for you. And you're hardly an injured bunny rabbit."

"My father didn't want me safe. He wanted me to live."

"Same thing."

She let out an emotionless chuckle. "Not even close, Frank. That's why you could never fill his shoes."

The tension in the SUV rose a notch. Doucet gave a silent signal to Dyer to stop antagonizing her. "Alex, how did you get out of the hospital in New York? And where did you go?"

"I don't remember."

Doucet paused, studying her. "Did you see a doctor? I mean, our doctors said you would be crippled."

"I don't remember." Alex held his stare in the dark.

"I'm sorry we couldn't find you, Alex," he said.

"How do you feel?" Ong asked, changing the subject.

"Angry," she replied.

"I meant your ribs and any other injuries you might have from today," Ong told her. "And what about residual injuries? Chronic pain? Lack of movement or strength?"

"Nothing I can't deal with," she said.

"I have a med kit," Ong told her. "It has some pain killers in it."

"Not interested," she said. "Definitely not interested in pain killers or anything that makes me feel good and makes me lose control."

"You were drunk," Dyer pointed out. "That didn't seem to be a problem."

Alex arched an eyebrow at the sergeant. "There are six dead mercenaries who might disagree. If I'd been sober, maybe things would have ended less traumatically."

Doucet suddenly realized that he hadn't patted her down for weapons. He saw a smirk stretch across her full lips as if she'd read his mind. Her eyes didn't miss much and they held no emotion at all. He felt a flutter in the pit of his stomach, the feeling he got when he was in the midst of a mission and the shit was about to hit the fan.

"Yes," she told him, leaning forward with a wince. "You should have checked me for weapons, Captain. And yes, I am carrying. However, I don't intend to kill anyone who doesn't deserve it."

"Who makes the decision?" he asked.

She chuckled. "You believe in God? Maybe God. A god. Maybe just me." She shrugged. "Life is a risk. And you've reached the edge."

The SUV got very quiet. The tires hummed along the highway.

"You think God is telling you what to do?" Dyer asked carefully. He exchanged a look with his team members.

Doucet shifted and reached into his jacket, wrapping his hand around the butt of the weapon holstered inside his jacket.

Alex yawned and leaned back. Her right arm wrapped around her broken ribs. Her left arm didn't move from its limp spot on the seat, three months of practice. "After you get off the highway in Sandusky, find a hotel, Prince," she said. "I need a few hours of sleep if I'm going to get you all to the last bomb."

CHAPTER FIVE

The cave should smell like blood. It should reek of it, but Alex couldn't smell anything. Her nose was broken and filled with dried blood. She breathed through her mouth, tasting metallic blood and bile. Her throat felt raw. The skin on her face felt hot and tight, she could feel the tracks of dried tears. The shame of crying and begging and screaming had fled long ago.

Her shoulders hurt. Her back and her legs throbbed with pain. Between the drugs and the periods of unconsciousness, she'd lost all sense of time. The cave had no access to outside light. This was her world: this cave and the one they dragged her to between sessions of torture. Enough time had passed for her to forget anything but the routine—the pain, the drugs, the humiliation, the violation, the dark cold of unconsciousness, and the sting of waking up repeated over and over again.

Her heart beat a slow rhythm. Normally, her heart pounded against her chest like a terrified sparrow being taken into a mineshaft to die. That was their new tactic: amp her up on speed so things hurt more. She stared down at the stone floor, covered in a fresh coat of blood. Maybe the drugs had just bled out of her. Either way, despite the pain and the blood and everything else, she planned on taking advantage of the reprieve. Ideally, she should give up. But something inside her, curled into a tight ball, refused. Something would not let her give up, not ever.

The two mercenaries in the room played cards near the door to the torture chamber. They were blurry around the edges. They played with lackluster energy. She could only see them with one eye—the other eye had swollen shut. This was the first time they'd pounded on her face; Peter had warned against it before. He wanted a pretty face. But apparently that had changed.

The end was nigh. The thought almost made her chuckle.

The mercs glanced up from their card game. She realized she'd chuckled out loud.

The mercs turned away, mumbling something about crazy chicks.

While the mercs weren't looking, she lifted herself up to take some of the pressure off her shoulders. The end might be coming, but she could still lift herself up. If she could just gather up enough strength she might be able to get the ropes off the hook imbedded in the ceiling of the cave. Her freedom counted on the anticipated dump of adrenalin to get her through a fight and a chase after she managed to get loose.

As she contemplated escape, the torturer returned to the room. He wore a fresh white lab coat. He scowled when he saw her pulling herself up. He reminded Alex of an Asian Cheech Marin from that movie her father had laughed at and forced her to watch, *Up in Smoke*. Her father had been a pot smoker—she really thought she could use some of that right now. But she had the heroin…and the heroin would come if she lived. They needed it to control her; she needed it to go on.

The torturer's hand tightened on a long curved blade in his hand. The handle of the blade was carved white ivory.

Alex doubted if it had ever been used before, the white was too white, and no one would ever be able to get blood out of those intricate details. Some damn ceremonial blade. She rolled her eyes. Figures the asshole would turn out to be some kind of fanatic.

He punched her hard in the gut, knocking the air out of her lungs.

She wheezed to get her breath back.

He swung the blade.

The blade cut the ropes.

She fell to the stone floor into the pool of blood and maybe piss too, who knew. Maybe she'd die of an infection since she wasn't lucky enough to break her neck on the fall. She just couldn't seem to let go enough to crack her head open.

The torturer shoved her to her back. He straddled her chest pinning her arms with his knees.

Alex didn't try to fight. The exercise in futility had been tried before.

The man brought out a small vial filled with silver liquid. The liquid inside seemed to bubble and churn.

Alex thought she might be hallucinating.

"No more games," the torturer said. He spoke Chinese, a regional dialect which Alex knew. She'd travelled all over the vast country and most of the Far East and she'd grown up having to pick up languages and dialects quickly. Still, there was something about his decision to use Chinese now that made Alex's heart jump.

The fucking video equipment mounted to the wall still blinked green. She suspected Peter watched her torture from the safety of some well-appointed room. The torturer had spoken only English to her until now. She'd cursed his heritage in a dozen languages; but he'd never reacted. She'd cried and screamed and begged for her father in a dozen other languages. She couldn't remember if she'd used the dialect he spoke now. But now that he used it, she fell into a panic.

He pulled the stopper off the vial, held it up over her shoulder and tipped it.

Alex watched it fall. It seemed to come in slow motion. *Oh shit, oh shit, oh shit, not this not this not thisnotthisnotthis,* a voice in her head started to shout. It felt like a real voice, like a voice that wasn't her own. It felt like something alive inside of her. The voice created a panic of its own which made her heart pound faster and harder.

The liquid hit her shoulder.

It was heavy. Like molten lead.

Pain to awaken the Soul of the Sword! the voice in her head yelled, almost gleefully, but full of terror. Alex felt nothing in her shoulder. But the voice felt like it was taking over her body.

"Where is it? Where is the Sword of Souls? Tell me where you've hidden the Sword of Souls," the torturer demanded in Chinese. "Tell me and I will neutralize the compound."

Alex furrowed her brow and laughed at him. This is how he thought he'd get what he wanted when he hadn't been able to get what Peter Van de Moeter wanted? This liquid? This was nothing. She turned to her shoulder. Smoke was rising from it. The smoke formed into the image of her teacher, Chen Sakai. She had a fleeting thought that she was hallucinating something from a Star Wars movie, which sucked because she really didn't want to be Luke Skywalker. No, if she had a choice, she would have chosen to be Chewbacca—intimidating and half wild. Don't mess with the Wookie. Let the Wookie win. She wanted to be Chewbacca. She wasn't the hero.

"Do not speak the name of the weapon. It is not to be spoken," Sakai's smoke ghost told her. "Those who speak the name must die."

The pain hit.

Alex thought she'd felt pain.

Nothing compared to this.

This was pain.

Her shoulder started to dissolve into a pool of liquid. She screamed in agony. Her mind searched for any escape.

"Tell me where," the torturer demanded. "Give me the Sword of Souls! I will end it."

She screamed a curse in the language he used. She didn't even comprehend what kind of curse.

The torturer paled. He fell back off of her, stumbling across the floor on his butt. His eyes were wide and filled with terror of his own.

She screamed until her vocal cords ruptured. She started to choke on the scream and the pieces of her shredded throat. Her pounding heart shuddered and stopped. *IT IS FORBIDDEN!* screamed the voices in her head, ripping through her brain and tearing it to shreds. *WAKE UP!!*

She was vaguely aware of shouting. Of Peter's whine that he couldn't have a disfigured trophy wife. Of doctors screaming that she was dying, that her heart had stopped, that she was stroking out. Her eyes rolled back in her head.

"Wake up, Alex!" A voice screamed at her. "Alex!" Hands shook her.

She jerked awake. She didn't know where she was. She started to fight the hands on her arms.

"Easy! It's me! It's Sinjin!"

Alex rolled out of the bed to get away from him, stumbling when she got caught on the sheets. She was gasping, her right hand grabbed her left shoulder to make sure it was there. She moaned as the memory of the pain lingered with her. Her clothes stuck to her sweat-covered body. She'd been sleeping in her clothes.

The hotel room had a balcony. Alex opened the door and staggered out into the cold March air before the walls could close in on her. Living on the streets hadn't been so bad. She sucked in the cold air and fought back the nausea that threatened to leave her heaving over the side.

Her hands gripped the iron bar of the rail and she leaned out into the darkness. Three stories below sat the dark SUV which belonged to the Division. A few cars scattered around the parking lot. A line of trees separated this side of the hotel from residential homes. None of the homes had lights on. She could hear the sound of traffic on the highway. She tried to focus on that.

The memory of the taste of blood lingered in the back of her throat, refusing to let her release the dream into the darkness.

A hand touched her shoulder.

She stumbled away from the big body invading her personal space. A hand caught her before she toppled over the railing.

"Sorry, I didn't mean to scare you," Doucet said, holding on to her. He rubbed her arm before handing her his jacket. "Put it on or you'll get sick."

"I've been living outside for three months," she managed. "This feels like spring." Still, she grabbed it and slid it over her long-sleeved t-shirt.

"Ah, *cher*," Doucet said softly, his Cajun accent thick. "*Mo chagren. Pauve ti bête.*" He reached for her and pulled her in to his arms.

Alex fought the urge to get away. She swallowed bile.

Doucet rubbed her back. "It was just a dream, *bebe*. I will not let anyone hurt you again."

Alex looked up at him. She could feel the warmth of his body seeping into hers. Once, they'd been friends. They'd flirted and danced around mutual attraction, but never acted on it. They had to work together; it would make things awkward.

He sighed. "Tell me where those bombs are, *cher*; and, come back to New York with me. I'll take some time off; we'll go to the *dojo* and train with Sensei Master Daisuke."

The Japanese name sounded strange through the Cajun accent. Alex met his dark eyes. She felt his heartbeat change against her hands. Guang's voice was in her head, telling her not to sleep with him. There were other good reasons not to sleep with Sinjin Doucet: she knew he was a womanizer and, in fact, he'd gotten a lot of good scores over the years because women tried to compete with her. Her father had a patent distrust of officers and had warned her against him years ago.

"Maybe Sensei Daisuke can help your nightmares," Sinjin told her. His voice rough.

"Maybe you can help me with my nightmares," she said. And maybe he could. Maybe sleeping with him, just a casual, fun exchange of comfort would erase the rapes. She had been her father's daughter once, always game for a roll in the hay without any strings.

He leaned down.

Alex steeled herself and her racing heart.

His lips found hers.

She returned the kiss, shoving the pending panic out of her mind.

His big hand spread open on the small of her back and moved down.

Alex tilted her head and opened her lips.

He took advantage and picked her up at the same time. He carried her back into the room and to the bed.

Alex put all thought out of her head and desperately yanked at his belt buckle. As their mouths attacked each other and their tongues wrestled. She felt his hand cup her breast.

He groaned when her hand slid into his pants and broke the connection to her mouth only long enough to yank his shirt over his head.

They were both breathing hard as they went back at each other.

Someone pounded on the door.

They both froze.

Doucet's hand covered her breast, her hand was inside his jeans.

Alex grabbed his neck with her free hand and pulled him down to her mouth. "Ignore them. They'll go away," she said. She kissed him.

He kissed back, easily forgetting the knocking.

The pounding returned. "Doucet!"

"Fuck," Sinjin growled and uttered another curse in Cajun. "It's the general."

Alex pulled her shirt down as he stood up and pulled his zipper closed again.

"Doucet! Open the fucking door!"

Alex waited for him to start for the door, then rolled off the bed. She grabbed the sheathed sword from its spot propped up against the night stand.

Doucet opened the door and stepped out into the hall. "General, I wasn't expecting you."

"Yeah, well I wasn't expecting you to be thinking with your dick."

Alex opened the balcony door. Three stories up with balconies all the way down. It would be easy for her to escape that way. But she didn't really want to escape. She just wanted to make it look like she wanted to escape.

"What the hell are they doing here, General?!" Doucet demanded. "I thought you were trusting us with this."

Alex wasn't surprised the general hadn't come alone. General Gregory knew her father and probably had access to her CIA training records. He'd ordered her into situations he wouldn't have ordered anyone else. Not because it was his job to do so, but because he knew she could do it—or so he'd told her one day when he accused her of being better than anyone knew. If Powell had been smart, he would have clued in Gregory to some of the other training the CIA had given her. If Gregory had been smart, he would have told Powell some of the things she'd done. If the men had compared notes, her gig would have been up. For a fleeting moment, she worried that maybe her return to their radar had forced them to compare notes. She quickly ruled that out; Powell was CIA and CIA never showed their hands.

She slid under the mattress, pulling her sword with her. She wasn't going to make it easy. She swallowed the claustrophobia and the threat of a panic attack. There'd been an extended period of time where she'd been put in a cave that was barely wide enough for her to breathe. She hadn't been able to move her arms or legs. Spiders and bugs crawled over her and she could do nothing about it. She couldn't even take deep breaths because there just wasn't enough space. She preferred the beatings.

"Step aside, Captain," General Gregory growled. His voice muffled by the mattress.

Alex forced herself to breath slowly.

"General, I can explain."

Heavy bootfalls rushed into the room. Alex heard them circle the bed and head to the open doors.

Gregory gave a sour laugh. "How about you explain to me why you look like some high school chump who's just been caught by his girlfriend's father?"

Alex bit her bottom lip. A minute later and the general would have been interrupting something a hell of a lot more than some high school dry humping.

Doucet was silent.

"Yeah, I thought so," Gregory said. "The man who raised her was an infamous mercenary and she's a trained CIA agent. She's playing you, Captain."

"That's not true, Sir."

"Stop thinking with your dick."

"General, the room's empty and the balcony door is open," a stranger's voice announced. "She won't get far."

"See that she doesn't," Gregory barked.

Boots thumping the ground again as they rushed out of the room.

Gregory cleared his throat. "So, a group of highly trained mercenaries managed to get the drop on you and your team, four of the most highly trained and competent soldiers in the United States. But one woman, one drunk woman who almost certainly has Post Traumatic Stress Disorder if not some more serious mental issues, this one woman managed to completely neutralize the mercenaries by herself. You want to tell me that she's harmless? Is that what you are going to tell me, Captain?" Gregory's voice came gruff and demanded attention.

"General, you want the bombs," Dyer said. "And you wanted us to convince Alex to tell us. We wanted to get her to trust us. You told us to do what we had to."

"You think letting her seduce your commanding officer is the way to get that done, Sergeant?" Gregory growled. "You knew her father better than any of these men. You know what he trained his daughter to be. And then, in the government's almighty wisdom, we added CIA operative training to the mix. Do any of you really believe she wouldn't use everything she has to get what she wants?"

"Alex isn't that way," Doucet said.

Gregory snorted a laugh. "Captain, her father knew she would be able to resist unimaginable torture and live to avenge his murder. He probably knew he wouldn't be able to resist it; he probably made sure they'd kill him so they would try to get the information from her instead of him—his secrets were better kept with her than with him. There's a special place in hell for fathers who send their children on paths of destruction and Joe McBrady is sitting on the throne. A year ago, we all thought Alex wasn't able to kill someone; and, today, I got a lot of bodies which suggest that was incorrect."

In the darkness, Alex waited. She heard Doucet come back into the room. She heard him collect his shirt and shoes. He sat down on the other bed and put on his shoes. She closed her eyes and tried to think of her martial arts kata as the mattress sank down towards her.

"Only one bed slept in?" Dyer asked.

"I wasn't sleeping, I was watching," Doucet said, his accent completely gone. "And Sergeant, I don't appreciate you making sure it was just me and her alone in this room together."

"I figured since you and her did all that Bruce Lee stuff with a sword together, that she'd trust you sooner than anyone else. I didn't think you'd make the moves on her."

"I didn't," he said.

There was a long pause.

"I kissed her. She kissed me," he said. "She had a nightmare. I was comforting her. It just happened."

Dyer grunted. "She said she needs us to retrieve the last bomb. That means she has the others. She'll have hidden them.

Van de Moeter got all of Joe's storage units and property," Dyer said. "Joe didn't leave her a thing. Where would she hide them?"

Alex heard Doucet stand up.

"Which means she has other resources we don't know about; doesn't it?" Doucet asked, his voice moving away.

Alex heard them go out into the hall. She heard the door shut.

She waited a few moments; but, the claustrophobia had her shaking and nearly hyperventilating. She slid the mattress aside and climbed out of the empty space. She brushed the thick dust off her clothes and swung her sword over her shoulder, so it was strapped low across her back. Her heart skipped a beat when she saw her boots sitting right next to the night stand. Perhaps she'd gotten lucky and none of the four highly trained Marines had noticed the boots.

The fleeting hope was dashed by the perfection of the silence behind her. Then the sound of a pistol slide being pulled back to chamber a round.

She slowly lifted her hands above her shoulders.

"Rookie mistake," Frank Dyer said. His voice was even and empty of emotion. All business.

"I'm out of practice," she replied.

"You move and I'll have to shoot you."

"Are you aiming for my head, my heart, or the back of my knee, Uncle Frank?" she asked. She threw in the "uncle" part in hope that it would make it harder for him to hold the weapon on her. She'd deliberately not used it since their reunion. She also had no reason to believe anyone would actually shoot her.

"I don't want to hurt you," he said. "You're like a daughter to me. A stubborn, belligerent daughter in need of boarding school."

"Another reason you were never good enough to be my father," she replied.

He grunted like the words were a punch to his gut. "The captain is going to cuff you," Dyer said. "Make a move on him and I pull the trigger."

Alex heard Sinjin move. She felt his hand on her shoulder. It moved down her arm and brought it down to the small of her back. A zip tie plastic cuff went around the scars.

"I'm taking your sword," he said, his voice close to her ear.

"Don't pull it out of the scabbard," Alex told him. "It will kill you." She felt his body stiffen slightly. She wasn't doing real good with having her hands trapped either.

"Okay, *cher*?" Doucet asked just as softly and privately as he'd mentioned the sword.

She took a deep breath and let it out slowly. She nodded. She stepped into her untied boots.

"Put your weapons away," Doucet ordered his men as Alex turned to face the room.

The three members of the extraction team all had their weapons trained on her. Three red dots centered on her chest. The three dots came from the weapons of the Marines from the Division assault team who stood behind in the room as well, one of them had never left the balcony. Kudos to them. She let Doucet lead her around to the foot of the bed.

"Alex," a gruff voice familiar voice barked.

She faced the owner of the voice as he moved into the room between Dyer and Prince. General Gregory was shorter than her, but he felt bigger in the room. *Five of the six suspects here*, the voice in her head said. *You could take them all out and then go to New York and finish off Powell in his sleep. Stop listening to a monk for advice.* "General," she replied, pretending the voice wasn't compelling.

"You going to tell me where those bombs are," Gregory said.

"I'm fine, General. Thanks for asking. You and Frank have shown such concern for my well-being, I'm a little overwhelmed by the support. You've both always been like family. I hardly miss my father at all," she said.

He scoffed. "I'll get Van de Moeter for you. I'll throw him in a cage. Don't be an ass."

"You have a way to get him to surrender?" she asked with sarcasm.

He sighed. "We're going back to the Division to talk about this," he said. "You took all his money and you have the bombs, so I think we can negotiate something with him before his own people kill him."

Alex licked her lips and smirked. She'd tested all of their security. They couldn't keep her locked down forever. And they weren't going to torture her because she'd proven that tactic didn't work. She'd die before she talked. She had died and she still hadn't talked.

"You're going with these guys." He indicated the assault team.

She shook her head. "I'm only going peacefully with Doucet and his team, General."

"You're not really in a position to negotiate," the assault team leader told her, moving to stand next to the general.

Alex ignored him, pretended he wasn't even there. "Doucet keeps my sword." The tension in the room rose. She felt Doucet's hand tighten around her arm. "It's old and expensive and I don't trust it in the hands of people who don't appreciate swords. I want him to give it to his martial arts teacher in New York for safe keeping, until I can retrieve it. I want to make sure that neither the Division nor the CIA have it—disagree with this and we're going to have issues."

"You aren't going to be able to retrieve it for a while," the leader of the other team said, stowing his weapon in the holster on his thigh.

Gregory sighed. "He can keep your sword," Gregory said, defusing the suspicion a touch. "He'll deliver it to his *sensei.* That's my only compromise, Alex."

She gave him an amused look. "No. It's not. But since you're being so generous, I'll compromise too. I will agree not to kill any of these gorillas who have guns pointed at me; I'll just put all of them in the hospital and hurt them enough to end their careers. We can avoid the hospital if you accept that I'll go with Doucet and Dyer."

"How about you go in a body bag?" the leader of the other team said.

Alex ignored him and held the general's gaze.

Gregory shook his head. "Not going to happen, Alex. Doucet's team is too emotionally involved. I am certain you'll use that against them."

Alex wondered if he really believed he was calling her bluff. "You should remember the soup kitchen, General. I have nothing to lose. The only person I gave a shit about is dead. I don't care if I live or die. No one in this hallway has been in a fight like the one I bring to the table and none of them have been in a fight with someone who really doesn't care if they survive the fight or not."

"You want to live long enough to see Peter dead," Gregory said.

Alex sighed. "Keep me in check with the promise of Peter. Keep Peter in check with the promise of survival. It's going to collapse around you. You're holding on to a house of cards and I'm the wind."

Gregory made a face. He lifted his jaw at the leader of the other team who was ready to haul her off.

The man stepped forward and grabbed her left arm, pulling her out of Doucet's grip. He turned and started to move through his gauntlet of armed men.

"General, you probably should have told him to grab my good arm," Alex said as she passed him.

He spun, shock on his face. "Alex, no—!"

Alex waited until she was sure he was watching before she exploded into action as if a trigger had been pulled or a switch had been flipped. Using the wall opposite the open door of the hotel room as a launching point, she flipped backwards with a tuck and curl which brought her cuffed hands in front of her body. She jumped forward and up onto the wall again to avoid one of the assault team members grabbing her. On the way down, she dislocated a knee and knocked the leader out cold and used her zip ties around a third man's neck like a garrote. She shoved her boot into the back of the man's leg and forced him to his knees in front of Gregory.

The man being choked tried to get at the plastic cutting into his neck, but Alex had it digging into his flesh. If she'd had a wire garrote, it would be cutting into his flesh. His big combat boots tried to kick and he tried to elbow her, but she stood where he couldn't get her.

A fourth man, the one she'd jumped over, pressed his gun to her head. His eyes were cold and Alex figured he had no qualms about pulling the trigger and sending a bullet into her brain. "Let him go," the man with the gun to her head ordered.

"You said you weren't going to kill anyone," Doucet said from behind his own weapon. He aimed his 1911 .45 at her heart and she didn't even wonder if he'd miss. The man was a good shot and often took on the sharpshooting duties of his team.

Alex stared into his eyes over the gaping black barrel of his weapon. She bit at her bottom lip, reminding him that moments earlier he'd been the one biting at her lip. "Ain't nobody dead yet." She smirked at them all. "General? I want you to know that I am thinking about breaking this guy's neck before taking this other guy's weapon and putting two rounds in his brain."

"Even you aren't that fast," Gregory growled.

Alex saw the doubt in his eyes.

"No one is that fast," he said.

"I don't have to be that fast. He's going to hesitate before he pulls the trigger. He knows I have a bunch of dirty bombs that could potentially kill millions. He knows if I die, anyone could find those bombs. He has orders to keep me alive at any cost; doesn't he?" The struggles of the man she was choking were getting weaker; she loosened up a touch.

General Gregory growled. "Sergeant, lower your weapon."

When the man did so reluctantly, Gregory arched a bushy gray eyebrow at her.

Alex stopped choking the man. He fell forward gasping as the blue drained out of his lips.

"Doucet, take her down to the cars. Search her for more weapons before you put her in."

Alex smiled. She knew it looked like madness danced in her eyes. Perhaps it was madness. One of them would be pushed to desperation; one of them would reveal themselves a traitor. And then the game could end. *I still think you should just kill them all,* said the voice in her head.

CHAPTER SIX

Nothing like cold water in the face. Alex had regained consciousness in worse ways, however. She gasped at the shock of it and sucked in a lung-full of muddy water. Her thoughts came lucid enough to decide that perhaps this was one of the worse ways to regain consciousness after all. She'd been trained to go from sleep to alert without a transition, to regain consciousness without confusion. Both her last teacher Chen Sakai and the CIA had drilled it in to her. It helped her not to panic now.

She ignored her body's urge to expel the water, knowing it would only lead to sucking in more. She needed to preserve as much oxygen as she could. A quick assessment of her situation told her that she was still strapped into the SUV with her hands cuffed behind her. The last thing she remembered was Doucet leaning towards her to check if the seatbelt was tight enough. She'd barely seen the punch coming and didn't have time to react to it.

The current of the cold water pressed against her and it tugged at the flowing hair covering her face. Unable to see, the world seemed dark, mucky, cold, and eerily quiet; underwater was a horrific place to be. She'd been tortured with water on some days, left to drown than pumped back to life. That hadn't been nearly as bad as the tight cave cracks she'd been shoved into where she couldn't move—cracks where she'd been hanging upside down and that they'd filled with water.

Alex tried to lift her knees and kick something, but something was pinning her legs. Doucet had woven the seatbelt around her zip-tied wrists so that she could barely move. She'd been fighting the claustrophobia which is why she hadn't seen the punch coming. She leaned to the left to see if her head could find the window.

She hit her head hard. Her lungs screamed for air, or at least the ability to cough out the water she'd sucked in. Her body was quickly reaching the point where it would ignore her commands and involuntarily try to breathe. When it did that, she would drown. She didn't particularly want to drown; if she was going to die, she preferred to die almost any other way. Mostly, she wanted to die fighting.

She shook her head to get the hair out of her face and try to see something. When she managed to get her hair away, she found herself face-to-face with the unblinking, foggy eyes of Travis Prince. His face was right in front of hers. From its position, she guessed that it was his body pinning her legs down. A round hole had punched through the man's forehead, a thin trail of blood leaked from the hole into the murk.

Alex stared at him, shocked and upset despite the fact that she had been contemplating his death. The fact that he was dead didn't exonerate him, but she felt it went a long way.

A hand grabbed her arm. Right arm.

If she'd been able to breath, she would have let out a shriek of surprise.

A knife flashed. She couldn't see anything other than a man's hand and the black cuff of a long sleeve. It came from behind her, where the open cargo area of the big government Excursion was.

The knife made quick work of the seatbelt. The hand holding her arm tugged. It let go of her arm and reached forward, planted itself over Prince's face and shoved the dead man back.

She felt the weight shift off her legs. The hand grabbed her and yanked again. This time, she floated free. Letting her body go limp seemed to be the best plan of attack because her vision was tunneling and the cold numbed her body. She couldn't survive or win any kind of struggle at the moment. The hand pulled her in the opposite direction of what she thought was up. It sent a wave of panic through her that made her control over her breathing slip. Her body gulped for air and only got water. She could taste the mud and muck as she fought the hand pulling her. The muck tunneled with blackness and the world went away.

Minutes later, Alex coughed water out of her lungs. The freezing cold air felt like needles against her skin. She forced herself up to her hands and knees. Her wrists were still tied together with the zip ties. She retched up water as her body shook violently from the cold. There was a roaring in her ears that kept her from hearing anything. She forced her eyes to focus. Silent images like some kind of old movie ticked away in slow motion.

A man pointed an assault rifle over the hood of a big pickup truck. His body jerked with recoil. Fire flashed from the muzzle of it. A layer of low-hanging smoke filled the air. Her nose stung with the smell of gunfire and burning rubber. She looked further than the shooter. There was a van with its side panels open facing in the direction that the shooter was firing. She could see through the doors to a big box truck this one facing her. There were more men pointing weapons on the other side of the van and using the box truck for shielding.

Someone shouted behind her.

The noise came out of the silence.

She jumped and spun in surprise. The twist made her lose her balance and she fell back on her butt, numb hands scraping on the rough asphalt road. Another guy shielded himself behind the back wheels of the truck. He was drenched, and his clothing had started to stiffen with the cold. The ends of his spiky hair looked shiny as they started to freeze. He was struggling with shaking arms.

He looked at her.

Eye contract brought the sound of gunfire through her haze. The pings of bullets as they jabbed through sheet metal into the truck. Dark smoke billowed up into the air as weapons fire made the van's engine catch fire and start to burn. The wind brought the thick black smoke over the pickup truck. The smoke isolated her and the two men.

These men had been trained by her father. She'd seen her father stage an ambush like this. Three vehicles blocking a road. They'd executed perfectly it appeared; however, they did not have the benefit of her father to adapt them to a new threat. Her father never would have brought a threat behind his line of attack; and, Alex knew she was a much bigger threat to them than the Division's black ops Marines. She couldn't figure out why they hadn't just loaded her up in their vehicles and taken off, leaving the Division to pick up the pieces.

She looked around for an answer. Beyond the man hiding behind the wheel well, the gray bay water danced and spat against big boulders. It was March. Ice covered the boulder break wall. In the slushy water beyond, four tires stuck up out of the opaque surface. The front two barely visible in the depths. It had felt deeper than that. She was going to have to go back in and get her sword, she realized with a shudder. She needed her sword. She looked back at the man using the back wheel and axle as protection from the flying bullets.

He pointed his pistol at her. His aim shook violently. There was no way in hell he'd hit her.

Alex wanted the Glock he was holding. She preferred bladed weapons; but, her father and the CIA believed people shouldn't bring swords and knives to gunfights. Right now, in the middle of a firefight with her Sword submerged in a nearly frozen bay and her own rapidly progressing hypothermia, Alex needed a fucking gun. *You don't need the Sword*, the voice whispered slyly in her mind. *You are the weapon, the Sword is merely the tool.* She shook her head to get the voice to go away.

She saw the man with the shaking gun widen his eyes as if he knew she'd been hearing voices.

Her eyes narrowed.

If he knows, he can't live.

Alex started to roll from her butt up to a crouch. Something hit her hard. It felt like a truck. It picked her up, flipped her over and slammed her down hard onto her back. The air punched out of her lungs. An instant later white-hot pain seared through her side.

She tried to sit up.

Stabbing pain iced through her and held her down.

She grabbed her side, lifted her hands and looked at the bright red blood dripping from them. She tried to breath and coughed. The taste of muck in her mouth was replaced with the metallic taste of blood. She groaned and rolled to her side, curling up around the pain.

"Fuck! Fuck!" shouted the man from behind the wheel well. He raced over to her, putting his weapon in its holster as he did. He grabbed Alex's shoulder and rolled her to her back.

She didn't have the inclination to fight him at the moment.

The guy ripped off his sopping wet shirt and shoved it at her side. "Medic!" he shouted as he shoved away Alex's hands.

Alex's back arched and growled against the pain as his wet shirt slapped and squished against the bullet wound. It wasn't spurting blood, but it was coming out in waves. She knew she was bleeding to death, but it would take a while for that to happen. Maybe a couple of hours. Which left her plenty of time to end this.

She turned her head and looked under the truck.

Twenty feet away from the wedge of mercenary vehicles, a second Division SUV lay on its side. It was smoldering and the smoke was getting blacker. Soon there would be flames from it too. Three feet in front of the vehicle lay a body of one of the

Division's assault team, his body twisted, bloody and broken. Three feet in front of the body lay her sword.

Glass glittered on the pavement around the matte black weapon which seemed to blend into the blacktop. It lay hidden amid the glass and broken pieces of plastic and metal. If she didn't feel it, she might have missed it. It seemed to almost melt into the blacktop.

Alex felt it waiting. She felt it, throbbing cold in her veins. *Now*, the voice in her head whispered like a lover whispering some secret enticement in her ear. *Now, it begins. Choose. Hesitate and it will not be forgiven this time.* A wave of *déjà vu* whispered through her; back to an alley in New York City. *Choose. Do not hesitate this time.*

Alex did not hesitate. She reached for the weapon. She forgot about the person kneeling beside her applying pressure to her side. She forgot about the difficulty breathing. She forgot about all of it. She stretched for the weapon.

Pain leaped through her as her torso twisted.

The pain brought on a surge of overwhelming anger.

The mercenary working on her gunshot wound shoved her shoulders back to the asphalt. "Stay put or you're going to bleed to death, you dumb bitch."

Alex moved quickly and without real conscious thought. She grabbed the survival blade which hung on the mercenary's belt, ripped it free of its sheath, and cut the wrist ties.

The mercenary tried to catch her hands to stop her, but he was too slow.

Alex cut his outstretched wrist with the sharp side of the blade and cut deep. Blood sprang up from the gash.

The hand which had been pushing down on Alex's side reached up to clamp over the gushing wrist.

Alex took advantage of his inattention. She rolled to her stomach and belly crawled under the truck to the other side. Alex pulled herself out from under the truck and stood up. She glanced down at the drops of blood hitting the pavement beside her waterlogged boot.

It looked like a battleground on this side of the mercenary road-blocking wedge. Glass, car fluids, plastic, blood, and things that had been inside the vehicles littered the area. Alex's squishing, water-filled boots crunched over the broken glass. She wrapped her left arm around her stomach, holding her hand over her bleeding side as she moved and scanned. To her right, a mercenary faced the ditch between the road and the raised railroad track. He held a weapon to the head of a shorter man with a shock of white hair cut in a high and tight Marine Corps fashion. The shorter man's suit was wrinkled and flapped in the wind coming off the water.

The Division people in the ditch had apparently seen her and chosen to hold their fire. The mercenary out in the open didn't realize this. His people were still yelling behind the vehicles, but their voices were all mangled together and unintelligible.

The mercenary concentrated on the ditch where his current enemy had taken up positions. "You shot her! She got hit by a stray bullet and she'll bleed to death if we don't get her to a hospital soon," the mercenary yelled at the hunkered down people. "Throw out your weapons and we'll just leave. I'll drop this guy off a couple miles down the road."

Alex stumbled to the sword. She dropped to both knees in front of it, oblivious to the sting of glass cutting into her knees. The dead Division man stared at her. She saw her shadow reflected in his eyes in front of a growing light in the sky behind her. She took a deep breath, tilted her head back and stared up into the sky.

Take it!

She reached out a bloodstained hand and wrapped it around the scabbard.

A soft whooshing sound filled the chilly morning air. At first, she thought it was inside her head, but then she caught a glimpse of a flicker of flame from the SUV.

The SUV's gas tank exploded. A huge cloud of black smoke billowed out around her.

Coughing didn't help the pain in her side.

Alex picked up the weapon and flung it across her back. She gripped the survival knife and turned towards the spot where she'd seen the mercenary threatening General Gregory.

The mercenary and Gregory appeared in the cloud in front of her as if there'd been a special clearing made just for them. Both of them stared right at her. She could only imagine what she looked like. Wet. Bloody. Frozen. Her temper unleashed.

It must have been bad because the mercenary stopped pointing his weapon at Gregory's head and straightened his arm so the weapon pointed at her.

Alex stopped. She could feel the heat of blood still running from her side. She dropped her left hand to her side. The sword strapped across her back throbbed in time with her slow heartbeat. She lifted her hands up, revealing the survival knife still in her hand, its blade resting along the inside of her wrist and arm.

As expected, his eyes darted at the weapon.

In that instant of inattention, Alex launched. She tackled both men.

They all went down hard. Alex shoved the blade into the mercenary's eye, nicking the General's ear with the sharp blade on the way in. She shoved it deep into his brain, using her momentum and all of her body weight. She could feel the blade scraping against bone.

The merc's body flailed, but he had two bodies on top of him holding him down. He screamed, high pitched and feral. His hand started involuntarily squeezing off rounds.

Gregory grabbed the wrist to direct the flailing arm away from himself and Alex.

Alex twisted the knife with every ounce of strength she had.

The body went stiff then collapsed.

Gregory turned to face her.

Alex punched him in the face and grabbed the gun. She pushed off the body and up to her feet. She pulled back the slide with her bloody hands. The chambered round flew out. She tossed the weapon away into the black, gritty smoke.

Gregory knelt on the ground. His gray eyes resigned and accepting. There was no fear.

Alex was breathing hard. Her side bled. Her hand, covered in blood from her own wound and the mercenary's death, held on to the knife.

Gregory's eyes drifted down to her side. "Do you need a doctor?" he asked. His gruff voice holding sympathy and concern, real concern.

Alex shook her head once. "Stray bullet—from the direction of that ditch."

Gregory's eyes narrowed. "They should know better. They should be better. No one should have been able to plan an ambush." He lifted his bushy gray eyebrows. "Fuck. That's what this is about; isn't it, Alex. It's not just Peter. You're chasing a mole."

"Stop chasing me, General. It will be bad for your health. You won't live a second time." She slipped into the smoke, hoping the move was all ninja-like because, to be honest, she wasn't feeling it. She moved to the wedge of mercenary vehicles.

She slipped between the van and the truck. The smoke thinned here.

A mercenary came at her from inside the van.

Instinct took over. She twisted, grabbed her sword, and took off his head. Movement behind her, attracted the point of the blade as if it were a magnet. She pivoted to see that she'd impaled a man. He stared at the weapon sticking out of his gut.

Alex pulled the blade down and out of the man's side. He dropped to the ground, but she didn't watch him die.

A civilian car stopped about ten paces back. The man was talking on a cell phone and standing outside his car, a nice Toyota Avalon. The vehicle shone with extra coats of wax. The color drained from his face when their eyes locked.

Alex would have felt bad for him because she could tell he was frozen in place with fear.

A mercenary shot at the ground in front of her. The bullet ricocheted off the pavement in front of her boots.

Alex could hear sirens in the distance. She couldn't afford to engage much longer. But she moved towards where the bullet had come from and used the sword to take the merc's arm. Before that even registered in his brain she was behind him and cut his throat.

She continued to the civilian in the business suit.

The man made some kind of noise like he was trying to speak, but no words came out.

"I need your keys and your phone," she told him. She slid the bloody sword back into its scabbard.

The man blinked at the weapon as if it'd disappeared.

"I'm not really asking and I'm in a hurry."

His shaking hands dropped the phone in her outstretched palm. He pointed at the car with its open drivers' side door. He squeaked.

Alex interpreted that as "keys are in the car" so she walked around him and got into the vehicle.

She started up the car, pulled the door shut and cranked up the heat before making a three point turn to drive away from the scene.

It was difficult to not speed, but she made herself drive obediently. She even pulled to the side of the road when police, with sirens blaring, raced toward the accident and gunfight. While pulled over, she checked out the phone and quickly figured out how to dial. She only knew one number in her head.

"Hello?" a voice asked, uncertainty in the tone.

"It's me. This phone took pictures or video. I need it expunged, also this call. Any social media. You know the drill...fuck him up a little digitally."

"Alex—"

"I need Guang to meet me with some new clothes by Sandusky, Ohio with some new clothes." She swallowed and shook her head as the road seemed to tunnel ahead of her. "And the phone," she said. "You need to erase this call."

"You just repeated—Alex are you okay? You don't sound okay."

"Fix the phone. They'll follow the GPS. And the car has GPS."

"Right," the man on the other end replied. "Leave the phone on. Hit speaker so you don't have to think about it."

She hit the speaker phone button and tossed the phone onto the passenger seat. "How did you know I was in a car?"

"The phone you're using is moving faster than you can walk. I can hear the background sounds and you just told me you were in a car, Alex," he said. "Were those sirens?"

"Yep."

"There's a report of a gun fight on a street in Sandusky, Ohio, and a car upside down and underwater in the Sandusky Bay."

"The phone, DJ," she said. "I don't want my picture all over social media."

"It's called multitasking. You should learn about it. Are you okay?"

"Fuck you, DJ, I just crippled a guy for life, shoved a knife into another guy's brain, decapitated a third and nearly cut another man in half. Now I'm driving and bleeding to death. Multitasking is overrated, asshole."

The voice on the phone chuckled uncomfortably. "Right. Okay. In 200 yards, turn right."

"The Bay is on my right. It's too cold to swim. I know this for a fact."

"Shit, you were in the water? You're probably suffering from hypothermia, that's why you sound so weird."

"I'm fine," she said. "I just need—" She watched the bay start to retreat and give way to land. Then ahead on her right she saw landing strips and some small planes. Near the row of small hangers, sat two black military helicopters. Which explained how Gregory and the Division's assault team had gotten to her and Doucet's team so quickly. It also explained where they were taking her before they got ambushed. She yanked the car back into the correct lane.

"You just need what?" the voice on the phone asked. "Stay with me, Alex."

"I need to…," she said. She groaned slightly, losing her train of thought.

"Slow down, Alex. Slow down and turn right."

She listened to him and turned into the airport. She saw a man wearing a red and black plaid flannel shirt standing outside one of the hangers.

His jeans were too short. He wore black high-top sneakers and a chain belt. His dark hair was thick and wavy above thick glasses. He concentrated on a tablet computer that he held in his hands.

Alex recognized him and rolled the vehicle to a stop.

She had to concentrate to put the thing in park. But she did. With a deep breath, she got out of the vehicle.

"Give me the phone," Dorije Jennings ordered without looking up from tablet.

Alex obeyed.

He looked at the bloody fingerprints then at her. "Wow," he said. "That's a lot of blood."

Alex couldn't seem to catch her breath. "Not all mine," she said, pulling her shirt away from her side so he wouldn't see the hole in it.

"Not there," he said. "There." He pointed behind her.

Alex frowned and twisted.

Blood covered the inside of the vehicle. It pooled on the leather driver's seat.

"Oh," she said. "Yeah." There was a trail of blood from the vehicle and along the ten steps between the vehicle and herself. She looked down and saw a big drop of blood fall from her shirt in slow motion. It fell to the toe of her boot and exploded there like some kind of bomb filled with red paint.

She moaned as the pavement flickered and became stone. The stone floor of the cave.

Her eyes burned. She wanted the comfort and warmth of heroin in her veins, it felt like what she imagined a mother's embrace might feel like. Instead, the craving for it was scratching at the inside of her veins. Things crawled under her skin. She stared at her raw and infected arms, certain she'd see that someone had delivered Egyptian scarabs to her and they were eating her from the inside out.

She heard movement and struggled to lift her head.

A shadowy figure filled the doorway of the tiny room. She pounded her head against the stone wall, trying to get her thoughts to line up and obey. She saw the needle in his hand and she wanted to say no. She wanted so badly to not want it.

"Do you want it?" the shadow man asked, a fake English accent on his lips.

Alex pounded her head back against the wall. She wanted to say "no." But when she tried, the word that came out was "yes." She started crying. "Where's DJ? What happened to him?" The sting of a needle slid into her tortured arm.

CHAPTER SEVEN

Alex blinked. She had no idea where she was and no idea how long she'd been unconscious. Her heart pounded with the sudden realization of how vulnerable she was—or rather had been. She jerked up and hit her head on a low bulkhead. But, she barely felt it compared to the pain that shot through her gut. She gasped and reached for her side. Her hand found a cotton t-shirt and bandages wrapped tight around her midsection.

She vaguely remembered being shot—a stray bullet. Still, white hot anger burned through her. She felt the pain at the press of her fingers, but it wasn't as sharp as it should have been. She healed fast, normally, but this was something else, something numbing. She took a deep breath to get her racing heart under control and felt the room move around her. It wasn't a completely unpleasant feeling, kind of like floating in a warm bubble bath. "Goddamn it," she cursed out loud. Her throat was dry, her lips chapped; she coughed and part of her brain knew she should be feeling the broken ribs inside of the dull pressure of the bandages. "Fuck. Fuck. Fuck." She growled, punching the bulkhead in a rage.

The bulkhead cracked. She wondered vaguely if she'd broken her hand.

"That'd just be fucking perfect," she said out loud. Her hoarse voice mixed with a steady hum vibrating through the room. Dull recessed lighting lined the top of the curved bulkhead. She'd been staring at the lights, thinking they were stars. Remembering she'd been here staring at those lights thinking they were stars just made her angrier. The roar in her ears she'd mistaken for ocean surf suddenly sounded a lot more like airplane engines. She forced herself to sit up, shoving away a heavy comforter. She had to fight the urge to crawl back under the warm and cozy protection.

The movement gave her vertigo. She growled like a dog keeping the vertigo and its friends "nausea" and "tunnel vision" at bay. Her tangled hair fell in disarray around her face, disorienting her as she stood up. She caught herself with a hand on the wall to keep from falling. Embarrassment flushed her cheeks. The effort of controlling the vertigo left her shaky and a bead of sweat trickled down her spine under the bandages. She shoved hair out of her face. She let go of the wall and tested her balance for a minute, then moved towards a darkened space beside a wall of drawers.

It didn't take a rocket scientist to figure out where she was. Somehow Dorije Jennings had gotten into the country and followed her to Sandusky, Ohio. Somehow Guang had gotten to Cleveland. Somehow the big private luxury jet was carrying her somewhere. She could be fucking halfway to Japan by now. And real high up on the list of her current irritations was that someone had drugged her. She added a few more curses in a few different languages as she felt along the wall and found the lights.

The private bathroom flickered to life. She had to squint against the brightness. It was done up in gold and white, and wood with a slight green stain to it. The towels on the rack were green. She could smell the dampness on the towels.

In the mirror, she could see the mess of her hair from falling asleep without drying her hair. Another irritation to add to the bubbling volcano of fury. She put her hands on the counter, on either side of the small sink and leaned towards the mirror. All color of her eyes was nearly swallowed by huge pupils. "Goddammit," she cursed again.

The woman staring back at her would have been a stranger to the woman who'd appeared in mirrors a year ago, before her father died, before she spent six months being tortured, before she spent three months living on the streets waiting for killers to get their heads out of their asses and find her. She turned on the sink and cupped cold water in her hands, then splashed it on her face. Her eyes had been filled with mirth and a fun a year ago, now there was not an ounce of mirth to be found. She wondered if her father would approve. He'd always told her that he wanted to keep the darkness out of her eyes for as long as possible. She had never known what he meant. Not then.

One early morning, on the rocks that circled his private island in the middle of Lake Erie. She'd just finished her work out and the sun was just beginning to light the horizon. Her father had been sitting in the shadows watching—silent. He'd been very serious. More serious than she'd ever really seen him. She closed her eyes and remembered what he'd said to her. "Ivan Norvensky," he'd told her. He'd grabbed her shirt and pulled her close and whispered it hard and hot in her ear. "Ivan Norvensky. Don't forget that name. It's going to save your life." She'd asked him what he was talking about. She wouldn't forget his reply. "I'm talking about saving your life; I'm not going to be able to save your innocence. Someone is going to kill it and I might not be there to save it. It's inevitable, considering what you are, but I need you to stay alive." She'd laughed at him and assured him that she was hardly innocent.

Ivan Norvensky had been the name of the KGB operative who'd hidden the dirty bombs around the country. And she'd been wrong about not being innocent. So wrong.

She'd already killed by then, but it wasn't the same. Chen Sakai had forced her to kill and she'd had to kill to save herself on different operations for the CIA, despite what they believed.

But, those killings have been nothing like what she'd done to escape Peter Van de Moeter, or in the soup kitchen or in the street after nearly drowning. Hell, even in the soup kitchen she'd been drunk and trying to save people and survive. It was the street that took the last of it. Something snapped. Or cracked, like an egg. And something else had slithered through that crack. She could see it in her too large pupils, writhing in the cold, dark void. It stared back at her, unmoved by sentiment. At least, it hadn't been Peter who'd set the last stone. A fledgling monster had been born.

Water dripped from her gaunt features. She'd lost too much weight and she'd lost even more in the last three months living on the streets. A plain gray-blue t-shirt and black sweatpants were baggy on her frame. The bandages felt like they were practically rubbing against her rib cage instead of muscle. For three months, she'd been working out despite living as a homeless person. The work outs had been desperate, frantic even. The masters at the *dojo* were too in awe of her to try to correct her, too impressed with her credentials to offer advice.

She opened a drawer and found a comb. She worked out the tangles. She forced herself to stay calm and not yank or get the sword and just cut them all out. Her heart slowed as she worked, her anger retreated, emptiness remained. When she was finished, her hair hung straight, feathering over her shoulders. She lifted the shirt up and used the front of it to dry off her face. Because she was so thin her eyes and her mouth looked a little too big for her face, it made her lips look pouty and her eyes doe-like. "Like some goddamn supermodel," she hissed at the reflection.

A smirk tugged at her mouth. The amusement on her lips didn't reach the blackness in her eyes, but it made the words cold and menacing, especially with the hoarseness of her voice. The voice that had plagued her mind for the last months both inside Peter's torture chamber cave and on the streets remained silent.

Her stomach growled in hunger.

She pivoted around and left the room. The vertigo hit again, but she'd trained to fight through vertigo and dizziness. She'd trained drunk, sleep deprived, sensory deprived, drugged, and much worse. This time, she was prepared for it. Her training hadn't been about trophies or even spiritual harmony; her training with Sakai had been about brutality and finality and the training she'd received before Sakai had been from monks who'd developed the martial arts to fight their oppressors. She opened the door of the bedroom area.

The next section of the plane was lit with the same track lighting. It offered three computer work stations separated by partitions. Only one of the three computer stations appeared worked in. The computer monitor wasn't on, but a soft yellow light glowed around the power button. The work space held papers in folders and a few pens in a black cup. Neat, tidy and compact, the space still suggested work was done here. Alex knew who it belonged to.

She relaxed a touch. Until just this moment, she hadn't been aware of the tension across her shoulders, the thought that possibly she could be in enemy territory. But of course, everything was enemy territory. She had three people she trusted, but she had no expectations that they would stand up against certain pressures. Those pressures would come if they hadn't already. She walked down a corridor which held another bathroom and a closet. At the end of the corridor was the main section of the aircraft.

The lights were on in this section and it was occupied.

Amid the lounge chairs, the three people on the planet whom she trusted held a sort of court.

Alex paused and leaned against the wall. The drugs made her aware of the touch of the door frame on a shoulder which should not be there. The smell of subtle perfume drifted in the air. The section had track lighting along the fuselage interior; the light outside the oval windows was dark. Through the windows, she could see the red lights blinking at the ends of the wings.

Akiko Tanaka, the CEO of Nyx International, stood by the bar and nearly out of Alex's view at the other end of the fuselage on the same side as her. She wore a gray suit and a blue silk blouse which were tailored to her petite body. She had short, black hair. Wire-rimmed glasses magnified her eyes. Her small, delicate hands held a wine glass half filled with white wine. Her red lipstick had formed a crescent on the edge of the glass. She stared down into the pale golden liquid. "They ordered me to take this plane immediately back to Tokyo and deliver her to them," she announced to the room, her back to the other two occupants.

Dorije Jennings, Alex called him DJ but most called him "Door", lifted his attention from the computer screen in front of him. He sat in a one of the lounge chairs with his back mostly to Alex. Alex could see some first-person shooter game on his computer screen. "What did you tell them?"

Akiko shrugged. She lifted the wine glass to her lips and took a sip. After a swallow and a sigh, she spoke again. "I told them I wasn't the one making decisions at the present. And that we had to stop in New York to refuel regardless. I have business in New York."

"I bet they didn't like that," Jennings replied. He reached into the bag of Doritos sitting on the table next to him. His headphones hung limp on his shoulders. Alex could hear the faint sound of heavy metal coming from them.

Akiko leaned against the bar. "No, they did not."

"They are not the power," Guang spoke softly. He stood directly ahead of Alex, near a small Buddha statue set in a niche in the wall. His voice was heavily accented, but firm, and even.

Alex felt his tone run with the warmth of the drugs in her blood. It sapped some of the rage away from her. She felt empty without the rage. Her stomach growled. She lifted her hand back to the bandages. It felt hot against her hand. She glanced down and saw a spot of blood staining the t-shirt.

"They are dangerous people," Akiko told the monk.

"They are powerful people," Guang corrected. "They are not dangerous."

Akiko sighed. "They made threats about removing me from my position and freezing all the funds. It's not exactly cheap to race across the United States in a private jet while buying off doctors."

"They can't do that; can they?" Jennings asked. "Cut you off. Cut her off? I mean, the money is hers. She stole a lot from Peter; but that's not unlimited."

Alex smirked. Money was not an issue; although she couldn't access the stuff she'd stolen from Peter. The Division was watching that. She couldn't get the nest egg she'd built as an operator for the CIA either because surely they were watching that as well. But she didn't need the luxury of a private cabin on a private jet; she could sleep in roach infested hellholes. She didn't need money to survive. Still, it made things easier for these people to help her.

Akiko shook her head. "Chen Sakai's heir has never shown up to a board meeting. I have been given full by-proxy voting privileges, but they could conceivably file a legal injunction challenging that. Hayashi-san remains chairperson of the board as well as leader of the Offspring. They don't think she's Sakai's legitimate heir and there's no paperwork. Only the weapon which cannot be named."

The Sword of Souls, whispered the voice in Alex's head.

The lights in the cabin flickered slightly, but no one other than Alex noticed. A tick of air travel, perhaps.

Guang took a step closer to the center of the lounge area. He moved on the balls of his feet like a monkey in the jungle, Alex thought: graceful, agile, powerful. He had a squared body that could move with incredible flashes of speed. Few people could challenge his *wu shu* skills. Alex could never count on defeating him with speed alone, which was one of the reasons Guang was a sparring partner she enjoyed and actually found challenging. Sparring with him only required that she limit herself to one system of martial art. She only had to pull back her attack slightly when she battled him.

Guang's voice filled the room, seeming to melt with the sound of the engines; Alex felt a little mesmerized by it. She grabbed on to it to ease a flair of vertigo. "For generations, the holder of the weapon has followed the directives of the Offspring," Guang told the others. "They are no longer the group of followers who wanted the small man to win. Now they are a cult concerned about political and financial power. They have become what the Sword stands against. History tells us this. They would like everyone to forget they sent the last True One back to the halls of the dead."

"By accident," Akiko said, slightly defensively. "They didn't know and they've sworn to uphold the ideals that the True One was unable to accomplish."

Guang shook his head. "Even then they would not accept that the True One cannot be controlled."

"They're going to kill her," Akiko told him. "I care about her. I'd rather not see her cut down in some dark alley."

"They will try. That's not unexpected," Guang replied calmly. "Alex is aware of the danger the Offspring represent. And it will not be a dark alley, it will be an elaborate arena. Of that we can be sure. But her battle right now is not about the Offspring or putting them back into their place. Her battle is the battle to become, the battle for genesis."

"She's stacking up bodies," Akiko said. "You of all people should be against that, Guang. Murder and destruction follow her; it is not the right way."

He shrugged. "Tigers hunt down antelope; should I tell the tiger not to do what it was born to do?"

"That's different," Akiko said.

"The cold air will kill a man who exposes himself to it; should I argue that the cold should be more tepid? Alex does what her nature drives her to do. She can no more help herself than the cold can stop being cold or the tiger can stop being a tiger. I merely remind the tiger to choose its prey carefully rather than wantonly. The wrong prey can kill the tiger." His eyes sparkled with amusement at the Japanese woman's frustration.

119

Akiko sighed and sipped from her glass. "She spent three months pretending to be homeless. She spent a lot of that time drinking heavily. She could have bled to death from that gunshot wound today. And what about the flashbacks?"

"She would not have bled to death," Guang said, his voice lowering with seriousness. "The Soul, the True One, can only die by the weapon which is not to be named."

Akiko rolled her eyes. "Old tales from our parents told to keep us in line with the Offspring's doctrine. You don't really believe all that supernatural stuff; do you, Guang?"

The corner of his mouth twisted up in a quirk, lop-sided smile. "I believe no simple human could have lived through what happened to her. I believe only someone inhuman would escape unscathed."

Akiko frowned at him. "You can talk in riddles all you like, Guang, but she's out of control and the Offspring are just trying to make sure the legend stays secret. The trail of bodies is getting difficult to hide. The Offspring will not tolerate it for long."

"An awful lot of people know about this thing that no one is supposed to know about. Someone must be talking about it or there wouldn't be so many people who knew about it," Jennings said. "Either way, she's decommissioned for a few days after that gunshot wound so we can figure out what to do."

Akiko shook her head. She sipped her wine. "They have people in New York. If we don't go to them, they will come to her. They will come for us."

Alex felt cold shiver through the marrow of her bones. "Did they threaten to come after you?" she asked.

All three of the people in the lounge jumped.

Akiko nearly dropped her wine glass.

Jennings let out a little shriek and cursed out loud.

Guang's eye twitched, the only sign of a crack in his stoic demeanor.

Alex would have laughed at their reaction if the lounge area wasn't spinning. The thought of someone threatening people just because they were helping her, for the mere crime of being loyal friends, bothered her. The cold pulsed through her veins.

"What?" Akiko asked.

"Did the Offspring threaten anyone other than me?" Alex asked, her voice slurred slightly.

"You should be in bed," Akiko said.

"You should not have drugged me," Alex replied. Even now she could feel her body relaxing into it, wanting to drift. She'd spent three months fighting the urge to get wasted again.

"The doctor wouldn't operate without drugging you," Akiko argued.

"I'm not a fan of doctors," Alex mumbled. "I'm less of a fan of drugs. I'm an addict, for fuck's sake."

"You were unconscious," DJ told her. "We figured no one needed to die if you woke up in the middle of surgery. No one would die if you woke up unaware of where you were."

Alex felt the corner of her mouth twitch. "The night's still young," she said.

DJ shook his head. "Actually, the night's over. You missed it. It's morning."

Alex rolled her eyes and instantly regretted it. If she hadn't been leaning against the bulkhead already, she would have fallen. Guang's reaction came as a barely noticeable twitch. "Did they threaten to come after you three, Akiko?" she asked, managing to keep her voice steady.

"They only threatened to remove me from my job," Akiko said. "But that's not as easy as they think it is."

"When I'm done, I'll pay a visit to a Nyx International board meeting. They will never threaten you again."

"They want to kill you."

"Their own rules say they need an audience and a recognized challenge."

"You're very popular with people wanting to kill you," DJ said.

"Did you open your stitches?" Akiko said. "You're bleeding."

Alex arched an eyebrow at her. "I don't feel a thing," she said. She winced as she stepped into the lounge. "Except hungry. I'm hungry."

Guang arched an eyebrow at her.

She gave him a dirty look. "You keep on discussing me while I go find something."

The airplane hit a bit of turbulence as she let go of the wall. She would have fallen if Guang wasn't fast. He caught her.

She growled at him. "I hate being drugged up," she said.

He nodded patronizingly and led her to the couch instead of the galley. "I tried to talk the doctor out of it. I told him that if you regained consciousness while he was sewing up that hole in your side, you might think twice about getting shot again. He seemed to be more concerned about you waking up and cutting off his head."

She grimaced as she sank into the couch. She put a hand over her side. "It wouldn't have been his head."

DJ snorted. "He said he gave you enough to keep you knocked out for another 6 hours."

"I'm hungry," she said again.

Guang nodded. "I will go and get you some food if you promise to stay on this couch."

"The doctor said she shouldn't eat because of the anesthetic," Akiko said to Guang.

Guang nodded. "Yes, but she has an iron stomach. And her body needs the energy to heal."

"If she gets sick, she'll rip out more stitches."

"She needs food."

"She needs to get healthy."

"Another reason to eat."

Alex frowned at both of them. "Hey, I'm right here. And neither of you are my parents." She leaned forward and grabbed some Doritos out of DJ's bag. She popped one in her mouth. "Now there's no point arguing," she told them.

DJ snickered. "You are really stoned; aren't you?"

Akiko waved Guang away from the door to the rest of the plane. "I can't have a monk serving anyone while I am around," she said. "It's just wrong."

Alex arched an eyebrow at Guang as she walked out of the room. "Did you tell all these people that you're a real monk?"

Guang chuckled at her. "You could be a comedian, Alex. A poor one."

She managed a laugh that surprised her and hurt her side. "Goddammit, Guang."

He grunted as he got a bottled water from the bar and loosened the cap for her.

"You're usually not this pleasant to be around," DJ said.

She gave him a dirty look. "I dislike all of you right now."

He laughed. "It's good to see you when you aren't passing out and bleeding everywhere."

"Sorry about that."

"I'm just glad you are okay. I thought you had bled to death."

Alex saw a shadow cross Guang's face as she took a swig from the water bottle. "I'm hard to kill," she told him. "How many of the bomb locations has Peter found?"

"He just found the second one," DJ replied. "I think he's figured out how to connect them."

"Ivan Norvensky," she said with a yawn. "I'm ditching Plan A."

"Uhm, wasn't Plan B just killing everyone?"

"New Plan B," she said. "I have a few things to tie up in New York, then I'm going to Vegas. You need to get out of the country. Richard Powell and the Division will figure out you are my computer genius if they haven't already."

"I'm not going back to prison."

"They won't do that," she said. "They'll use you as bait to get to me. And then, they'll force you to work for them and tell them everything you know about me. You'll connect me to Akiko and Nyx International; you cannot be caught. I'll have to forget about Peter for a while and kill a lot of other people to rescue you. It throws off the time table."

123

Akiko returned with a tray of food. She set it down on a tray in front of Alex.

Alex's stomach growled. She sat up and grabbed the spoon. Okayu, Japanese rice porridge, steamed in a large bowl in the center of the tray. Smaller bowls held tofu, shitake mushrooms, chopped green onions, sliced ginger, a pickled plum and some fried egg. A mug filled with green tea topped off the tray. She stared at it and realized suddenly that she was starving. Her hand with the spoon actually shook.

She started dumping the smaller bowls into the rice.

"Go slow or you will be sick and I will be forced to acknowledge I am not as wise as I pretend to be," Guang warned her.

Alex nodded. As if to prove that she would, she took a sip of tea first. She burned her tongue in her haste to get to the food. "You aren't all going to stand around and watch me eat; are you?"

"I've never seen anyone inhale okayu before," DJ said.

"I'm not going to inhale it."

"You look like you haven't eaten in two days."

Alex started to reply, then shut her mouth.

DJ's eyes widened. "Seriously?! You haven't eaten in two days?!"

"What day is it?" She filled the spoon and filled her mouth. She glared at DJ.

He shook his head and put his headphones back on, going back to his game.

Akiko rolled her eyes and sank into one of the chairs. She pulled out her smart phone, mumbling something about people who didn't know how to take care of themselves.

Guang studied her as she ate.

"What?" she asked in his native language.

"Something is different."

"I'm drugged up to the gills and starving to death," she said.

He nodded. "Perhaps that is it. Perhaps it is something else entirely. Your brain was still damaged last time we spent significant time together."

She shrugged. Let him stare. Fuck it. She was eating. She intended to eat the entire bowl, but by the time she got halfway through it, the carbs and the drugs and the injuries were ganging up on her. She slowed, fighting to keep her eyes open.

Worse, the food was leaching the drugs out of her system faster and her side had begun to throb.

Taking a break from the food, she leaned back. She told herself she'd just close her eyes for a second.

CHAPTER EIGHT

The sound of the engines changing and the tilt of the plane woke Alex up. Somehow, she'd ended up back in the private bedroom again. Early morning light came through the windows. She yawned, scratched at an itch on her side and frowned at the bandages that separated her from the itch. She climbed out of the bed easier than hours earlier and quickly found her sword and a small switchblade along with a change of clothing.

She cut away the bandages. The bruises on her side from the broken rib had turned dark purple and blue and black overnight. The stitches of the bullet wound were tugging at the edges of the wound. She stifled a yawn and slipped the switchblade under the stitches to pop them open. Pulling them out stung and there was a little blood which she washed away. She found some makeup in the bathroom—Akiko's most likely—and she used it to make the wound look healed and to dull the intensity of the bruises. Her fresh outfit consisted of jeans and a black sweatshirt. She towel-dried her hair.

Sucking up the pain, she stared at herself in the mirror. In her eyes, horror danced with the hints of a broken psyche.

When she had it under control, she walked out into the lounge area finding the others just waking up and stowing things away for landing.

"Feeling more yourself?" DJ asked.

"I'll let you know when I figure out what that is supposed to feel like," she joked. She ignored the way Guang stopped what he was doing and narrowed his eyes at her. He'd been in Thailand when she'd woken up three months ago, five hours after collapsing in an alley in New York City. Instinct would have her avoid his intense gaze; but, she knew that would be a dead giveaway.

"You really need to rest, Alex," Akiko said. "That bullet wound needs time to heel."

She lifted her shirt to expose the pink circle of skin and the dulled bruises. "I'm fine." She dropped the shirt as Guang took a few steps closer. Close examination would reveal the make-up.

Akiko's mouth dropped open and color drained from her face. "How?" Her eyes darted from Alex to Guang, neither of whom were talking.

"I'm hungry," Alex said, crossing the room. She felt Guang's dark eyes follow her.

"We're landing," DJ said.

Alex made a face. "Isn't there an energy bar or something left? And how long does it take to fly from Ohio to New York City?"

DJ laughed. "Oh, yeah, because all the hoity toity stuck ups who normally fly on this plane just love energy bars for breakfast. And we had to fly to Los Angeles to get the doctor and then you were operated on. And then we had to get Akiko to some stupid meeting in Sacramento."

Alex crossed the lounge to the bar and grabbed a bottle of water. She plopped down into the lounge chair beside him. It took just about everything she had not to grunt in pain at the motion. "Got any Doritoes left?"

He laughed at her. "I'm not sharing; I've seen you inhale food."

She gave him a hurt look. "Wow, that's cold, DJ. I rescued you from prison and gave you a job."

He nodded. "Yeah, and I cleaned your blood out of a stolen car and saved your life yesterday. We're even. The Doritos— and I'm not acknowledging that there actually are any left— will remain mine. What's the plan here?"

Alex yawned. Something flew through the air towards her, from mostly behind her. Without even thinking she caught it. Her mind registered that it was an apple a moment later. If she'd been in a spot where she felt anything less than perfectly comfortable, she would have drawn the sword.

Guang had one of his own and he bit into it as he sat down in one of the other chairs. He said nothing.

Alex shined the apple on her sleeve before chomping down on it. Normally, she might have shined it on her stomach, but there was no way she was doing that against the broken ribs and the gunshot wound. "You have everything I asked for last night set up?"

DJ nodded.

"Then go back to Tokyo with Akiko. Decide where you want to have a home base. Make a wish list of everything you'd like to stock your dream office. Make sure it's not in a country with an extradition treaty with the US, that's the only requirement."

"I'm setting up an office?" DJ said.

Alex nodded.

"For what?"

"I'll tell you when I get to Tokyo."

"What if you die here?" Akiko asked. Her normally steady voice shook slightly.

Alex swallowed another bite of apple. The healed bullet wound had unnerved the CEO more than Alex had anticipated. "Then I won't be in Tokyo." She looked at Guang. "I'll need you to help me get out of Ohio and into Canada afterwards."

"Afterwards?" Akiko asked. "After what?"

"After I meet up with whoever is behind Peter kidnapping me and stop him."

"You plan on meeting this man?" Akiko asked.

Alex nodded. "He won't be able to resist the bait."

"What bait? The bombs?"

Alex shook her head. "He doesn't want the bombs."

"What does he want?"

"A weapon more dangerous," she said.

For a second Akiko looked confused then realization came to her. "You're going to use yourself as bait? Alex, that's foolish and stupid. What if he shows up with six other people?"

"He knows what he's hunting. There will be six with him. When Peter is dead and his contact inside the Division is dead, he will have to come for me himself." She finished the apple and watched the landscape and roads start to grow larger.

"Alex—"

Alex sighed and looked up at Akiko. "What makes you think I have a choice in this, Akiko?" Her voice sounded tired, resigned, fatalistic. She'd spent a lifetime fighting who everyone wanted her to be. Now she was going to give them all what they wanted.

The rest of the flight was spent in silence. Alex let the three think about things. She had no idea where their thoughts were going, but she couldn't risk caring. None of them would willingly betray her—for different reasons. She didn't plan on giving them enough information to bury her even if they were forced to betray her. If she'd known the answers Peter wanted, she would have told him. She shouldn't have held out for six months. When they finally asked a question that she did know the answer to, it'd taken the shattering of her mind to keep from talking. There was only one topic on which she would never talk and they'd asked it—but Peter hadn't known to ask. Absently, she flexed her hand over the hilt of the ancient weapon laying across her lap. The scars of that moment of resistance remained as surely as the scars on her body. She didn't expect anyone one else to hold out when she hadn't been able.

She hitched a ride with Akiko's waiting limo and had the driver drop her off near Central Park. Akiko had offered her money, but she'd refused. She didn't need any money.

Guang stepped out with her.

Alex stared at him as he closed the door and the limo drove off. "You're not going to be my chaperone," she told him.

"Do you think this is wise?"

Alex furrowed her brow. "What are you talking about?"

Guang's his normally stoic face broke into emotion. He threw his arms out in exasperation; but with a force made to seem intimidating.

Alex twitched in reaction to the movement, unable to stop herself.

Guang shook his head at her twitch and rolled his eyes. "You're hurt, you've got a bad case of Post-Traumatic Stress Disorder, the Offspring have a strong presence in this city and they want to control you, the CIA is here and they want to control you, your former co-workers are here and one of them turned you over to a maniac who tortured you for six months." He sighed. "Have I left anything out?"

"Melodramatic much?"

His hand jabbed out and caught her over the bullet wound.

The blow hadn't been fast or hard, just a whisper that she might not have noticed any other time. But now, she would have gone down to one knee if it hadn't been for Guang's other hand holding on to her elbow and keeping her on her feet. Her vision tunneled. She had to struggle to breath and she wondered if one of her broken ribs had just punctured a lung.

Guang cursed under his breath. "It's worse than I thought."

Alex resisted the urge to check if the gunshot was bleeding again.

Guang sighed. He pointed at a bench. "Sit. I'll get us breakfast. Don't leave."

"Nothing that smells like grilled meat," she said through clenched teeth.

Guang nodded, his frustration softened a touch.

Alex winced as she sank down onto the bench. She watched the morning traffic, the businessmen and women hurrying to their jobs many of them on cell phones or talking via blue tooth devices in their ears, the taxis and trucks and busses rushing around. An occasional jogger moved by, on the way to Central Park, fewer than there had been earlier in the morning—Alex had been one of them once, jogging from her efficiency apartment to Central Park and back before going to either a private *dojo* or the *dojo* where she would spar with Sinjin Doucet.

Guang returned with two paper cups on a tray and a box. "Only in America."

Alex opened the box and her eyes widened at the wide variety of donuts and pasteries.

Guang shrugged and sipped from one of the two cups. "You need to gain some weight," he told her. "You ate well on the plane."

Alex pulled out a big donut and took a big bite out of it. She actually moaned it was so good.

Guang chuckled. "Crème brulee donut…apparently they are famous."

Alex nodded with her mouth full.

Guang sipped his tea and watched her finish one and dive in for another. "It is said that the weapon controls those who are bonded with it. It is said that the weapon, being that it is a weapon, has a blood lust that cannot be controlled."

Alex started on a raspberry and something else donut flavor. Guang had bought six different donuts. She was thinking at this point she might be able to devour all of them. If listening to him talk was a price to pay for the food, it was one she would pay enthusiastically. Besides, she told herself, she owed him more than she could ever repay. More than anyone, Guang was her friend. If she'd gone to Guang instead of tried to work when her father died, Peter never would have gotten her. She reminded herself to make that mistake into a lesson.

131

Guang's voice was deep and it moved with a hypnotic cadence. The sound of it often reminded Alex of monks chanting in ancient temples and of times when she spent quiet and silent moments inside temples—the temples of Northern Thailand, the ones that not many tourists frequented, were her favorites. She could close her eyes and feel the heat and smell the ancient air. "The Offspring believes it is necessary to exert control to prevent the power of the weapon from creating an unstoppable serial killer."

Alex finished the second doughnut and eyed one of the pastries. She leaned back in the bench and let the food settle a little.

Guang stared out at the traffic. "It is said the True One controlled the weapon. One must spend years fighting for control of the weapon before gaining mastery—that is why the Offspring believe one must be older to hold the weapon. They believe your youth is why the sword hasn't devoured you yet. They believe the time is near for their chosen champion."

Alex reached for an apply crumb pastry. "Perhaps the one you refer to wasn't the True One. Perhaps it was just a talented imposter. The Offspring killed the last True One and on his dying breath he swore he would never return. He swore his soul would roam the halls of the dead so that he could laugh in the faces of each of the Offspring and their descendants as they passed through over and over again, suffering under the thumbs of the gods who would keep them from free will."

Guang arched an eyebrow at her. "I was not aware that you knew the stories of the Offspring."

Alex rolled her eyes at him. "I'm not psychic. I broke into the library at Sakai's house and spent hours reading the diaries."

Guang snorted a laugh. "Of course you did."

"I'm not the True One," Alex said. "I am just me."

"If I believed that, Alex, I would turn you over to the Offspring myself."

Alex snorted. "You could try."

"Said the woman who nearly passed out from a brush of my hand."

"You caught me by surprise."

Guang grunted. "You know why all the other children in the village were afraid of you when we were toddlers, Alex?"

"Red-headed, fearless wild child. Father hired to hold back an army. Superstition."

Guang shook his head. "No. Because when they looked into your eyes, they saw something. Something scarier than the soldiers who tried to wipe out our people, something more terrifying than the stories of dragons and demons. Your skills are supernatural."

"You can beat me in *wu-shu*."

"Not if it were life or death."

"If it were life or death, I wouldn't stick with one discipline," she said. "What does this have to do with what I'm doing now? We're getting side-tracked and I have things to do this morning. Aren't you going to eat any of these?"

Guang smiled at her as she finished the third of the six items he'd bought. "You have a certain blood lust going on yourself. You suffer from flashbacks—I was with you in Thailand and I listened to Jennings describe what happened to you when you saw all your own blood in that stolen car. Your body and your mind are still healing. It takes a lot of energy. Energy you don't have to fight the will of the weapon which is not to be named. You need to stop fighting your personal battles so that you can fight the one that matters."

"I have to stop the man who is paying Peter."

"Why? I understand the traitor. I understand Van de Moeter. This is simple revenge. I do not condone these things, but I understand them. I don't understand why you even care about the man paying him. There are a hundred people, maybe more out there wanting to kill you for that weapon right now. The Offspring have been plotting for nearly 15 years now— soon they will be ready to formally challenge you."

Alex sighed.

"Why must you flush out this man? He is nothing."

"You know those medical reports DJ has from the Division? How I shouldn't be able to walk and talk or use any of my limbs? I don't remember escaping from the Division hospital. But I remember a dark, dirty alley. I remember falling in a greasy dirty puddle seeping out from a pile of garbage. I remember my brain on fire and craving drugs." She took a deep, shaky breath. Her eyes stared out at the streets, but she wasn't seeing any of that. "I remember the pain. I remember the madness. I remember big fluffy flakes of snow falling against my burning face. I could hear the rasping of my breath and the slow weak pounding of my heart. I remember thinking that my heart was tired of pumping, that it just wanted to stop. My lungs tasted like metal and they ached ten times worse then when I was on top of *Chhogori*. It was just so relentless. Death is relentless, Guang."

Guang stared at her.

She winced as she shifted position, her hand holding onto her ribs. "After all I'd been through, I was there, lying in this repulsive puddle of filth. I had finally just reached this point where I couldn't get up any more. The minute I stopped fighting, it was gone—the pain, the craving, the madness. I stood somewhere dark and empty and cold. Sakai was there. He made me an offer." She closed her eyes and breathed deep, smelling exhaust fumes and the grit of the city. "Kill the mastermind. Promise to kill him and you will live to avenge your father." She opened her eyes. "The next thing I remember, I was waking up in Thailand and you were there to stop the madness."

"Are you saying you negotiated with the weapon for your life?"

Alex let out a laugh. "I don't believe in any of that shit. But, I can't explain how I got from New York to Thailand in under five hours. I also don't know how I showed up half healed from my injuries." She absently rubbed the scars around her wrist. "All I know is that I'm willing to sell my soul to kill Peter Van de Moeter and I'll do just about anything to avoid the consequences of not paying the debt. I will die another way, not that way. That was bad, in that alley." She pushed herself to her feet and grabbed another doughnut. "I will see you in 24 hours. Secure my trip to Vegas for me. Please Guang."

Guang stared at her. After a minute, he gave her a curt nod.

"And Guang?"

"Yes, Alex?"

"I'd appreciate it, if you didn't write all that down and give it to the Offspring until after I'm dead—if at all." She pivoted on her heal and jumped over a small fence to disappear into Central Park. She could feel Guang's eyes staring at her back for quite some time.

After picking enough pockets in Central Park and in Times Square, she was flush enough to head to a second-hand shop for her first change of clothing. She bought black jeans that hugged her long legs, a form fitting taupe colored top with buttons that strained over her chest, and a bright green jacket. In another cheap shop she found a gold necklace with a green pendent which dangled at the top of her cleavage. She tied her hair up in a ponytail with a gold clasp. On a whim, she added black-rimmed glasses. She was loathe to lose her boots, but she changed them out for knee high boots with spiked heels that matched the color of her top. She bought a pair of running shoes too. With the last of the money left over, she went to a drug store and bought alcohol, cotton balls, bandages, and string. She cleaned the make-up off the bullet wound, sewed it back up and put a bandage over it. She considered wrapping up her ribs again, but she figured the tight top did that well and good enough. She made another pass of picking pockets—it was a lot easier dressed like she was. She bought a large bag to be used as a purse and inside she stashed boots and a few changes of clothing.

After walking down the street to make sure she turned male heads and picking the pockets of all the men who leered, she hailed a cab and gave the driver an address. She paid in cash. She had to walk three blocks to get to where she wanted. In the first block, she stashed a gray hoodie; in the second block, a pair of nylon jogging pants got shoved into a mailbox slot, and in the third block she stashed the tennis shoes in a dark corner by an abandoned storefront. The building she wanted was one of New York City's nondescript office buildings. This one had a canopy over the door. Alex looked down to adjust her top as she walked by the cameras hidden in the canopy. She carried the big purse under her arm.

Just inside the door was a large reception desk. Alex made sure her heels clicked on the linoleum as she walked up to the desk where two burly men in security uniforms sat. Around her, men and women with briefcases moved through the lobby to the two elevators. They flashed ID cards hanging from lanyards around their necks to the vigilant men at the desk. Both men turned to eye her as she approached.

"Ma'am," the older one said. His eyes rolled up and down her body, checking for bulges in her clothes that would indicate a gun. Their eyes didn't even see the bag with the clothing.

Her clothing selection barely disguised the sword she constantly carried with her. And to be fair there was a bit of a trick involved with the Sword: the kind of illusion that magicians used to make things disappear. Not unlike the trick she'd used earlier in the day to make the bullet hole disappear. Still, she would not have brought a gun. Her father had trained her; she was a natural with a gun, almost as good as with a sword. However, she held the opinion that if someone needed to die, the least you could do was try to make it personal.

She'd chosen clothes that looked like she couldn't hide anything at all. She smiled and nervously pulled her ponytail forward over her shoulder. At the same time, she made her cleavage stand out.

The younger one's jaw practically hung open, his eyes were right at boob level.

"Hi," she said. She couldn't hide the raspy aspect of her voice, but that didn't mean she couldn't add in a healthy dose of bimbo. Both men were new to their jobs. Or at least, she'd never seen them here before. She'd not come in through the front door often, but she would have remembered. In her job it helped to remember people who might recognize you. "I have an appointment."

"An appointment?" the older one asked.

She nodded. "Well, an interview actually." She smiled sheepishly. "With Mr. Powell. He said he's on the third floor. He's kind of a big deal I guess." She pushed her shoulders back to strain the buttons on the tight shirt. She'd kept her own bra, which was a little lacy, part of it peeked out from the shirt, just a hint.

"Ah, Mr. Powell. I wasn't aware he was looking for another secretary," the older man said.

"He told me to come here and get a pass. He told me not to tell anyone what I was interviewing for because he hadn't fired his other secretary." She leaned forward and whispered to the two men. "I guess she's kind of incompetent."

"Imagine that," the younger man said, staring straight down her shirt.

The older man cleared his throat. He passed her a visitor card. "Take that elevator there ma'am. Go up to the third floor and turn right. Mr. Powell's office is at the end of the hall."

She nodded. "Thank you," she said, trying to figure out where to clip the pass. She finally decided on her jacket lapel.

She turned to the elevator and walked letting her ponytail swing back and forth. In the elevator, she pushed the button for the fifth floor. She hid her face in the filled elevator and watched all the clueless civilian workers get off at the second and third floors. She palmed her visitor pass and slid it into her back pocket before the fourth floor; then, stepped out on the fifth floor.

The fifth floor was a series of cubicles, all manned by serious looking people staring at computer screens and talking on secure headsets. The overhead lights were bright; and, the carpet was clean and industrial grade. She turned to her left and started to walk. People seldom paid attention to people who behaved as if they belonged. Alex had once proven this point by walking through the middle of a high security prison yard which was filled with rapists and prisoners—while CIA psychologists pissed their pants and the warden of the facility nearly had a stroke. She proved it again here, in the middle of a CIA program so covert that it wasn't even housed in Virginia.

At the corner office, a secretary sat at a large oak desk, blocking the closed door. She looked up at Alex who'd stopped directly in front of her.

The busty blonde secretary did not disappoint. Her blue eyes rolled down the jaunty ponytail, the form fitting top, long legs in the tight jeans, and the spiked heeled boots. Women who depended on their looks to impress often hated Alex instantly and the busty blonde didn't disappoint. She scowled.

Alex resisted the urge to warn her that the scowl would cause wrinkles. She would look old before her time. Hell, she figured this one would be a Botox queen before that ever happened. "You're new," she said to the blonde in a kind of accusatory tone.

"I've been here six months," she replied haughtily.

"Ah," Alex said. "I'm Richard's girlfriend. Is he in?" She managed not to smirk when the woman blanched.

"No—"

"Okay, well, I'll just wait for him in his office until he gets back," she said. She walked right around the woman and opened the office door.

"You can't go in there!" she exclaimed, jumping up.

Alex walked into the big, spacious corner office. Peter's fake office was on the third floor, but this one was where the CIA handler did most of his work. She wondered if he had another bombshell secretary down on that floor and if the women knew about each other.

"Ma'am, you have to leave." The blonde secretary teetered on heels higher than Alex's and her balance wasn't nearly as good, the girl could hardly walk. She'd gone from pale to flushed with anger in an instant.

Alex turned around to face her. She smiled. It was an antagonizing smile. If the woman came at her trying to scratch her eyes and pull her hair, Alex thought she would laugh out loud.

The woman huffed.

Alex tilted her head to the side. "Not the fighting sort, huh?" she asked. "Shame. How long have you been sleeping with my boyfriend?"

"He's not your—"

"Charline, is Powell back?" a man's voice asked.

"No, this woman just barged in and---"

The man, a behavior analyst who Alex recognized because he was the one who debriefed her after missions, looked into the office.

Alex waited.

Recognition hit him.

The folder he'd been holding slid to the floor, papers cascading and catching wind and floating away.

The blonde secretary gasped and started to collect the fallen papers, but then noticed that the analyst wasn't moving. He was staring.

"Better call the boss, tell him you fucked up again," Alex told the small nerdy analyst. "How do you even keep your job with all these miscalculations?"

"I'm calling security!" the blonde snapped.

The analyst grabbed her arm as she tried to march back to her desk in her tottering heels and tight pencil skirt. "Don't. Don't call security. There will be a bloodbath."

Alex smirked. "I guess you're not wrong all the time. My bad."

The analyst's eye twitched behind his thick glasses. "You shouldn't be able to talk. Or walk."

"You shouldn't rely on third party reports."

"I didn't."

Alex chuckled. "You're going to have some firsthand reports today, bud. You might want to reassess."

The analyst stared at her. "Call Mr. Powell," he told the blonde. "Tell him to get here as fast as he can. Under no circumstance call security. Tell him Fireblade is in his office."

139

Alex snickered. "Fireblade? Really? That's the best you people could come up with?"

The woman hesitated, clearly not wanting to leave people alone in Powell's office.

Alex saw the thought roll over the blonde's face. She tilted her head. "You better be more convincing, she's thinking she's going to call security despite what you just said."

The analyst turned on the woman, he hadn't released her arm. "Page Powell! Page him now! Just him. Tell him Fireblade is in his office."

His high-pitched, panicked squeal moved her into action.

Alex yawned she walked around Powell's desk and sat in his high-backed chair. "Close the door on your way out and make sure Powell is the next one through that door."

"What are you doing here?" the analyst asked her. His voice shook slightly. He squared his shoulders and tried to look her in the eyes.

Alex wondered if the show of confidence was supposed to hide his shaking legs. "Well," she said carefully, "you've been trying to find me and bring me here; haven't you?"

His mouth moved as if searching for words that wouldn't come.

"Leave," Alex told him. "Close the door behind you. Make sure the next one who comes in is Richard Powell. If it's not, I will make what happened in Cleveland look like a picnic."

He obeyed, quickly.

When she was alone, Alex searched Powell's desk. She wasn't concerned about what was in his computer. He'd never put the good stuff into a computer. In the top drawer, she found a piece of paper and a pen. In the locked drawer, which she picked with a paperclip in about three seconds – you'd think a black ops chief would have better locks on things – she found a stack of filled files and a Colt .45 1911 pistol with laser sights. The magazine lying next to the weapon was filled with 8 hollow tipped bullets. She locked the magazine into the weapon and pulled back the slide to chamber a round. She laid the big pistol on the desk next to the blank piece of paper and pen. She moved it so the barrel was pointed at the door. Then, she let her attention go to the files. She leafed through the top one, then a few of the other others.

She briefly considered searching for a lighter to set the files ablaze. She couldn't take the files with her. She sighed and quickly changed clothes into something more practical and more typical for herself. After using the bimbo top to wipe the makeup off her face, she tossed the tight bimbo clothes into the drawer with the files and locked it back up.

With the Colt tucked into the waist of looser jeans, cold in the small of her back, she sighed to herself. "One problem at a time," she mumbled.

CHAPTER NINE

The office door opened. A thick, wood door without windows; the kind of office door that suggested both power and privacy.

Alex sat in the executive chair, leaning back with her boots up on the corner of the desk and watching the door. Her hands were folded over her flat stomach. The Colt bit into her back.

Richard Powell stood in the doorway. He stared at her. He wore a dark, tailored suit; a pressed, white dress shirt; and a yellow tie. His hand gripped the door knob so tightly that his knuckles were white. He pressed his lips together into a thin line. His eyes were slightly red, slightly surprised, and more than slightly scared.

The blonde bimbo stood behind his shoulder. Her painted face was etched with wrinkle-free concern. Her hand reached out and touched his arm, blood red lacquered nails against dark cloth. Her mouth pursed, bright red lipstick matching the nails. Her eyes narrowed over Powell's shoulder.

Alex sighed. "Do we do this the easy way or the hard way?" she asked the man who'd been her handler for years. Her gravelly voice hung heavy in the air. The question had a certain irony. Nothing about this was going to be easy, least of all her escape. If they managed to catch her, she might never get out of this building again.

He arched an eyebrow at her. "The hard way for whom? You or me?"

Alex shrugged. "If I planned on killing you, I wouldn't do it this way," she said. "So, you still have hope. If you play it right."

He released the breath he'd been holding. His eyes darted to the closed drawer of his desk. A bead of sweat trickled down from his temple. "Hold my calls, Charline," he said. She started to protest, but he stepped into the office and closed the door on her.

Alex heard the door click tight.

He did not lock the door; but then, he'd probably be safer locking himself in a cage with a hungry polar bear.

"You still get laid talking to her like that?" Alex asked him.

"Get out of my chair," Powell ordered.

Alex laughed. A genuine laugh. It'd been a long time since she'd felt that, but it amused her that this man believed he could have her back in his corral so easily, with just a stern tone and an air of authority. "In a second, I'm almost done with my resignation letter. I'm just contemplating the exact words I want to use. Choosing just the right words can be so very…very important; wouldn't you agree?" Despite her laugh her words held a chilly warning.

He opened his mouth to speak, then closed it again. He took a deep breath as he ran a hand down his tie to smooth it over his shirt. "There's no resigning."

Alex shrugged. "You can fire me. I promise I won't apply for unemployment."

"I should fire you for dressing you did," he said. "You looked like a tramp."

Alex grinned. "Everyone believed I was interviewing for a job as your secretary. You might want to consider that before you try insulting my costume."

He flushed.

143

"How unstable does your little squeaky analyst think I am?" Alex scratched at the stitches in her side. She dropped her feet from the corner of his desk.

Powell twitched at the movement, his shoulders nearly turning to the door to run before he caught himself. He took a deep breath and released it slowly. "He thinks you're here to kill me. I barely convinced him to let me come in here alone."

Alex gave him credit for keeping his voice steady. "Well, it takes a bit to set up a burn team inside the actual black ops offices of the CIA, I suppose. Someone would have to delay me or something." She signed the letter and put the pen down.

Powell's eyes darted at the letter even as he pretended that tension wasn't eating at him behind his calm smile. "Are you here to kill me?" he asked.

"I'm here to resign."

"You know that doesn't happen, Alex."

"Yes, I vaguely recall your attempts to get me to kill one of your so-called rogue assets."

"I vaguely recall you telling me you didn't have the stomach to kill."

Alex smirked. "Actually, I told you I didn't kill people for money. A subtle difference; you really didn't pick up on it at the time. It amused me. I would have lied to you just as easily, but not lying to you was more fun. I'm here to resign. You need to stop chasing me."

"You could have resigned over the phone."

Alex nodded. "Could have. But I thought I should be polite."

"The United States government put in a lot of time and money training you. You can't just leave," Powell said. "We have more resources and more money than you can possibly imagine. You leave and all of those resources will be used to hunt you down."

"I spent six months being tortured, I'm addicted to heroin, and I'm working on a drinking problem. All the paychecks you ever paid me are still in the direct deposit account that you set up all those years ago, Powell. I never spent a dime of it. Take it all back with the interest," she said. She rose to her feet and deliberately looked at the drawer holding all the folders and Powell's research. "I shouldn't be able to work anymore anyway. They would have lost all that training and money if I were anyone else on the planet. I should be dead."

His eyes darted at the drawer. He swallowed hard.

Alex saw the perspiration break out on his upper lip. "I should be dead. But I'm not that easy to kill. Take the money back and we'll call it even. It's a generous offer and it gets you out of this alive."

"Taking all your father's money back from Peter has made you generous," he said. "But what about Door Jennings? He might like to spend some of that." He looked smug.

Alex didn't make any noise as she walked around the desk. When she was a child, to occupy her always restless mind, the monks had made her practice imitating the movements of the animals she saw in the jungle or the mountains. The one's which had been hardest were the silent stalking of the big cats. She'd worked so hard that it became her natural gait. Most of the time, she hid that—it alerted dangerous people to just how dangerous she was. Not now, however. Now she used it for its full potential to inflict the kind of instinctual panic that the ancient parts created when confronted with danger, primal danger.

Panic and fear danced in eyes that Powell struggled to keep stoic. His hips were partially turned towards the door as if to give him an advantage in running. He'd never make it. It would be like running from an attack dog. She could kill him easily, before he could even make a sound.

The voice in her head didn't chime in to agree with her or urge her on. She licked her lips and took a deep calming breath before she spoke. "I don't have a lot of friends, Powell. I don't have very many people whom I trust. Even thinking about threatening one of those people is very hazardous to your health. I will destroy you, disembowel you, and dice you up into pieces. I will do so without hesitation and without remorse. I am much more than the killer you wanted to make of me. More powerful, more intelligent people than you have tried to control me. They failed. You will fail. Stop and live. You don't understand the rock that you're trying to look under. It will destroy you."

He twitched. He swallowed again, then gave one of those uncomfortable laughs like you want to pretend that the person threatening you is joking but you're reasonably sure that they are not. "I want you to work for me, Alex," he said. "I want you to become a weapon for the good guys. I've never hidden that from you."

The tremor in his voice made Alex want to smirk at him. She walked to the big windows overlooking the city. Below the office was the street and the doorman, five stories below. Further down the building was a flag pole jutting out over the street—where it had been over a year ago when she'd last been here, where it had been for all the years she'd worked for Richard Powell. She wanted to make sure he noticed the weapon stuck in her waistband. "I won't kill for money."

"I just got done debriefing General Gregory. He says you slaughtered those mercenaries even while they were running away from you. You could be legendary. You'll be killing bad guys. That's what you want to do, right?"

Alex turned to face him. She watched his eyes dart at the desk. She wondered if he was thinking of the Colt or the files hidden there. "Like my teacher before me." She smirked at the sick look on his face; he'd been the one to tell her to never ask a question you didn't know the answer to.

"You'd have the resources of the United States behind you, not some shadowy organization. You could be the point of the spear of the free world, Alex. With unlimited resources and protection."

Alex nodded. "Yes, those resources and protections worked so well for me this past year. A secure text sent me into Peter's ambush. Did you send it, Powell?" She watched his body jerk in surprise. The discovery of the files had changed things, she realized suddenly. If he believed even part of what was in those file, Richard Powell would never have betrayed her to Peter.

His eyes darted at his desk again.

"Your lack of attention to my plight is beginning to piss me off. I don't think you understand the danger you're in. That burn team building up behind your door won't be able to save you in time."

He paled and involuntarily held his hands up. "It's not a burn team," he said, but his insistence was weak.

She crossed her arms and leaned back against the glass windows. "I want to know if you sent me into Peter's ambush. Did you hang up and erase my distress call? Did you think that his torture would make me into the killer you've always wanted?"

He loosened his tie and shifted his weight from foot to foot. "Someone set you up? There's a traitor inside the Division. I will help you find him."

"Peter needed inside help. He tried to get me alone for weeks after my father died, but I never liked him and I didn't give a shit about my father's money and estate passing to him instead of me. I was distraught. I should have followed my gut and left for the Far East. But instead you convinced me to stay. You convinced me to stay and work through the grief."

He took a deep, steadying breath and straightened up. Some of the fear dissipated.

Alex narrowed her eyes and tilted her head.

"Alex, I swear I would never do anything to intentionally get you hurt. I have never done anything to put you in the position that made you suffer like you did."

"Maybe you didn't think it would come to that. Maybe you didn't think Peter had the stomach for it. Maybe you thought I was so depressed over my father's death that you could push me over the edge and make me into your assassin."

Richard Powell started to reply, then bit off his words. "I would never have condoned what happened to you. Peter Van de Moeter is crazy; I knew that before your father's death and I

147

know that now. I knew he had an unhealthy obsession with you. I spoke to your father about that."

Alex sighed. She crossed the room to him and stopped so that her shoulder was touching his. She leaned forward slightly so that she could whisper in his ear. At the same time, her right hand slid to the small of her back and wrapped around the Colt. Her instincts were starting to twitch; she could practically feel the team behind the door breathing through the adrenaline pumping through their veins. "Burn those files, Powell. The ones about a legend which isn't supposed to be talked about. Burn them or I will come back and burn this place to the ground with you and everyone in it."

"Alex—"

She straightened. "All I have to do is tell the right people that you have them, and the US government will fall over themselves to deliver you to a Chinese prison. By the time you realize that would have been the best option, it will be too late for you."

"I want those bombs, Alex."

"No, you don't," she said, a cold smile stretching her mouth. "You want something much more devastating. You just haven't figured that out yet. The bombs are just something you can hang your hat on. No one really wants those bombs."

He paled noticeably and wrung his soft hands. "You expect me to believe in fairy tales?"

"You must have been very proud of yourself when you found me in a little state college in Ohio."

"Why do you even want those bombs? You can play mind games without them."

She glanced up at the door to the outside. She stared at the door knob. If they raced in now, they'd have to shoot through Powell to get to her.

"Hell," Powell continued. "It's not like you're going to use them."

She blinked at him.

Whatever color he'd had left in his face drained away. "Alex, I will send everything I have after you to stop that. If someone inside the Division betrayed you, I will help you find out who and we can deliver them to justice. You cannot use those bombs."

She said nothing.

Instead, her finger slid inside the trigger guard of the weapon. From the outside, the windows of this building looked like mirrors. No assassins would be able to take position and shoot inside with any certainty. Which meant they probably hadn't splurged for bulletproof glass. At least she hoped that was the case, because if she could help it, she'd prefer not to kill any CIA agents today.

"Alex, you expect me to believe you would kill thousands just to get to one man? This is a bluff."

She chuckled at him, but her attention was on the slowly turning door knob. She spun, lifted the 1911 and started squeezing the trigger eight times.

The window shattered.

The door burst open as Richard Powell dove for the floor, covering his head.

Alex jumped through the broken glass. The ledge outside the windows was wide enough to stand on. She'd climbed ice walls and mountains in the Himalayas during blizzards. One of the things that had made her an obvious phenom of the martial arts when she was a toddler was an uncanny sense of balance.

Instead of running across, however, she dropped down, holding on with her fingertips and dropping on to the ledge directly beneath Powell's office.

Above her, the strike team looked out and over and down.

"Where in the fuck?" one of them said, his voice carrying over the wind and the sound of traffic below.

Alex pressed herself against the wall of the building so they couldn't see her. She hurried along the ledge to the corner of the building. It was an ornate, older building and the architecture provided plenty of hold for someone with experience climbing. She climbed down the corner, using her bare arms and legs to hug the building.

The pedestrians she'd startled with her drop to the sidewalk gave her a wide birth. But this was New York, nothing much phased New Yorkers. They believed they'd seen everything. Most of them didn't even glance up to see where she'd come from.

Alex moved quickly. She heard shouts behind her and assumed it was the strike team rushing out of the building. None of them would attempt to climb up or down without ropes and gear. When she was a teenager she used to freak her father out by climbing some of Thailand's island cliffs without safety gear and sometimes nothing more than a bikini. Climbing. Heights. Not a problem.

The tennis shoes were right where she'd hidden them. She changed out the boots.

She kept moving until she found a pedestrian wearing a hoodie. She pointed the weapon in the man's face.

He started for his wallet, his eyes wide.

"I just want your jacket," she told him.

"Wha—"

"Your hoodie!" she snapped. "Hurry."

He was running away from her without a jacket when the first of the strike team came around the corner.

"Fuck," she said.

She shoved the empty Colt into the hoodie pocket and started running. She found her stashed clothing along the way, transforming from herself into a jogger who no one payed attention to.

Unfortunately for the strike team, she had a huge advantage. She'd lived in the city; and, while here, she'd discovered a thing called Parkour. She'd run these same streets whenever she was in town. She leaped over walls and vaulted down stairways. They couldn't shoot into crowds of civilians.

Running full speed, she felt good. Hell, she felt wonderful as her lungs sucked in the cold air. While she wouldn't have made it to the Olympics with her running speed, she was still fast. She had reserves of endurance from a lifetime of physical training and activity even without being in her top physical condition. Running wild was almost as much a part of her genetic code as the Sword. She had to admit she loved the chase; she loved the adrenalin.

She lost the strike team long before she reached Central Park. But she kept on running. She pulled the hood up so any surveillance cameras wouldn't spot her and send more spooks her way. Her plans for the rest of the day weren't anything fancy: more picked pockets, a couple of falafel pita sandwiches, and then an afternoon to run around the city avoiding the CIA and the Offspring. To her it was a game, to the CIA it was very serious. Alex figured it would be good training for them.

Later, Sinjin Doucet would go to his nightly session with his martial arts teacher, he was predictable when he was in the city and his *sensei* insisted on that. So, then she would show herself again.

Alex wandered the city and changed outfits a few more times. Her instincts for hiding and moving unseen helped, but the CIA had trained her to avoid being followed. It seemed like years since she'd used the skills they'd taught. However, the skill wasn't just caution now; it was how she would survive. The CIA had hunters out on the streets of New York. She spotted them a couple of times; their orders might be to eliminate her as a threat.

Her mind wandered as she scanned the crowds for faces she'd seen more than once. Through all her studies, the monks and her teachers had always been most frustrated with her inability to meditate and focus – and then had become irritated when she excelled despite her apparent lack of attention. All of her teachers except Sakai. Sakai had somehow known her inattention did not mean she had not noticed details. He'd known all along. She'd run from him in the end, from his training and his legacy. Her face flushed with embarrassment. It'd taken a bullet in her side after nearly drowning for her to accept what Sakai had given her when not even dying in an alley and six months of torture could convince her.

151

The Offspring, the cult which managed the money and the property for generations, thought she was disloyal as well; for other reasons. Over the centuries, they'd created ceremony and rules to contain the Sword of Souls. They had expectations. Sakai had been a teacher and Sakai answered to them. He pulled the weapon out at their behest and their call. They controlled where he went and who he saw. The only thing they hadn't controlled was her, but they'd allowed Sakai to have her as a student out of an indulgence to an old man. The Offspring never suspected.

She'd run to the one place the Offspring had the least resources to contain her—the United States. She'd enrolled in college and tried to be a normal 18 year old. Normal proved boring.

Richard Powell played on the boredom. He'd recruited her. However, the paperwork in his desk suggested it wasn't just luck which brought him. He'd claimed it was reports from the *dojo* where she practiced every day while in college and the fact that her father was a mercenary. In the end, those papers, while they'd condemned Powell, had saved the CIA controller's life. Powell had known that Chen Sakai was the Japanese assassin who'd been known as the Great One, an assassin with a sword who'd devastated the enemies of the Far East. He'd known that Alex was a student of Chen Sakai—the Offspring hadn't taken her seriously enough to protect her identity—she was female, she was Western, she came after they'd already chosen who they wanted to take on the reign of the Sword of Souls after Sakai passed.

It was said that the Sword of Souls controlled the one who bonded with it. It was said that the True One, the Soul of the Sword, would be reborn and would control the weapon. Under no illusions of her impending greatness, Alex knew she had an advantage, she didn't believe in the legend. The Sword of Souls was just as blood-thirsty as any other weapon.

Powell's people covered the city; sudden appearances of CIA personnel throughout the day indicated that his people had probably hacked traffic cameras and surveillance cameras throughout the city. Her own computer expert, DJ, was on the corporate jet headed back to Japan but he'd help here and there, to make things difficult for the CIA. She moved often, never lingering in one place too long.

She ended up in Chinatown. The swarm of people felt comfortable and familiar. Without Guang's steady voice, this was as close as she could get to calm the anxiety which threatened to swallow her. There was this nagging voice that despite her disbelief in the power of the Sword of Souls, she could not explain how she'd been near death in a New York City alley five hours before waking up in the jungles of Thailand. She did not want to be a slave to the Offspring or the weapon or a madness that consumed her. She feared losing her freedom.

She shouldn't feel comfortable here; this was probably one of the most dangerous places in the city. The Offspring drifted among these people—after she'd come to the United States, they'd migrated spies here. Her snub of their rules once again would mean they would be hunting her, like owners looking to get a leash on some escaped dog. Powell would think of this place as a possible destination. He would cover all his bases, covering the three surviving members of the Division rescue team led by Sinjin Doucet – and he'd cover Doucet's teacher's *dojo* which was exactly where she intended to go. However, a squared away Marine would never leave the apartment where he'd been ordered to stay—at least not until after dark. The team watching his place would report to the team watching the dojo. She had time to kill before sneaking into the *dojo* and confronting the Cajun Marine officer.

Alex wanted to spend her down time with what felt familiar. Her father had worked to give her freedom for as long as he could; she believed he'd actually sacrificed himself to make sure she had it. But his sacrifice had been used up—as he must have known it would eventually. She was Chen Sakai's chosen heir. The ancient sword had been handed down for thousands of years and she sure as shit wasn't going to be the one to stop the legacy.

With Travis Prince dead, she cleared him of betraying her—the bullet in his head had to have been placed by a sharpshooter and Peter would not have let a sniper kill his foot inside her world. General Gregory and Richard Powell proved neither of them had delivered the orders to send her into Peter's ambush or had hung up on her call for help. Alex had three suspects left.

She'd come up with a plan—a crazy plan that would draw out Peter's money-backer along with the traitor. The crazy was about to get racheted up a few notches. First, she needed to control the actions of the three suspects. Frank Dyer had been her father's best friend and an uncle to her. He was family. Mitchell Ong knew the legend; and now, he knew there were people perpetuating it. Ong's family owed her a debt; however, Ong hadn't known what or who she represented and he could have betrayed her. Sinjin Doucet had a background in martial arts; he was the only one she might have called a friend. None of them seemed likely to turn her over to a madman; but, one of them had. The way to manipulate a closely knit team was to control its head. She didn't want to make things complicated and Doucet was the easiest to manipulate; whether friend or foe, he could be controlled.

Rather than continuing on in the disguises, Alex opted for a final outfit change which was more comfortable than costume. The broken ribs and the bullet wound throbbed. She wore sturdy work boots, blue jeans just loose enough to fight in if needed, a black t-shirt advertising the band Godsmack, and a worn dark brown Carhartt jacket. She'd splurged most of her stolen funds on the boots—good puncture resistant, steel-toed, waterproof work boots with brown tops and black soles. Many martial arts masters had this thing about bare feet and all that; but Alex had never been under an illusion she was strong enough to stop a sword with her bare feet. Judo experts needed the flexibility and mobility of bare feet; Alex wasn't under the illusion she could win a wrestling battle either. She'd lose any direct battle of power versus power; her skill was in finding ways to negate or evade the other person's strength: speed, precision, and anticipation.

The smells of Chinatown made her hungry.

Her body needed lots of fuel to heal itself; she hadn't been kind to it these last three months. She couldn't bring herself to eat meat; the smell of it made her gag. Chinatown had a boatload of hole in the wall restaurants. She chose one which did not have a menu with an English translation posted outside the front door for the tourists. It was a Vietnamese place specializing in Pho, a noodle soup. It offered vegetarian Pho and imported beer, and that was enough for her.

With a stifled yawn, she stepped inside to the warmth. The smell of spices filled the place. Her stomach growled.

A young girl in a fitted white top and black pants stood behind a small counter with a cash register on it. She lifted her eyes to Alex as she shut the register drawer. Her face was a mixture of boredom and resentment. She stood with her hip jutting out slightly, her black ponytail hanging over her tiny shoulder. Her eyes rolled up and down Alex. The girl had porcelain skin and delicate features; she was beautiful. The instant hatred from women made no sense to Alex; but, at least, it was predictable. The girl all but slapped the label of "bitch" across Alex's face.

Alex scanned the rest of the patrons in the place. A pair of Koreans in business suits sat at a table near the back of the room. An old couple sat by the window taking in some people watching. The place was decorated with palms in big clay planters and the walls held photographs of scenes around Hanoi. Some of the streets were familiar, the close neighborhoods pressing against narrow streets between wherever her father had chosen to house her and wherever the dojo had been where she'd been training. She'd learned how to pick pockets on the streets of Hanoi; of the rich tourists who came to the streets to gawk at best; at worst, they came to buy children and enslaved women. She did a double take on a framed piece of parchment on the wall above a table near the kitchen door. The parchment had black ink painted on it, black careful brush strokes forming three ancient symbols.

Alex sighed and shoved her hands into her pockets. Her father always said she had the worst luck and the best luck, but nothing in between. The sword strapped across her back seemed to press cold steel through its plain black sheath and her jacket. It'd been there, this sword. All this time. Somehow, no one saw it. Somehow. A cold metal chill ran down her spine. The three symbols on the parchment were also scarred into her flesh and into the metal of the sword.

"One?" the girl asked her in a heavily accented voice.

Alex tore her eyes from the framed parchment. The girl's voice carried a New York accent behind the Vietnamese one—a faked Vietnamese accent. The girl was more American than she was. She also figured the girl used the accent to be purposefully difficult to understand for all the Western customers. All an act for the tourists. This place wasn't tourist friendly; it was Offspring friendly.

Alex contemplated leaving. Although she was fairly certain the Offspring wouldn't deliver a description of her to everyone in its ranks, she knew she was inviting trouble by staying. She was hungry, tired, and hurting...not exactly a good combination for her temper. She let her hunger win out. She needed a second wind. With a nod, she let the girl lead her to a table. What could possibly happen in this place besides getting cold pho? she asked herself.

As she followed the girl to a table, her eyes drifted back to the parchment. The three symbols were as familiar to her as the back of her hand. They were the scars that had formed over the spot where Chen Sakai had impaled her when she was just 18. Three little symbols separately they were words for death by a sword's edge, a restless and wandering soul, and the focal point between good and evil. Together they were sometimes called *tamashiikatana:* roughly translated into a spirit who carries the sword of one's death. Good and evil. Sanity and insanity. Life and death. Alex felt like she was the "and" between all these concrete things—meaningless but necessary.

156

The girl put her at a small table for two people set against the back wall. It was a good seat for someone on the run. She could watch the door and all the other patrons, plus she had a view of the door into the kitchen. She sat down.

The girl put a menu down on the table and walked back to her podium.

After taking off her jacket and hanging it over the back of the chair, Alex glanced through her options on the menu. It had no translations or pictures.

A heavy-set woman emerged from the kitchen. She was clearly the teen's mother. She smiled at Alex. "Hi. Welcome. Can I get you drink?" Her accent was real.

Alex nodded. "Beer. I don't really care what kind as long as it isn't dark."

She nodded. "Okay. Do you need help with menu?"

Alex shook her head. "I'll have the vegetarian pho." She pronounced pho as "foe" rather than "fuh" just so the woman would think she was trying to act smooth but really had no idea what she was doing. You had to assume a Vietnamese place would serve pho, the noodles and broth were practically a national dish in Vietnam. The young girl grimaced as she leaned on the podium and texted on her phone.

The woman took the menu. "Okay. I be right back with you drink then." She returned to the kitchen and started speaking Vietnamese.

Alex listened as she leaned back in her chair.

In the kitchen, the woman was laughing at the tourist who was "trying to act cool." Someone else suggested spicing up the soup. From their tone, Alex doubted they'd go through with it; but she wouldn't mind if they did. It'd been cold wandering around New York City all day. She leaned back against the wall and glanced out the window. Traffic, both pedestrian and motorized, moved along smoothly. She didn't see any shadows lingering in alcoves. She scanned for people she'd seen more than once, but each face that passed seemed unique. Somehow, she'd managed to get though Chinatown without alerting the CIA or the Offspring. It seemed too good to be true. Her hand rested against the bullet wound in her side.

A teenaged boy emerged from the kitchen with a beer bottle and a clean glass. He put it down on her table and bowed twice as if he didn't understand English at all.

Alex practically rolled her eyes at the act. She lifted the beer bottle to her lips and winced at the bitter taste. They'd given her the worst stuff they had. She should have considered that before being so nonchalant about the order. She sighed. Not that it mattered, it wasn't going to get her drunk anyway. One beer wouldn't even get her buzzed after the tolerance she'd built up the last three months.

In the kitchen, people rattled on in Vietnamese, talking about mundane things: the cold weather, baseball's spring training, and school. The old couple at the big window barely spoke to each other as they watched the world race by. Each of them had big bowls of noodles in front of them. They slurped and watched. The man wore a scowl on his round, wrinkled face. His eyes kept darting at Alex.

The boy and woman soon emerged from the kitchen with a steaming bowl of soup and all the condiments that might go with it—sweet hoisin sauce, Sriracha sauce, and tangy Vietnamese fish sauce. They also set a plate filled with fresh bean sprouts, basil, lime, and chilies. But the chilis looked like jalapenos, something pretty tame. Alex thanked them. Before being kidnapped, Alex had always eaten well—when she remembered to eat. She could burn calories quickly and Chen Sakai had taken to leaving food laying around. She'd munch without thinking, packing away twice as much food as the boys being trained by Sakai—dried vegetables, sticky rice wrapped in seaweed, pieces of fresh fruit, pretzels, peanuts, and when the house cook wanted to experiment with new recipes, he sought out Alex for taste testing.

These last three months, she couldn't even think about food without feeling nauseous. Until she'd let loose the demons inside her. Now, she couldn't seem to fill a bottomless hole in her stomach. It was like she was attempting to get all the food she'd missed into her body during the last year. She picked up the spoon and tasted the broth. She had to admit that the stuff was really good and really didn't need anything added.

The two businessmen got up and paid their bills with the girl at the front podium. Neither of them glanced Alex's way.

Alex used her chopsticks and her spoon both to slurp up the noodles with the broth. She was only about a quarter of the way through the bowl and starting on her second beer when a group of young men entered the place. They were older than teenagers, but not by much.

Alex saw the girl stiffen and pale as the five of them strolled in: loud, confident, and arrogant. The old couple's posture changed from casual and relaxed to nervous and on guard. Guang's warning echoed in her brain as the tingle of cold started to seep into her bones. Her father's prediction that she could walk into a bank and it would get robbed on that day--the worst of luck and the best of luck—rang in her thoughts.

The leader of the boys grabbed the girl and pulled her to him. "Are you on the dessert menu?" he asked.

She pulled free. "Let go of me. Get out of here," she ordered them as they laughed.

The older woman, the server, emerged from the kitchen. "Go away. You no cause problems in front of customer."

Alex sighed as she continued to eat. Maybe she'd get lucky and finish.

A man and the teen boy came out of the kitchen. The man was clearly the cook. He was a small man who wore a t-shirt and an apron wrapped around his waist. He frowned at the boys and waved a skinny arm at them. "Go! Go!" he ordered them, his accent real and thick.

"What? We're paying customers! You're not going to turn us away; are you, old man?" the leader asked. He flashed a stack of bills.

"You no welcome here. I call police."

One of the other guys grabbed the teen girl again.

Alex stiffened. When she was fifteen, four men, who trained in the same martial arts school in Hong Kong that she'd been training in, cornered her in a quiet alley. Her father had warned her not to take the short cut, but she'd been stubborn. They'd behaved very much like these men were behaving. But there'd been major differences: no one around would come to the aid of a stupid white girl and Alex had "earned" her attack by besting the leader of the boys in a fight inside the dojo.

This girl's brother, who seemed to be about the same age as the other boys, rushed forward. "Let go of my sister," he said.

One of the intruders shoved him backwards while a third man ripped the phone out of the wall.

Alex's attention kicked into a higher alert status. The Sword stirred like a waking beast in a dark cave that'd just been stumbled upon.

The leader of the group smiled at the family. "Your daughter is a cock tease," he said in Vietnamese. "And you—" he pointed at the man "—you are very disrespectful to us. We don't like how we were treated last time we were in here. My father is the leader of the Offspring. We own you." He cursed the man in about the most repulsive way possible in Vietnamese.

The old woman at the table by the window gasped at the mention of the Offspring.

Alex groaned.

"This is none of your business, so keep your old lady panties on," the leader of the group told the old woman. At the same time, he put a Converse sneaker on one of the clay pots and knocked over one of the palm trees. His eyes challenged the cook, the father.

Alex slurped her soup and watched the owner of the place freeze. She saw the fear and the shame of that fear in his eyes. She wouldn't let them hurt the teenage girl, but she found her biggest irritation was the way the leader had spoken to the old woman.

The scars on her side started to burn cold. In her case, she'd fought the man-boys off, but refused to finish them off. She wasn't ready to kill. Her endurance had been fading. That's when Chen Sakai had appeared. With flashing Sword, he'd cut them all down. He didn't stop until they were all dead, he even killed a man in the alley who'd refused to step in to help. He'd killed everyone except for himself and for the nearly exhausted fifteen-year-old redheaded white girl.

The teens manhandled the girl and ripped one of the sleeves of her shirt off for effect. She tried to get away, but was picked up and manhandled.

That young girl who'd been afraid to kill no longer existed. To Alex, it seemed like that event had happened to someone else. Chen Sakai trained that reluctant part of her away while her father had tempered the training by sheltering her as much as he could. To do what was necessary required cold dedication; and her veins froze with it.

The brother from the kitchen was cursed with the hot-headedness of youth. He rushed the teens who were hurting his sister.

This time, the biggest man in the group didn't just push the teen. He deflected the charge with a pretty good execution of a *VoVinam* move. Alex had never studied any of the Vietnamese styles of martial arts. But she'd done some street fighting in the dark seedy depths of Bangkok against men who had studied those styles. Enough that she recognized the technique. She also recognized that these were the kind of thugs who relied on fear and intimidation rather than real skill—they'd die quickly in a real fight, even quicker in an underworld fight like the ones they held in the big cities of Southeast Asia; the ones run by organized crime, the ones where people died. Alex thought all these things as the teen flew backwards and landed on her table. The bowl of pho flew up in the air.

Alex finished the noodles hanging on her chopsticks. She watched the liquid fly out of the bowl as it rolled in the air. She watched it reach the top of its arc and start to come down. It had still been steaming so Alex moved in her seat to shove the teen out of the way so he wouldn't get scalded. She made it look like he'd rolled on his own. At the same time, she caught her still full beer in midair without spilling a drop. The *pho* splattered on the floor beside the kid.

She stood up and took a swig of beer to wash down the last bite.

"This doesn't concern you," the leader of the gang told her. He pointed a finger at her, jabbing it in the air with each word. "You need to leave. No charge for dinner."

Alex sighed. She took another swig from the beer bottle to finish the nasty stuff. "You don't really think I'm going to just leave and let you hurt that girl; do you?" she asked. She resisted the urge to move forward and break his finger.

His eyes rolled over her. "Maybe we'll have fun with you too. You don't look so bad for an old bitch."

"Well, I'm not a scared teenager," Alex said. "I'm not sure if you could get it up around a real woman." She eyed him in the same lurid way he'd ogled her. "And even if you could; I doubt I'd notice. Size does matter, no matter what the girls tell you, PeeWee."

The four men behind him got quiet. Their eyes widened a little.

"Please," the father said desperately. "You no get hurt. You customer. I am sorry. Dinner free. This not your problem. You leave, safe."

Alex ignored him and watched the leader of the group. Her eyes dared him to come after her. She really hadn't left him much choice. The big guy in the group could clearly overpower him. The only thing that had granted him leadership had to be reputation. When the guy didn't react fast enough, she figured he needed another shove. "I see you're scared. You people aren't ever going to get any taller if you all keep cowering around us white folk."

"Let me fuck her and then kill her, Brian," the big man said in Vietnamese. "Fucking cunt. Your father and the Offspring will get rid of the body just like they'll shut up the girl and this family."

Alex felt a smirk stretch her mouth. She switched to Vietnamese easily enough. She'd grown up in various Asian

162

countries learning English simultaneously with a dozen other languages. They all came naturally to her. "When I want the dog to bark, I'll throw it a cookie," she said to the big man.

The big man's eyes widened. His face flushed red. He charged and took a swing, off balance and slow. Most big guys were slow. Most big guys without training were not accustomed to conserving energy for a prolonged fight—not that he'd need any endurance for this one. His mallet-sized fist came in a long arc, slow and meant to deliver devastation.

Alex moved it, redirecting its momentum. She shoved her boot into the back of his knee as he spun like he was Alex's dance partner and Alex had been leading. He went down in front of her, his own beefy arm locking his own neck in a choke hold. Alex held him in a pressure joint lock with minimal effort.

All the while, Alex had never dropped the stare of the group's leader.

Fear flittered across his face like a green cloud. He pushed it down with anger.

The big man struggled in vain to free himself. However, if he moved too far from where she held him, his joints flew into excruciating pain.

The leader reached into his jacket.

Alex felt her stomach drop. The monsters beating at the back door in her brain had stopped pounding on the door. They stopped demanding to be released; now, they just sat back and waited for the doors to open and the flood gates to be released. "Don't do it," she hissed at him. "If you pull that weapon, the Offspring are going to have to come here to pick up your body parts."

The mention of the Offspring brought silence through the restaurant.

The old man rose from his seat. He stared at her, his face pale. Then he turned to the teens in the gang. "You must leave. Run away. There is no shame in running. Your fathers are powerful men and they would tell you there is no shame in running from here. If you continue, you and all of us will be dead."

One of the gang members pointed at Alex, ignoring the plea of the old man. "You can't possibly know about such things. It's forbidden to speak of those things. You're about to meet the wrath of the Offspring."

Alex felt the monster inside of her flex its muscles. Guang's warning that she couldn't control her reactions was coming true. She shouldn't have had that beer. She was going to prove the Offspring right. "No," she growled at him, her voice not quiet her own. "I can fucking talk about the Offspring as much as I fucking want. The gods don't want *their* name silenced. The Offspring need to remember their place if they want to survive another generation." She held the big man, barely conscious of his struggle to free himself. "Let go of the girl and leave. Don't pull a weapon. If you make me fight, I will fight. I don't fight for status, I fight to finish. I'm not usually this generous with options; you should take advantage of them while you have them."

The others looked at the leader.

The leader of the group sneered at Alex. He pulled out a switchblade. "I am of the Offspring. I will not let some white woman besmirch the legacy of the Sword of Souls, I will—" His voice trailed off.

Alex winced when he spoke the name of the weapon. The cold pain of the weapon seared through the marrow of her bones. The words combined with the flash of the knife—if it had been a gun, she might have been able to keep the door shut. The monster pushed the door open and stepped out.

She broke the big guy's neck. The crunch stopped the leader's brave words in his throat. Alex smirked at the irony of that. The big guy had not been expecting to die. He had been concentrating on not breaking his arm. Over powering his spine had been almost easy. She let go of him. "That is what is forbidden by the gods," she said in a cold, empty voice.

The big kid's torso fell forward. It twitched on the floor.

"Jesus Christ!" exclaimed the man still holding the teen girl.

"Wrong god to ask for help," she sneered at him.

The leader lunged. He'd had some training. She wondered if he had trophies or black belt displayed in his childhood room. He took a long time to get to her in his slow-motion world. Alex took the knife out of his hand, grabbed the back of his shirt and hurled him into the wall behind her. She heard his skull crack.

The framed parchment with the three symbols fell off the wall. The glass protecting it shattered.

While her back was towards the group of men invading the small restaurant, one of them charged her.

The old man cried out a warning.

Alex didn't need the warning. She moved low, then lifted as he reached her, lifting his feet off the ground and flipping him. Without thought, the sword was in her hand. As the man fell out of the air, she cleaved him in half. She used the handle of the weapon to crush the throat of the fourth man, then kicked his knee out so he could writhe around on the floor trying to breathe through his crushed airway.

The last man threw the teen girl at her and tried to run.

Alex jumped over the dead big guy and vaulted over a table to intercept him. She grabbed his shirt and slammed him hard against the wall; the Sword slid under his chin. She could feel the need in the blade, the thirst. She growled against its pull. However, the terror in the man's eyes told her she could use him for something else. Fear could drive a man insane. Fear could kill a man as easily as a sword, but it took longer. Alex figured she should make the most of the time he had. The Sword of Souls didn't agree; it was made for drawing blood. She could practically see it throbbing with a blue-white light beneath the sheen of red covering its blade, throbbing in time with her own heartbeat, which was surprisingly calm. Her arm shook with the effort to hold the weapon back.

The white was visible all the way around the irises of the man's eyes. His heart raced against her fist balled up in his shirt, like his ribs were a cage and his heart was hurling itself against them to escape.

"Put your hands up," she ordered, each word deliberate and strained through the effort of holding back the weapon.

She thought he was too afraid to pull a knife and stab her in the gut. But in the same situation, that's what she would have done. So, she would not take that chance.

He lifted his hands up, putting the backs of his hands against the wall near his head. They shook.

Alex leaned in to whisper in his ear. His breath came fast and shallow against her shoulder, but she barely heard his begging to be spared above the roar of the monster, the war cries of a thousand Mongols racing across the steppe, Spartans screaming as they charged. All of it was free and stampeding through her brain, following the edges where her mind had shattered, filling in the gaps. All of them were pissed off and demanding blood.

She struggled to keep from killing him. Her hand flexed over the handle of the weapon. None of the internal struggle revealed itself in the cold killer holding the last survivor. As she whispered, the ammonia stench of hot, fresh piss twinged her nose.

"I will," the kid said loudly, his voice breaking. "I promise. Please don't kill me." He started to cry.

She ripped the sword back from his throat with a growl. The effort to put it back in its scabbard physically hurt. She grunted and winced. Her hand went to her side where the scars burned and the bullet wound itched. She felt someone come at her back. "Don't," she growled through clenched teeth. "Don't touch me."

She looked over her shoulder at the family and the old couple.

It'd been the old woman who had moved toward her.

Her husband had his hand on her arm, holding her back. He had fear in his eyes. "The weapon that cannot be named kills all who see it," he said in the silence of the room.

Alex did her best not to bend over at the pain in her side from the burning scars. "That's not going to happen today," she hissed, her hoarse voice sounded shaky with the pain.

The man's eyes widened slightly. "It is impossible for the Great One to resist the will of the gods."

"Fuck the gods," she said in Korean. "Just don't run. I'm like a dog that can't help but chase."

He nodded.

Alex didn't think his shaking legs would carry him fast enough to really run. With a grunt of effort, she grabbed her jacket off the back of the chair. "Call the Offspring. Have them clean up the mess."

The owner of the place nodded. The others were in shock.

Alex bit her bottom lip. "I'm sorry."

He furrowed his brow in confusion.

Alex left them all confused. The cold air helped ease the pain in her side. She hurried out of Chinatown and away from the *dojo* where Sinjin Doucet's teacher lived. There was no way she was going to be able to spar with him now; there wasn't going to be any sparring tonight at all. Plan B was going off the rails.

CHAPTER TEN

After what she'd done to Powell earlier, Alex McBrady didn't expect Sinjin Doucet's apartment to be unwatched. She hadn't expected to go to Doucet's apartment. Alex had spent a lifetime watching her father plan strategy against superior forces on top of being trained by the CIA to avoid detection; Powell didn't compare to her father when it came to strategy. The CIA would not be positioned anywhere on the street; Powell was smart enough not to have some panel van parked on the curb. Unfortunately for the CIA asset handler, Alex was smart enough to know he would hide.

Alex huddled in a dark shadow and waited for them to show themselves. Patience had never been her strong suit; but, she knew they would show themselves before she had to move. Surveillance took a lot of control. Some men took it seriously and could have outlasted Alex; but, Alex knew those would not be the people Powell would send after her. The people who came after her would have to be high strung and pumped full of adrenalin; men or women too wired to sit still for long. Alex waited, motionless in the chilled dark. Plan B and moved on to Plan C or Plan D, or whatever.

After an hour, a man left the building across the street from Doucet's apartment. The man's eyes scanned up and down the street on both sides of the road. He seemed more vigilant than just some guy heading out for cigarettes or another case of beer. Moving her position slightly, Alex studied the man's building. After a few minutes, she found the window with a rifle scope pointed out of it—third floor, middle of the building.

Alex grinned to herself. Sliding through the shadows, she crossed the street a block away and returned. The apartment's lock picked easily—there would be no engaged deadbolt or chain because one man had left and was expected back. The door slipped through the darkness inside the apartment. Alex followed it, low to the ground. She pulled the survival knife out of the holster at the small of her back.

The efficiency apartment had a single window. In front of the window, a man lay prone on the floor, his eye to the scope of a McMillan Tac-50 rifle. Alex thought the big sniper rifle was a bit of overkill for her—no pun intended. The bullet from the thing could probably go through her and through the building across the street. The window was open an inch to accommodate the silencer and to hold up the end of the rifle rather than a bipod stand. The gun was a matte black color designed to prevent reflection of light. A more reasonable AR-15 leaned against the wall next to the window.

The man behind the Tac-50 rifle breathed slow and steady. The tip of his finger rested on the trigger. His eyes were open, one of them trained on the scope on top of the rifle.

Alexandria Rae McBrady shut the door behind her. Her hand flexed over the grip of the knife—a habit which often lulled enemies into believing she had poor control over the weapon—because they'd all been taught to hold a knife or a sword with a firm but relaxed grip, never a loose grip, never a too tight grip.

When she got within range, the man spun suddenly. He kicked the knife out of her hand.

169

It flashed in the moonlight and flew across the room. When it came down, it stuck into the floor.

The man tackled Alex at the knees.

Normally, having the wind knocked out of her wouldn't hurt so fucking much. But the damn broken ribs. Alex spun and smashed her elbow into the man's face.

He grunted, but instead of backing off, he caught her ankle and pulled her in before she could escape. He landed a fist in her side.

She cried out in pain. However, pain didn't slow her down. Not now, that she was clearly in a fight for her life. She punched him in the jaw. The punch hurt her hand probably as much as it hurt his face. His head snapped back though. She scrambled to get the knife.

He leaped up and tackled her, going for the knife as well.

They struggled to get the weapon and keep each other away from it at the same time.

Alex knew he was stronger. Her teacher had told her that her biggest weapon was an opponent's over-confidence. She'd just handed that to this CIA guy.

He pounded her side again.

She felt her side gunshot wound rip open again.

He took advantage and got her in a headlock.

Her boots slid on the floor as she tried to find some leverage to get him off her neck. Her vision tunneled.

The man laughed through his heavy breathing. "You fucking remember me, bitch?" he snarled. "We were in psychopath camp together."

Psychopath Camp, the name the residents of CIA assassin training had given to their training location, had shown Alex a lot of things. The men had been dangerous and enjoyed killing too much. She'd been the only female, although she'd been told that there were other females who'd gone through the camp. It hadn't taken twenty-four hours before one of them had tried to attack her in her sleep. She'd dropped three bodies in near-by sinkholes—thank you Texas—before she managed to get herself flunked out of the camp.

"Remember Rocky? How he suddenly disappeared one night?" he said. "I know you killed him. I've been waiting all this time to return the favor. They said you washed out because you didn't have the stomach for wet work, but all of us saw the monster in your eyes. You're no fucking different than the rest of us; no better."

Alex couldn't get out of the hold. She faked passing out; hoping he wouldn't break her neck.

He held the hold for a few seconds after her body went limp.

Forcing herself not to suck in air when she had an airway again took a lot of effort. Instead of breathing, she pushed her body up off the floor, balanced on one hand and whipped her legs up. She got his head in her legs and flipped him around so his own weight did a lot of the choking. She allowed herself to breath when she had him pinned.

Unfortunately, he landed too close to the knife and managed to rip it out of the ground.

Before he could stab her legs, she let go of him and scrambled away. She stumbled, still dizzy from lack of blood and air to her brain.

The man was on her. He swung the knife.

She managed to avoid it and land a hard blow to a nerve cluster which numbed up his arm. She liked that one because it took away the superior strength.

The knife dropped to the ground.

Alex punched him again in the same cluster to make sure his arm wouldn't be returning to the fight any time soon.

He staggered back a few steps, but came at her again.

She blocked most of his blows, and he blocked most of hers. Not all of them though.

Alex was having trouble with her side, protecting the throbbing ache too much.

Like the feral animal he was, the CIA assassin smelled the weakness. He landed two jabs to the bullet wound, his hand coming back coated in red with her blood.

Alex landed hard against the wall.

171

He pulled back for the blow to knock her out.

She moved at the last minute, flinging herself across the room to the survival knife.

He dove after her to stop her.

But his right arm didn't work well yet and it came too slow. He landed on the ground where Alex had been an instant before.

Alex jumped on his back and drove the knife into the base of his skull, separating brain from spinal column.

All two hundred pounds of psychopathic muscle spasmed and went limp.

Blood poured out of his mouth and nose onto the floor.

Alex pushed herself off the body and staggered back against the wall beside the rifle still rested in the window sill. Everything hurt. She put her hand over the bullet wound and could feel the heat and the blood.

The adrenalin wore off quickly. She groaned.

As she sat there trying to catch her breath, the door opened. The man she'd seen on the street looked at the dead man on the floor, then saw her against the wall. He reached for his weapon.

Alex grabbed the AR-15, pulled back the bolt, pulled the stock in tight to her shoulder as she released the safety, and fired.

The rifle barely bucked against her. It made a slight *pfft* of air. Instead of a bullet, a dart appeared in the man's chest, right above his heart.

He didn't even have time to realize he'd been hit when his eyes rolled back in his head. He dropped like a stone.

"Fuck," Alex said. Whatever was in that dart worked fast. She tossed the rifle aside and forced herself to her feet.

She checked to see if the man was still alive.

He was.

She broke his neck.

He wasn't.

She stared down at the two dead men. She glanced towards the bathroom and the shower. "What the fuck," she said. "Why not?"

She turned on the lights and made sure the front door was deadbolted and locked.

The men had a duffle bag. It was big enough to accommodate the rifle. However, it also held more darts, ammunition, and an emergency kit. The emergency kit had probably been the idea of the other CIA guy—assassins really didn't think of packing CIA field kits.

Alex took the kit to the bathroom, stripped off her clothes and took a hot shower. She didn't have anything to dry herself off with so she dripped on the floor naked while she cleaned her wound and sewed it back together for the third time. This time it hurt a lot more. She had to stop a few times to keep from passing out. Her hands shook. She stared at her face in the mirror. "You fucking forgot pain fast enough; didn't you?" she asked the reflection.

Part of her was relieved that the bruised reflection didn't talk back.

Searching the men after getting dressed, she found a couple hundred dollars.

She could have walked right over to Doucet's place. However, she felt a little sick at the prospect of what she intended to do. So, she went to a store down the street and bought ice packs, Tylenol, and two bottles of Johnny Walker Black label.

As she paid, the clerk slid her a business card for a women's shelter. "You can get out," he whispered to her.

She took the bag and nodded at him.

She walked back to Doucet's apartment. It didn't take much to bypass his security and break in—she'd been here before and she habitually analyzed security. Once it had been her job to assess security systems and break them. She closed the door and walked into the place. Her eyes were adjusted to the darkness so she didn't bother with lights.

With a sigh, she put the shopping bag on the coffee table and sank into the couch. Two Tylenol went down with a swig of Scotch. It all sounded impossibly loud in the silence of the dark apartment. However, it did not cover the sound of a bed spring squeaking.

Alex squeezed the ice pack and felt it get cold. She put it on her side where the broken ribs were and held it there with her swollen left hand. Two birds, one ice pack.

Across the room, a door knob started to turn.

Scotch burned down her core in contrast to the cold. She slouched back in the couch and closed her eyes. Left hand on the ice pack on her side, right hand wrapped around the neck of the open bottle of Johnnie Walker.

Something moved in the darkness. Soundless so most would have missed it, but Alex didn't just listen. She felt the air move, felt the hairs on the back of her neck stand on end. She wondered if that was what had tipped off the CIA assassin across the street. Was it that feral instinct which had alerted him? She didn't open her eyes to look at the shadow approaching her. She didn't react to the sound of the safety being released despite the cold which leached into her bones and tried to drive her into another attack.

"The aspirin aren't working," she said. "Make sure it's a head shot." She lifted the bottle to her lips and took another swig, half expecting it to explode with a bullet headed towards her head.

"Alex?"

She grunted in the affirmative. The Scotch burned going down but settled nicely behind the ache of her ribs.

"Fuck, I could have shot you," Doucet grumbled. The lights switched on.

Alex squinted at the big Marine. His Sig Sauer pistol pointed at the ground now and the safety was back in place. Sinjin Doucet stood between her and the open bedroom door. His long hair hung loose over his bare shoulders. Dusky skin glowed with a red cast in the artificial light. Despite years of black ops service his skin was smooth and unmarked by scars.

Alex had the bizarre thought that if someone put a feather in his hair he could pass for some Native American romance novel cover model. She chuckled at the thought.

"Glad you think getting shot is funny," he groused.

Alex moved the ice packet and winced. "Some things are funny." She took another swig from the bottle.

His brow furrowed and his dark eyes stared down at her. "You look like shit, Alex."

Alex smirked at him. "Wow, no wonder all the women throw themselves at your feet, Doucet. You're so charming."

He sighed and put the gun down on the coffee table, pointed away from both of them. He'd also carefully put it just out of her reach.

She chuckled to herself as she lifted the bottle again.

He snatched it out of her hand.

"Hey!"

He put it out of her reach on the coffee table and pushed the other bottle back too. "Why are you here?"

"I don't figure they paid the rent on my apartment while I was a guest of Peter Van de Moeter."

"Let me be more specific. Why are you in New York?"

Alex grimaced up at him. "Are you trying to intimidate me by hovering up there?" she asked. It hurt her neck to look up.

Shaking his head, he walked across the room and grabbed a leather string to tie up his hair. "Last time I trusted you, I ended up losing a member of my team," he told her.

"Don't blame Travis on me," she hissed at him. "If you will recall, I was unconscious at the time because someone sucker punched me."

"It's your fucking game, Alex. People have died. Good people. Travis was a good guy."

Alex stood up. She glared at him. "I thought I needed your help to get those bombs. Clearly I was mistaken." She turned to the front door and nearly doubled over, going down on one knee and catching herself on the arm of the couch.

Doucet grabbed her arm and helped her back to the couch. He crouched beside her. "Lift up your shirt."

She gave him a dirty look.

He rolled his eyes. "Whoever beat the crap out of you might have pulled the stitches you probably did a piss poor job of putting in. Lift your shirt."

"No one beat the crap out of me," she grumbled.

He arched a dark eyebrow over his dark eyes, not looking away from hers. He kneeled on one knee next to her.

She lifted her shirt to reveal the bandages wrapped tightly around her ribs.

"You're bleeding through the bandages."

Alex dropped her shirt. "Yeah, I'll just go see a doctor or something." She reached down and grabbed the open bottle that he'd taken from her. She downed another swig. "Thanks for nothing."

He caught her arm again. "You need a doctor."

Alex took a deep breath. Her eyes dropped from his earnest look. "I'm not going to a doctor, Doucet. I'll be fine. I will find someone else to help me get those bombs. You stay here and follow your rules." She watched his jaw twitch slightly as his brain worked.

"I have a battle kit. I can sew you back up and get you some antibiotics so it doesn't get infected. Stay here."

"That didn't work out so well last time."

"Gregory and the CIA pulled me and the team off the job. Dyer and Ong are on leave like I am. I'm the only one who knows where you are." He hesitated. "Please, Alex. You don't know what it was like chasing you through the streets of New York City thinking that if I didn't find you, you'd die alone in some alley."

Alex felt him loosen his grip on her arm.

He stared into her eyes as his big hand fell away from her arm. "Take off your jacket," he said, clearing his throat and taking a step backwards. "I'll go get that kit."

Alex lifted the bottle.

"And lay off the bottle," he told her. "It makes you bleed more."

She grunted and rolled her eyes as she swallowed. The burn was barely noticeable now.

Doucet disappeared into the dark bedroom.

Alex took a deep breath and let it out slowly. She put the bottle down and winced as she took off her jacket. Everything hurt. She could feel the bruises from where the CIA man had pounded her in a few spaces. Over-confidence will kick your ass every time, she thought to herself.

Doucet returned with a towel and a black bag. He put the items on the kitchen table. "Come over here, the light is better," he said. He'd pulled a shirt on. "Can you make it?"

"Fuck you, Doucet. I can make it." Alex crossed to the kitchen area.

He opened the fridge and handed her a bottled water. In the bag, he found a packet of antibiotics. "Take these," he said.

Alex ripped open the antibiotics. "These will go well with all the Scotch," she grumbled.

He frowned. "Did you kill whoever did this to you?"

"Why would you think that?" she asked.

"Because what I saw in Cleveland wasn't the Alex McBrady I remembered. The book on you says you don't have the stomach to kill."

"That mercenary would have killed those people if I hadn't stepped in. They didn't deserve to die just because they tried to be nice to me. They were helping people in that soup kitchen. I feel bad about destroying it. You and your team were committed to making sure there were no civilian casualties; you weren't going to succeed. That merc was a killer; he wasn't going to leave witnesses." She started to say something else, but the words stopped in her throat when he pulled out a pair of scissors. The fluorescent lights in the kitchen area shone off them. She banged the small of her back against the counter's edge and grunted at the jolt of pain that radiated to her ribs.

"I have to cut off the bandages and cut out these stitches. You suck at sewing, Alex," he said.

She nodded. "Hard to sew when your hands are shaking."

"You going to be okay?"

Her eyes darted at the bottle of Johnnie Walker.

"Alex, look at me," he said. "*Cher*, it's going to hurt. Are you going to freak out on me?"

She swallowed.

"I'm going to need you to take your shirt off," he said.

Alex was surprised at how much her hands shook. She pulled the shirt up over her head, gasping in pain. Doucet helped her. He draped the shirt over the back of a chair. "First I'm going to cut off the bandages."

Alex let him do it; her breath got ragged as she fought the looming flashback.

Doucet tried to be careful pulling the bandage off the bloody gunshot wound, but it was half stuck to the injury even though she'd cleaned it not too long ago.

Alex's fist clenched and a moan escaped.

Doucet dumped the bandages in the trash.

Alex looked down at the injury. Her side looked worse than it had on the plane, black and dark purple. The ragged circle which had been stitched up twice already bleed, trailing blood down her hip into the waist of her jeans.

"Okay to go on?" Sinjin asked carefully.

She sucked in a deep breath. "Just do it."

He nodded. "I have to clean it first. Then we'll put that ice pack on it and try to numb it up. There's a needle with some numbing agent in there."

"I'm not going to let you near me with a syringe," Alex said, clenching her teeth.

Sinjin nodded. "I thought that might be the case. We'll manage. I'll be as careful and as fast as I can be."

Alex leaned on the counter for support. She managed not to make a sound through the cleaning and the removal of the torn stitches. But the first new stitch pulling the edges of skin together, ripped a cry from her lips.

Sinjin froze.

"No," she said through gritted teeth. "Just do it fast. Get it over with." She forced herself to stand still for him, but she couldn't stop the heaving breath pushing in and out in an attempt to control the pain. At least she could be certain the broken ribs hadn't punctured a lung.

Doucet finished quickly, but to Alex it felt like it had taken forever. He tied off the stitches and cleaned around the wound with alcohol. Finally, he taped a bandage over it. "It's done," he said. His hand reached for her face. He cupped it gently and his thumb brushed away tears.

She hadn't realized she'd been crying. She looked up at him with the raw pain of it.

"You're okay, *cher*," he told her, his Cajun accent thick.

She felt the heat of his body close to hers.

His hand moved down her cheek to the bruises on her neck. Then it moved down to her bare shoulder.

She didn't move. She watched his face and the heat building in his eyes.

His lips lowered to hers.

She closed her eyes and fought back the bile and the urge to flee. Once, as little as a year ago, she'd been a free spirit. She liked sex just as well as the guys and a roll in the hay without strings was fun. She'd come from a world that wasn't hung up on sex. Whatever had changed inside her over the last six months was something she didn't want to contemplate. She stamped it down and buried it and returned the kiss.

She gasped in pain when Doucet lifted her up to the countertop.

"Sorry," he said, breathing heavy.

Alex took the opportunity to pull his shirt up over his head. She ran a hand over his hairless chest. Her hand looked pale against his skin.

His mouth trailed kisses over her collarbone. His hand slowly pulled the strap of her bra down over her shoulder.

Alex buried anxiety. She'd gotten very good at closing doors and building walls. She stopped thinking and let herself feel. The alcohol helped. She let her body react; and, when it didn't, she pretended it did.

Later, in his bed, she made her breathing deepen and slow. She closed her eyes.

But she didn't sleep.

It took a while, but she felt the mattress move slightly as Doucet shifted his weight.

She moved in response and felt him freeze. She kept her breathing even and didn't open her eyes.

After a minute, he moved again, sliding out of the bed.

Alex listened to him move across the bedroom floor, then go into the living room and close the door. The instant, the door closed, she opened her eyes. She moved quickly, collecting her clothes and putting them on as she headed to the restroom. She could hear Doucet whispering to someone in the other room. She didn't really care who he had called—it would either be Peter Van de Moeter or General Gregory. But in the end it didn't matter. In the bathroom, she opened up a tube of toothpaste and used it to scrawl a message on the mirror.

After the message, she found a shirt which belonged to Doucet and put it on. She rolled up the sleeves.

The conversation in the other room sounded like it was starting to wrap up.

Alex opened the bedroom window. The place had no balconies or ledges, but it was a brick building and brick provided mortar between the blocks. It wasn't much, but it was enough. Plus, the window was only on the second floor.

She slid out the window feet first, clenching her teeth when it came to balancing on her ribs. She silently thanked her father for insisting that she learn his hobby so they could do it together. She'd spent a good portion of her youth cliff climbing, ice wall climbing, and mountaineering. She had no fear of heights nor of falling. She hung by her fingertips.

She dropped and rolled when she hit the ground, wincing again at the stab of the broken ribs. The stitches in her side pulled but they didn't rip out. Doucet had done a good job sewing. She'd never been good at sewing up her own injuries—she preferred to avoid them. After she was 16, after a year of training with Chen Sakai, no one with a knife or a sword had been able to get close enough to her that she'd needed to think about cuts that would need stitches. She had a problem with judo and Brazilian jujitsu...all those fancy grappling arts which the mixed martial artists favored these days; but never with a blade.

As she hurried down the dimly lit street, she tied her hair up in a ponytail. Her walk changed from athletic and graceful to slow and confused. She rolled the sleeves of the shirt down and let them hang over her hands. She clung to the shadows and became a different person. Two black sedans rushed down the street towards Doucet's place. Neither of them slowed down to check out the lone traveler. Alex felt a sense of relief that Doucet had called the Division and not Peter. The relief bothered her. She heard Guang's warning in her head and she realized she'd changed her walk to something bouncy and carefree. She started walking quicker.

Behind her, the sound of tires squealing as a vehicle raced around a corner.

She turned to look.

One of the black sedans was coming back.

Alex ran.

CHAPTER ELEVEN

Alexandria Rae McBrady came out of the small bathroom. She frowned at the monk sitting on the seat by the window. The Great Plains rolled by to the rhythm of wheels on a track. Her lifelong friend, and to be honest with herself, probably her only real friend in the world, was watching her. His dark eyes were veiled against the attempt to read them, but she felt the disapproval. "What?" she asked in an old, obscure Chinese dialect.

Guang shook his head. "Nothing."

"Good," she groused. "I don't want to hear it anyway." She climbed up onto the top bunk and lay down. She put her hand on her side where she'd been shot, then moved it quickly when she caught Guang taking note of it.

"There is really nothing to say," Guang said. "I mean, it is perfectly normal. To get yourself involved with a man who has no compassion for what you have suffered and leaves you vomiting—that is normal. You are planning something crazy which could destroy you and everyone around you. Also reasonable."

Alex rolled to her side. "We're stuck in this tiny cabin on this train for the next fourteen hours, Guang. Do you really want to do the passive-aggressive sarcasm thing?"

Guang shook his head. "You are correct. I would much rather sit quietly listening to your nightmares in between bouts of your retching."

Alex swallowed. "I spent three months barely eating. I just over did it."

Guang snorted. "I am not sure why I thought six months of being tortured and raped, followed by an experience that had to be even more emotionally traumatic for you, might actually put a clue in your thick head. Some of your stupidity must have rubbed off on me."

Alex sat up and turned to him. "What I did has nothing to do with why I'm sick," she told him, pointing her finger for emphasis. "Not the torture, not the six months, not – " She stopped herself.

"Not the what? What happened?"

She took a deep breath and looked away from him. Outside the world rattled by. Small downs, open fields, America as she'd never seen it before. This wasn't her country. This wasn't her home. She missed the jungle. No, not just the jungle. She'd spent three months on the streets of Cleveland and she even missed the streets of Thailand, the narrow, filthy alleys of Bangkok. She missed the lights and the noise and the tiny little bars of Tokyo. She was tired of playing in this playground. "Maybe it's food poisoning."

Guang sighed. "It is not." He stood up and took the single step that put him next to the bunk bed. "Alex, a year ago, you could pick up some random guy, have some fun, and move on. Now, you are not having fun, you are using your body to manipulate someone. In effect, you are torturing yourself all over again. It is difficult for me to watch this happen. And it angers me that this man allows it to happen. If he cared for you, he would not."

"I'm tired," Alex said softly. "Guang, I want to go home."

He frowned. "So, we get off this train at the next stop and we find a plane and we go to the east. Until you are better."

Alex felt her stomach roll. She swallowed the bile, absolutely refusing to get off the bunk and rush back to the train cabin's private bathroom. She'd have to push Guang out of the way to get there and it'd be proving him right.

Guang sighed. "Is he the one who betrayed you? This man you are using? Who is using you?"

Alex closed her eyes and took in a deep breath. "I don't know. Maybe it was the dead one."

"You could not be that lucky," Guang said dryly.

She managed a humorless laugh.

"You could have found another way other than sleeping with him."

"It was faster this way. And I'm not going to turn into a nun," she said. "Faster. I want to go home. I think I need a vacation."

"I am your friend, Alex. I wish for you to find someone who can replace bad memories with good ones; someone to care for you rather than someone who looks at you and sees only the surface."

Alex sighed. "That's not going to happen, Guang. It can't happen."

"You have forgotten how beautiful the world can be."

She turned her head to look at her friend. "There are no flowers or sunsets in my future, Guang. I died in an alley in New York City and I woke up in a cave, without my mind and I almost killed you."

"Well, you are not happy with me now either, but at least you have enough sense not to kill me."

Alex managed a grin. "Well, who else is going to call me stupid and stubborn?"

"Everyone says it behind your back."

"They're afraid of me. You aren't."

"I've known you since we were toddlers. But, Alex, I am afraid *for* you. You are sleeping with a man who does not see behind your façade. He does not accept you for who you are.

So instead of healing that scar inside you; he is giving you mortar and bricks to make the walls thicker and higher."

"It's not going to matter," she said.

"What do you mean?"

"I shouldn't be alive."

"Will to live."

"Sold my soul," she replied.

"That is not true."

"You weren't there."

"Tell me what happened in that alley. After you escaped the hospital and ran."

Alex grimaced.

"If anyone is your counsellor, it is me," Guang said carefully. "I cannot walk the trails you walk, I cannot walk with you on this journey you are on. But I am here now. I can listen. What happened to you."

Alex sighed. "I don't remember it all. I was kind of insane."

"What do you remember?"

Alex jumped slid off the bunk and moved to get away from the earnest monk. She shook her head. "I remember voices yelling." She went to the window and stared out at the landscape as the train raced through it.

"What were they saying to you?"

Alex arched an eyebrow and smirked. "They weren't yelling at me. They were arguing. About..." she narrowed her eyes and stared out the window. The train rocked around her. "About whether or not I had the strength to survive with a broken mind. About if I should be forced to move on or allowed to continue. About how the world wasn't ready to accept what had to be done. About abandoning the world to its own horrors." She sucked in a deep breath, it shook.

Guang stared at her back. He said nothing.

Alex let her head fall. She stared down at her hands. Her hair fell over her face, hiding the sun and the world. She saw too much out there; too many details that would have flashed by other eyes. Cars that needed repair, families starving, fat executives, abusive husbands, drug addled mothers, children without souls. She bit her bottom lip to keep it from starting to tremble. She forced herself to not let her hands wring.

"Alex? What did you do when you heard this argument?"

"I let go."

Guang's brow furrowed. "I do not understand."

She swallowed and turned to face him. "I let go."

"Of what?"

"The bars that are holding in that thing inside of me which everyone is afraid of," she said. "That thing everyone sees when they look at me, that I can't see myself. The thing that makes people look away."

"And?"

"I can't control it. It took over." It was as close to she would come to admitting that she somehow had glimpsed what she was capable of and it had terrified her.

"You are not out of control."

She shook her head and ran a hand through her hair, shoving it back from her face. "I hear it roaring in my skull. I can almost understand its whispers."

"It?"

She shook it off and pulled back from the confession. Her eyes got hard again. "Guang, I know you want to believe that I am something I'm not," she said. "I won't live as a slave. Peter dies, the man who betrayed me dies, the man who is pretending to want those bombs dies." She set her shoulders. "I made a deal to live. I don't expect to live beyond that deal. I should be dead. This thing inside me, this thing that Sakai gave me. It's not going to win."

"I have known you a long time. I know you will never live as a slave. You do not have to convince me of that."

Alex shook her head. "It's like being in a choke hold that isn't set well. You just get that trickle of air and you keep sucking it in without passing out."

Guang sighed. "All of what you just described, it has nothing to do with who you are and everything to do with what you've been through this past year."

"You're wrong."

"You are afraid for the first time in your life."

"I'm not afraid of anything."

"And you are a liar."

"I'm dead already, my body just hasn't given up yet. No wishes. No flowers. No happy moments. Nothing but pain and agony and blood and revenge. My soul is lost and I'm going to throw my humanity in after it."

"I think you are wrong and I'm afraid you will not be able to live with the consequences of what you plan."

She chuckled without humor. "What I plan. Guang, I don't see any way I can survive what I plan. The man behind Peter Van de Moeter wants power. He has to die. He's bringing insurmountable odds. But he's never fought someone who is willing to die just to win."

"You will win."

"Take my body, Guang. Throw whatever pieces are left of me in the jungle in Thailand. When this is over let me sleep. I want to go home to the jungle."

Guang's eyes narrowed, his lips pressed together. "I will pick up the pieces, Alex. That is my role. I will pick them up and put them back together. No matter what you do to destroy yourself. And when this is over, wyou might get a short reprieve before the Offspring come after you for their Rule of Sevens tournament; your reprieve better be spent training." He walked out of the cabin and left her alone.

Alex flinched when the door slammed. She stared at the closed door for a long time before climbing back into the bunk.

When she closed her eyes, she dreamed she was back in the alley months ago, she dreamed she was dying. She dreamed her teacher came to her and carried her from the alley.

She stood in a room made of white light. The voices spoke simultaneously in a thousand languages. The noise was deafening. She covered her ears and screamed, sinking to her knees. But the sound was unrelenting. It drove itself into her brain like a thousand white hot needles. The light blinded her.

Simultaneously, the crescendo of voices stopped. The light switched off. She was lost in nothing.

Panic came.

She reached out and fell into the blackness. Blackness with no bottom. Just her stomach in her throat.

It seemed to go on forever. Soundless. Lightless. Sensory deprivation to an extreme that only a madman could conceive of.

Then a voice.

Soft.

Teasing.

Mocking.

Deadly.

"Choose."

Alex didn't understand.

She didn't know what she had to choose. She didn't know the choices. Her stomach was gone. Her heart didn't race anymore because it was gone as well.

There was nothing.

"Choose."

"What?"

"Remember," another voice said, another language.

"No! Choose without remembering!" a third voice said.

"Get me out of here," Alex begged. "I'll give you anything. Just get me out of here."

"Anything?" the first voice asked, intrigued.

"Anything!"

"Your soul?"

"Yes!"

"Your freedom?"

"Yes."

The voice laughed. "You're lying."

"I swear."

Laughter. "I call your bluff, Alexandria Rae McBrady. Deliver your revenge. Take our revenge to battle. Survive. Without a soul. Without your freedom. Survive and continue to exist. This is your choice. When your task is complete we will meet again."

"Just make it stop," Alex begged. "Please, make it stop. I can't—no more—"

She gasped and jumped awake.

Sweat made her clothing stick to her body. The light out the window was dimming. Guang sat in his chair reading. He looked up from his book at her.

She saw his eyes go from her face to her hand. Her eyes did too. She saw her hand shaking and gripping the handle of the Sword of Souls. Her breath came in harsh gasps.

Guang spoke softly. "I made reservations for dinner. You have time to shower and change. I also bought you some clothes more appropriate for the weather. Akiko knew your sizes."

■■■

"What are we doing here, Alex?"

Alex looked at Sinjin Doucet in the mirror of the Las Vegas motel room.

When she'd found him, he'd been the focus of female attention as he nursed a beer. He'd been there for hours and hadn't so much as glanced their way. He'd beaten her to Vegas by a couple of days, the benefits of being able to take a plane. She and Guang had taken a series of busses and trains. Still, she doubted the tall Marine had gone to bed alone every night he'd been here. Frank Dyer had positioned himself at a Blackjack table which had a view of the bar. He watched the captain and the crowd and played poorly. Mitchell Ong sat at a quarter slot machine losing the government's money.

They'd waited for her. She'd finally showed herself to them.

She took a deep breath and released it slowly. She wanted to go back to that moment. She wanted to see them and instead of showing herself, she wanted to turn and walk away. But, she hadn't.

Sinjin Doucet stood by the side of the queen-sized bed, pulling on a pair of black jeans. His white briefs stood out against the dark tone of his skin. He'd practically ripped her

189

clothes off when they'd gotten to the room. He'd gotten what he wanted. If she'd allowed herself to think, she would have plunged into a panic attack. Alex didn't hold his actions against him; she'd encouraged it and had done nothing to stop it. Her body had taken some satisfaction from it too; even if her brain and her gut didn't. If she'd wanted to stop him, she could have.

Guang's warning echoed in her head.

Doucet's room was high up on the corner of the Luxor Hotel on The Strip in Las Vegas, Nevada. The window was slanted because of the pyramid shape, beneath it, a Jacuzzi tub stood empty, waiting for some romantic night. It was the promise of some event Alex never expected to experience. The room felt used, worn.

She wondered if Doucet imagined a life of honeymoons, or what he expected. Had he gotten a Jacuzzi room because he'd dreamed it might happen or had he gotten the room because it was high up and the windows were sealed? She could not escape from this room like she had from his apartment in New York. She wondered if the Black Ops Division team planned on expensing this trip.

The days on the road had tested her patience; but, she had to admit she'd needed the rest. Next to the buff figure of Doucet, she looked even more gaunt and pale than she imagined in her head. Her eyes were haunted, but the dark smudges under her eyes and the redness had gone away with sleep. Guang's steady presence allowed her to let down her guard enough to drift off and catch an hour or two at a time before the dreams woke her up. Her sleep resembled something close to unconsciousness these days. She just passed out when she couldn't take it any longer.

Sinjin looked good in his civilian clothes.

Alex dressed the part of tourist. A form fitting white t-shirt with sleeve caps was tight enough to reveal the bottom of her rib cage and to emphasize the swell of her breasts. She wasn't a female athlete who lost all her female parts. Her loss of weight only made it all the more noticeable. Acid washed jean shorts were rolled up to just over her knees. With her hair down and a flush on her face, she was the perfect trophy for the ego of the man behind her. She wore sneakers rather than boots—white Nikes—a concession to her tourist character. "You're the first who claimed I'm not memorable. Thanks. That's flattering."

He walked towards her, pulling his black t-shirt over his wide, smooth chest. He put a hand on her bare arm and looked into the mirror. "That part I'm pretty clear on," he said. "I would say more than just memorable. I'd say unforgettable." He leaned down so that he could smell her hair and inhaled deeply. A groan rumbled in his chest. "But, it could be better if we didn't have these bombs hanging over our heads."

Alex bit off the reply she wanted to give. Those bombs weren't hanging over her head. They were hanging over his and everyone else's. She wasn't worried about the bombs.

Sinjin brushed her neck and kissed it.

A shiver ran down Alex's body. She couldn't help it. There was a spot there that set off a reaction in her body and Doucet had found it. She felt his lips smile against her skin. She took another deep breath and released it slowly.

"Com'on, *cher*," he said. "Tell me where they are. I'll call in a team to go get them. We'll go back to having fun."

She turned to face him.

His hand went to her face, his thumb brushed her cheek near the corner of her mouth. He groaned. "Ah, *cher,* I could kiss dis *bouche* all day and den some." He kissed her mouth. "I can-na believe I thought of you as one of the guys."

Alex let his tongue slide between her lips. Her hand moved up to the thick mane of black hair falling over his shoulder. "You think you can seduce the answers out of me?" she asked, her hoarse voice a little breathy when she broke her mouth free.

He didn't stop kissing her as he replied. "Nah, *cher*, dis is all pleasure. But, I have to do my job. You can't ask me to forget that."

191

"Maybe I'll fall asleep and you can call Gregory again." She frowned at the bitterness in her voice.

Doucet's attention wasn't focused on her tone. He was watching his hand move over her body and cover her breast as he nuzzled her neck. "Your message on my bathroom mirror was clear enough—toothpaste is hard to clean off by the way. I did done learnt the lesson you wanted me too, boo. I will not spook you again. Just me and the boys. I'll send Gregory after the bombs, not after you." His Cajun accent as thick, his voice deep.

Alex felt his body's reaction to hers against the front of her hip. "We need to meet Dyer and Ong for dinner. They'll wonder where we are."

Doucet shook his head. "Nah, we're goin' ta be late," he said. "And I'm pretty sure they know where we are." He grinned and nibbled at her ear. "Although I'm pretty sure the Sergeant doesn't approve." He chuckled. "God, you're so beautiful."

Alex's breath caught as the hand cupping her breast squeezed. She buried her thoughts and just went with the action. She was, after all, a physical creature. That's what she told herself. Doucet was six feet five inches of sculpted muscle. She could appreciate that. The roar in her ears. Her pounding heart. The edge of the dresser bit into the top of her thighs, pain to match the growing ball of anxiety in the core of her being. Easy to forget what she was waiting for.

So, this. Again. The action before the action. She figured it was better than waiting.

She expected to wait until dinner at the very least.

She let him turn her and back her onto the bed. She let his leg move up the inside of her thigh.

His hand was warm on the cool skin of her hip. They were hard and calloused as they worked the button at the top of her pants.

She did not expect the window to explode.

Because it was safety glass, it didn't shatter all over the Doucet's back as he suspended himself over Alex's body.

The roar of the dry hot wind and a whump, whump growl of a helicopter too close to the building filled the room. Somewhere alarms began to wail.

Three men dressed all in black with their faces covered, jumped out of the side of the chopper, their belts attached to ropes that led back into the helicopter. Their boots crashed in the shattered window and landed on the edge of the window Jacuzzi tub.

Their rifles shot tranquilizer darts into Doucet's back. His body collapsed onto hers, protecting her from the darts and pinning her to the mattress.

Sluggish and slow Doucet's hand moved towards the Kimber Custom 1911 which he'd left on the nightstand, still holstered.

Alex knew he wouldn't make it. She'd been trained to have a tolerance against drugs and alcohol. She'd trained drunk to build muscle memory. Her body reacted even when it was numb. Doucet's biggest vice was a few beers. He had his addictions: clean living, trips to the *dojo* near his apartment, and women. Alex had a natural resistance to the effects of drugs to start with. Six months of being pumped full of heroin and whatever else Peter had done to her probably made her practically immune. She wasn't planning on letting anyone know that however. Back when Peter first kidnapped her, the number of darts it'd taken to actually put her down almost killed her. Fortunately, along with the torturer, Peter's unknown buyer had also provided several doctors.

She shoved Doucet's body towards the gun, sliding her own body away from him and the window. She fell on the floor and scrambled towards the room door as she pulled down her shirt.

A dart hit the wall beside her.

Instinct had her rolling away from the spot.

She started for the door, in the hallway which had a closet and a door to the bathroom.

The room door smashed open and off its hinges.

The sound of a fire alarm going off blared from the hall. Smoke filled the hallway. Men in black, wearing gas masks flowed into the room with the smoke. The lead man held a canister of pepper spray in a gloved hand.

Alex skidded to a stop; she didn't turn away fast enough. Pepper spray blinded her. She cried out and fell backwards. Instinct took over. She had left the Sword of Souls with Guang as well as all her other weapons; if she hadn't, all of these mercenaries would be dead. Without a weapon, she would be less likely to stay free after an organized assault. After all, only idiots brought pepper spray and tranquilizer darts to a sword and knife fight. Blindly, she grabbed the arm with the pepper spray and broke it. Before the guy could recover, she took the pepper spray and sprayed it into his mask. He screamed; but the scream was short lived as she shoved his head into the edge of the open door.

Someone grabbed her around the neck. She figured it was one of the other mercenaries who'd come in from the hall. He leaned back, lifting her feet off the ground, stretching her back, forcing her to concentrate on keeping her neck muscles tight so her neck wouldn't break. She lifted her legs, found leverage on the wall and started to push up and over to switch out the guy's choke hold with one of her own. She might have pulled it off; but, she got jabbed with a stun gun in her side.

Thanks to all the fun torture she'd experienced, along with plenty of tazers and stun guns from the sadistic CIA trainers, she thought she might be a little resistant to them too. She told herself she only went down because they hit her right in the healing bullet wound.

She dropped with no control over her contracting muscles.

Through blurry vision, she found herself looking across the carpet at Sinjin Doucet's dilated eyes. He managed to move a hand weakly in her direction. He mouthed her name.

Guang had asked her what she would do if the mercenaries killed Doucet. She never thought they would. They couldn't because it would narrow the search for Peter's inside man or perhaps Doucet was the inside man. Either way, she saw him reach out, wanting to help her and she felt nothing.

"Get her hooked up and into the chopper," a voice shouted over the noise. "Security and police are on the way."

The stun gun hit her in the neck and the world went dark.

CHAPTER TWELVE

The familiar warmth of heroin coursed through her veins and made waking up difficult. Her eyes burned. Her side hurt. She didn't care. What bothered her more was that she was in a chair when she wanted to lay down, curl up, and sleep. A weak attempt to get her arms out from behind her back accomplished nothing other than a flair of pins and needles in her hands.

A hand gripped her hair and pulled her head back. "You're awake. Hello, Alexandria." The voice was thick with a fake English accent and higher pitched. "Open your eyes."

Alex took a minute to remember how to do that. She groaned at the bright light outside her shut lids. She tried to turn away from the light. The hand gripping her hair at the back of her head would not allow her face to turn. Something familiar about bright white lights, but it didn't go with the voice. Alex couldn't get her thoughts organized enough to figure out why.

"She's still messed up," the voice said. "How much shit did you give her?"

"Enough for someone with a tolerance," another voice replied, a German accent.

Alex wondered why there always seemed to be a German around when things were about to go bad.

"Hello, Alexandria," the voice with a thick, faked English accent said from beyond the light.

"Peter," she said, her tongue felt thick. Her words slurred. "Pretty desperate move. You must be running out of time."

"There is no time limit," he hissed at her.

She snickered. She had no doubt that was a lie. "He's pissed off about your lack of results; isn't he?"

"You're going to tell me where those bombs are, Alex."

She must have drifted back to sleep or wherever heroin sent a person. They were shaking her and slapping her again. She laughed. "You're stuck with an Interpol warrant. You can't leave the country even if you did have the bombs."

"That warrant has nothing to do with me fucking up and everything to do with you exposing some of my men! You do not know what the fuck you are talking about! I am free to go wherever I please. You, on the other hand…"

A shadow stepped into the light. A hand moved quickly.

Alex felt the sting of being backhanded. She laughed. "Fuck, Peter, you punch like a girl. Six fucking months of torturing me and you still can't throw a fucking punch?"

Someone in the room snickered.

She got slapped again. This time she tasted blood. Her face burned. She spat in the general direction of the shadow, hoping she got blood on one of his pastel suits.

He grabbed her jaw. Bony fingers dug into her face.

Alex grimaced as his face came down close to hers, close enough to be in focus.

Peter Van de Moeter was a tall, skinny, ugly man. His eyes were pale, his skin sallow, his lips thin and gray like earthworms on a sidewalk after a cold rain. He wore his blonde hair in a pompadour. Alex could smell the hair spray and the cologne. "I need those bombs, bitch," he hissed. His breath smelled like overly sweet coffee and Gouda cheese.

The memory of that smell made her stomach roll. She felt a flashback twitching at the edge of her unconsciousness. She

197

smelled it in her dreams. She felt it clinging to her skin on really bad nights as if she'd been rolling around in rancid flowers. "You're not the badass that you pretend to be."

"Have you forgotten how you begged to have me inside you? I especially like that little whimper you get in the back of your throat when you cum."

A cold sweat had broken out on her skin, leaving her feeling cold. Addiction did crazy things. "You better step back," Alex warned him.

"What?"

"You're inspiring vomit."

"You're not—"

Alex threw up. She got a little satisfaction out of the way Peter leapt away with a yelp.

"That's disgusting!"

Alex turned her head and spat away as much of the sour bile as she could. She laughed. "Yeah."

"You know what repulses me? That you've sullied yourself with that Cajun—"

Alex laughed, honestly. "Gosh, I was really hoping you and I could make a go of it, Peter." She laughed harder. "Fuck, you are a dumb shit. I can't believe my father let you shoot him." The laughter brought tears. The tears cleared out the sting of the pepper spray. The talk of her father sobered her up some.

"Your father didn't let me shoot him."

Alex grinned at him. She stared into his pale eyes with as much focus as she could muster. "He would have told you where to find the bombs, Peter." She felt the twitching need of the heroin jump inside her body. It felt like Mexican jumping beans of anxiety hopping around at the ends of her nerves. The adrenalin was eating up the effects of the heroin. She was afraid. "He would have told you the first time he heard me scream. That would have broken my father, Peter. This is a colossal fuck up with your signature at the bottom. Your buyer knows. That's why he's coming here to oversee things himself. The attack on the hotel. That was desperate. He must be coming soon."

Peter blinked. "You can't possibly know that."

Alex smiled. "No matter how much cologne you wear, you can't hide the smell of failure." She laughed to herself.

Peter hit her. Then suddenly he was going to town on her.

The chair she was tied to fell over. Pain shot through her shoulder. She missed the vomit, although it wouldn't be the first time she'd fallen in her own vomit. Torture wasn't pretty and clean like it was in the movies. The movies made you think you could resist it. You could sit there on your couch with a big bowl of butter popcorn and say things like "I'd never talk, that guy is a pussy." Not in real life though. In real life there were scars and unimaginable pain coupled with huge amounts of indignity. The pain was better than the indignity, it was easier to deal with and it went away.

With the light out of her eyes, Alex could see the room. It wasn't some cave or some basement. She was in a wine cellar. That explained the chill in the air. The wine racks along the wall were empty. Two mercenaries still wearing their black garb were in the room with her and Peter. One of them had been the person responsible for pulling her head up.

Peter stood near the door breathing hard from the effort of beating on her. His pastel blue suit was stained with vomit and blood spatter. His narrow nose flared. The fist clenched at his side, with its long thin fingers looked thick and red around the knuckles.

Alex smirked at the thought of breaking his hand with her face. Failure had stalked him. When he found the location of the first bomb, he'd opened the container and found a laptop computer that showed his bank accounts and balances. Then, a program began to run, draining all those accounts one by one and transferring the money to somewhere no one could touch it. It would be difficult to trace, but not impossible. She suspected the CIA would have found it by now. When Peter found the second location, he'd been more cautious. She couldn't blame him, the withdrawal of all his money had been triggered by his fingerprint on the laptop—top of the line technology that had been stolen and traveled around the globe to underground agencies, completely untraceable. He had experts which would have told him as much. The money couldn't be withdrawn without a fingerprint confirmation. But at the second spot, his men had found a piece of paper with the word "BOOM" on it. There'd been an unfortunate cave in, trapping and killing the mercenaries. The third location prompted the sudden release of a nearby septic system. Pretty impressive for a homeless drunk living on the cold streets of Cleveland, Ohio, if she did say so herself.

Peter's buyer wanted the Sword of Souls. Alex figured he'd be afraid Peter would actually kill her if he got his hands on her again. Not to mention the aggravation her obvious capture would be for the Offspring, putting them on alert and making the buyer's goals more difficult. Every failure and indignity she laid at Peter's feet tainted the buyer's future image by association.

Alex knew better than most that image and reputation mattered more than actual skill. They would call her legend and they would whisper about supernatural things. Two things she couldn't explain plagued her: how she'd gotten from an alley in New York City to a hidden retreat in the jungles of southern Thailand and how she could strap a sword to her back and sheath it and no one seemed to see it until she grabbed it.

"Bitch," Peter said. He hauled back his shoe and kicked her.

The world went dark again.

Alex was getting damn tired of being unconscious. She woke up with a pounding headache and shaking from the heroin withdrawal. The metallic taste of blood and bile coated her mouth. She started to lick her dry lips and flinched at the pain from a split in her lips. As the world came into focus, she realized she was no longer in the wine cellar. However, she was still tied to the chair. Her shoulders hurt from the strain. Her hands and feet were asleep. She swallowed and narrowed her eyes at the man sitting on the couch in front of her.

The man came in to focus. He had black wavy hair and a thick black beard with dark olive skin. Empty cold eyes regarded her, unreadable. He lifted a highball glass filled with ice and some clear carbonated drink. He sipped. The ice clinked in his glass. He sat back in the couch, one leg bent over the other. One delicate hand on the glass, the other resting on the cushion beside his khaki pants. An expensive watch sparkled in the dim light.

Alex was having trouble seeing out of one eye, so she had to turn her head to take in the rest of the room. It was a big game room. In addition to the couch the man sat on, there was another couch set at a 90-degree angle. Behind the man, a pool table was covered and silent. A dart board on the wall. Cue sticks and a rack neatly displayed. To her right at the open end of the "L" formed by the couches. A big television hung on the wall with an elaborate sound system stacked in a built-in shelving unit beside it and a fire place. To the left, behind the man's shoulder, a dark wet bar held a display of expensive whiskeys and crystal glasses. The room had no windows. The only light came from a small table top lamp on the end table— the other lights in the room were dark. The circle of dull yellow light provided a respite for Alex and the man and the illusion of a kind of intimacy that made Alex's gut curdle.

She brought her eyes back to the man. Inside, she felt the stirring of the unleashed monster.

"Miss McBrady," the man said in the Queen's English with an Arabic accent. "Welcome back to the world." He pronounced his words carefully and spoke slowly.

Fear spiked through her. The muscle at the back of her jaw twitched. She couldn't stop it and she knew instinctively that the man had taken note. She carefully tested the strength of the restraints holding her legs and ankles to the legs of the chair, but they provided no give. The same was true of the restraints around her wrists which were held in place partially by her own body weight between the small of her back and the back of the chair; but her numb hands were tied to the chair back as well. She couldn't tell but she assumed that another rope

201

connected her bound wrists with her bound ankles, effectively trussing her up like a hunter's prize.

The vacuum of emptiness in the man's eyes sucked up every detail of her movement. "Mr. Van de Moeter was ordered not to damage you or hurt you," he said. "I must apologize for the rough treatment you received."

Alex's arm started to jump. The familiar craving for heroin coursed through her, enhanced by the anxiety this man seemed to bring out. Three months of self-imposed cold turkey and now she was right back where she'd ended; too bad she didn't have time for rehab.

"My employer would have preferred to meet you when you are in your best health. I would have preferred to meet you in your best health. It would have made our conversation so much more satisfying. As you know, there are complications regarding him killing you when you are not at your best."

Alex let out the breath she'd been holding and tried to assess her injuries. Her broken ribs had been rebroken; she probably had a concussion, and now she was going through heroin withdrawal. Her eye was nearly swollen shut from where Peter had kicked her in the head. A burning tingle coursed through her blood and bones, but she couldn't be sure that wasn't the withdrawal. Hell, it could have been because she knew deep in the pit of her gut that, while the mercenaries were dangerous men and sick men, this Arab trumped them all with depravity and coldness on another level. Whatever her immediate future held, it was not going to be pretty.

"Brutality is not the answer," the man continued in a slow even tone, oblivious to where her mind traveled. "Your current activities seem to present some doubt as to the accuracy of the reports telling us how thorough your previous questioning was. The man was a professional; I'm surprised he lied. My employer only hires the best. However, I warned my employer that tradition questioning would never work with you." He paused, frowned and reached out to touch her face by her swollen eye.

Alex jerked at the touch.

"Fascinating…it's already healing. I can practically see it heal." His land lingered on her skin. It was cool and soft against the heat of the fresh bruises. "To think that we understand all there is to understand in the universe is arrogant. We have forgotten more than we remember." He leaned back in the couch again and took another sip. "Like the Sword of Souls—"

Alex groaned at the flare of cold pain in the marrow of her bones. She swallowed and sucked in a shaky breath. The monster inside her growled low and tensed for a strike.

"Hmmm," the man said. "Fascinating. I will have to report this to my employer. He does not really believe. He just craves the power. But I believe, Alexandria. I believe that the Sw— the weapon which should not be named—I believe that the weapon which should not be named has power. I believe it wraps its cold steel tendrils around the soul and inflicts its will on the one who is bonded with it. And even though he doesn't believe in its actual power, my employer believes he is the True One, the only one in the universe who can tame the Sword of Souls. Of course, there is arrogance to those rich enough to want this type of power."

Alex breathed through clenched teeth. A trickle of cold sweat rolled down her back. Her vision was improving. Her brain was clearing. The thing in her chuckled and sat back on its haunches, waiting.

"You are younger than I expected."

"You're more Arab, than I expected," she replied.

He smiled as if he'd just won something. "You were expecting someone Asian, I suppose. The legend has never belonged to Asia alone. You should have done your research better so you could pull off this act you perpetuate. Still, intellect is not what you excel at; is it? I mean, you have no formal education. You have only the stories of monks and mercenaries dancing in your head. Perhaps the songs of all the warriors who have held the weapon before you? Just enough of their skills to get you by?"

"You want the weapon for yourself?"

203

He smiled. "No, Alexandria. I have no desire to be a slave. I desire to be what the Offspring has always aspired to—the master who pulls the strings of the slave. I'll walk the step of the True One's protector and companion and let him do the fighting."

"That hasn't always worked out so well for the Offspring recently."

He nodded. "True. But these days, they carry the burden of killing the last True One and driving him back to the halls of the dead." He sighed. "I can see why Chen Sakai became so smitten with you. You are a beautiful and intriguing woman by anyone's standards. Beautiful, quick-witted and brave, with an intriguing mind. It's an attractive combination in a female. Probably intoxicating to an old man who'd been enslaved his whole life. However, history tells us that the weapon does not pick any master without forty turns of the seasons behind him. You're not even close to forty years old. And a female holder of the weapon? Honestly? I am shocked by how many of the Offspring have actually bought into this tale. However, you have managed to pull off your charade quite well. Until now, of course."

Alex licked her dry lips. "History is nothing more than the lies of men trying to explain what they cannot understand. You just want me dead."

The Arab arched an eyebrow. "My employer has no interest in seeing you dead. In fact, he is willing to let you turn your bombs over to the US government and he will make sure you get whatever revenge you desire on the man who murdered your father. All he wants is the location of the weapon. He believes it is a tool for power over nations. He does not believe in abstract forces behind modern explanation."

"He's right. It's all a lie."

The Arab grinned. "I have seen how you resist physical torture. I know better than to expect an easy agreement. But, Alex, I think you should consider some things that your youthful exuberance has hidden from you. You need to take the advice of someone who is older and more experienced. You and I, we could be friends."

Alex spat blood to the floor.

The man grimaced slightly. "Right now the Offspring is nearing the completion of a great arena for the Rule of Sevens to play out. In two months, the man they believe to be the next Great One turns forty years old. In two months, the Offspring will no longer be content to allow you to wander around with their weapon. It was brash to steal the weapon. My employer appreciates such brashness. We have resources which indicate certain powers inside the CIA are already rumbling about removing you from service. What are you going to do when you're facing seven sword masters who want to murder you in front of an audience, while putting on a good show? At the same time, you will be dodging bullets from CIA assassins. You will crumble. Your charade cannot survive the onslaught." He finished his drink and put it down on the table. His hand returned holding a big syringe with a thick needle. The syringe was filled with a dark green liquid.

"Shall I tell you a story?"

Alex swallowed and tried to keep her eyes from bouncing back to the syringe. "Not like I'm going anywhere."

He smiled. "You Americans. You all think you are funny. You all act brave in the face of your fear. It's stupid."

"You have a lot of American friends?" she asked.

"Friends is a strong word."

"Yeah," she agreed. "I actually agree with you."

"Under different circumstances, we might have been friends."

"Nah, I'm just a pretend psychopath, you're the real thing."

He leaned forward. "Which brings us to the story actually." He held up the syringe.

Alex tried to convince herself that her shaking was from withdrawal, but she was having issues convincing her own mind of that so it probably wasn't fooling this guy.

"This is a type of truth serum. Not sodium pentothal, which I'm sure your government work exposed you to. I would imagine they inject you with it and interrogate you just so you know what it would be like. I'm curious; did it help you resist the torture at all?"

Alex met his cold gaze. "No."

He arched an eyebrow. "Do you think that by telling me the truth now, that I will not inject you with this? Do you think you can convince me to trust you and you can just tell me where those bombs are?"

"You and I both know that I don't give a shit about those bombs and neither does your boss," Alex said. "I will give you the bombs." She'd give him the location of the bombs right now if she knew for sure his boss was on his way.

He studied her for a long time, searching her eyes.

Alex watched him think. She wished she could go into those black, lifeless eyes and pick out the thoughts in his head. The bombs would make him rich. Perhaps he would take the bribe. Perhaps he valued money more than he did inflicting pain. She doubted it.

"The legends say that the Offspring were given the Rule of Sevens by the gods in order to stop the slaves of the Sword of Souls when the weapon's blood lust is out of control."

Alex twitched at the mention of the name, she felt a wave of cold crawling through her bones, especially her ribs. Part of her had the urge to start digging into her own gut to get that feeling out of there; but her hands were tied and numb.

"Sadly, they misused it and killed the last True One. On his dying breath, the True One vowed he would never return from the Halls of the Dead and from that point on, humanity would be denied their free choice by the evil which walks among them as well as face the dangers of the Sword itself which lusts blood above all else. How did they get the True One to participate in the Rule of Sevens? Because by definition, he was a great warrior who controlled a great power. Well, they made this serum and they gave it to him. It reveals the true self. It rips away all the masks that we layer on ourselves. It makes it impossible to lie. When they used it on the True One those centuries ago, they questioned him and found people he cared about to force him into the fight—because even he could not fight the effects. It stripped away everything, the layers that the Sword gave him in his life including the muscle memory of the training of all his past lives. He gave away what he cared about; he became just a man with a sword. They used those things to force him into the battle. Those who had trained to be warriors easily defeated him." He smiled. "Some say he was just a great warrior and not the True One at all. They say that the True One, when unmasked would slaughter all mortal enemies before giving up answers."

Alex sighed. She bit her tongue to keep from telling the guy that it didn't exactly happen that way. She'd read the ancient handwritten accounts. She'd read between the lines of the Offspring justifying their actions.

"Sadly, it's been used on others who have held the Sword of Souls since then. They all, every last one, believed themselves to be the True One reborn, the one in charge of the Sword. However, the serum makes them see the veil that the power of the weapon has draped over their eyes. They are forced to face the unhappy truth that their skills come from the Sword of Souls and not from themselves. It's quite devastating to the ego." He paused. "You can avoid that. Just give up the Sword of Souls. You've had a good run and lived your dream; but, it's time now for the adults to take over. My employer's ancestor was supposed to hold the legendary weapon and it was stolen from his family by the Offspring. He is the rightful owner. The Sword of Souls must be returned to the proper blood line. He will be here in a few hours."

"You just said the True One wasn't going to return ever. Quit fucking up your doctrine and get this over with already," Alex snarled at him. She wasn't afraid of seeing her true self, six months of torture had unburied all of that. She was afraid of it getting loose and not being able to put it back in its cage. Of course, if the boss was going to be around in a few hours with Peter, she didn't really care. She felt her heart slow down, she felt the cold flow through her veins, she felt the monster calm down and stand back knowing it was just a matter of time, no more clamoring needed. She let go.

The Arab grunted. "You have surprised me, Alex McBrady. That doesn't happen very often. Good for you. Of course, the result will be the same. You think you are the True One. You think this will not work on you as a truth serum." He held the needle up and removed the cap. Then he tapped it with his fingernail and pushed out the air and a single bead of thick green liquid.

Alex couldn't maintain the stoic air in the face of the needle and caught herself trying to escape. She thrashed against the restraints. She had to fight hyperventilating as the man tied a rubber strip around her upper arm and tried to find a vein in the arm tied behind her back. She tried to head butt him, too, but he stayed out of range.

He ran a hand over her hair, more a caress than a touch. "Shh," he whispered. "Conserve your energy. You are going to need it to face up to all your self-delusions." He pulled her hair back. "Oh, and to deal with the pain. The process is excruciating. You will scream. It takes about an hour for the pain to stop. Afterwards, you will answer truthfully everything I ask of you."

"You should have taken my offer," she said. "Because afterwards, you're going to die."

He clicked his tongue at her. "I know you believe you are the True One. But you are not and you will see that when the weapon's shadow is stripped away. You are a pawn of the ancient gods. You are a thief who stole a legend from a sick and dying old man. You will see this yourself soon enough."

Alex wasn't expecting the needle to plunge into her neck. He'd fooled her with the rubber band around her arm and the search for the vein. He grabbed her head and chin to keep her head still. She struggled and strained. She felt the sluggish stuff hit the ice in her veins and push through it like a ship cutting through winter.

He let her go, pulling the empty syringe out of her neck.

She gasped and gagged, leaning her head forward as much as she could with her being tied up like she was. She was prepped for pain, but none of it came.

"It exhausts the body to deal with the pain. I will cut you free when it hits to keep you from hurting yourself. When the pain passes, we will talk. When we talk you will tell me, what I want to know. When we have the weapon, we will still give you Mr. Van de Moeter. You might as well kill him if you still have the stomach for it. When this unpleasantness is over, you can have a normal life. Get married, have beautiful babies. That is what women are meant to do. Not this stuff you have been playing at." He moved back to the couch and sank into it.

CHAPTER THIRTEEN

Alex took a deep breath and let her head hang. She controlled the pace of her breath; she put a calm look on her face and froze it there. She knew about pain, she knew she had a high threshold for it, and she had a gut feeling that this was going to exceed that threshold. Whoever Peter's benefactor was, he knew about delivering pain. Lifting her eyes, she found the Arab's cold stare.

He slowly, dramatically retrieved a knife from a sheath hidden on his belt. The piece was two sided and about three inches long—the kind of blade used for a close assassination in a crowded room. It had a metal handle encrusted with various jewels and gold inlay. "Everyone tries to resist," he said. "They all fail." His manicured hands with his shiny nails and soft pads laid the blade on the cushion beside his creased, khaki pants. The hand lifted up and came to rest on his thigh.

Alex's eyes followed the knife before returning to the cold darkness in the Arab's face. The stuff was burning down from her neck, tracing her veins and arteries with fire. It burned like sports cream after a hot shower and it was getting hotter and spreading. The world slowed down and the Arab seemed to move in slow motion. That feeling of the monster in her head, locked behind bars disappeared as if the growing heat had melted away the bars.

The Arab held her gaze.

Alex's lips parted slightly as the heat hit the bullet hole in her side. The heat seared through her veins and arteries and into the capillaries where the restricted space intensified the heat. In response, Alex relaxed the tension in her shoulders and let go of resistance other than the intensity she put into the stare.

A flicker of uncertainty skipped through the vacuum of his black eyes.

Alex let the corner of her mouth lift in a smirk.

The uncertainty grew larger than a flicker, it grew into a flame which began to melt the cold in his eyes.

She couldn't hold back the flush that started to take hold. She'd been in sunless Ohio for three months, hiding from the cold. Her skin was pale and her face had a tendency to flush at the most inopportune times: sex, embarrassment, anger – all of that made her face red. Maybe her skin would just spontaneous leap into flames. Maybe blisters would pop up from the inside, sizzle into black before flaking away to ash.

"You have remarkable control," he said. "Most cannot fight the pain at all." His voice didn't sound as confident as it had before.

Alex yawned as cold sweat began to trickle down her spine.

The Arab frowned. He started to speak, but stopped himself. He pressed his lips together and furrowed his brow. A touch of fear began to grow in his uncertainty.

Alex waited. The pain moved from her veins to her skin, her heart, her lungs, her fingers and hands. She sucked in a breath and released it slowly. Her stoic façade burned. She felt the trickle of sweat roll down her face.

He arched an eyebrow, relief came to him.

Alex felt the heat fusing her ribs, sealing the hole in her side. Cold sweat broke out over her skin because the knitting ribs and closing wound hurt more than the stuff he'd injected her with. It was uncovering the façade and revealing the true self. The monster inside was losing its definition and growing larger, starting to fit inside her skin and wear it like a suit. She was losing her fight against the drug and the monster was taking advantage.

The Arab's frown deepened, furrowing the skin above the bridge of his nose. Thick black brows knitted together over the furrow, like a bridge. "You have," he paused and tilted his head, "the most unusual eyes."

Alex could see better out of the one that had been nearly swollen shut. She could feel the flames burning away the swelling. Her leg started bouncing despite the tethers holding her to the chair.

"I will cut you free when you give in to it," the Arab told her. "I do not want you to hurt yourself before we can talk."

Her leg bounced. She clenched her teeth, locking her jaw. Bright light appeared at the edges of her vision. The pain squeezed and clawed into her bones. The heat hit the cold adrenaline pumping through the marrow of her bones. She gasped and tilted her head back staring at the ceiling.

The muffled tones of the Arab's perfect diction barely made it through a growing roar in her ears. "It takes about an hour to get through the entire system. You lasted fifteen minutes, easily three times longer than anyone else. The power of the Sword of Souls serves you well."

Alex's broken ribs snapped back together at the mention of the Sword. A gasping, ragged cry burst from her lips. Unrelenting waves of pain rolled over her, always increasing in size. Knocking her backwards over and over again as she kept trying to come up for air. Her poor ability to focus saw the Arab's hand move. Only it didn't move toward the knife, it moved toward the bulge in his khaki's.

She groaned as the brightness at the edge of her vision closed in and took over. The pain took over.

It took her vision first, but hearing anything other than the roar of her own agony quickly followed. It seared the ends of her nerves to make her body numb. The smell of sweat and the dust on the floor and *Sprite* filled her nose. Her mouth filled with the taste of metallic blood and something chemical. Still the pain went on, increasing until thought boiled away. Eternity passed. Trapped in bright white blindness.

After eternity, she slowly became aware of nearly hysterical gasping and sobbing for breath. Her forehead pressed against hard industrial type carpet. A string of drool hung from her lip all the way to the carpet. She sat with her legs folded beneath her. Her torso bent over them; her arms wrapped around her stomach, hugging herself. She hurt all over. Not the after-torture pain, but the dull kind of all-over ache that came from physical exhaustion. She shivered uncontrolled and wondered if she'd ever feel warm again.

Sakai had been the only one to ever get her to the point of internal exhaustion. His house near Hiroo, Japan sat atop a cliff which overlooked the ocean. The house was ancient. A narrow, steep stairway had been carved into the rock. Sakai made his students run those steps. Most couldn't make it up all the way without taking a rest, the combination of the steepness, the treacherous footing, and the altitude made it unsafe. A crude iron railing had been installed to prevent deaths—the Great One before Sakai had apparently gotten tired of his students slipping and plunging to their deaths. A few of the elite students could run up the steps, down them and back up without faltering. On Alex's first day as Sakai's student, she'd run up and down the steps four times. Sakai refused to tell her when to stop and she'd refused to quit. The last run up had ended with her crawling because her legs wouldn't support her any longer. Sakai had given in and told her to stop, but he ordered the servants not to help her inside.

Even as she got better and fitter, she still ran those damn stairs until she couldn't any longer. It became her punishment; whenever Sakai got frustrated with her belligerence or her natural instinct for rebellion. He'd just look at her and bark "Stairs" and off she'd go. She ran them in the snow and the rain and Sakai always left her outside until she could find a way to get herself inside. Once she'd crawled in, her hands and

213

knees bloody from the stone. But those steps had taught her something. "I need to go back," she said, her voice shaky and breaking.

"There is no going back, Alexandria," a man's voice said. Perfect diction cutting through the air so sharp she could almost see it.

Alex jerked her head up. Her body twisted, unbent, moved to be able to strike.

The room spun around her, slower than her vision. She groaned and fought for balance. Her back found a flat service. It took her a minute to make sure it was a wall rather than the floor. She rolled, her back against the wall.

"The disorientation is normal," the voice said.

Alex licked her dry lips and forced her eyes to focus on the shadow sitting on the couch in front of her. She remembered the Arab. She pulled her shirt down over her stomach where it had ridden up. She let one leg stretch out in front of her, the other stayed bent. She rested an arm on her knee. The other arm wrapped around her stomach, feeling for broken ribs, heeling bullet wound, anything.

"How do you feel?"

"I do not feel good." She leaned her head back against the wall and looked up at the ceiling, forcing herself to get oriented to gravity. He expected honesty, the inability to hide the truth, the inability to remain silent. Inside her brain, she could feel the compunction. She searched a moment for the monster, but she couldn't pinpoint it. She chuckled slightly.

"The effort of resistance takes all one's reserves of energy," he said. "They say that Chen Sakai was the greatest teacher the Sword of Souls has ever commanded. They say his students exhibit nearly superhuman endurance. Still, the records say that Chen Sakai broke you."

Alex shook her head once. The room moved behind her vision, rushing to catch up. "Not records. Human interpretations. I've read the old books too." The Offspring considered their library of journals off limits to anyone not in their high ranks. The punishment for betraying that edict was death. Alex had been 16 and sneaking into their library to read.

The Arab smiled, his white teeth too bright against his full black beard. "It's forbidden to read those texts if you are not a member of the Offspring. Did Sakai let you in the library?"

She filed away the information that the man was one of the Offspring. It meant his boss was also one of the Offspring. "I broke in," she said. "I don't like locked doors." She frowned and glanced toward the wet bar and the stairs behind it.

"The door is locked," he said. "We will not be disturbed until my employer arrives."

Alex turned back to the man. "When will that be?"

"An hour or two yet," he said. "Van de Moeter went to go get him. When they will return, I will give them the location of the bombs and the Sword of Souls. Then my employer will decide your fate."

Alex chuckled. It came out with the exhaustion tinging its edges, but it was genuine.

"You find that amusing." He paused.

Alex arched an eyebrow. "Was that a question?"

The Arab frowned. "You are not supposed to be circumvent or belligerent," he said.

"I simply did not know what response you expected from me."

He pressed his lips together. "Of course. Why do you find the arrival of my boss and Peter amusing?"

"Because I came here for him," she said.

"They brought you here."

"Beats going hunting. Easier to just sit in the stand and let the prey come to you."

"You allowed yourself to be recaptured?"

"Fool me once shame on you, fool me twice – oh wait, that doesn't happen." She chuckled. "I got tired of waiting. I want to go home."

"You are bluffing."

Alex rolled her eyes. "You're the idiot who wanted me unmasked and all honest and shit. And now you think I'm

215

lying? You should make up your mind on how you think this is going."

The man tilted his head like a dog.

Or perhaps, Alex thought, she only thought it did. The room didn't seem real stable. She felt restless. She wanted to move through the liquid of the room. She wanted to fight. She groaned with the sudden realization that she wanted to fight, she wanted to destroy things and people.

"It must be devastating to be faced with how much of which you thought was yours belongs to the Sword of Souls. How your skills are no longer there, no longer instinct, but a faded, distant memory. Like something you read in a book that you don't quite remember. At least, it healed you. I've never witnessed that before. Paranormal. A miracle. Perhaps it is your youth and the gods themselves feel pity for your tortured soul."

Alex moved her left hand over her flat stomach. The gunshot was gone, the ribs no longer caused pain. She could see out of her eye again. The scars on her side felt like ice woven through her skin. "At least, it healed me," she agreed with a laugh. No one had ever felt sorry for her soul.

"Where are the bombs?" he asked.

She smiled at him. "In a safe place."

"Where?"

"After I collected them all, I put them in a storage unit here in Nevada. A unit my father used to own."

"Here? On what was his compound?"

She arched an eyebrow. "This place belonged to my father? I've never been here before."

"So somewhere else."

She nodded. Her eyes studied him, his movements, the exposure of his vulnerable spots. She thought about the many ways she could make him die. She considered which one she would choose. She had an hour or two before the main event.

"But Peter owns all of those storage units does he not?"

"He does," she said. "And still does. They are the only assets which I let him keep."

"Clever."

"You flatter me." She leaned her head back against the wall and laughed.

"And the Sword of Souls?"

"You need to stop fucking saying that. Sword of Souls this. Sword of Souls that. It doesn't matter what language you say it in. You're making the difference between dying well and dying long grayer. The weapon that cannot be named was given to a friend and he hid it so even I don't know where it is."

"Clever. You are so clever, Alex. What is his name?"

"He's a monk. I can't pronounce his name," she said. "Some damn Chinese thing. I can't seem to remember how to speak that language."

"You gave the Sword of Souls to a Chinese monk?"

"It seemed appropriate."

"My employer will want to find this monk."

Alex grunted. "He should probably worry more about me."

"You are nothing," the Arab said. "You are a tool. Nothing more."

"The irony is that we were both hoping for that to be true," she told him.

He frowned again. "First Chen Sakai broke you. Peter Van de Moeter broke you. Now, I have broken you."

"You do realize that technically I killed the first two names in your little list, right?" she frowned and shook her head. "Oh, sorry. I forgot. I haven't killed Peter yet. An hour or two before he and your boss come back?"

"That's right."

"Time seems very confusing right now."

"An effect of the drugs. Thank you for telling me this, Alexandria."

Alex shrugged. "Not a big deal. You're going to be dead before you can talk to anyone else."

"How do you intend to kill me?"

"I'm leaning towards cutting open your gut and letting you watch your entrails spill out into your lap," she said.

His hand unconsciously went to the blade's handle.

Alex smirked.

He stared at her. "Your father's perseverance. Your mother's cunning. And your American arrogance. They suit you well. No wonder you managed to cajole Chen Sakai into giving you the Sword of Souls."

"You're wrong. I don't know what the Offspring recorded in their little diaries, but no one was there other than Sakai and I. I begged him not to. I tried to stop him. I've done nothing for the last 10 plus years other than run from that one night when he stuck that blade in me and forced me to make it feed on his soul and attach itself to mine. Just like I begged the gods to let me live long enough to avenge my father. They said I could avenge him as long as I killed your employer as well." She sighed. "He's been rather difficult to find using the traditional methods."

The Arab shook his head. "That is insane. You're hallucinating. The drugs have revealed your mental instability."

Alex yawned.

The Arab stood up and pointed his finger at her. "You are insane. You cannot expect me to believe that you are the True One!"

"My name is Alexandria Rae McBrady. That is all that I am." She shrugged. "I don't expect you to believe anything other than that. I am the daughter of a mercenary. I am the weapon he chose to unleash on Peter. I was born to be a weapon. But I am just Alex McBrady. That is all."

"Yes. It is all that I believe."

Alex smiled at him.

His eyes widened.

Alex wondered what he saw in her eyes.

The color drained from his face. He jumped to his feet.

Alex launched herself at him, like springs unloading. She had a habit of breaking necks. Mostly because any professional killer knew it took strength to break a neck. But she couldn't do it without speed and surprise and every ounce of her strength. She had none of these advantages now. So, she tackled him, over the back of the couch where he'd been sitting.

She straddled him and punched him in the face. Maybe not so hard, but fast. Four, five, six punches before he managed to throw her off. She somersaulted backwards, ending up on her feet crouched down. Like Spiderman. She laughed at her analogy.

The man scurried back until his back hit the couch. His hand covered his bleeding nose, but it dripped down over his crisp shirt and filtered into his beard. He glared. "You fucking bitch," he snarled. Blood covered his teeth. He reached for the knife.

Panic flashed over his face when he found the sheath empty.

Alex grinned and held up the knife.

He managed to get his legs under him and scrambled over the couch with a mewing sound like a kitten looking for its mother.

Alex attacked again.

He kicked at her.

She avoided it easily. She might not be at top speed at the moment, but she was faster than him. Adrenalin was pumping into her veins as well.

He started for the stairs.

Alex caught him at the bottom of the steps. She led with the blade, sinking it deep into his spine. She fell on top of him when his body stopped working.

With a groan, she climbed up a couple of steps and sat down. The world spun. Her breath came hard and fast, but not in gasps. "Wow," she exclaimed. "Head rush."

The Arab sat against the wall, unmoving except for his eyes. His body struggled to suck at air.

Alex wiped her hand off on her shorts. Red blood streaked across the denim.

She chuckled at the look in his eye before sliding out of the stairs through the gap under the railing. She walked to the bar.

If this place had been her father's then she knew there was some good stuff hanging around.

The man made a small whimpering sound.

She glanced over her shoulder.

His head didn't turn, but his eyes were following her.

The bar was pretty empty. She found a bottle of Jack Daniels, dusty and unopened. "Fuck me," she said. "This wasn't my dad's place." She spun the cap off the bottle with her thumb. It flew off the bottle, bounced over the bar and hit the carpet with a soft pat.

She took a deep swig as she walked back to the steps. She had to step over the Arab's body, but the guy didn't make any moves to trip her.

The Arab wheezed.

She sat down a couple of steps up from him and took another drink. She winced as it burned down to her empty stomach. She studied the man's dark eyes. If it was true that the eyes were the window to the soul, then his soul was black and filled with fear. "Chen Sakai found me in an alley in Hong Kong. I was 15. Four men from the dojo where I was training were pissed off that they'd been humiliated in class by a girl. I fought them off for two hours before Sakai stepped in and scared them away. Sakai-sensei told me I should have killed them. My father told me I should have killed them. They said I was being too nice. I said the world wasn't a brutal place. After so long humanity should have evolved into something less violent, I said." She rubbed her shoulder, the one that had been melted away by acid, it had a dull ache in the bones. "I wasn't afraid of what your drug might show me about myself. I was afraid that it might force me to accept that they were right." She pointed at him and laughed. "You totally misjudged that one, dude. And about now, I bet you're wishing you hadn't said the name of the Sword of Souls so often and you're finding the sad truth that you didn't really believe in it as much as you claimed. Faith is a fleeting thing and assholes have a problem really holding on to it." She pointed at him as she took another swig of the whiskey. "You are an asshole."

Drool fell from his mouth, his eyes were wild, moving and jumping.

"You are going to die," she told him. "No one can get a doctor here fast enough to save you. Even if they could, you'd never walk or breathe on your own again. So, maybe it's better to die. You're an evil, sick man and this is what you deserve. But then, I suspect you know that." With a final deep swig from the bottle, she stood and walked up the steps. "It's unfortunate that I don't have the weapon with me. It would like to feed on your soul. It likes guys like you. The extremes. The really good guys and the really bad ones." She laughed and headed up the steps.

The door at the top opened into a shadowy kitchen; it wasn't locked like the man had said. It was the kind of kitchen that impressed people but seldom got used. A big center island would be perfect for catered trays. The appliances were stainless steel. Alex opened the fridge, shivered in the cold air that spilled out over her. The fridge was clean and empty. Alex closed the door again, preferring the darkness. Her tennis shoes made no sound on the burnt orange colored tile. She moved to the only thing sitting on the counter top: a wooden knife block. She had good night vision, even with the drug coursing through her system. "Convenient, that knife block," she whispered aloud in the dull glow of light. "Oh, and good knives too. The preferred knives by many high end chefs. Thanks J.A. Henckels. Jesus, you're talking a lot, Alex." She grabbed the handle of the chef's knife. It was heavy and balanced; it was made to fit in the hand. The nightlight from the stove vent glistened off the thin edge of the blade. She lay the knife down on the counter and pulled out some of the others. "I should just do eeny-meanie-miney-mo," she mumbled to herself. In the end, she chose the slicing knife and the paring knife. The big chef's knife would make her job easier, but she didn't want to deal with the size of it. She could always come back later.

She made two parallel slits in her jean shorts to hold the paring knife. She put the slicing knife in the belt loop in the small of her back. The handle pointed to her left hand, the blade pointed down against the thick denim seam. Then she stretched her shoulders and walked out of the kitchen.

Thinking twice, she turned back and turned off the light over the stove.

The kitchen doorway led to a small staging area with doorways on each of the walls. She stopped and stared at the three closed doors—single doors to the right and left, double doors straight ahead. "Wow, it's like a real-life video game," she said. She was starting to bounce with the excess energy coursing through her veins. "Unintended side effects," she mumbled. "Sorry about your luck, Peter." She chose the door to the right.

The door opened to a dark dining room with a long table. The opposite wall was all glass doors. Although there were sheer curtains covering the windows, she could see a fire burning and several figures sitting around the fire.

She opened the doors and stepped into the cool night.

Three men lounged around a built-in fire pit. Four chairs had been arranged around the fire. Empty beer bottles littered the ground. The firelight reflected off the surface of a dark pool covered with some kind of plastic cover.

"More beer!" one of them demanded. He raised an arm like a battle cry charge. "I'm not sitting here knowing Joe's kid is getting tortured without more beer."

"Wow, you really do care," Alex said. "I wasn't feeling the love."

The three men jumped up. All three fumbled for their weapons. Only one of them actually had his weapon.

Alex waved at them. "Hi guys."

"How'd you get up here?" asked one of the unarmed ones, the oldest of the group. These three were all in their late thirties, early forties. They were professionals: professional drinkers and professional soldiers. Which meant they were getting sober quickly. But their eyes showed recognition and a touch of something that wasn't quite anger or greed.

Alex couldn't say the same about getting sober. The swigs of alcohol seemed to have made her energy ramp up even higher. She was having trouble slowing down. "Stairs. I used the stairs."

"What happened to the Arab?"

"I killed him. Sort of. He's dying. Not quite dead." She laughed. Her hand was shaking from the adrenalin and the drugs. Her heart raced. She wanted to fight so badly, she could practically taste the blood.

He frowned and tilted his head. He put a hand on the arm of the man with the gun and forced it down. "You're fucked up."

She shrugged. "I don't think you should hold that against me."

"How about we go inside and talk about this?"

She laughed. "I'm high, not stupid."

"What are you planning?"

"Ooh, good question." She smiled at them. "I was going to give you the opportunity to run, but I'm not sure I should."

"If we don't, what then?"

"Well, then I guess you've tied yourselves to Peter; haven't you? And Peter is the fucking *Titanic*." She smiled at the expressions on their faces. "You're thinking about the money he's promised you? But, I took all the money he stole from my father. The only thing he has right now is an Interpol warrant and an empty storage unit. And he's going to die. He's been trying to get those bombs for more than a year. Do you really think after all that time and all the torture and all the other shit that I'm actually going to just give them up?"

One of the men whispered to the other. "Truth serum. Fucked up Chinese truth serum."

"Would you tell me where they are?" he asked.

She smiled. "Wow, you're a smart one. You might even have been the one my dad wanted to take over his operations. Peter probably stole that from you too. But the answer to that question is yes, I would tell you if you asked." She laughed. "But if I told you, I'd have to kill you."

"We have a gun."

"You better kill me instantly with one bullet. Because I brought some knives to this gun fight." She laughed. She felt movement behind her. The silence of the dining room was marred by a barely audible jingle of glass bottles.

"You'd just let us leave?" the mercenary in front of her said. His eyes were careful not to leave her face, but his body and the bodies of the other two were tensing up.

Alex stayed loose and relaxed. "Yeah. I'm after Peter and the buyer. Don't really give two shits about the rest of you. You can all go as long as you don't get in my way." Her elbow came up as she twisted and moved around the body behind her.

She smashed a foot into his instep, grabbed the gun slide, pressed the magazine release. The magazine fell to the floor.

The man tried to grab her around the neck with his free arm.

Her shoulder buried in his chest. She flipped him, never letting go of his gun arm. She felt the cartilage tear as the shoulder dislocated.

Before he could cry out in pain, she stomped on his head, making it bounce off the concrete with a brutal crack.

His hand fell from the useless weapon. His body went limp.

She loosened her grip on the slide, allowing the single round to slide into the chamber. Alex looked up at the three mercenaries. The crazy giddy feeling had been replaced by something cold and hard. She saw the men react to it. One of them actually took a step backwards. She racked the slide to expel the bullet, then dropped the useless gun on the dead body.

The one who'd spoken lifted his hands in surrender. He turned to the other two. "She's Joe's daughter. In a fight with Peter, I'm picking her."

The other unarmed man nodded. He lifted his hands too. "I'm out."

"Fuck," grumbled the man with the gun. He lowered the weapon, his thumb hit the safety.

The leader of the trio nodded at the house. "There are five more inside. They're younger, never worked for your dad. You need help?"

The man with the gun offered her his weapon, butt stretched out to her, hand off the trigger.

She shook her head. "I don't like guns. How long before Peter and the buyer get back?"

"Two hours. Are you sure you don't want us to help with the five guys here?"

Alex glanced down at the dead mercenary at her feet. She arched an eyebrow at him.

"Right." He nodded. "Around dawn. That's when Peter should be back. When the horizon starts to get lighter, you worry."

"I'm not worried," she said.

"We're taking one of the SUVs in the garage."

"Go south. Cross the border. There's a special forces team tracking me. If you cross paths with them, they will kill you."

"How do you—"

She pulled a small metal disk out of her back pocket. "Tracker."

"Dumbasses should have searched you."

Alex shrugged. "If I see you before Peter and the buyer are dead, I will kill you."

The man nodded. "Understood." He and the others started towards the side of the house where a gate led to a courtyard and then stopped and looked back. "Alex?"

"Yeah?"

"Not all of us wanted your dad dead."

"Not all of you were stupid."

"Good luck."

"Don't need luck. But thanks."

CHAPTER FOURTEEN

Alex watched the three mercenaries leave. She twisted the cap off one of the sweating bottles of abandoned beer and sucked it down while she waited to make sure they didn't return. The night was dark, but the sky was filled with stars and a crescent moon.

After a few minutes, the headlights of a vehicle came around the building, then turned south and drove away. Alex turned her attention to the north. A ridge overlooked the compound from that direction. When the vehicle's lights were out of sight, she stepped over the body of the dead one and went back into the house. She took another beer from the six-pack sitting on the table. She twisted off the cap and took a deep swig from the sweating bottle. The dining room had a set of double doors pointing in the same direction as the double doors in the kitchen's staging area.

She figured this was where the man had come from. She opened the door slowly, and saw dull darkness. A huge ballroom opened up. In the middle of the ball room was a pile of gear including several ice chests. "Not planning on staying long, not even unpacked," she said.

She found the five mercenaries in a large living room beyond the ballroom. They were all watching a huge television with a basketball game on it. They were yelling and laughing. Empty beer cans and bottles covered the tables, along with two open pizza boxes. Three slices of pizza remained in the grease stained boxes. Rifles leaned against the couches, handguns laid discarded under the boxes and surrounded by empties.

She considered grabbing one of the rifles and just shooting all of them. But, she really didn't like guns. Knives, she thought, were so much more personal and she had such a lovely set.

She walked into the room, grabbed the head of the nearest cheering mercenary and slit his throat. Blood gushed out, spraying everywhere in the room. The cheering stopped. Stunned silence except for the commentary from the TV. After that stunned, frozen shock, the room burst into chaos.

Alex already had the paring knife in the second merc. She twisted low so a bullet hit him in the chest. As she moved, her left hand grabbed her second knife and brought it up into the femoral artery of another mercenary. Hot blood spilled over her. The man dropped to the ground, his hands trying to stop the bleeding, but it gushed out of his leg and between his fingers.

The guy who'd found a weapon missed again, hitting the man coming up behind her.

She landed a roundhouse kick on the guy's jaw and sent him flying backwards. Another weapon discharged into the ceiling. Plaster drifted down over her head like snow, collecting on the blood stains that stained her clothing. She grabbed the end of the rifle, ignoring how it burned her hands and shoved hard. The stock bashed the guy in the face. Then she grabbed it from his hands and swung, filling the air with a wet crunching sound. She buried the last knife into the last man's gut, grabbing his shoulder for leverage as she shoved all of it in and pulled down.

His eyes widened. He grabbed her throat and tried to squeeze. Alex pulled the knife up through his belly. His guts spilled out over her hand.

He fell backwards.

Silence.

Alex stood in the middle of the carnage, breathing hard, her heart racing, and listening and hoping for more victims. The stench of metallic blood, opened bowels, and stale beer filled the room. She turned slowly and glanced at the television. Blood spattered over its surface as a basketball team made a drive for the basket. Blood covered the leftover pizza too.

She grimaced slightly and walked back out of the room, leaving a trail of blood.

She went back to the big ball room area and started sifting through the equipment and the coolers.

The duffel bags contained a lot of fire power and some clothing. She changed out her blood-stained shirt for a green t-shirt, a camouflage jacket and pants which she had to roll up. She went back to the bodies to see if she could find boots that fit and weren't filled with gore, but there was nothing.

The horizon was still dark.

The house was a big thing, decorated in "modern desert" with indian patterns and paintings of American indians in headdresses. "If Dad owned this it was only because that stupid idiot he was seeing wanted it," Alex mumbled to herself as she walked through the place. "And they hired some generic idiot to decorate it." It would be just like the wench dating her father to have a kitchen that never got used but showed off every modern convenience. The woman had liked her father's money a lot, almost as much as Peter liked the money.

Alex sucked in a breath and shook the thoughts out of her head. She had tolerated the woman because her father seemed to like her; but, truth was she'd be hunting her father's lover down, if the woman hadn't died in a car accident shortly after Peter inherited everything. Because of that woman and some bogus claim that she was married to Joe, Alex had watched her father get buried in a casket in the ground in Ohio. She growled at the boiling anger. "I shouldn't have killed them all then," she muttered.

On the second floor, a banister looked over the tiled floor of the foyer. She looked up at a domed ceiling with skylights and a thick chain holding a huge chandelier. She climbed up on the banister and reached for the chandelier, but it was further away than it looked. She sighed and walked around the second floor on the banister. She almost lost her balance once, but got down and wiped the blood off the bottom of her feet. When she got back up on the narrow wood banister, it was better.

Pleased with herself for getting all the way around, she put her arms out and lifted one foot. She leaned forward slowly, reached with one hand and did a hand stand in the darkness. Her heart beat hard and sure. She concentrated and slowly let go with one hand. As she balanced, the front door below her opened.

Three armed men bled silently into the darkness.

"Hey!" Alex shouted at them.

Three weapons shot up at her.

"You can't be down there," she said. "Peter will see you when he comes in."

"Alex?" said a deep, familiar voice. "What are you doing?" His voice was tense.

She sighed and brought her feet back down to the rail. She stood up and stared down at them. "Stop pointed those fucking guns at me or I will shove them up your ass, Doucet."

"Captain?" Mitchell Ong said tentatively.

Doucet lowered his weapon. He pushed the night vision goggles up from his eyes. "Alex, you need to get down from there. And you need to talk softer. This place was crawling with mercenaries—"

"The only things crawling in this house are three uptight Marines," Alex sneered back at him. "Don't fucking patronize me. God, I hate when people patronize me."

"Are you okay?" Frank Dyer asked, heading for the stairs in the middle of the foyer which spiraled up to the second floor in a wide spiral.

"I'm fine," Alex snapped, agitated. "Actually, I could use another drink. There's some beer in the dining room and half a bottle of Jack on the steps to the basement by the dead Arab." She did a cartwheel on the banister. The rail wobbled from the pressure. "I'm just restless and killing time until Peter and his buddy show back up."

"Alex," Doucet said, his voice tight and his accent nearly non-existent. He lifted his chin at his lieutenant.

Mitchell Ong shut the front door and flipped a light switch.

The chandelier lit up. A thousand crystals blazed like individual flames.

"Wow," Alex exclaimed. She straightened up in awe at the light. She wobbled but managed to hold onto her balance.

"Alex," Doucet said again. He reached out his arm as if he could push her back off the rail from fifteen feet below. "That rail wasn't made for gymnastics."

Alex moved back and forth, making the thing sway more. There was a cracking sound somewhere down the rail near the closest wall. She frowned at it, tilting her head.

"Holy fucking hell," Mitchell Ong muttered.

Dyer had frozen on the staircase.

"They don't make things like they used to," Alex said. She had climbed all over thousand-year-old monasteries with no issues. "Who makes a bannister out of balsa wood?"

"Alex, Peter could be back anytime," Doucet said.

"I know," she growled at him. "That's why it would be nice if you turned off the light and got out of the way. When he comes back, I'm going to kill him and his little buddies."

Dyer stepped onto the second floor. "Alex," he said holding out his big hand. "Why don't you come with me?"

Alex turned, wobbled slightly and whirled her arms.

Dyer dove forward.

Ong and Doucet cried out and ran to spots underneath the banister.

She danced out of his Dyer's reach and laughed. "You guys are all so uptight."

"That wasn't funny," Dyer scolded.

She laughed at him. "There's a bunch of equipment back in the ballroom," she said. "Maybe they have three sets of clean pants since you all just shit yours."

"What kind of drugs are you on?" Dyer asked.

Alex laughed and tossed her head back. "A kind that really fucking backfired on them," she said. "But I feel awesome. I mean, I was a little crazy, but I think the alcohol is counteracting that. I'm fine." She frowned when all three of them exchanged looks.

"What's that on your face?" Dyer asked. "Is that blood?" He moved forward.

She stepped backwards away from him and lost her balance.

The guys all yelled.

Instead of windmilling her arms, she compensated and used her other foot to push off the banister. With the balance gone, she wasn't going to try to get back—what was natural instinct in another person had been trained out of her years ago. She stretched, her eyes focusing on the dazzle of the chandelier and the bar of the frame holding all those crystals.

She caught it and swung.

Her weight on the chain, made it fall fast. It stopped with a jerk after about 5 feet, leaving her about 10 feet above the ground...almost within reach of the two men still on the ground.

One hand slipped off the narrow metal strip. It was cutting into her hands.

She swung her legs up to the center bracing bar and hooked her knees around it. Then she let go of the bar with her other hand and tried not to be dazzled by the lights and sparkle.

Mitchell Ong and Sinjin Doucet stared up at her.

"This is a fucking rush," Alex told them.

"Alex," Doucet said in a low rumble. "Get down from there. We need to get out of here and we need to go get those bombs you're playing this game with."

She rolled her eyes at him. "We can't go get the bombs." She bent her body to make the chandelier swing, the crystals shot darts of light around the room.

"Why not?" he asked.

"You don't have a truck," she said. "You think you can just go and get all those nuclear bombs with a duffel bag?" She laughed again. "Fucking truth serum or something. Fuck me. It kind of works." She nodded. It made the world spin with the blood rushing to her head and the lights flashing around her. "Wow, this is a trip. You should get up here and try this," she told the men.

Mitchell chuckled. "How about you very carefully come down?"

"We'll help you," Dyer said.

Mitchell shook her head. "She doesn't need help. She's got some training."

Alex laughed and held her hand out with her thumb and forefinger slightly apart. "Just a little training," she said. She met his eyes with a warning. If he said too much, he wouldn't make it out of here alive.

She was starting to get sick to her stomach though.

She bent her body up to grab the chandelier frame again. She let her legs drop, then let her arms stretch out as far as they could. She dropped to the linoleum and rolled like paratroopers were trained to roll and eliminate the potential for broken ankles.

Doucet stepped up to her and grabbed her arm. It wasn't an aggressive grab, but Alex reacted as if it was.

She jerked away, slipped on the dry dusty tile and fell on her butt.

He looked down at her, shocked.

She made a face. "Don't touch me," she said.

"Did they hurt you?"

"Yeah," she said because she couldn't lie. She turned away from him, not meeting his eyes.

"Alex," he said, his voice softer, the accent stronger. "Is that your blood?"

"No," she said. She held up her hand and showed him a small cut on the webbing between her thumb and forefinger. "That's the only injury you can see." She rolled herself up to her feet. "I think I'm going to be sick."

She turned and ran out the door to puke over the railing of the porch.

The light went off and as she heaved, she heard the men follow her outside.

"We have a vehicle," Dyer told her as she managed to get herself under control and put her forehead down on her folded arms which were on the rail. "Over the ridge. Can you make it?"

"I need to wait," she told him. "For Peter."

"You really think you're in any shape to fight Peter, his bodyguards, the buyer, and the bodyguards I'm sure the buyer has with him?" Dyer asked. "Alex, please. For once in your life, be reasonable. You may think you're Wonder Woman, but it's pretty clear you are strung out and haven't slept since they took you."

She lifted her head and looked at him in the first hint of dawn. His dark skin made him look like a shadow even in the first dull glow of light. Behind him, Sinjin Doucet watched the driveway and the distance expecting Peter's return any minute. He barely glanced at her. Mitchell Ong's face was purposely blank and his eyes scanned the first glow on the horizon for approaching vehicles; however, his thoughts were somewhere else. "I can make it over the ridge," she said.

"Good girl," Dyer said. He smiled at her. "I know your father isn't here any longer, Alex. But I'm his best friend and I will make sure no one hurts you any more."

She wiped her mouth on the sleeve of the stolen jacket. She closed her eyes and let her forehead hit her arm again. She sank down to her knees in front of the rail. Her hands lifted up to her face and covered it.

"Alex?" Dyer said, his voice softening. "Honey, it's okay. Everything is going to be okay. Just stop this stupid game."

233

She sucked in a shaky breath and wiped away the tears welling up in her eyes. She refused to look at any of them as she pulled herself back up and walked down the steps. She turned off the walkway to the driveway and headed for the ridge.

She heard them scramble after them.

Sinjin fell into step beside her. "What happened to all the mercenaries in that house?" he asked. "If the police—"

"Peter isn't going to call the police. And even if he would, his buyer is a Middle Eastern terrorist trying to buy nuclear bombs that he doesn't have to smuggle into the United States. I doubt if that guy is interested in cops," she said. Her hoarse, ruined voice came out abrupt, angry.

"I tried to save you. I tried to find you quicker. You can't blame me—"

Alex stopped walking and turned on him. Her fist clenched and unclenched at her side. The anger burned inside her like a volcano spewing out freezing cold. She could feel the "You want to know what happened to those mercs? I cut their throats and disemboweled them. I left them to die on greasy pizza boxes surrounded by empty beer bottles." She took a deep breath. "I looked them in the eyes and sliced them up with some pretty expensive kitchen knives. And you know what? I enjoyed every second of it."

He shook his head. "You don't mean that."

She gave out a bitter laugh, turned and started walking again.

"Alex," he said, catching up to her. "Did you tell them where the bombs are?"

"I am actually having issues lying at the moment," she grumbled. "So yes, I told them. Or rather just him."

"Him?"

"The Arab."

"Where is he?"

"I shoved his pocket knife into his neck and separated his brain from his spinal cord. Then I left him to die slowly, suffocating in his own body but completely aware of what was happening."

"You left him alive?! Are there any others you left alive?"

Alex eyed him. "I let some of them go."

"What?" Dyer said. "Why?"

"To prove that I could," Alex said.

"To prove to whom?"

A smirk tugged at her mouth. She turned to the headlights bouncing down the road towards the dark house. She started to turn around.

"Where are the bombs?" Dyer asked.

She stopped and stared at him.

"Where?" he repeated.

She gritted her teeth together, but the words spilled out. "In a storage unit in North Las Vegas." Her body shook, her looked like she might be sick again.

"What's the name of it?" he asked.

She glanced back at the road. Three vehicles were turning onto the long driveway that led to the dark house. She hadn't realized they'd walked so far. They were nearly at the top of the ridge. Below the three cars made a parade towards the house.

"I don't know," she said, starting towards the cars. Her heart raced. She had all three of her targets in this one spot. It would just take a--

"How can you not know?" Doucet asked, interrupting her thoughts.

Alex's eyes darted at him. "I'm not the one who sent them there."

"How can you find them?"

Her eyes darted from him to the house. The car had stopped in front of it. "I have a map. In my head," she said, distracted.

Sinjin stepped towards her.

She jumped back, tripped and fell over a rock.

"You're going over that ridge and to our vehicle and you're going to take us there."

She saw Peter in a pastel suit get out of the front car.

Others started getting out of the other vehicles. A man in a robe and turban stepped out of the back car. He stopped, with a hand on the car door. His eyes scanned the desert.

Alex felt his gaze travel over her. She felt him linger.

"Don't move," Sinjin hissed softly.

"We're too far away," Mitchell replied. "It's still too dark."

Alex's hand reached for a sword she didn't have. She looked down at her empty hand. "I need to sleep," she said, only slightly conscious of the fact that she had spoken out loud.

The man in the white robe and turban continued his scan of the dark emptiness around him. Then he stepped out from behind the door and walked to join Peter. Six men fell into step behind him.

Alex had known there would be seven of them.

"The car is just over the ridge," Sinjin said.

She looked up at him. "Then let's go."

CHAPTER FIFTEEN

Far off the Las Vegas Strip, the lobby of a non-descript hotel had several areas of chairs and couches. Big tinted windows looked over the busy street. The sun was bright. People walked down the sun-bleached sidewalks. People wearing casino uniforms waited under a poorly shaded and graffiti-ed up shelter for a bus on the opposite side of the road. Behind the lobby, a small casino took up most of the bottom floor of the place. It was the kind of place which might attract locals or a travelling businessman after a long day rather than the kind of place tourists frequented. The advertisements in the hotel room where Alex McBrady had caught a few hours of sleep in between the nightmares suggested the place had a truly remarkable gym on the fourth floor. She had not checked out the gym. Actually, with the way Doucet, Dyer and Ong watched her, she could barely get the privacy to go to the bathroom.

Alex sat in one of the low cushioned chairs in one conversation pod in the lobby. Her leg bounced with pent up energy. The drugs had left her body for the most part, but the boiling energy had not. Across from her Captain Sinjin Doucet and Sergeant Frank Dyer sat in identical chairs. Their long legs and buff bodies looking awkward in the chairs. She felt their eyes on her, boring into her as if they could sift through her guts and find out what she was thinking.

She was thinking there wasn't much difference between the good guys and the bad guys, and she wasn't quite sure which one was which any longer. They hadn't let her out of their sight, even checking bathrooms to make sure they didn't have windows. She'd managed a shower alone, to wash the smell of blood and the Arab off her skin. She'd written down her sizes for Dyer who'd gone off to buy her clothes. She slept in an oversized t-shirt they'd bought in the hotel gift shop; but when she woke up the clothing had been there. Along with Doucet sitting in a chair watching her.

She hadn't said anything to him and he hadn't made any move to touch her. He seemed a bit confused about what to do around her. She could see in the way he looked at her what he wanted to do. She had her "stay back" vibe in full strength. The clothes fit: a white top with three-quarter dark blue sleeves, jeans, and black hiking boots. The boots didn't have steel shanks or toes, but they were an improvement over the tennis shoes.

She watched the people coming in the place. A few people came with gym bags and headed for the elevators. All of them buff and wearing too tight clothes. This was how Sinjin and Frank fit in without drawing attention. Alex figured that fit her as well; but the clothing Frank had picked for her was very conservative. Not the kind of clothing a woman who joined an expensive gym would wear. The women who came in with yoga mats over their shoulders or gym bags were wearing skin tight spandex pants which curved over their butts and showed off narrow hips and strong thighs. Their tank tops were equally tight, bunched up over their flat stomachs in a way that emphasized those flat abs at the same time. Women with long hair had it tied up in a single ponytail; short haired women wore their hair spiky and casual. She didn't fit in, but also, the clothes didn't draw male attention away from those women with their asses looking as hard as the marble floors.

Dyer's eyes followed some of those female butts. Sometimes arching his eyebrows in appreciation.

Doucet watched her, which surprised Alex. His dark eyes didn't hide his thoughts. If her vibes of demanding people stay away from her weren't enough to discourage someone, Doucet's possessive glower should do the trick. He oozed frustration and possessiveness.

The lieutenant had been sent off to get a box truck. He was probably happy to get away from the tension. He'd been the only one to try to talk to her. He hadn't gotten far with the conversation; but, Alex figured he counted getting her to take some ibuprofen as a small victory.

The drugs had been in a brand new, still sealed container and Ong had made sure she watched him open the seal, pull out the cotton, and take one of the pills himself. He'd left her with a still sealed bottle of water and the bottle.

She'd taken four. They helped with her headache and a serious of aches throughout her body. She had bruises all over. A big hand print bruise on her inner thigh reminded her of the night before. She didn't remember what the Arab had done to her while she'd been lost in the rolling waves of pain, but she had a good idea. She sucked in a breath and tilted her head back to stare up at the ceiling. Her leg bounced faster.

Across from her, the two Marine Corps veterans sat up straighter. Their grim set expressions pulled in towards the center of their faces.

A cold dump of adrenalin surged through her veins. The surge wasn't unfamiliar, but it didn't often surprise her. Except this morning when it seemed to have a mind of its own, like the opposite of menopausal hot flashes. She clenched her fist, feeling the emptiness of her hand. She felt the need for a weapon; she craved the need for freedom. She wanted to run out into the desert, climb some cliffs and stand at the top under the endless blue sky to feel the wind in her hair.

Years ago, she'd been to Vegas with her father. On a break from whatever martial arts school she'd been conquering at the time—before Sakai, after a teacher conceded that she had surpassed them in technical skill—he'd brought her out to Red Rock, a conservation area within driving distance of the city. His passion had been rock climbing and mountaineering; it is what Joe McBrady did for fun. The hot dry air had its appeal for Alex after the sauna of the Far East. She'd stood at the top of a particular difficult cliff, on the edge with the desert spread out in front of her. Below, looking small, a sedan had pulled up next to the Jeep her father had rented. A large, dark skinned man stepped out of the sedan. The sun reflected off his bald head. He shielded his eyes and looked up at the cliff. Alex threw up her hands and waved at him. She yelled out a hello, her voice carrying out on the wind which was pushing at her back, making her sweaty shirt cling to her spine.

She remembered her father's grin as he watched her, his tanned face marked with laugh lines and his eyes with their gold and green sparkles of glitter sparkling in the bright sun. His hard, calloused hands worked, hauling in the yellow and green climbing line they'd used. She remembered him laughing and saying, "Go ahead."

She'd turned over her shoulder at him, arching her eyebrows at him. Her heart started to beat faster in excitement.

He took his gloves off his belt and pulled them on. Without a word he walked up to her and checked the safety harness. He pulled on the rope still threaded through the waist tie-in loop and checked the belay loop. "Put your gloves on so you can slow yourself down without ripping up your hands," he ordered. "Don't let your legs get twisted up in the rope and watch the cliff when you come back at it." He grinned at her and reached up to mess up her hair. "When Frank stops screaming like a little girl, make him help you anchor the rope so I can follow you down."

"Running jump?" she asked.

He'd rolled his eyes. "Why can't you just fall off the cliff like all the other kids?"

She grinned.

He fed out forty feet of rope. "This is all you got. And let me get behind that rock so you don't pull me off after you. Concentrate on what you're doing and not on seeing Frank's face."

She'd grabbed the rope about ten feet from where it hooked into her safety harness. She hadn't wanted to wear the harness, but now, it proved to be a good idea. In retrospect, Alex figured her father had an ulterior motive in letting her jump. And she did jump, as far as she could. Arms out like she thought she might be able to fly. She'd spun in the air, grabbing the rope to make sure it didn't get tangled around her legs and snap off a limb. For a minute, she felt like she was floating. She flipped in the air and used the sudden tension of the rope to complete the flip.

She caught a flash of the man below lifting his hands to his head and yelling, she could see the white all the way around his eyes. Then the cliff wall rushed at her. Her fluorescent yellow rock climbing shoes hit the wall, her knees bent to absorb the impact. Her legs were like springs, pushing back against her momentum and flying her back out into the air. She already had the rope in one hand, found the guide rope below her butt, and controlled her slid down the rest of the way with her father feeding her rope at the same time. She was laughing when she hit the ground.

Frank Dyer was cussing loudly and yelling up at her father.

She looked up at her dad and saw him standing at the edge, waving down at them. She walked back to the Jeep and started to tie off the rope; he'd given her instructions and she would follow them. "Dad says when you're done with your heart attack you need to help me anchor the rope."

"Fuck your dad," Frank snarled. He turned angrily. "Seriously does he not care that you could be killed? Sometimes I think he doesn't care about you at all."

Alex opened her eyes with a start, realizing she'd fallen asleep in the chair despite the restlessness. She looked up at the older version of Frank Dyer.

His brow furrowed. "You okay?"

She wiped the sleep out of her eyes, noticing the scars around her wrist. "Do you miss my dad?" she asked.

"He was my best friend," Frank replied.

She sighed and stood up.

Doucet stood up too.

She felt like she was jumping off the cliff but had ropes tied all over the place. There wasn't any freefall, just people above her pulling on the ropes trying to force her to move the way they wanted. Turning away from him, she walked to the glass wall and looked out at the street.

A couple in motorized scooters came down the sidewalk in front of her. They were older, Asian and dressed like locals with pastel clothing, sun hats, and dark sunglasses. They slowed in front of the doors of the hotel. The doorman opened the door for them.

Alex didn't turn to watch them. She saw their reflections in the glass.

"Thanks Harry," the woman said to the doorman, her voice gravelly—from years of smoking probably although it sounded as rough as Alex's own. "How are the slots running today?"

"Let's just earn enough points for a free buffet," the man on the scooter groused before the doorman could answer. "I'm hungry."

"You don't be careful and people are going to start thinking you're a Buddha statue," the woman told him. Her scooter humming into gear.

They continued to bicker back and forth as they crossed the lobby to the casino entrance.

Alex hooked her thumbs in the belt loops of her jeans. She looked up and down the street for a box truck.

A kid screeched, high-pitched and echoing in the mostly empty lobby.

Alex turned and saw a toddler running away from two Asian parents. The man wore a business suit; the woman a small, conservative sun dress. She carried an infant in her arms.

The toddler stopped at the windows right next to Alex, pressing her noise against the glass. Her pudgy hands left fingerprints on the glass.

"So sorry," the man said rushing up and scooping up the toddler. He scolded the child in Japanese. He had a lanyard around his neck and the toddler grabbed it.

Alex was quick, quicker than he was to hide the lanyard again. It identified him as a participant in a convention for home security systems, his name, and underneath his name, the company he worked for: Kyoto Security, a subsidiary of Nyx International. "Sorry. Not good, my English. Not mean to bother you."

Alex knew that was bullshit. If she'd been sleeping, that kid would have raced over and somehow managed to wake her up. Alex spoke in Japanese because her Japanese was better than his English and because she knew neither Doucet nor Dyer could keep up with her in attempting to translate her words. She told him the child was adorable and made all the appropriate compliments about his English.

He bowed slightly thanking her a few too many times.

Alex made similar comments to the woman who looked simultaneously embarrassed and awestruck as she hurried over to help collect her daughter.

The man nodded, bowing over and over again.

"You don't have to keep bowing," Alex told him.

He blushed slightly, but his complexion hid it well. "It is a great honor, Great One."

Alex nodded. She turned from him to look at the two Marines.

Alex looked at the two Marines. "I'm going to translate for these people to get them checked out easier," she said. "Do you want to hover over my shoulder? Maybe put some handcuffs on me or some leg irons? I mean, I might be planning something sinister or try to escape."

"Alex, you aren't a prisoner," Doucet said.

She'd had an opening to escape when they'd hit the buffet for breakfast. However, she didn't want to escape. She wanted to tie off the rope and follow her father's instructions. Then she wanted to follow the instructions of the Sword of Souls. Afterwards, she wanted to go home. Home, that retreat in Thailand on the beach that only she and her father knew about. An old couple served as guardians of the place, making sure it was maintained and always ready for an unannounced visit from the American owners.

As if to prove his words and convince her of his sincerity, Doucet sat back down in the chair. "Go on," he said. "Help them."

Alex indicated with her arm that the couple should go to the check-out desk. They put the toddler down and the girl promptly ran ahead; her tiny sandals slapping the marble. The woman's sandals clicked as she walked; the man's business shoes made a soft shuffling pat. Alex walked silently. Her eyes scanned the lobby. The doorman and a woman in a uniform behind the desk. A bank of four elevators, two on each side of the wide hallway which led to the casino area. A woman in dark gray yoga pants and a pink top waiting for the elevator. Two abandoned scooters just inside the casino area. The bells and whistles and lights of organized confusion inside the casino. Almond shaped eyes staring back at her from the confusion.

Alex said something to the toddler about how she ran too fast.

The toddler stopped and turned back, laughing, a playful glitter in her eyes.

Alex pointed at the girls red sandals. There was a nursery rhyme about red sandals. She couldn't remember all the lyrics, but she recited how it started.

The child gasped in surprise and laughed and clapped her hands. She joined in.

Alex screwed up the lyrics and the toddler quickly corrected her. The child's mother looked horrified at the harsh way the child issued the correction, but then relaxed when Alex grinned and laughed. The honest laughter felt strange inside her gut.

At the counter, the woman in the uniform smiled. The counter lowered on her side, providing room for a keyboard, a computer screen, a stack of room cards, a card reader, some pens with the hotel's name on them, and a few extra supplies. Those extras were a katana, a switch blade, a set of thin throwing spikes, and a remote detonator. The desk worker didn't even glance at these items.

Alex asked the kid what other nursery rhymes she knew. She crouched down in front of the kid to straighten a bow on her sundress.

The mother helped start up another one. The kid sang loudly, her light voice filled with happiness and simplicity and filling the lobby. The baby giggled too.

Alex met Doucet's eyes over the head of the child. She wondered what he was thinking because suddenly he looked very sad. She straightened up and turned away from him, moving so the mother of the toddler blocked her from the eyes of the Marines. The woman was smaller than she was, but she provided enough of a buffer so that Alex managed to get the three items over the counter and hidden. The sword wasn't the Sword of Souls, it was an inch shorter, but it was in a black matte sheath and didn't have a blade guard.

She didn't so much as translate for the man but made sure she was paying for his bill. When she was assured that it had all been taken care of she made sure the toddler got a sucker. She smiled at the kid and bowed at the couple. She walked back to the two Marines, who'd been joined by Ong. A big white truck sat on the curb. It had air vents about six feet from the bottom and a coolant unit on top of it.

"Horse transport," Ong said. "It has a 3 ton haul capacity and won't get too hot inside in the desert. I was a little nervous about the temperatures considering the age of what we're going to be hauling.

"Let's get this over with," Alex said.

"Where are we going?" Doucet asked.

She held out a hand.

He shook his head.

"Cell phone," she explained.

He unhooked it from his belt and passed it to her.

She resisted the urge to check the recent outgoing calls. She figured he might have erased them anyway. She brought up the internet function and did a quick search. She found what she was looking for and pulled it up. She passed it to him.

"Henderson Storage?" Sinjin said. "I thought you said you didn't know the name of the place."

"I wasn't in my right mind at the time," she replied. "I'll give you the password when we get there."

"Maybe you should stay here," Dyer said. "You've only had a couple of hours of rest and after what happened…"

"Sitting around with nothing to do but think about it, isn't going to help," she said. "I'll ride in the back."

Doucet joined her in the back, letting Dyer and Ong take the front cab. He pulled the back closed. His phone rang as fans came on and began to cool the interior of the box.

Alex slid down to her butt with her back against the wall, facing the doors.

"Yeah, I have reception," he said. "We're good." He caught himself as the truck began to move. He slid down next to her.

Alex fought the urge to move away.

"You want to talk?" he asked.

"No," she said.

"I have five sisters, Alex. I know that normally women need to talk when—"

"I'm not a normal woman."

Sinjin chuckled. "*Cher*, I know that."

Alex took a deep breath and let it out slowly.

"I'm sorry I wasn't there for you," he said.

"I seriously do not want to talk about it."

"You were good with that kid."

"So?"

"I didn't expect you to be good with kids, I guess."

"I'm full of surprises."

He frowned. "Alex, don't push me away."

"Is that what I'm doing, Sinjin?"

He leaned over and kissed her.

She pulled away.

He followed. "Let me make you feel better," he said.

She didn't pull away a second time. It was a long ride and she couldn't think of another way to pass the time. Plus it had the extra bonus of avoiding conversation. She shifted so he wouldn't find the weapons she had on her before shutting her brain. She let herself forget as her body took charge of enjoying itself and not needing to think.

CHAPTER SIXTEEN

Alex sat on the edge of the box truck and looked at the storage unit. It was in the back of the maze of storage units. It looked like a small town without windows. The sun beat down hot and dry. She wished she'd thought to bring water. She rolled the sleeves of her shirt up to her biceps, exposing the bottom half the tattoo on her arm and more scars. The sun was turning her scars pink.

The three Marines stood in front of the unit staring at the lock on the unit's door. She heard cars driving by on the highway. As she listened, she heard a vehicle slow down and turn into the storage unit complex. She looked down at the ground, at her swinging boots. She had a sick feeling in her gut, but it was tempered by fury.

This unit had been owned by her father. It had been transferred to Peter before she'd even been aware that he was dead.

"I can't believe you hid the bombs in a storage unit that Peter owns," Dyer said. "He had them all the time. What if he came out here looking for something?"

Alex swung her legs. "Peter didn't even know he had it," she said, using the past tense because she'd taken it back from Peter. Each time he found an empty bomb site, she took a little more. She'd lied to the Arab. "It was one of my father's secret weapons stashes."

"One of?" Dyer asked. He frowned.

Alex watched his eyes as his brain calculated how many times over the years Joe McBrady had been out here in Vegas before heading to Mexico.

Dyer frowned. "How many did he have?"

Alex shrugged. "One or two others." She jumped down and walked up to the lock.

"We're going to need bolt cutters," Doucet said.

Alex sighed and shook her head. "Men," she mumbled. She lifted the lock and spun the dial quickly. The lock fell open into her hand.

Doucet stared at her.

She shrugged. "Lucky guess."

"Peter might have changed it."

She rolled her eyes. "Then he would have known he had this unit. Plus, that would require work and Peter is all about taking the easy road. He killed my father and stole all his shit instead of working for it. He's planning on selling these things to some stupid Arab. In addition, I had the bombs delivered here so I already knew it worked." She pushed the lock into his chest, bent down and lifted the overhead door.

In the middle of the storage unit, a pallet on wheels held a large sealed crate marked for the US Army with the letters MRE on the side. She stepped back.

Doucet stared at it.

Dyer moved into the unit. He grabbed a crow bar that was conveniently lying on the floor. He pried open the crate's lid.

Two briefcases lay inside thick cushioning inside two smaller boxes. Both cases were cracked and dried leather, one was faded more than the others. The leather seemed to be worn bare at the corners. Wires came from the seam and wrapped around the handle of the case before attaching to a crude 1980s clock radio with digital numbers. The clock had stopped running so that all that remained was a gray screen.

"Fuck," Dyer said. "Damn you, Joe. I don't get why he didn't just contact us."

"Maybe because he's dead," Alex said.

Doucet made a disapproving face at her. "Let's get this sealed back up and out to the base. We made arrangements to have this stuff destroyed at a secret Air Force bunker about twenty miles into the desert."

Alex shrugged. "Whatever."

He narrowed his eyes. "These are the bombs, right?"

Alex nodded. "Why wouldn't they be? I promised you the bombs when I had Peter."

Right on cue, Peter strolled around the end of the line of storage units. Four men were with him, pointing their weapons at Alex and the others. "But you don't have me," he said. "You will always be one step behind, Alexandria."

"How in the hell?" Ong muttered, pointing his weapon at the approaching mercenaries.

"You left quite the mess in my rental property, Alexandria," Peter said.

Alex yawned and leaned against the wall of the storage unit.

Another set of mercenaries appeared from the opposite direction, trapping Alex and the Division rescue team in the storage unit with the nuclear bombs.

"Let's see your weapons," Peter ordered the Marines.

Alex crossed her arms over her chest and crossed her legs at the ankles. She made no move to show hers. Still the mercenaries eyed her warily. She smiled coldly at the one she'd let go the night before. "Nice to see you again," she said.

He licked his lips. "You don't scare me."

She smirked.

"Pat her down for weapons," Peter ordered the guy.

"Unless you're afraid," Alex said. "Then I suppose one of the others can do it."

The man narrowed his eyes and swung his rifle onto his back. His jaw set as he marched up to her. He grabbed her shoulder and spun her into the wall roughly. Alex glanced at Doucet.

He muttered a curse under his breath.

Alex moved at the first contact the mercenary made with her. Her elbow slammed back into his face. To his credit, he'd been expecting her to lash out. He wasn't fast enough to escape complete injury. She knocked out his teeth instead of breaking his nose. "Ow," Alex said. "Son of a bitch, that hurt my elbow." She spun and decked the man as something like a bar fight broke out around her.

Suddenly the confined space worked to the advantage of herself and the Division men. The mercenaries had to avoid each other while Alex and the others could basically hit whatever was in front of them.

Alex retrieved her survival knife and shoved it into the gut of the man behind her. She pulled him in close and shoved deeper. "I told you not to let me see you again," she whispered in his ear as he leaned against her. She let go of him and the knife.

He grabbed her sleeve as he went down, ripping it off.

Alex frowned and glanced at the fighting going on around her. Someone was pulling the box truck away from the storage unit giving the mercenaries more room.

One of the mercenaries pulled a weapon and pointed it at her face. "Don't move," he ordered.

Alex lifted her hands and leaned back against the wall of the storage unit. She made no move to do any more damage. She watched the fighting. It looked pretty good and the Division didn't do so bad considering only two of them fought for their lives. The third one knew he wouldn't be killed.

It didn't take them long to subdue the Marines.

Ong took the worst of it, barely able to stand. However, no one was in great shape when it was all over.

Peter strolled up to the crate. His suit was a light blue-gray color. He wore it with a white silk shirt and a dark striped tie.

All of them remained perfectly pressed. He glanced at the counters. He glanced back at one of his men. "Check and make sure they're not fakes," he said. He turned, his pale eyes rolling over the three Marines, then finding Alex.

Behind him the Geiger counter erupted with static when it neared the crate.

Peter smiled at Alex.

Alex smiled back. She pulled out the detonator that she'd palmed and pushed the red button.

"System armed," a woman's voice announced from the crate.

A collective gasp jumped from all the men in the room.

"Detonation in 180 seconds," the voice said.

"What the---" Peter gasped, he spun on Alex. "You're bluffing. Stop it." He pulled a small .22 caliber revolver from his jacket. He pointed it at Doucet's head. "Stop it. Stop it or I will shoot him."

Alex made a face. "What the fuck is that?" she asked. "Is that a real gun or a cap gun?"

Even some of the mercenaries snickered.

"It's a real gun."

Alex sighed. "Jesus Christ, Peter, you're supposed to be a mercenary." She dropped the detonator to the concrete and crushed it under her boot. "Shoot him," she said. "He's got less than three minutes to live anyway. Besides, a .22 isn't going to kill him, Peter. For shit's sake, did you buy that gun because it looked big next to your dick." She smiled all charm at the mercenaries. A couple of them grinned back despite themselves.

"One hundred seventy seconds," the voice said.

Alex lifted her chin at the big .45 Smith and Wesson pointed at her own head. "You need a gun like this. At least it has some serious stopping power. I get shot with this, I'm probably not going to kill this guy afterwards."

"If this bomb goes off—"

"Eight bombs," Alex corrected. "Eight bombs wired together with enough C4 to make this storage unit facility nothing but a crater. Enough radiation to ruin your buyer too. I'm sure he's not letting your leash out too far these days."

Peter stared at her.

She waved her hand impatiently. "Go on, Peter. You were going to threaten me. I was just making sure you did it properly."

"You can't be serious," Dyer growled at her. "You're not going to go blow us all up. You want us to believe you fought so hard to stay alive just so you can blow yourself up?"

"One hundred sixty seconds."

A panicked silence fell over the group of mercenaries and beat-up Division soldiers like a shroud. A calm fell over Alex. She leaned back against the wall, crossed her arms over her chest and crossed her ankles. With a yawn she waited.

Peter lowered his weapon from Doucet's head. "Kenner, check this thing. It's not a real bomb."

One of the mercenaries let out a laugh. "You fucking check it, Peter, did you see the radiation readings on that? Those bombs are 40 years old. I'm not opening them up."

"One hundred fifty seconds."

"If it explodes, you'll die too," Peter said. His voice losing the fake English accent.

Alex's smirk twitched in amusement. "You may recall me begging to die," she replied casually. "And I've already got radiation poisoning. I'm dying anyway."

"Bullshit."

"Let me point out my recent propensity for vomiting," she told him. If she'd had time, she would have found a way to act like she was losing clumps of hair too. She should have had Guang hide some red hair around the storage unit and shave a patch out of her hair. Hindsight is always so much better.

"One hundred forty seconds."

Peter's eyes left hers and he stared at the crate. A bead of rolled down his face. "You'll kill them, too." He waved his hands at the three Division men.

Alex arched an eyebrow at him. "They're Marines. They knew the score when they took up the pledge. Like all of your guys here, Peter. They all knew they were risking their lives when they came out here today. Of course, they didn't realize they were going to get blown into a thousand bits which will be irradiated so no one will be able to pick up the pieces and they'll just lay out here in the desert until something comes along to consume the roasted meat—and then what ever that something it, it will most likely die before it can digest its meal."

The man named Kenner who Peter had looked to for disarming the bombs turned to Alex. "What's the radius of that thing?"

Alex shrugged. "You have about 60 seconds to get in your vehicles and get out of here, at 80 miles an hour, you might escape lethal dosages. If you do, go to a bar called the Soap Bar in Hong Kong and tell them the word *yaojing*. He'll ask you what you want to drink. You ask for a shot of Johnny Walker Blue. The shot will come with a 20 thousand dollar paycheck." She paused. "Or stay and die with the rest of us."

Kenner and a couple of the men exchanged glances. They lowered their weapons and took off.

"What?! You can't leave," Peter shouted after them.

"Fuck you Peter, we've been waiting a long time for a payoff that's never coming. We're taking the sure thing."

"She's lying. She doesn't have any money to give you."

"One hundred thirty seconds."

Alex shook her head. "All that time with my dad and you never learned how these guys tick? You're as pathetic as that gun."

Peter lifted his weapon.

Kenner took it out of his hand. He and several of others, including the one with the gun on Alex, left. The squeal of tires and the revving engine filled the hot, still air.

"One hundred twenty seconds."

"We got this now," Doucet said. "Stop it."

Alex laughed at him. "Fuck you."

"You wouldn't kill them," Peter said. "Your lover. Your father's best friend. Some slant-eye—I know how you have a soft spot for the yellows. You going to let them die too?"

"One hundred ten seconds."

Alex said nothing, just watched him start to unravel.

"What about the innocent people? You're going to kill innocent people here. The guy at the guard shack. He's probably got kids and a family."

Doucet grabbed Peter. "He'll go to jail, Alex. He'll pay for what he did to you. Stop the bomb."

"One hundred seconds."

One of the remaining mercenaries ran to the crate. He examined the timer in the middle of the crate, a new modern timer. He reached forward and punched in few numbers.

"Incorrect passcode," the computerized voice said.

Peter looked up from the ground. "There's a password! What's the fucking password?"

"Ninety seconds."

"Alex, what's the password?" Doucet demanded.

She shook her head, a dead look in her eyes as she watched them all. In addition to Peter, three mercenaries had remained, hoping for the big nuclear bomb payoff rather than the sure thing. Maybe they didn't trust her about the cash. They would have been smart about that, the *yaojing* was a female spirit known for seduction and eating souls. The owner of the bar called Soap in Hong Kong would kill anyone associated with Joe McBrady who'd once used a hooker to act like a *yaojing* to seduce the owner's superstitious father and destroy a very profitable shipping line.

Peter tried to get away from Doucet.

"Eighty seconds."

"Alex!" Doucet ordered. "What's the fucking password?! Now!"

Alex narrowed her eyes at him. "You want to spend the last moments of your life yelling at me?" she asked him. You should probably call your mom and your sisters.

"What about their families?" Peter asked. "You'd do that to them? Or make this part of the desert useless for a thousand years?"

"Seventy seconds."

Alex rubbed her elbow. She stepped out of the unit and tilted her face up to the sky. Hot sun tightened her skin. She really wished she'd brought water along. "It's a good day to die," she said. "Too late for you guys to appreciate the little things at this point. But hey, we're all here for a reason."

Behind her, she heard a pistol slide being cocked back.

"I'm going to need that password," Dyer's deep voice said.

Alex pivoted around.

The muscled sergeant held a weapon to Doucet's head.

Peter pulled away from the big Cajun. He brushed off his suit. Smug, thick lips pursed once.

"Sixty seconds."

"If I don't get that password," Dyer said, "he's going to start losing body parts."

Alex didn't give a shit about Doucet. She felt sick to her stomach. "Why, Frank? You were like an uncle to me and like a brother to my dad."

"You think this is a fucking movie where you get the bad guy to explain himself to you? Fuck you, Alex. Fuck you and fuck your dead father. Fuck all your fucking money that he got for hiring himself out like some kind of military whore."

"You killed him."

"Not me. I just set him up. He was supposed to give up the bombs and live. It's his own fault he's dead. Then you were supposed to give up the bombs."

Alex nodded. "Yeah, and then everything was going to be fine."

"Fifty seconds."

Dyer continued, oblivious now to what she did. "I stayed in the Marines. I didn't get kicked out like he did. I worked hard. I served a cause. I have nothing to show for it, just a shitty pension on the way. Not enough to do anything. Your father had everything and he didn't deserve it. Fuck, Alex, he set you up to be Peter's target."

"And you made sure that Peter got me," she replied softly.

His mouth twitched. "Don't fucking try some of that stupid ninja stuff with me," he said. "I will shoot you. You didn't have to be tortured. You should have just told us where the bombs were. What happened was your own fault. You don't give a shit about those bombs or this country or anything. You're a fucking psychopath."

"Forty seconds."

Peter ran up to her and grabbed her arm.

She twisted with lightning speed and shoved him face first into the wall.

He gasped grabbing his nose and his split lip. His pale eyes turned on Dyer. "Make her!"

Dyer's finger tightened on the trigger.

Doucet took a deep breath. "Sergeant, don't."

Dyer glared at him. "You're an asshole, Captain. I'd be doing the female half of humanity a favor by getting rid of you. I can't believe you fucked her."

"Thirty seconds."

"What's the password!" Dyer screamed at her.

Alex heard the panic in his voice.

The mercenaries who'd remained, turned and started to run, taking the box truck.

The tires kicked up stones at Alex.

She laughed at Dyer and Peter.

Ong groaned against the wall. He only had one eye that wasn't swollen shut and it stared at Alex.

"I will kill him!" Dyer said, shoving the end of the barrel into Doucet's head.

Alex took a deep breath. "Well, one of us is going to do it in the next minute either way," she replied.

"You are in love with him."

Alex rolled her eyes and laughed. "I'm a psychopath. I can't love anyone."

"Liar!" He started to pull the trigger.

"Ten seconds," the computer voice said.

Dyer and Peter both froze. They stared at the crate.

"What the fuck happened to twenty?" Peter screeched.

"Nine seconds."

Alex moved away from the wall.

"Eight seconds."

"Alex—" Doucet said. "Please stop this. Innocent people will die."

Peter threw himself at the crate and started to push buttons and pull wires.

"Incorrect password. Seven seconds."

Alex stretched her shoulders.

Doucet's brow furrowed.

"Six seconds."

"No!!" Dyer shouted.

Alex moved forward a few steps.

"Five seconds."

Dyer spun and fired into the spot where Alex had been standing.

Alex grabbed Peter's jacket and threw him at Ong. "Hold him a second," she told him.

The slide was open on Dyer's semiautomatic, its magazine emptied. His big figure still tried to pull the trigger.

"Four seconds."

Alex watched him.

He threw the weapon at her.

She evaded it easily.

"Three seconds."

"Fuck you and fuck Joe fucking McBrady," Dyer hissed.

"Two seconds."

Dyer threw a punch at Alex.

She leaned out of its way. And lifted her own hands as if she were willing to spend the last seconds of her life boxing with him. She grinned. She actually was willing to spend her last seconds alive in a fight, unfortunately, she had two more people to kill after Dyer.

CHAPTER SEVENTEEN

"One and three-quarter seconds," the voice said.

All four of the men in the small space did a double take at the talking crate.

Alexandria Rae McBrady laughed. Her muscles felt warm and loose; her bones felt icy cold and hard as steal. Despite the distance from the Sword of Souls, she felt its song in her blood. She felt the monster stretch its limbs.

Dyer turned back to her first, realization drawing up the curtain in his eyes. "You planned this. You brought Peter here on purpose. You let him kidnap you."

Alex yawned. She nodded her head at Ong who remained on the ground, leaning against the wall of the storage unit, bleeding. He had a weapon on Peter. "I thought he was the smart one."

"One and a half seconds," the voice from the crate said.

Dyer's jaw twitched, his face seemed to grow even darker than it was. "Are those even the bombs in there?"

"You heard the Geiger counter," Alex said. "We are all going to die here."

"You're a bitch."

Alex smirked. "You're a fucking traitor."

"One and a half seconds," the voice from the crate said.

Dyer's ham sized fist tightened, and his shoulder pulled back for another punch.

To Alex, the swing seemed slow and awkward. Still, she had no doubt that if it connected it would hurt. She easily dropped under the arc, coming up like a piston inside his immediate space and driving a knee into his ribs and her elbow into his mouth.

Dyer fell to the ground. Clouds of dust rising around him. He felt directly in front of Doucet.

"Alex," Doucet shouted. "Don't!"

Dyer turned and decked the Cajun as he scrambled to his feet.

"Sergeant, she's going to kill you, then me if you don't stop her," Peter said. His pale eyes glittered like a snake's eyes as it slithers around for the kill. The only thing missing was a pink forked tongue flicking out of his too thin lips.

Ong managed to keep a weapon on Peter, but he couldn't get up. His face was a bloody mess.

"One second," the voice said.

"Alex, forget about him! Stop the bomb," Doucet ordered.

A bead of sweat rolled down Alex's spine, traversing scars which cris-crossed her skin like a Jackson Pollack tapestry. Her heart was slow; her breath came from the center of her core. The world seemed to stop turning. Time seemed to stand still.

Dyer swung with one hand, feinting, and brought the other fist up hoping to catch her by surprise.

Alex spun and swept her leg under his at the same time, she brought her elbow up into the side of his head.

He fell hard again.

"Half a second. Oh, what the hell. Fuck this," the voice from the crate said. "I'm going home."

Alex grinned.

Dyer came at her low, trying to tackle her.

Alex grabbed one of the throwing spikes she had on her and slid down and under Dyer's charge. She used his momentum and her boot in his gut to push him over her body. As he passed, she shoved the spike deep into his thigh.

Dyer cried out in pain. He stumbled out into the sun, hoping to avoid weight on the damaged leg. He pulled the spike out and stared at it. Then he threw it away.

Alex listened to the spike chime as it bounced over the asphalt baking in the sun. She shoved her hair back from her face.

Sweat glistened on his bald head, trickled down his face.

"You're as fucking crazy as your father," Dyer said. "I'm not going to kill you, Alex."

"Well, I know you aren't going to kill me, Uncle Frank." She spit his name out to him. "I did expect you to try to fight to keep me from killing you, but I guess it doesn't surprise me that you're just going to stand there and take it. You're pretty good about doing nothing."

"Fuck you! I cared about you. I didn't risk your life taking you on dangerous mountaineering treks. I didn't expose you to ruthless teachers who sent you back to your dad with bruises all over your body. I didn't keep you from going to school. And I didn't put the target on your back. That was your father. He pointed Peter at you. It's his fault." He spat as he shouted. He stumbled backwards, trying to escape her.

Alex walked after him, slowly. "I got a call on a secure phone to show up at the warehouse where Peter was waiting for me. That was you."

"Peter said he wanted to talk to you. He said there was a lot of money in it for me. He said he wanted to protect you from your father's enemies. All you had to do was answer his questions."

"I called in the distress signal. You blocked it and erased it so no one in the Division would know it was made. So, they wouldn't look for me."

He nearly tripped over a two by four laying on the ground as he continued to back up towards the chain link fence that circled the storage unit property. His big hand wrapped around the board. "You were only supposed to be gone a couple of days. You're a spoiled brat. Always calling daddy to bail you out while he made sure you had no career prospects, no future, nothing. You were no better than those trust fund brats."

Alex nodded. "Yeah, that pesky government job I was doing could have been done by monkeys," she replied.

He rolled his eyes. "They just wanted you for your daddy's connections and your looks." He swung the board at her when she got too close.

She avoided it with ease.

"Alex!" Doucet yelled from inside the storage unit. "Dyer. Stop."

"He's going to have to kill her to stop her," Peter said.

"Shut up and don't move," Ong ordered, his voice rough with pain.

Dyer looked over her shoulder at his team. He swung the bat again.

At the ends of the road that was in front the line of storage units, several black SUVs skidded around the corners and bore down on them.

The distraction was enough to make Dyer think he had an opening. He tried to hit her with the two by four. She caught it in her side, rebreaking the ribs. But she grabbed the piece of wood and held it in place as her leg kicked out and broke a couple of his ribs

Dyer let out an "oof" and stumbled back, catching himself on the fence. He pulled the board, pulling Alex into his space where he could fight her.

But, Alex went willingly. She brought her knee up in his groin hard. Then up into his side again.

Dyer vomited over her shoulder. His grip on the board released involuntarily.

Alex took it and tossed it aside.

Sagging against the fence, nearly doubled over, Frank Dyer looked up at Alex.

Her face stayed completely blank. She met his eyes.

"Alex," he gasped as he tried to control gagging. "Please! I loved your father like a brother! I love you like a daughter."

Alex pulled out the sword. Her head tilted to the side. "You'd sell your daughter to a psychopath?"

He pointed at her. "Don't give me that shit, Alex! Your father set you up. He did the same God damned thing! He made sure Peter and I and every merc around knew that the only person he trusted was you and that you would be the only one who knew where the bombs were."

Alex's hand flexed on the handle of the sword. The metal flashed in the bright sun. Sweat made strands of hair cling to her face and neck like slashes of blood, like the welts of the whip across her back. When she spoke, her voice was low and dangerous. "Don't spend your last breath with my father's name on your lips, Frank Dyer." She spat his name like a curse. "My father did that for two reasons. He didn't want someone using me to make him talk and he knew I never would. He wanted to make sure that if he died, he'd still win."

"This isn't winning. This is murder."

"Don't do it, Alex," Doucet shouted as he struggled to keep Peter from running.

Alex lifted the sword.

Frank Dyer held up a hand. "Don't!"

The sword flashed.

His hand, still reaching out for Alex, fell to the ground.

Alex stepped to the side to avoid the spray of blood.

Dyer screamed, high-pitched and almost inhuman.

Behind Alex, men's voices were shouting.

"Put down the sword!"

"Federal Agents! Put down the sword!"

Alex couldn't hear her own thoughts over the screaming charge of a thousand charge Huns in her head. The world itself seemed a long way away. The shouts seemed like nothing more than squeaks from mice at the start of a maze while she stood at the cheese with the trap about to spring.

Her heart thumped slow. She grabbed the sword with her second hand, sucked in a breath and let out a loud *kiai*. The

263

sword swooped through the air. It moved in slow motion to Alex, she heard the air scream around it. It hit the fence before it found Dyer. The metal on metal sent up sparks as the sword bit through the chain links.

Dyer's eyes were wide, his mouth starting to open in a scream.

The sound of the voices behind her raised in a crescendo of panic and horror.

The sword pulled though the fence and Dyer's neck.

Muscle memory brought the sword through and then down by her side. If she'd had the sheath strapped to her belt, the weapon would have slid in it smoothly without hesitation. In her head, she saw her first teacher nod approval, his dark eyes never allowing the surprise to enter, never conceding that she was better than everyone else in the class, never allowing a cocky six-year-old child to recognize that after only two years training, she'd reached levels that some masters would never reach. Nothing had been given to her by a sword she did not yet know existed. These skills were hers, earned.

In front of her, the body slumped harder against the fence. The edges of the slash in the fence stained red and glistening in the sunlight. Blood shot out of the neck because the heart didn't realize the body was dead yet.

The head, mouth open, eyes wide, rolled off the man's wide muscular shoulders and bounced once on the concrete with a wet sound. The body slide to the side, red pouring out and spreading on the dusty concrete.

Behind her, the shouts had turned to stunned silence and the sounds of several people retching.

Her hand flexed on the handle of the weapon.

She turned pivoted away from the first checkmark on her to do list, the promises made to keep her alive.

A dozen men in black riot gear had swarmed around the storage unit. Four black SUVs with tinted windows blocked off the road out of the area.

Richard Powell stood in front of one of those SUVs, his suit jacket flapping in the breeze, his face not as pale as those of the men who normally worked the field. His eyes met hers.

She frowned, her brow furrowing. She glanced over her shoulder.

The fence was eight feet high and topped with a coil of cheap barbed wire. It wouldn't be a problem for her. But beyond was an endless flat desert. Perfect for her father's needs—no one would be able to spy on him without him spotting them—but pretty awful for escape from a dozen of the best trained commando units in the United States.

She turned back to the storage unit.

Peter stood up, looking smug. One of the masked commandos tended to Lieutenant Mitchell Ong.

Doucet stood to the side and one step back from Richard Powell. The Cajun's pretty face was hard, twisted between concern and horror and sick and upset. He'd worked with Frank Dyer, entrusted his life to the man, for years.

Alex didn't blame him for being upset. She was upset. The man had been a consistency her entire life. He'd joined her and her father on vacations. He'd joked with her and played with her when she was little. She'd never been much for tea parties, but she distinctly remembered days at fairs with her father and Frank squeezed into seats on the kiddie rides, their knees up to their chins, stupid grins on their faces as she laughed and wanted to go faster.

Her eyes drifted back to Peter.

She felt the red dots of the rifles on her shirt and on her skin like lasers burning into her.

Her hand flexed on the sword. People often mistook the flexing habit of hers as a nervous habit or a sign that she didn't have a good hold on her weapon.

This was a mistake.

Peter made a point of smiling thanks at one of the commandos in the unit.

Alex glanced back at Richard Powell.

For a second everything seemed to stand still.

Alex smirked at her former handler, the man who would do anything to make her an assassin controlled by the government. The man knew what she was. She'd seen the proof in his desk drawer.

Richard's eyes widened. His head turned to Doucet.

Peter's smug smile fell away. He started to back up deeper into the storage unit. His delicate long-fingered hand lifted up and pointed, like the grim reaper trying to make a designation of who should be next.

Richard was shouting.

Alex planned on impaling Peter and watching the light leak out of his eyes like he'd watched her father die. She moved forward.

The commandos shouted for her not to move, for her to let go of the sword, for her to get down on the ground. They threatened to shoot.

However, Richard was shouting at them not to kill her.

Doucet grabbed a handgun from Richard Powell. He pointed and fired.

Doucet was a natural marksman. He'd won competitions.

The gun didn't explode. It let loose with a puff of air.

Like the weapon the assassin watching Doucet's apartment had carried.

Alex knew a single gunshot wouldn't have stopped her before she could get to Peter.

But the dart was something else. She'd watched it drop the guy who'd been watching Doucet's New York apartment in an instant.

She didn't know what the hell was in it, but it was bad.

The dart hit her in the chest, right under her collar bone.

Pain exploded through her body.

One of her legs gave out.

The sword fell from her fingers.

It clattered on the concrete.

A cold sweat broke out over her body.

She couldn't catch her breath.

Peter applauded. "Nice shot! Hell, what the fuck is that stuff? It took me more tranqs to put her down than it would take an elephant."

Alex reached up and pulled the dart from her chest. Her jaw was locked and sweat beaded up on her forehead. Her eyes narrowed, but focused on Peter. The hatred burned away the pain, locked it away. The irony that Peter himself had taught her how to compartmentalize the agony did not escape her. She was down on one knee. She forced herself to get back up.

Doucet held the weapon steady. He shook his head. "Please don't make me, *cher*," he said, his accent thick.

Alex stood facing him. The world swayed and spun around her. If she weren't so focused on killing Peter, the mess would have disoriented her.

"A second dose will kill her," said one of the men kneeling near Ong with a medical bag. He rose to his feet, his eyes jumping between Doucet, Richard Powell, and Alex.

Alex glared at Peter Van de Moeter, smirked at the terror on his face. "How's it feel, you mother fucking asshole?" Her words were slurred. "To know you're going to die soon."

"I can't let you murder someone else," Doucet said.

She tried to focus on him.

"Don't take another step," he warned. "I love you, *cher*, but I will shoot you."

She took a deep breath and shoved one foot forward.

"STOP HER!" Peter screeched.

The gun puffed again.

A second dart hit her in the neck.

Alex wondered how Richard Powell was walking on the walls, running towards her in slow motion.

Then he was gone and she stared up at a blue, cloudless sky.

The Sword of Souls chuckled from its safety.

"Medic!" Doucet shouted from a long way away.

The blue sky faded away.

267

Richard Powell rolled Alex over onto her back. Her eyes were open, staring up at the sky. Her arm flopped off to the side, lifeless. Her mouth was open, but she wasn't breathing. All that flashed in his head was the medical report that had said she'd suffered several heart attacks while being tortured; suggesting that, should she recover, care should be taken to avoid physical exertion and stress.

The medic was at Alex's side, on his knees. He dropped his bag and pulled the cap off a long needle that stayed in his hand. Without hesitating, he stabbed the long needle in Alex's chest.

Immediately her body jerked and started to shake.

"She's seizing," he yelled. "Donnelly, hold her still."

Another man swung his rifle onto his back and shoved Powell back. He held Alex down as she started to convulse. The violent convulsions slowed and got weaker as the plunger went down until they stopped all together. She started foaming at the mouth.

The medic turned her head and cleared her air way. "CPR!" he ordered the man helping him.

The commando obeyed immediately. He started pushing down on her chest.

The medic pinched her nose and breathed for her. "Com'on," he yelled at Alex.

Richard Powell felt nauseous as he watched the desperation in the two commandos. He figured it had been this way that last moment when Peter's torturer went too far just before she escaped.

Powell looked up at Captain Doucet who stood at the edge of the storage unit watching. The man looked broken. His chief non-commissioned officer had been beheaded in front of everyone after admitting he'd tried to sell out his country. He'd been forced to shoot the woman he'd been sleeping with. And now people were doing CPR trying to save her. "She's going to be okay," Powell said.

"The world is better off without her," Peter chimed in. "Did you see the look in her eyes? That's evil. Pure evil. I've never seen anything like that. It's a good thing you stopped her before she killed all of us."

Richard made a face. "Get that asshole out of my sight before I let her wake up and kill him."

"I want to make a deal," Peter said. "I have information you can use. I need protection though. Witness protection program or something. I can give you names, all of Joe McBrady's contacts with arms dealers and commandos. I can tell you who wants to buy stuff and who has the resources to hit the United States. You need me."

Richard looked at the man in disgust. "That doesn't mean I've forgotten that you're a rapist and a murderer," he hissed.

The commandos dragged Peter out of the storage unit.

Mitchell Ong, pushed away the people trying to help him. He staggered across the space to Alex's side, falling to his knees beside her. He lifted Alex's hand with his own bloody, swollen hand. His fingers felt her wrist for a pulse, leaving bloody fingermarks. He looked over his shoulder at Richard Powell. "What in the hell did you give her?"

"Box Jellyfish venom combined with botulinum toxin," Richard replied. "Or something derived from both of those. It works fast, sends the body into shock almost immediately."

Ong frowned. "Box jellyfish venom is supposed to be one of the most painful venoms known. You don't think maybe she suffered enough?"

Richard's spine stiffened. "She knew that dart had stopping power. She killed the two assassins I had outside of Doucet's apartment. She saw what it did. She could have stopped."

Ong spat at the man, blood and spit hitting the ground in front of Powell's Italian leather shoes. "She spent six months being tortured. Even your analysts had to tell you that she's not thinking straight. Dyer sold her out; he sold all of us out. Peter tortured her and raped her and was going to sell nuclear weapons to the enemy. They were our enemies as well as hers. You could have shot her before she took Dyer's head."

Powell blinked. "We were too far away."

"Bullshit," Doucet said. "You wanted to see her commit murder of one of ours. You wanted it for leverage."

"Do we give her more antivenom, Doc?" asked the man on his knees pumping Alex's chest.

"We're not giving her any more drugs then are absolutely necessary," Ong said. He winced as he shifted his postion.

The medic looked at him. "If she wakes up, we have to shoot her again."

"Breath," Ong ordered. He looked up at Doucet. "Captain, you're going to have to relieve him, we might have to be at this for a few hours will the venom works through her system. I can't do it, I kind of need a doctor myself."

"We can't stay here for a few hours," Powell argued

The medic looked up as he gave up breathing so the other man could pump her chest. "Get a gurney," he ordered another man. "We can keep up the CPR while we take her to one of the vans. We can go to Nellis and get her on a machine." He bent over and breathed for Alex again.

Suddenly her body gasped, started choking.

Ong pushed the medic out of the way and turned Alex's head to the side, he pulled her hair out of the way as she vomited. "Her heart is racing," he said, wincing over his split lip. He coughed, spraying blood over Alex's shirt. "Shit, we're going to need to sedate her or she's going to seize again." His eyes got hard. "No more venom. No more pain; do you understand me? She's suffered enough."

The medic nodded, grabbing a clear bag filled with fluid out of his kit. The bag was connected to a long tube and a capped needle at the end. "Which arm, Lieutenant?"

"Her left arm," Ong ordered. "She's got less scarring there."

The medic hooked up an IV into her left arm which had less needle tracks. It took him a few minutes to find a vein.

Richard's gut tightened when Alex's right arm lifted off the pavement.

She managed a half-conscious sob of pain.

Ong spoke to her in rapid Chinese.

Powell stared at the woman who looked small and vulnerable surrounded by three burly soldiers. Her face had gone pale, he could see the dark rings under her eyes. He wondered when she'd slept last, when she'd eaten. He wondered what it was about this woman who could kill and surmount physical trials which few could. She didn't take care of herself; she didn't worry about her own pain or mortality. She would endure to finish what she started. It made her a dangerous enemy and a formidable weapon. Powell wondered if it was that self-denied suffering which invoked such a strong feeling of care? Maybe it was the fact that one just could see in her eyes that she'd sacrifice everything to achieve her goals.

Either way, Ong worked desperately to keep her alive despite the fact that she'd just murdered his long-time team mate. Powell clenched his jaw as he watched the interaction and wished he spoke Chinese.

Eyes fluttering, semi-conscious, straining against what was most certainly agonizing pain, Alex's arm stopped moving. Her hand folded into a fist.

Ong spoke softer, leaning down closer to her face.

The medic managed to get the IV needle in her other arm. He held it up and opened the valve under the bag. Liquid began to drip through the tubing. "Jesus," he said, "her heart is racing."

Ong ignored him. He continued to talk to Alex.

The tightness of her fist started to loosen. Her arm started to move back down to the pavement.

She let out a sigh.

Ong sat back and wrapped his arm around his ribs.

The medic passed the IV bag to the man who'd been helping with CPR. He grabbed a needle out of his pack and stepped over Alex. He ripped Ong's sleeve further than it was already ripped and stabbed him in the arm with the needle. "That'll get you through until Nellis," he said. "What did you say to her?"

Ong shook his head. "It wasn't what I said, it was that it was in Chinese. The Far East is a place where she feels safe. She grew up there."

Powell watched the exchange. He glanced at Doucet and was surprised to see that Doucet had a cast of doubt on his face. The Marine Captain didn't believe Ong any more than he himself did.

CHAPTER EIGHTEEN

A dull, steady roar rolled through Alex's head as she regained consciousness. Instinct kept her breathing slow and deep and steady. It kept her eyes shut. The roar came with a dull vibration which her mind quickly put with an airplane. She sat in a chair, reclined back, wide enough to suggest this was a private plane or first class. Definitely not coach. Definitely not a military transport. Definitely not Akiko and the private jet. Her head leaned against a pillow with her hair shielding her face to a degree. Her mouth felt impossibly dry. She ached all over. Cold handcuffs held her wrists together. Tight bandages hugged her broken ribs. She wasn't wearing shoes and heavy manacles weighed against her ankles. Because of the bandages, she couldn't tell if they'd put a belt around her waist to keep her hands close to her body as well.

She could smell fresh shampoo in her hair, soap on her skin. She remembered turning away from Dyer's body to go after Peter Van de Moeter. She remembered Sinjin Doucet pointing a weapon at her. She remembered the pfft of a dart. Then nothing.

She risked opening her eyes a slit. The lights were off in the cabin, just a slight glow. It was nighttime. She was facing a window with the shade drawn. She suspected whoever had put her in the chair put her face that way on purpose. The only way she could assess her surroundings would be by moving her head; and, if she moved her head, they would know she was awake.

"Can I get you another coffee, Sir?" a woman's voice asked, her voice a little hushed as if there were sleeping passengers around her.

Alex bit her bottom lip. A flight attendant meant a commercial flight. A commercial flight limited her options which hadn't been many to begin with. She couldn't fly a plane, not a big commercial one and not a small one.

"No, I'm good," said a voice that Alex did not recognize.

"Does—Is--?"

"She's drugged up," the man said. "She'll be out long after we land in New York."

"What did she do?" the flight attendant asked. "I know I'm not supposed to ask, but---"

"International terrorist," the man replied. "One of the most brutal I've ever tracked down."

"Oh," the woman replied. "Are you with the FBI or something?"

"Homeland Security," the man said. "We don't normally transport dangerous criminals on commercial flights, but we have to get her back to New York for processing before we send her down to Git-mo."

"Oh my goodness," the woman exclaimed. "I think I'd be terrified of dealing with people like that all the time."

"It's a calling," the man replied.

Alex rolled her eyes.

"You're very brave," she said. "I'm scared of her and she's not even conscious."

"She's harmless right now," the man said.

Alex didn't see the poke in the ribs coming, but she felt it. Her body reacted before she could stop herself.

The man let out a yelp of surprise as his hand was caught, twisted and put into a control hold.

Alex would have broken the arm, but the chains and cuffs holding her stopped her short. She adapted in the blink of an eye; switching from the control hold to a manipulation hold and forcing the man's head into the seat in front of him.

The person in the seat ahead grunted awake with the jolt.

The flight attendant let out a squeak of horror.

The soldier who'd been assigned to babysit the unconscious prisoner, took advantage of Alex's short reach, the close space, and his superior strength. He reached over his body and grabbed her wrists. His elbow drove towards her face.

She twisted around to avoid the elbow. At the last minute, it lowered and hit her in the ribs.

The air flew out of her lungs. She released the guy's arm and curled towards the side of the plane, pulling her knees up a touch. There wasn't quite enough room to curl into a fetal position. She groaned and coughed. The cough made her ribs. She forced air through clenched teeth against the knifing pain in her gut.

The soldier grabbed her arm to twist her around.

Alex saw his fist pulling back for a blow to knock her back into unconsciousness. She wasn't going to be able to defend herself against it either. Not the first time she'd been shackled up and forced to take a blow. She eyed his fist with resignation.

The soldier hesitated. "I don't want to hurt you," he admitted.

Alex bit her bottom lip and eyed his fist hovering in the air. Behind him in the aisle, the man from the seat in front of him had risen to his feet.

Richard Powell had a hand on the elbow of the flight attendant. He wore a wrinkled blue dress shirt with the sleeves rolled up and a loosened yellow tie. Bags and dark rings under his eyes and stubble on his jaw suggested she'd been unconscious for a while. His eyes were red, lines traced down around the corners of his mouth.

275

He held a capped syringe in the hand resting on the back of the chair.

Alex swallowed against the panic that rose up in her at the sight of the syringe. A muscle in the right side of her jaw twitched.

The soldier's fist fell and he let go of her arm. "Easy," he said carefully.

Alex's eyes darted to him then back to the needle. She heard rattling and looked down to see her hand shaking. She made a fist to stop it.

"We're thirty thousand feet in the air, Alex," Powell said. "You are trapped."

Not a good thing to tell a person in danger of a panic attack. Alex felt sweat pop up on her forehead. Her breathing sped up to match her racing heart.

"No," the soldier told her. He reached over her.

His body over her made her shove herself back into the corner of the chair, as far away from him as possible. A slight whimper might have escaped her.

The man threw open the window shade and quickly backed off. "No panic attacks or flashbacks, not in this place," he told her. "Stay here, with me. Don't go all Twilight Zone on me, kid."

She managed a strangled laugh at the analogy. Outside dawn was breaking and the clouds were glowing beneath the plane. She didn't see a wing so she didn't see any little goblins pulling wires and trying to make the plane crash.

"Breathe," the soldier told her. He turned over his shoulder and said to Powell, "Put the needle away, Sir. It's a trigger for her flashbacks."

"She's faking them."

"She's not faking this one," the man replied. "I've got too many buddies in VA hospitals to be faked out."

Alex felt him move away from her, out of the seat. The space made it easier to breathe. She leaned forward, pressing her forehead against the seat back in front of her. Voices whispered in her head in a dozen languages. The plane seemed to fade in and out of her consciousness with the cave where she'd been held for six months. She fought the pull to the dark place; wishing she had Guang around and his steady, deep voice speaking to her.

The thought no sooner crossed her brain than she felt the Sword of Souls. Its cold fingers reached across the distance and squeezed her soul. One down. Two to go. Her fist tightened. She turned her head to look at the trio staring at her from the aisle: the flight attendant, the soldier, and Richard Powell.

The flight attendant stared with wide eyes, fear rolled off her in waves. She pressed against the man she'd been flirting with. The soldier held an unopened bottle of water out to her; condensation was starting form on the outside. He had lost interest in the woman and looked at her with both concern and pity. Richard Powell tried to look in control, but a hint of fear rolled off him. Alex figured he was the only one who had any concept of what might happen if she had a flashback and freaked out in the middle of a flight. He'd hidden the syringe; his hand was empty as if she'd only imagined it.

"Okay?" Powell asked.

The threat of a flashback had calmed. The Sword of Souls' hold on her grew stronger. Alex nodded. She glanced at her hand which was still shaking. Her eyes rolled from him to the bottled water.

Powell nodded. "Do you have a straw?" he asked the flight attendant.

She nodded and quickly moved towards the front of the plane, relieved to get out of the way.

Powell took the bottle and nodded at the soldier. "Take my seat."

The man made a face, but nodded.

Powell slid into the chair beside her. When the flight attendant brought a straw, he thanked her and asked her for food.

"Pretzels, chocolate chip cookies, or fruit?" she asked. "Breakfast will be served in about an hour."

Powell looked at Alex. He sighed. "How about one of each of those if you have them?" He opened the bottle of water and dropped the straw in it.

Alex took it from him. She still had to bend her head to reach the straw because her hands wouldn't come up high enough, but she didn't care. She sucked down water. The straw kept her from gulping it. She could always try the old "I-have-to-pee" thing when they got to the airport, but she had a feeling she'd be peeing with an audience. Her mind ran over escape options. They would be taking precautions to tighten up the weak spots—the transfer from the airplane to some other kind of transport would be the first one. Ideally, she wanted to take advantage of the transfer—she still had two people to kill.

The Sword of Souls growled in her blood.

She coughed on the water.

"Take it easy," Richard Powell said. "You'll make yourself sick. Do you want something to eat?"

Alex's stomach growled. She couldn't remember the last time she'd eaten. She'd skipped dinner to let Doucet take her to bed. Before that, she'd had lunch with Guang in a small temple where she couldn't eat with the monks and Guang had shocked the other monks by taking his plate and eating with her in a separate room, drawing several of the other monks with him. But the lunch had been sparse and when Guang had attempted to make her eat his portion, she'd refused. The days that followed up to this point were a blur.

Richard pushed the call button.

The flight attendant was there immediately, smiling at him while her eyes watched Alex warily.

"Do you have any meals left?"

"Of course," she said. "The beef or the chicken?"

Alex's stomach rolled at the thought of meat. Worse than meat was the thought of airplane meat. "I'm a vegetarian," she growled before Richard could answer.

Richard arched an eyebrow at her. "Since when?"

"Since someone used a blowtorch on my back and made me smell like a barbeque," she replied without breaking eye contact.

Color drained from Richard's carefully controlled face. He swallowed. "Do you have vegetarian meals?"

The woman nodded, apparently not believing the story or not comprehending it without the benefit of having watched Peter Van de Moeter's edited digital copy of her torture. She moved back to the front of the first-class area. She returned quickly with a tray that offered a salad, a roll, fruit, and pasta with a red sauce and mushrooms.

Richard pulled the tray out for her and set the tray on it and her water. With a second thought, he took the plastic silverware, opened it and took the fork and knife from it before returning it.

Alex eyed him. "You want me to eat a salad with a spoon?" she asked.

"Yes, I do."

"I don't need a plastic utensil to kill someone," she said.

"Probably not the best thing to say in your situation."

"I can't fly the plane," she replied. She used the spoon to launch a grape up in the air and caught it in her mouth.

"Good to know. Not sure if I believe you."

"I'm not sure where you think I might have found the time. You've been watching me since I was twenty years old." She saw something flitter across his eyes. "Wow, earlier than that?" She managed to get some pasta on the spoon and took a bite before it fell off. Actually, she'd known he'd been close to identifying Chen Sakai as an infamous assassin—from the paperwork in his desk. He'd found her by mistake; probably a flag on her forged high school paperwork to get into college after Sakai died.

Richard Powell frowned, turned away from her and reclined his seat.

Alex concentrated on the food and used the movement to disguise her test of exactly how much movement she had with all the shackles. The waist chain wasn't a chain at all but a thick leather belt with a metal loop sewn into it to hold her wrist shackles to the center of her body. She watched the people who moved down the aisle to and from what she assumed was a restroom nearer the front of the plane. Not a single one of them managed to not stare at her while at the same time trying not to stare. She kept her hair down over her face to keep them from getting a good look. As she finished, someone walked by and hesitated. She froze. Her fist tightened on the spoon. Her head turned around the veil of dark red hair and looked up at the person standing at the end of the row of chairs.

Her sudden tension made Powell open his eyes. He looked from her to the aisle where Peter Van de Moeter stood. His hand went to his pocket where he probably had stashed the needle. Alex had every intention of shoving it in his eye if he attempted to take it out.

The thin Van de Moeter wore khaki pants and a pastel green shirt. Unlike Richard Powell, he looked like he'd just ironed everything. His pale face showed no signs of stress or long nights. He smiled. His short blonde hair was perfectly coifed without a hair out of place. He stood straighter and ran his long-fingered hand down over his beige silk tie. His long tongue flickered out to wet his thin lips.

Alex let the spoon drop back onto the tray.

"What are you doing?" Richard growled at Peter.

The soldier in the seat in front of Powell stood up. His eyes on Alex; his hand hidden under his jacket.

Doucet stood up from the seat across the aisle from the soldier. His dark eyes locked with Alex's. He couldn't stand up straight in the middle of the aisle he was so tall.

"Need to use the loo," he replied with false innocence. "I thought you had that monster sedated for the entire trip. You're putting us law-abiding citizens at risk."

Alex's first instinct was to pick up the tray and throw it at him. Her temper shot into high gear. She wanted to rage against the restraints holding her prisoner. She wanted to wrap the chains around his neck and watch his face turn blue and his tongue fly out of his mouth. A dozen other ways he could die filtered through her brain. She could do it; she could launch out of her seat and break his neck before Richard Powell could get the syringe out of his pocket. The soldier probably had a taser in his jacket, he couldn't risk shooting a bullet in a pressurized cabin filled with civilians. But the end result would leave her unconscious again. She was tired of being unconscious.

The Sword of Souls shivered against the restraint. Somewhere in the back of her mind, Alex was aware that whoever was watching the sheathed weapon had woken up and was staring at it in the darkness, unsure of what had woken him up. That it wasn't Guang surprised her a little. But she knew that DJ would be tracking her on this plane and would already know her destination.

Peter smiled at her, gloating.

"Get the fuck out of here," Doucet said, reaching out to drag Peter forward.

Peter arched an eyebrow at Doucet. "Please do not touch me, Captain. As an upstanding member of society with no blemishes on my record, you can understand my misgivings about being forced to keep company with a murderer who is getting away with her crimes because she slept with you." He looked back at Alex, his smile getting wider. "That's what is wrong with this country; too many violent criminals allowed to breathe the fresh air of freedom."

Alex smiled back at him. He might as well enjoy breathing because he wouldn't be doing it much longer.

The Sword of Souls called her closer.

His smile faded. He swallowed and licked his lips.

"Alex," Powell warned softly.

She dropped her gaze from Peter and met Powell's.

"He's turning over names and places. You know we can't turn that away."

Alex knew what information Peter possessed to broker a deal: her father's network. Peter had most of that legitimately, too. But it felt like he was killing her father all over again.

There were people who had saved her father's life and protected her while she was growing up, there were safe houses and weapons caches and people who could forge documents or get weapons in almost every part of the world. Her father owed these people as much as they owed him. When Alex sold Peter's name to Interpol to make sure he stayed in the country, she'd known these dangerous people would be on alert. Some of them, the smarter ones, would already have implemented their contingent plans and escaped. But some of them would not be able to run.

The ones in the East would be calling on the Sword of Souls with requests; because that was the network that the Offspring had established. They wouldn't know that Joe McBrady and the Sword of Souls converged. The ones in Europe and South America would put a price on Peter's head, a dozen or more high bounties at the very least. That made Peter a job which an assassin could use for retirement, the last job of their careers. They would hunt him and the United States thought they could protect him.

"How many lives are you willing to sacrifice for those names?" Alex asked Powell. "How many have you sacrificed because you thought you could control me?"

"You know the game and so do the men and women who work for me. They know what the price might be."

Alex lifted up her cuffs. "I bet they don't, Powell. I bet they have no idea what you're sending them out to face."

Peter Van de Moeter laughed. "What they face? A shackled and broken woman who depended on her daddy to save her ass? That's real scary."

"Remember," Richard told her. "You can't fly the plane."

Alex smiled at him, cold and dangerous. "And you can't keep it up in the air forever."

He shifted slightly.

Alex felt her body get very calm, she felt the cold sear through her. "How fast do you think you are, Powell?" she asked him.

He carefully took his hand out of his pocket and showed her that it was empty. "Move along, Peter."

Alex swallowed bile as he moved forward. She shoved the remaining food away.

"Alex, you need to understand," Powell said. "I had to do this.

Alex turned away and stared out the window. She listened to the voices in her head, the ancient ones, the angry ones, the teachers, the fighters, the killers, the saviors. She let the anger get cold and hard. She promised herself that Peter Van de Moeter would not live long, not if she had to strangle him with the chains holding her captive, not if she had to use her teeth to pull out his throat.

CHAPTER NINETEEN

The plane headed into New York for an early morning landing. Alex watched the cars and buildings get bigger as it descended. She'd stared out the window as the sky grew lighter and the Sword of Souls grew closer. The sky looked clear and blue. The Sword was waiting for her. It made her calm.

Richard Powell had attempted to get her to talk. He'd talked a lot about his excuses for letting Peter Van de Moeter be free and for putting her in shackles.

She ignored him.

Powell eventually gave up. He switched seats with Sinjin.

The Marine tried to put his hand on her knee.

She pulled it away.

He sighed. "Alex, I know you're upset, *cher*," he said with his heavy Cajun accent rolling through his words. "I'm sorry about Frank. I had no idea he sold you out to Peter. If I had— well, things would be different."

Alex wondered how things would be different. More than likely Frank would be alive too—her father would still be dead. She mourned the loss of the man she'd considered family, but that man had never really existed. In a new light, she saw the envy sketched on his face. She adored her father. Part of her realized that he wasn't a great man. She'd watched him kill in cold blood. He hit women. He drank too much, he smoked pot. He took her to places that no one should ever take a little girl. But he would die for her—hell, he had died for her.

She felt her eyes start to well up. She closed her eyes and buried the grief. Not yet. She took a deep shaky breath. Let Doucet think it was about Frank. Fuck them all. She shifted in her seat. The chains rattled as if she were some cast member of a production of *A Christmas Carol*. Instead of her father, she thought of the Sword. She listened to its call. She felt the chains it used to bind her soul. Ice cold chains that scarred and froze, but at the same time promised power and held the skill of a thousand years of martial arts training. Shackles in exchange for power. It would be a sacrifice many would make. Alex had made it in order to survive long enough to kill Peter and the man pulling his strings. She pushed away the other gifts the weapon promised. Life was all she'd ever wanted, not power or more skill. Just life.

Peter sat somewhere behind her. She imagined his smug face reflected in an oval airplane window, watching the dawn of a chilly March day in New York City. The iconic city stretched out behind the airport. She wondered if Peter was imagining breakfast in some fancy restaurant, maybe being put up by the CIA in some five star hotel room. All those pleasant thoughts flittering through his evil head. He'd stood over her father's body and watched him die. He'd raped her over and over while she bled and hurt from broken bones and electrocution. He raped her until the fresh clothes he'd demanded she be dressed in before the rapes were soaked with bright red blood.

She took a deep slow breath, the kind she used to do when she was faking meditation. Her mind wasn't designed for calm. It raced, constantly. Always had. For as long as she could remember. The pent-up energy. Meditation had been torturous—before she understood what torture really was.

She'd learned to fake it in places where the slightest fidget would earn one a smack with a split bamboo staff. Now she grabbed onto the thought and wished it would silence the cries for blood in her head. She yearned for peace. But two-thirds of her target remained. First Peter. Then the man behind it all. Then she could sleep.

Doucet changed seats with Powell again.

Powell looked at her. "You're going to behave," he said, as if speaking to a child.

She wanted to ask him what he planned for her if she didn't. She was shackled and imprisoned and surrounded by armed men who would kill her if she stepped out of line. No one was on her side.

The tires of the plane hit the runway smoothly. Around the cabin, people started to fidget. The sound of a couple of seatbelts coming loose. Jump up, grab your bag out of the overhead bin, race to be first, end up waiting as people left row by row.

Alex ran through *kata* in her mind, her muscles remembering the moves even when she couldn't make them. This was the meditation she'd found rather than empty mind. *Kata* helped to calm the boiling anger. The *kata*, the structured moves of the martial arts, helped escape the torture. The close proximity of the Sword of Souls fed her rage. She'd read in the forbidden journals locked away in Hiroo, Japan, that the Sword brought considerable rage to whoever held it. The Offspring had been created to keep the intermittent holders of the weapon from going on murderous rampages. They'd been the buffer to control the surge of anger and to protect the people that the Sword of Souls was created to protect. However, they thought they controlled the Sword now. It'd been so long since the weapon had felt the touch of its master.

It called out to her.

Her blood answered. It vibrated in her veins.

She tried to deny it. She wanted to finish this and then to rest.

She wouldn't let the Offspring control her. She would die before she became a slave. To the Offspring. To the Sword of Souls. To a legend she did not believe in. One mission. One mission, revenge, and then a trip to the place she called home for sleep. Eternal sleep. Drifting infinite in the halls of the dead. Escape the pain of living.

The plane taxied up to a gate. Richard Powell stayed seated.

Alex felt eyes on her as all the civilians filed out of the plane. She stared out the window. A crew of three Asians drove a truck around, trying to look important. The flight attendant's voice was canned cheer as she wished all the passengers a good day and to enjoy New York City.

Alex kept her face hidden from the passengers and from everyone. She was afraid Powell and the others who knew her would see the surge of power in her eyes.

Powell helped her hide. He didn't want her face filling the minds of a bunch of civilians either.

She could have laughed out loud at his delusions of still having her go to work for him. She'd decimated his office and cut off the head of one of the best Marines in the Division of Anti-Terrorist Activities. Would the CIA be stupid enough to still put her on the pay roll? She wondered what they had for leverage to control her. She glanced around Powell to Doucet in the seat across the aisle.

He looked back and offered her a compassionate smile. The kind of smile that a lover might give a person they cared about. Alex wondered when he'd realize she'd used him. She wondered if his ego would ever allow him to accept that; she didn't think so.

Perhaps she was insane. The mumbled ancient voices swirled in her head, whispers she couldn't quite understand. Insanity would explain a lot. The Sword felt like a lover's touch in her mind. It fed the anger and stood behind her. It didn't care about right and wrong, governments or politics. It didn't even care about good and evil. That's where the Offspring were wrong when they thought it was a power for good. The Sword of Souls fought for balance, not good.

287

When everyone had disembarked, Powell stood up. He stepped aside and two soldiers moved in to position.

Doucet exchanged a look with Powell before he got off the plane. Peter with two guards of his own moved behind the soldier who'd taken up position at the end of Alex's aisle.

There was another soldier standing back a few rows, his weapon drawn and pointing at Alex's head.

"Stand up," ordered the goon at the end of the aisle.

"Be careful," Powell warned them.

The men were professionals. Their eyes watched. One stood back a few paces with his hand on his weapon. The other stood at the end of Alex's row, blocking any fast exit.

"Get up," the one at the end ordered again. He had a thick East Texas accent.

Alex sighed. The voices in her head rumbled with anticipation like an army's tense whispers before the first shot of battle. The Sword of Souls was close, so close, she could feel it, she could taste it. It sang in her blood, it fed her lungs, it pumped the blood through her heart. She let it loose.

Free reign for the monster that lived inside her.

It rejoiced. It stretched.

The anger boiled over into steam. Releasing it would be a relief.

"Follow their orders and they won't hurt you," Powell told her. "They're under orders to kill you if you do anything out of the ordinary."

Alex met his gaze. She didn't know what he saw in her eyes; but, she knew she'd lifted the veil that she'd used since returning from the dead. She'd died in an alley, of injuries she shouldn't have survived anyway, of withdrawal from heroin. She'd traded her soul for the chance to kill Peter Van de Moeter and the man behind her father's betrayer. What Powell saw was the last thing Frank Dyer had seen before she cut off his head, the thing that the mercenaries had seen in that house where Peter had tried to torture her again.

The color drained from Powell's face. "Gentlemen, do not underestimate her," he reiterated.

Alex smirked at the tremor in his voice. She tested the length of the chains as she slowly rose to her feet. She did it in an obvious way. The chains rattled. She wanted everyone tensed up. Tension made them fall back to muscle memory, to their training. It made them predictable.

Adrenalin made their pupils grow. The marshals controlled their faces, keeping them calm and stoic. They were men accustomed to the adrenalin dump. They were accustomed to working through it. Their bodies worked on instinct.

"Trying something would be really stupid," the guy at the end of the aisle said. "I don't care what kind of super ninja you are, you're not going to stop a bullet."

Alex stepped towards him on her socks. The leg irons rattled, the wrist cuffs were limiting.

"We should move her hands behind her back," the marshal told his partner. "While we're in a confined space."

Alex lifted her wrists up as high as they would go, offering them to the marshals.

"Do not remove her restraints," Powell growled. "Jesus, let's just get her down in one of the cars and get out of here."

The lead marshal rolled his eyes. He grabbed Alex's arm and pulled her out of the aisle. She stumbled slightly, for effect, and banged her leg against the armrest at the aisle. A bruise on her thigh was a small price to pay for getting the leg irons in the right position to be removed, with the welded area of the chain to the outside.

She tried to lean down to rub her thigh and get the wrist cuffs twisted as well, but the marshal lifted her arm and kept her from bending down.

He spun her around to the front of the plane and put a big hand on her shoulder. The muzzle of his weapon pressed against her spine in the small of her back. "We're going to take this real slow," he told her in an even voice. "Start walking." He had a strong grip, the grip of a man accustomed to working with his hands.

Alex yawned. She shuffled forward slowly so she didn't twist the leg cuff out of position.

The flight attendant stood back in the first-class galley. The door to the cockpit had been opened. The crew all looked back down the aisle, eyes curious. Alex noted that none of them could fathom why she was so dangerous. She didn't look all that dangerous. Not dressed in the orange clothes and cuffed up. Hardly a need at all for all the heightened security. They rolled their eyes at each other.

A Division operative with a machine gun stood in the telescopic tunnel. He wore all black and a helmet hiding his face. He blocked off the tunnel to the airport where all the civilians had gone.

"Turn right," the marshal ordered.

Alex did and pushed through a door to stairs that led down.

Cold air blasted her face. She felt the breath ripped from her lungs. Not because of the cold, but because of the sword. It'd been stuck on the inside of the portable stairway which had been put up to the door of the telescopic walkway, right on the inside of the handrail. The Sword of Souls. Invisible to anyone else. She saw it before she saw anything else. The dawn shadows hiding it further.

Alex glanced around and noted the snipers on the roof above the gate. A trio of armed men stood down at the bottom of the stairs as well all armed with submachine guns. Three black SUVs had been parked. All the major players stood around in the space between the bottom of the stairs and the vehicles, which blocked the wind: Sinjin Doucet, Richard Powell, and Peter Van de Moeter. All looking confident and in control. The wind flipped her hair over her face.

She shook it away and used the movement to scan the rest of the area. The crew sitting in a food service vehicle waiting for the prisoner unloading were all Asians. A big tarp had been hung over the windows so that no one in the gate could watch the little show of force. Alex stopped at the edge of the top step.

"Go down," the marshal said. He had to raise his voice above the wind. The cold added a tremor to his stress level.

The air tasted like jet fuel. Alex breathed through her mouth.

Alex lifted her jaw slightly to signal the Asians as she glanced over her shoulder at the marshal. The move was subtle, but she knew who was in that van. "I don't have enough chain in the leg irons," she said. "I can't get down without falling."

"Yeah?" the guy said without sympathy. "That's too bad. I hear you're an athlete. Hop."

"I'm going to fall," Alex told him. "I've had a bad few days. My legs are tired."

"The tarmac will catch you. Try not to break your neck on the way down." He shoved her with his weapon for emphasis.

Alex took a step down and faked a fall. She grabbed the sword on the way down. She tumbled head over heels. The Sword flashed free. The side of the stairway blocked her from the snipers.

The wrist cuffs came off first, the chain sparking as the Sword bit it into two pieces. Her legs were free by the time she hit the bottom and rolled up to her feet.

The roll put Doucet and the three armed men between her and the snipers.

The red dots of laser sights shone on their clothing, moving and trying to find a path to Alex.

"She's got a sword!" Doucet yelled at the men who were still at the top of the stairs, the only people who still had a clear line of fire. However, the big .45 round would go right through her and slam into Powell or Peter.

They didn't shoot.

Alex grinned.

Richard Powell moved between Alex and Peter. He held up his hands. But his hands shook. "Alex, stop."

Peter turned and ran towards the SUV.

The Sword whipped through the air near Powell.

Powell ducked to get away. A look of surprise and shock on his face. Alex didn't care. If he'd ducked in the wrong direction, she would have killed him. She didn't intend to have more than one casualty here; but, she wouldn't lose sleep about killing people who got in her way. Fortunately for him, he ducked in the correct anticipated direction. She punched Powell in the temple, the motion caused the strand of heavy chain to slap across his pretty face and break his nose.

Powell and his tailored suit went down like she'd ripped all the bones out of his body. Richard Powell hadn't been designed for physical battle.

Alex stepped over his body, ignoring the yells to stop. She grabbed the back of Peter's pastel suit and hauled him around so that he was between her and the guns. The only thing behind her now were the empty SUVs and the truck with the Asian crew in blue jumpsuits.

Peter held his hands up. "Alex! I didn't kill Joe! I didn't kill him. It wasn't me. I just did what I was told! I didn't have a choice—"

The Sword sliced through the air. Light flashed off it in a strong blue. The flash distracted. The Sword flung blood over the tarmac and over the Marines standing around.

Peter frowned and looked down at himself. His brow furrowed. "What the—" he began.

Then blood poured from his mouth.

He'd been cut from right shoulder to left hip in a diagonal.

His top half started to slide off the bottom half as his legs realized they didn't have any orders any longer.

Peter's eyes were wide in horror. His hands tried to stop the slide from happening.

Alex watched.

Gun fire.

A bullet hit the SUV behind her. She moved as Peter's twitching body smacked the tarmac next to Powell's unconscious body. A wave of blood and guts rolled out of Peter.

Some of the Division men lifted their visors on their helmets to throw up.

Alex slid between two of the SUVs.

The van's panel opened.

Two guys with machine guns stepped out.

Alex hurried between them as they riddled the CIA transportation with bullets. Alex sat down next to Guang.

"Go! Go! Go!" one of the two gunman yelled at the driver as the other man pulled the van door shut. "Keep the plane between you and the snipers."

Guang shook his head.

Alex grinned.

"It's an honor to meet you," the man with the gun said. "Are you injured?"

The van threw the around. Bullets pinged off the outside.

Alex arched an eyebrow.

"Armor," he said. "Guang-daishi is a very persuasive advocate for your cause."

She eyed Guang.

He shrugged. "I told them you were insane and needed protection from yourself." He reached forward and grabbed her jaw, forcing her to make eye contact. "I'm not far off. They have a doctor along with their skills."

She pulled out of his grip. "All I need is sleep and some food," she said.

Guang arched an eyebrow. "That would be a good start, American."

"We have a safe house set up for you," the leader of the van said.

"Who are you?" Alex asked. "What did my venerable advocate promise?"

The man smiled. "The current royal family has served among the Offspring for many generations. Five hundred years ago, the current king's relative supported the implementation of the Rule of Sevens. He later came to the understanding that the person they disliked so much and thought was a menace and a reckless fool was in fact the True One." He paused. "The royal family has carried that guilt around for generations. The Offspring have never taken the feelings of the family into account."

Alex frowned at Guang.

He shrugged. His dark eyes glittered with amusement. "A menace. A reckless fool. Someone people dislike. You're perfect for the job."

"I'm not the True One," she said. "I'm just..." Her voice trailed off. She shook her head. "I'm just a menace."

"It is said the True One will deny the truth. It is said the True One will try to thrust away the power."

Alex narrowed her eyes. "Where does it say that?"

Guang chuckled. "You think you read all the secret texts when you were sneaking into the library in Hiroo, American? Your child-self was much like you are now—impatient and impetuous. You only read the exciting stuff."

Alex bit her bottom lip.

"The royal family hopes this will be a step towards absolution," the man explained.

Alex noticed that the other man was staring at her with glazed awe. She mumbled something under her breath.

The man frowned. "What was that?"

"She says that of course it does. However, there is a faction within the Offspring who still deny," Guang said. He grumbled at Alex in his native tongue. "Go sit in the corner and pout. Akiko worked this out."

"This is..." She sighed and switched to English. "You're native tongue doesn't have a word for bullshit," she said.

The leader of the group smiled thoughtfully. "She is not what I expected," he said to Guang.

"That's part of her charm," Guang replied in a dry voice which indicated just the opposite. "Sometimes I think the weapon which cannot be named chose a Westerner just to torture the rest of us."

"The gods have been known to have a sense of humor," the man agreed.

"You both realize that I can kick both your asses, right?" Alex grumbled.

"Full of anger too," the man observed. "Has she always been this way?"

"No. The anger only came after she admitted to needing the power of the weapon. Before then it seems she effectively ignored it."

"Which only the True One could have done," the man said, nodded at Guang.

Alex was relieved that the van came to a stop.

The man handed Alex a bag. "Clothing," he said. "Per Ms. Tanaka's directions. We will wait outside the van for you to change, then another vehicle will take you to the safe house." He opened the door and he, his fellow gunman and the driver got out.

Alex sighed at Guang. "You going to stay to watch?"

"Do you need help?" he asked.

Alex started to snap at him, but he moved before she could. He grabbed her arm and shoved up the sleeve.

Her arm was covered in bruises, some old, some new.

"Rolling down a flight of stairs while restrained will do that to you," he said.

"Most of it isn't from the stairs," she said, before she could stop herself. She grimaced at her words and looked away from.

He frowned. His callused hand reached up and touched her face. He brushed a lock of hair off her forehead and sighed. When he spoke, all the mirth and sarcasm had left. He spoke in his native language. "Never in my life have I met someone who will sacrifice so much for what they believe in. Let go of the burden long enough to recover for this fight you intend to pursue. When do you schedule this great battle of yours?"

She stared at him. She thought about denying what she'd done. "There is no option to avoid this," she said. "This is the price I pay for being alive long enough to avenge my father."

Guang nodded. "The price is high."

"Things worth dying for are never sold cheaply."

"You don't expect to live through this fight."

"I shouldn't be alive to have it, Guang."

He frowned. He shook his head. "You can survive."

"I already sold my soul. There's nothing left to sell."

"When?"

"Two days."

"Two days of rest, then. Two days of solitude. Two days in the temple. Clear your mind. Prepare."

Alex nodded. "That's the plan. I want to make a good show of it."

Guang grimaced. "You look tired."

Before she could respond, Guang dropped his hand. He turned and left the van.

Alex stared after him for a minute, then opened the bag.

CHAPTER TWENTY

Alexandria Rae McBrady stepped out of the van and eyed the limousine. It had diplomatic plates. The man in the chauffer uniform stood beside the soldiers, there was a bulge of a weapon under his jacket. His eyes went to the sheathed sword that she carried. Her hand wrapped around the worn spot without thought. The strap that held it on her back dangled alongside her denim clad leg. The cold breeze off the Atlantic blew strands of long hair across her face like bloody claw marks.

It must have been tough for Akiko Tanaka to choose the clothing that she had delivered—nothing fashionable or name brand. The CEO had one guilty pleasure. She loved to shop for clothes. She'd tried to make Alex into her life-sized Barbie on more than one occasion. However, what Alex wore could have been something that she'd picked out herself. Black boots, expensive enough to feel comfortable immediately—the boots probably cost more than twice as much as the rest of the clothes combined, Alex figured. She had thick socks, jeans which hugged her body more than normal, but were denim combined with some stretch woven in so they allowed for full movement. Panties and a matching bra, in white lace. A gray, long-sleeved t-shirt and an insulated black hoodie completed her outfit.

The driver glanced away from the weapon and looked at the leader of the team that had rescued her from the CIA. They were on an abandoned dock, at the edge of the water. The city surrounded them.

Alex's hand flexed on the weapon; she felt its energy seep into her. She stared at the city behind, the smell of the water and car fumes filled the air. She walked around behind the limo to the edge of the water. Starbucks cups, water bottles, other unidentifiable stuff floated in the water. The sea wall supports for the dock were coated in white frost. She inhaled deeply. The cold stung her nose.

Without thinking, she swung the sword over her shoulder, the strap over her head to hold the weapon perpendicular across her back.

Behind her, she heard the men gasp. She heard one of them make low rapid comments, agitated, afraid.

Alex didn't listen to the words or strive to hear them. She tilted her head back and let the rising morning sun add some warmth to her skin. She closed her eyes and felt the cold steel in her bones. Road weary. Exhaustion threatening. She was afraid to go to sleep. Afraid of the dreams. But she couldn't remember when she'd slept, even tried to sleep. Unconsciousness and drugged stupors didn't count. Her body had reached its limit. Her task was done. The only thing left was the chore that had been her bargain.

"Alex," Guang's voice said, breaking through whatever reverie she'd found.

She opened her eyes and pivoted back to face the group.

The armed driver walked to the back door of the limo and opened it.

Alex walked back to the group. She bowed to the leader, forgoing the Western handshake. "Thank you. I will not forget your help."

"We are fulfilling our obligations," the man said bowing lower than her bow, a bow of reverence.

Alex winced at it.

The man rose and met her eyes directly. He shivered as if he felt the cold in her bones. "And alleviating a debt."

"Debts die with bodies," she said. "As far as I'm concerned, I owe you and the royal family." I bowed again.

He smiled and held out his hand.

Alex shook it.

"Save travels, *Sensei*," he said in English.

"I'm just Alex," she said. "Chen Sakai was the teacher."

He nodded. Then turned and ordered his men to the van.

Alex turned to Guang as they drove away. She gestured for him to head to the limo.

He entered first. He was a monk and the society they were keeping demanded it.

Alex didn't much care about chivalry. She felt a weariness in her bones. Even the chill of the Sword felt dull. The voices in her head yawned. She followed the monk into the back of the vehicle.

The driver shut the door.

Alex slid over the leather seats, letting herself sink into the cushioning. She felt Guang staring at her. Closed her eyes and let herself relax. Sleep wouldn't come. "Stop staring at me," she said as the vehicle started to move.

"You think you're going to die," Guang said.

"We're all going to die, Guang."

"You know what I mean. This fight you have planned. You think you are going to die. You really believe that you will die in two days."

"One person with a sword against seven men with guns," she said with a yawn. She didn't open her eyes, but shifted on the bench seat so she could stretch her legs out and lean her head against the back of the seat. "The math is pretty simple."

"How can you be so calm about this? When you've spent the last three months plotting and planning and drinking and suffering?" Guang said, his voice getting louder.

Alex opened her eyes and looked at him. She saw the driver glancing in the rear view mirror. He quickly looked away. "I'm tired, Guang," she said. Her hoarse voice was heavy with exhaustion. "But I don't want to die. I want to go home first. To the jungle."

"You should be passed out from exhaustion."

"So what's the problem?"

"You acted the part with those men back there."

"What part?"

"The part you don't want. It's not like you to grant absolution."

Alex stifled a yawn. She sank down in the seat. "I did what I came back to do," she said. "Now I just have to pay the tab, Guang."

"You're not going to die."

Alex sighed. "Do you really think I'll live like a slave? You know."

"I know what?"

"You know that there are…" she paused and furrowed her brow, searching for the right words. "You know there are things which cannot be explained."

"I have always believed that."

"It might be reasonable to assume those things are stronger and more powerful than anything we know; right?"

He narrowed his eyes. "They are greater than us," he agreed, choosing his words carefully.

"Fighting them would be futile, right?"

Guang narrowed his eyes. "When have you not fought? When has the idea of futility ever stopped you?"

Alex grimaced, crossed her arms over her chest, and snuggled into the seat. Sleep came quickly this time, sucking her under. The sleep was more than unconsciousness. Her body needed it and it collapsed into it with a sigh of relief. A dreamless sleep.

Hours later, when the dream came, it was not or torture or rape or reliving the pain.

She walked through a field. Mist rose from the ground and hid what lay beyond the gray-white clouds. She could feel the cool chill of the mist against her face. She held her hands out as she walked, spreading her fingers and letting her palms face forward so the mist touched them.

She breathed in deeply. The air smelled like wet trees, like a rain forest clearing first thing in the morning, that moment just before the heat kicked in, like the foothills of the Himalayas. Beneath the smell of the wilderness was something musky and woodsy and smoky. It was familiar and evoked a kind of craving that calmed her in the very pit of her soul. It wasn't unlike the effect of heroin.

The thick grass would have cushioned the fall of her boots to a dull thud; but she didn't make sound when she walked. With a straight back and squared shoulders, she took long strides into the unknown. The mist folding back from her passage as she moved. Her body seemed relaxed, but contained at the same time; like a big cat stalking through a jungle.

She felt things around her, surrounding her. Her eyes searched the white mist.

"Where are you?" she yelled out. Her voice felt hollow, but it wasn't scratchy or hoarse. It travelled through the emptiness with its lilting mélange of Asian and Western accents. Silence replied.

In front of her, the white mist got a little darker.

Alex picked up her pace.

A child's giggle.

Alex started to run.

The giggle got louder, surrounding her.

A log lay across the ground in front of Alex. It appeared out of the mist suddenly. She leaped over it just in time.

More logs appeared.

Alex didn't slow.

The logs got bigger.

She ran, breathing hard now. She went from hurtling the logs to vaulting over them. Then suddenly, a brick wall appeared.

She skidded to a stop. She leaned her back against it to catch her breath.

The wall disappeared.

She fell onto the wet grass.

"No fair," she said as the mist swirled around her.

"Did someone promise you fairness?" asked a voice.

Alex sighed. She stretched out spread eagle. "One can hope."

"Sorry."

"You don't sound sincere."

"Probably because I'm not."

"Why am I here?"

"You came. We didn't call. Perhaps you want to hear the agony of your tormentors as their souls—"

"Stop," Alex said. "Don't ruin my good mood." She closed her eyes and sucked in another deep breath. The white mist seemed to scrub her lungs and her soul. She could imagine that anyway. She didn't expect her soul would ever be scrubbed clean of all the blood stains.

"We fulfilled our promise to you."

"Two days," Alex said. "In two days, I will pay you. I need two days."

"Being alive has its drawbacks. Why two days?"

"Sleep. And to get my head in the right place," she said. "Killing Peter. Flushing out Frank Dyer. They weren't equipped to fight me."

"They were unworthy opponents. But collateral damage has always been necessary in the hunt for the blackest souls. And for corruption of the whitest ones."

"Good thing the world comes in colors," she said.

"Yes. Good thing."

Alex lifted her head and looked at the mist. "Is that sarcasm?" she asked. "Can you even do that?"

A child's giggle.

The mist sighed.

"You know, I almost felt sorry for your suffering. The suffering of the past, the suffering yet to come."

"There's only so much suffering I can do in two days," she said.

"The battle comes in two days. If you are so certain you will lose, why do you take two days to prepare?"

"Ego. I ant to put up a good fight."

"And what if your fight is so good that you win?"

"Statistically unlikely."

The mist laughed. "Statistically? You want to talk statistics? Really? When you've defied them your entire life?"

Alex scratched at the scar on her stomach. The ones that spelled out the ancient text. "Seven against one."

"It's a rule created by mankind, not by nature. You are a creature of nature."

"I am human."

"You are human," the voice agreed. "More trials await you. This is not the last."

"I will fight the seven. I gave you my word. That's all."

"The fight is not the trial; it is the payment. The trial you can see with the scars on your skin. I will take the nightmares from you. I will leave the scars as a reminder of the tests to come. When you pass the last test, I will take the scars as well."

"I'm not doing any more tests," she said, angrily. She rolled up to her feet. "One. I promised one!" She pointed her finger at nothing.

Suddenly, the ground beneath her was gone. She fell. She tried to grab something, but there was only mist.

She woke up with arms flailing. For a minute, she was disoriented and didn't know where she was. Her muscles were on alert in defense. The room smelled like incense, thick sandalwood and jasmine and sage and something unidentifiable but familiar. Sucking in a lungful of it was reflex.

She glanced around the room, squinting against a pounding headache which throbbed inside her skull. With a groan, she turned her stiff body and got off the bed, rubbing sleep out of her eyes and stretching out the stiffness. She was in a small bedroom with a twin bed. A tall narrow dresser sat against one wall. The room had no windows, but, a nightlight was plugged into the wall to provide enough of a glow to see.

Alex had been laying on top of the covers of the bed. She still wore the clothing that she'd been given in the van. Absently, she smoothed out the wrinkles and stood up. Memory of getting into the room didn't come to her; last thing she remembered was falling asleep in the limo. She rubbed her face again and stifled another yawn.

The door was only a few steps from the bed and she was surprised to find it unlocked. A door across the hall was open, revealing a tiny bathroom with a shower, a toilet and a pedestal sink. The toilet seemed elaborate with buttons along the side for various functions. A short hallway led to a living room area and an open kitchen area. There were windows at the end of the room. Alex squinted against the light which shot through her head like a knife.

In one corner of the room a small alcove held a Buddha statue and several items for a small household shrine. Guang meditated in front of it. His eyes were closed. He didn't move although Alex was certain he was aware of her presence.

She walked to the fridge and opened it. Inside were shelves of bottled water and nothing else. She frowned and grabbed a bottle. Turning as she opened it, she noticed a note on the counter. It was written in Japanese, in a female's delicate, crisp hand. Alex wondered if Guang could read Japanese. She assumed he could because he spoke it well enough, but she'd never thought to ask. She sighed and opened a drawer under the phone hanging on the wall.

Take out menus filled the drawer. Alex sucked on water while she glanced through them. She picked out two which looked good and picked up the phone.

It automatically connected.

A woman answered, *"Moshi moshi!"* Her voice was friendly and cheerful. Alex imagined some tiny Japanese girl in a cubical somewhere with Hello Kitty pencils everywhere.

"*Moshi moshi*," Alex responded. She leaned back against the counter and asked if she could order food for delivery like the letter on the counter indicated. The girl on the other end of the phone gushed that she would order anything Alex required. Alex ordered. She was hungry. She ordered for Guang too, vegetarian. She was hungry for meat though. Then she told the woman on the other end to wait ten minutes and order the exact same order again fro a different place.

The woman told her that she would call back when the delivery was ready.

Alex thanked her and hung up the phone. She chugged the rest of the water and went back for another bottle. She opened it and walked to the window. Between the buildings she could see Central Park and the stretches of water that divided the island. Rubbing her temple, she stared out at the city as the shadows stretched and the lights started to twinkle on. Reflected in the glass, she could see the shape of Guang sitting behind her.

With a straight back, he appeared as still as a statue. He wore the orange robes of his station, his uniform. Alex wondered how hard he'd had to fight to stay in this small space with her. Monks weren't supposed to mix with females. But she'd known why he'd stayed. He'd stayed to protect everyone on the other side of the door beside the fridge, the door that led out of this small apartment. She had a habit of waking up badly, still caught in the throes of nightmares.

Guang moved. His robes made a soft shuffling noise in the silence. He stood up in an easy, smooth motion and turned to her. "Are you okay?" he asked. He saw some of his old friend in front of him. He could see it in the set of her shoulders, in the easy way her arms and feet rested with her completely still body. She could be all motion and blurring speed and she could be more still than anyone Guang had ever met. Even the masters of the temple where he'd grown up and trained had never exhibited this stillness. Worse, she was unaware of it, completely and totally unaware. When she tried to meditate, at least as a child, she'd been hopelessly fidgeting.

When she turned to face him, her eyes lit on him. He felt a shiver as the light caught the colored sparkles of glitter floating in her eyes, like some internal power source. He could see the darkness too. Not as haunted and scared as it had been, but not gone completely. He knew there had been something about the sleep she'd fallen into in the vehicle. She hadn't so much as fallen as been sucked down into. He'd carried her up here and she hadn't so much as fluttered her eyes on the verge of waking up. She looked rested; she looked in control. She would have to be.

"I have a headache," she replied. She rubbed her temple as if just mentioning it had made it flair up. She spoke his native language, the lilt of her multitude of languages gave her hoarseness an almost hypnotic quality.

"You slept for nine straight hours."

"I was tired."

Guang frowned. "No nightmares?"

Alex squinted. "I don't remember," she said. She winced and rubbed the side of her head.

Guang would have missed the flash of confusion in her eyes if he hadn't known her since they were toddlers. He saw her dismiss the confusion just as quickly as it had appeared. Perfect denial. He chose to ignore it, just as he'd ignored the strange lapses in her memory when she'd shown up in Thailand, more than half insane. "You ordered a lot of food."

"I'm hungry," she said. She finished the second bottle of water. "Where are we?" She waved her hand at the small apartment.

"Japanese consulate in New York City. This apartment is one they use for guests who need diplomatic immunity. It is technically part of Japan."

Alex chuckled.

"You find something humorous?"

"I think it's funny that people think I need protection," she said.

"The CIA has people at every exit and in the lobby. You murdered a house filled with people, a decorated Marine, and a CIA informant." He'd watched her fake her fall down the airplane tunnel steps and pick up the Sword of Souls from where he'd hidden it. If he'd doubted that the weapon and she had a connection, the simple fact that she'd known exactly where he'd hidden it would have convinced him. Of course, he'd also watched her put it in its sheath and swing it across her back. He'd carried her out of the car and up to the bedroom of this apartment and the only hint that the sword was anywhere at all on her body was the stripe of freezing cold that cut across his arms from a matching cold stripe across her back.

Alex narrowed her eyes and tilted her head. "Guang, you are my best friend. But you are also a monk. I would understand if what I did is too much."

Guang sighed. Too much. Perhaps it should have been. He'd dedicated his life to peace, acceptance, and to giving up the struggle. She'd given up all those things and survived to challenge them. But in a way, she allowed others to find them instead. The monster which had destroyed Peter Van de Moeter had not been filled with heat, but rather the same kind of predator instinct that a tiger showed as it launched an attack on a deer, the cool brutal natural instinct of a python or a cobra striking its prey. "You are my best and oldest friend. The world often seems like a cruel, harsh place for those who do not understand it, so judgment is a waste of time. I will not abandon you."

Alex's mouth twitched slightly. Sadness filled her eyes. "I wish I could say the same."

Guang shook his head. "You will not die tomorrow."

Alex sighed. "I'm going to starve to death today if some of that food doesn't get here soon." She shoved the sleeves of her shirt up to her elbows.

Guang's eyes flickered over them. His heart skipped a beat. Her arms were tanned from the desert, the scars slightly lighter tan than the skin around them: circling her wrists, tracking up her arm, stitching over the botched surgery. But all the bruises had disappeared. They were healed as if they'd never existed.

"What?" she asked.

He shook his head. "Nothing."

Alex's eyes narrowed.

He felt his heart pick up its pace. His gut told him it was important not to expose her to her own delusions. "I thought maybe the scars would fade with the sun tan."

Alex sighed. "The scars aren't going to fade, Guang. That's why they're scars."

A knock at the door interrupted Guang's reply. He stepped towards it, eager to escape the conversation. He'd seen many things that could only be explained by the gods, but each time it stunned him and he wondered why his faith wasn't stronger. He'd seen Alex wake up in her bed in Thailand, the vomit still wet on her ragged, filthy clothes and the bandages ripped into rags and drenched with her own blood. He'd seen the bruises covering her arms after her escape from the mercenaries and the CIA, where she'd been beaten, drugged, and raped—again. But, the bruises had disappeared and she clearly did not remember them having been there. She didn't remember any more than she remembered the injuries that had been erased in those few slim hours between disappearing in New York City and appearing in Thailand.

Alex started towards the door.

Guang got to it first.

A man in a dark suit stood framed on the other side. He kept his hand on the door knob. He had an earpiece in his ear, the wire tucked into the pressed white collar of his immaculate shirt. "You ordered food?" he asked in Japanese.

Alex fell into speaking Japanese easily. "Is it here?" she asked without any hint of accent. Japanese could have been her first language.

Guang saw the surprise in the man's face, quickly hidden behind the stoic façade. People often mistook Alex for many things. The more stressed out she got, the more relaxed she seemed. Sometimes it lured people into trying to attack her;

like some snake charmer reaching into a bag for a snake he thinks is calm enough to pick up. Very seldom did she let go of her control enough to let loose with her real accent, that musical, mystical mélange of accents. But it had disappeared the instant the knock at the door came. Guang could imagine hearing the whoosh as it fled out of the room.

The security guard eyed Alex. After the surprise, he went back to emotionless. All business. This was one of the elite security guards, a man accustomed to protecting people who needed protecting. But, of course, Alex didn't exactly need protecting.

Alex sighed. "Yeah, I'm not what anyone expects," she told him.

The man touched his ear piece and started to turn from the room, pulling the door shut behind him.

Alex stepped around Guang. She caught the door and ripped the earpiece out of his ear.

Guang heard the whiff of her fist as it passed his ear. He took several steps back, not that he needed to. Alex's speed took control of the security man inside the small space of the threshold. She was the best master of the arts that Guang had ever seen; and, the gap between her and all the masters he'd worked with or seen practice was impressively wide.

He stood back and watched the master work. Maybe he would learn.

In response to Alex's overwhelming speed and intense aggression, the man's training kicked in. It was all muscle memory, the preprogrammed response to an attack which sped forward faster than the inevitable adrenalin dump into the security guard's system. But he'd been trained to deal with that adrenalin. His muscle memory kicked in. But knowing this gave Alex an advantage over his superior physical strength.

She had no idea what art he'd trained in. His response could have easily been from one of the hundreds of different schools of the hundreds of different forms. Perhaps he hadn't been trained in Japan. He could respond with Korean martial arts or Chinese. Her mind would just as fast as her attack, analyzing his body language to pick out his move. The instant she recognized how he moved, it was over. Although the man didn't know it.

By the time Guang recognized the man's move, Alex was already countering it.

The man moved to subdue her and send her to the ground. The man was impressively fast; but the gap between that and Alex was wide and he did not come close to crossing it. Guang almost felt sorry for the man. He hit the floor hard. The air bursting out of his lungs.

He jumped to his feet and spun back to her to attack.

Guang grabbed him in a choke hold. He held the man back. "Think about if you really want to do this," he told the man in Japanese.

Alex hooked her thumbs in her jeans. "I'm going to go down and get my dinner. Would you like to accompany me?" She was the epitome of relaxation. Her eyes were amused, confident. "I mean, now that we've established that I don't need a bodyguard."

He nodded.

Guang released him.

The man rubbed his shoulder where she'd used a pressure point to get him down. He eyed her warily. "The CIA is downstairs, you can't step across the line or you're out of our territory and they will take you in to their custody. You have to stay here."

Alex's eyes darkened.

Guang felt like some of the heat left the air.

"I will not trade one prison for another. And while I appreciate the hospitality of the Japanese government, I will go where I please."

"My job is to protect you."

"We'll pretend that's true." She yawned and lifted her chin at Guang.

He nodded. "Try not to kill anyone," he told her in his native tongue.

She smirked. "I promise you, my friend, that I will avoid that until tomorrow night."

He arched an eyebrow.

She shrugged. "Well, unless I'm pushed into it. It's not my intention."

"Your intention is to make sure everyone knows that you can't be controlled and to do it in the most obvious, blatant way possible so that everyone gets the message," Guang said.

Alex grinned. "I thought I was being mysterious."

Guang sighed. "As subtle as a black yak hiding in a snow drift."

She laughed.

Guang smiled. It was the first honest laughed he'd heard from her since her father had died. He mumbled about her lack of patience.

She shrugged and rubbed her temple.

CHAPTER TWENTY-ONE

Alex stepped into the elevator. She leaned against the back of it and yawned. She grinned at the grouchy agent who'd been protecting her by keeping her behind a locked door.

The Japanese equivalent of a secret service agent followed her inside the small room. He frowned. He straightened his tie and hit the elevator button for the lobby of the consulate. He faced the doors, his back to Alex. "You are very fast," he said, his English very heavily accented.

Alex nodded. "I am."

"But now that I'm prepared, you couldn't do that again."

Alex's eyes sparkled with amusement. "I could do it slower, but then it's just more embarrassing for you. You could have asked if I liked locked doors. I don't, by the way."

He looked over his shoulder at her. "You brag like an American."

"Well, that's what I am," she replied.

"Americans often call themselves masters when they are nothing but children with egos. I have been to some of these so-called *dojos* in America. They are nothing but pretenders."

Alex chuckled. "There do seem to be a lot of people calling themselves teachers in this country. There's a karate school on every corner."

He rolled his eyes. "Trophies and black belts and pretending."

"Is there a *dojo* in this building? I mean, you and your fellow security men must train somewhere."

He narrowed his eyes at her. "There is."

"After I eat, we'll test out your theory," she said.

He gave a smug laugh. "What happens when everyone finds out you're a fraud?"

Alex smirked. "This might surprise you, but nothing would make me happier," she replied. The elevator doors opened.

Three Japanese soldiers stiffened when they saw her. They stood in front of the elevator. Spread out in front of them was a lobby area. A high desk separated the row of soldiers from the open space where couches formed a loose waiting area and a flat screen television broadcast Japanese television. Photographs and paintings of Japan decorated the walls. In one corner, a Japanese suit of armor gleamed. Just beyond the suit of armor, a thick white line cut across the black marble floors. On one side of the line, the marble offered a green shape of the United States. On her side, the marble offered a green Japan shape. A sign on the wall beside the suit of armor announced that the line marked a separation between countries.

On the other side of the line Richard Powell stood with Sinjin Doucet and three other men. They faced five Japanese men in pressed suits with bulges under their jackets where they carried their weapons. The Americans perked up when Alex appeared. The soldiers moved so that their hands were closer to their hidden weapons. Doucet and Powell tried to meet her eyes.

Alex ignored them all.

Standing off to the side, having walked out of the elevator on the far side of the room, was a skinny kid in jeans and sweatshirt advertising one of the two restaurants Alex had ordered from. Alex saw him squirm as he stood on the

American side of the line. He held two filled plastic bags, one in each hand. He didn't look at the Americans, but he eyed the Japanese men.

Alex crossed the floor towards the kid. The bodyguard from upstairs on her heels. He barked an order to the other men to watch the Americans and make sure they didn't cross the line. "Hey," she said to the kid, making sure her boots stayed on the Japanese side of the line. "You got my food order?" English. No accent.

"Yeah," he said. "$75.93."

Alex lifted her eyebrows in surprise. "Damn. I've been in the Midwest too long." She pulled a wallet out of her back pocket.

Behind her, she heard the agent from upstairs blow out a breath.

She opened up the wallet and found a one hundred dollar bill. She pulled it out. She handed the wallet back to the guy tailing her.

He grabbed it angrily.

She watched him shove it back inside his jacket.

The delivery boy twitched at the action.

The bodyguard's hand froze. Some of the color drained out of his face.

A smirk pulled at her mouth.

He swallowed and dropped his hands from his jacket.

Alex turned her attention back to the kid. She held out the hundred.

The kid reached.

She pulled it back.

He frowned.

Alex watched the bead of sweat appear on his forehead. She smiled, but the smile didn't reach her eyes like it had when she'd grinned at the man behind her or when she'd laughed at Guang's words. The smile came with the awakening of the monster inside her. It yawned and stretched and wondered if it really needed to be woken up for this at all. "New to this game, huh?"

"What?' he asked.

"The CIA. Are you a new recruit?"

He laughed. "Lady, I just deliver food."

"Did you bug the food or the bag?"

"Listen, just pay me and I'll be on my way." He reached for the money.

She pulled the money back. "Did Powell promise you some grand adventure? I bet you jumped at it. I bet you think you want some adventure and excitement."

"Alex, leave him alone," Powell said, walking towards. "He's just a delivery boy."

Alex ignored Powell. "People die here, kid. Did Powell tell you what happened to the last guy he promised to protect? I cut him in half. He was alive long enough to watch his guts spill out and try to hold his halves together. Ever hear the sound of intestines being ripped out of a body cavity? Or smell it for that matter? That's something you'll never forget."

The kid turned a little green.

Alex glanced over her shoulder at the bodyguard.

Amusement flittered across his eyes along with a little bit of aggravation at having been manipulated into action. He stepped onto the white line. "The CIA thinks bugging the Japanese consulate is a good idea? I think I will bring this up with the ambassador and lodge a formal complaint."

"You're harboring a murderer," Powell said calmly.

The man sighed. "I see. You think your avoidance of confirmation or denial will save face? Let me ask you who did this refugee—"

"Refugee?" Doucet sputtered. "Really? You can't be serious. She's an American citizen."

The bodyguard tilted his head at the towering Marine. "Actually, she has dual citizenship. Mr. Powell, I hope you'll keep your dog on a leash."

Powell narrowed his eyes and glanced over the bodyguard's shoulder at Alex. "Some of my dogs are tamer than others."

"Some are feral and one would be a fool to try to tame them," the bodyguard replied in an equally calm voice. "I'm

315

sure you can find a more diplomatic avenue to request extradition. I surely hope that the American people don't discover that you offered immunity to a terrorist in exchange for the names of a couple of alleged gun dealers and are now interested in imprisoning the person who killed this terrorist—a man guilty of murder, kidnapping, gross assault, torture, rape, an attack on an American casino putting the city of Las Vegas on high alert, smuggling in international criminals, and a host of other crimes against both your charter and international law. Surely there must be some better route to travel than hanging out in our lobby."

"She won't stay here forever. She won't even stay here long. She doesn't stay in any one place long." Powell sighed. "Alex, this is a mistake. You don't want to put me in this position. You'll be on the run for the rest of your life. And it will be a very short life."

At the back of the room, behind Powell and Doucet and their armed men, the elevator dinged and the doors opened.

Another kid carrying bags of food entered. He looked up and froze. His eyes got big. "Whoa."

Alex looked back at the man from upstairs. He seemed to be in charge. "My dinner's here," she said in Japanese.

The man managed to keep his face blank of expression, but Alex could see the slight twitch at the corner of one eye. He sighed and stepped up to her. "Stay on this side of the line," he said. He snatched the $100 out of her hand.

She gave him a mocking salute.

He crossed the line, brushing passed Doucet and Powell.

Powell frowned at the other delivery. He turned back to Alex. "You think I can let you go with all that CIA training? I can't, Alex. I can't let you out there. No one retires from this job."

"You wrote me off as dead. I flunked out of your assassin's training. My scores on all your little tests were mediocre at best. You're the only one in the organization who believes I'm something more, Powell."

"I have proof."

Alex nodded. "Go tell them about an ancient legend. Tell them about magic and ancient gods and pulling swords out of rocks. See how long your autonomy lasts. I mean, you probably have a lot to answer for because of all that destruction at your office."

Powell's mouth twitched. "I have witnesses who saw you on that airport tarmac. Only a half dozen people in the world could have pulled off something like that—if that many."

"Anyone with a sword in the middle of a group of snipers who don't want to shoot could have done that," she replied.

He eyed her.

She shrugged. "That's what your analysts will say. Plus I had help."

"From the Japanese government."

Alex shook her head. "They're not stupid. They weren't involved in what happened at the airport."

The bodyguard returned with two bags of food. "The delivery kid wondered what was going on with the hot chick," he said, passing the two bags to Alex.

She grinned. "I hope you tipped him well."

"Minimal. I told him you were a bitch."

Alex chuckled. "Touché." She nodded at Powell. "Enjoy your dinner. Hope I ordered what you like." She pivoted on a heel and started back towards the elevator with the bodyguard in tow. She noted how he kept himself at her elbow, his body positioned between her and Powell and Doucet. She pushed the button for the elevator.

When the doors opened, she stepped inside and turned around to face the two Americans staring back at her. She held their stare as the doors closed.

The minute the doors closed the bodyguard turned on her.

Alex's glare snapped at him. "Don't make me mess up my dinner," she said in a cold voice. "I'm really hungry."

"Give me my weapon back."

She reached to the small of her back and lifted her shirt. She handed him his Sig Sauer. "Nice weapon."

"You prefer swords, I understand."

"I prefer to look someone in the eyes," Alex said. "If I kill someone, it's always personal."

The man stared at her. "The monk says you're not a sociopath."

Alex shrugged. "The monk sees what he wants." She walked out of the elevator and back to the small apartment.

Guang watched Alex and the bodyguard enter the apartment. The bodyguard looked useless. Like a third, but paralyzed arm. He'd realized that Alex had set out to show everyone who was in charge. Despite the easy-going façade, her eyes sparkled with cunning. This was when she looked most like her father. He'd had the intense eyes as well, built in to a face lined with laughter. Her father had been a very dangerous man. The bodyguard was apparently just picking up the fact that Joe McBrady's daughter was also very dangerous.

"No one died," she announced with false cheer. She spoke English, the universal language between the three of them.

The words made the bodyguard wince.

Guang tried to look impressed, but he didn't try hard and a glint of humor drifted across Alex's face. "Did you give him his weapon back?"

Alex frowned. "You noticed that?" She put the bags on the counter.

Guang walked to the kitchen's breakfast bar. He could smell Chinese food. It made his stomach growl. "I see more than you think."

Alex grunted.

The bodyguard chuckled at the exchange. "I will let you enjoy your dinner," he said with a bow. "When you are ready for the *dojo* let me know, Great One."

Alex started unloading boxes of food. "The name is Alex. Keep calling me that and someone's going to get hurt. It'll be about an hour."

"Don't you Americans have to wait two hours for your food to settle before you exert yourself physically?"

"I don't plan on exerting myself," Alex replied.

The man grinned at her. "We shall see."

Guang shook his head. He switched to his native language as the bodyguard left the apartment. "You might give him a little hope."

Alex shrugged as she opened one of the dozen boxes of food and grabbed a set of chopsticks. "I plan on giving him a lesson, not sparring with him. Idiot brings a gun in here and thinks he can lock me in a room. You know it was written all over his face that he thinks he's better than I am."

Alex opened a box and snatched up some of the chopsticks that Guang had laid out. She grabbed a mouthful.

Guang opened a bottle of water and set it in front of her.

"I'm starving," she said after swallowing.

"You've expended a lot of energy recently," Guang replied.

She grunted. She pulled up a chair and started searching for other boxes. They ate in silence until Alex leaned back and sighed. "So, I need to tell you my plans so you can help me if I need help."

Guang stiffened.

"He will bring a witness from the Offspring with him and six other sword fighters."

"Alex, this isn't official—"

"It is as official as it is going to get at this point. The presence of the witness will make it legit. The Offspring don't really care who faces their champion next year when their choice turns 40. It could be me or this asshole or whoever kills him after me." She sighed and drank some water. "If the worst happens, I need you to take my body out of there. Don't let the Offspring bastards have it."

"Alex, you are not—"

"Please."

Guang sighed. "Okay, Alex. No matter what. No matter where. No matter when. When the time comes, I will make sure that your remains are in my control." He closed his eyes and took a deep, steadying breath. "Do you have a preference on what I should do?"

Alex shrugged. "Burn it. Let it rot in the jungle. Throw it in the lake. Just don't let anyone dissect me or study me. Thailand by the cove is a nice place to spend eternity. But no fucking monument."

"Like the grave of the last True One in Nepal?"

Alex grimaced. "Pilgrimages, a bunch of whining people wanting someone else to fix their problems, a group of people standing around like gestapo trying to control the masses. If I survive, I might go to Nepal and destroy it."

Guang arched an eyebrow. "You know, whenever the sword which shall not be named bonds with another wielder, it is tradition to make a pilgrimage to that grave. You never went."

"Because they were waiting to ambush me and I was just a kid."

"And what if you survive this ambush?"

Alex pressed her lips together. "The chances are—"

"Since when do you quote chances?"

"If I survive, have a doctor ready. Get a boat, there's a dock on the north side of the island. It'll be over one way or the other by midnight. If I can make it to you, I will."

"A doctor?"

Alex shrugged. "The fights I pick are never the easy ones."

"You were pretty beat up from the torture a couple of nights ago and you have recovered well," Guang told her, choosing his words carefully.

Alex frowned. She rubbed her temple at the stab of pain. "This will be different. And I have not taken care of myself to be at 100 percent. And—"

"And?" Guang furrowed his brow and stared at her.

"I spent a lot of years running from my responsibilities. I am not trusted completely. But, don't worry. It will work out."

"You think you are going to die and you just asked me to arrange for a doctor and I should not worry?"

"No one can fight seven sword masters in a row or simultaneously and walk away unscathed. Even if I was the best in the world, Guang, which I can assure you that I am not." She paused and made a face. "Don't try to argue that. It's true. I'm not the greatest. If I ever learned a single thing from Sakai it was that there is always someone better. There's someone faster, there's someone stronger, there's someone smarter, there's always someone who knows a counter to your best move and they'll find it at the worst possible time."

Guang sighed. "Okay. I will make arrangements. I will take care of your body should you fall. That is the role of the spiritual guide; and that is the role I have taken for you."

Alex made a face. "The Offspring won't stand in your way; but the CIA might show up. You can't be caught by them."

"I understand, Alex. And what about you? Can you get out of this building?"

Alex nodded. "Not a problem. I'm going to find this *dojo* so I can give the bodyguard the lesson I promised, then I'm out of the city. I need some time alone."

Guang took a deep breath and released it slowly. "So, this is good bye until tomorrow night." He stood up.

Alex stood as well. She started to say something.

Guang held up a hand. He stepped towards her and embraced her.

She hugged him back, then let go, and left the room.

Guang stared after her for a long time.

Powell stared at the elevator where Alex had disappeared with bags of food. He glanced at the young CIA recruit he'd made pose as a delivery man, the first one to arrive.

He hated to be outsmarted. All this time, he'd thought he was one step ahead of her, just trying to contain her. But, he'd seen it in her eyes now. She'd needed him to flush out Dyer and to get at Peter Van de Moeter. She'd used him, played him, and manipulated him. She'd even slept with Doucet, who he'd thought might be able to reign her in; love could control many things; and, with her father gone and vulnerable from her ordeal, Alex was a woman in desperate need of comfort and love. Or so the analysts had advised him. Take away her support system and she would need to find another one—hopefully the CIA.

But Alex had defied those analysts. Instead of behaving in the way that'd been predicted, she'd used all of them. Powell had to wonder why he hadn't guessed that. After all, he had evidence that suggested most of the governments of the Far East considered her one of the most dangerous people alive. They'd warned him that, like Chen Sakai, she would be controlled only by some secretive dark organization which had to be negotiated with. However, she'd come to work for him and he was pretty sure they would not approve of her rampage across America or her hoarding of dirty bombs. She'd gone rogue from the Offspring and from him.

He closed his eyes. Behind his lids, he didn't see the horrific images of what had happened to Dyer or Van de Moeter; instead, he saw Alex's eyes when he'd told her that the men were under orders to kill her if she did anything out of the ordinary. What he'd seen in the glittering amber of her eyes, was perhaps a vision of her soul. It curdled his blood, dumped adrenalin into his system and made his knees feel weak. It was something cold and ancient and deadly, something that seemed curled up inside her like some serpent hiding in the darkness. And when he saw it, he could imagine its forked black tongue flickering out and touching his brain as if to say "Let them try."

The combination of those highly alert, almost other worldly eyes with the ultra-relaxed body posture had made him uneasy. It'd made the hairs on the back of his next stand up. He wondered when he'd stopped thinking about Alex as a kid, when he stopped thinking about her as a beautiful woman. Had it been when she'd been returned to New York City? Broken and bloody and insane. He'd like to think he wasn't that fickle. Perhaps it had been when she'd shown up in his office and threatened him about the research he'd done.

The secrets kept about the Sword of Souls had been protected for longer than written history. He'd only heard about it by mistake. It had taken a lot of work to find out the little that he had. First he'd tracked Chen Sakai. But the man was old, no one knew how old…someone had told him over 200 years old, but Richard couldn't find anyone who could separate the legend from reality where Chen Sakai was concerned. According to his research, Chen Sakai's successor had been chosen by the Offspring, the name of the organization that controlled the sword.

Alex had not been their choice. He knew the time when they would come to claim their weapon was coming quickly.

CHAPTER TWENTY-TWO

The sound of a helicopter approached. The noise of the blades soon got loud enough to drown out the sound of the wind and the waves of Lake Erie breaking on the rocky coast of the small island, smashing chunks of ice from the still partially frozen surface. The dark house shook as the chopper buzzed overhead.

In the darkness of the house her father had built, Alexandria Rae McBrady listened. She felt the vibration as it buzzed overhead. She knew the island well. It wasn't large; what wasn't rocky coastline was covered with trees. It was March, so most of the trees were bare, but still, a helicopter had only one landing spot. Spotlights shone over the windows. In the room where Alex sat in the dark, the beam of light reflected off the walls.

Alex opened her eyes. The walls of the room were covered with all kinds of weapons: swords, rifles, maces, halberds, kamas, sais, bows, crossbows. Glass display cases filled the room, containing weapons too small to be on the walls: daggers, throwing stars, pistols, blow guns, darts, and more. Her father had collected these over the years. This was his museum. Perhaps it would have all been guns if not for her interest in the martial arts. But he had been a man of war and conflict; so, anything was possible. She sat in a lotus position, the Sword of Souls resting on her knees. The backs of her hands rested on top of the weapon, the blood-stained handle against the skin of her right hand, the always cold, ever-sharp blade against the back of her left hand.

The helicopter engine moved away. She listened to the sound of it change as it found purchase. She heard the engine cut out which meant they hadn't brought an extra pilot, just the seven sword masters and the one witness. In her mind's eye, she envisioned them scrambling off the chopper into the cold wind. The night was dark, cloudy, damp, it would seep into their bones and remind them that they were far away from the dry heat of their homes. No doubt their skill levels would have taken them to places beyond the Middle East, but there was something unique about the chill of Ohio in March in the middle of Lake Erie. The cold sucked away breath quicker with the damp smell of dead fish and the decay of winter.

Alex's right hand flipped over and wrapped around the hilt of the weapon. The handle had been wrapped with strips of leather for a thousand years, the inner layers thinned with age, but held with the blood of all those who'd come before her the warriors and the teachers and the pretenders. The teachers outnumbered the pretenders, the pretenders outnumbered the warriors. Alex felt the connection to all of them, just as she felt the ghost of her father in this place. The house itself felt like a cobweb-filled monument to her father. Peter Van de Moeter had moved in, but it was clear he'd never come to this room. She felt her father here. She felt the memory of his voice on the sound of the wind. She felt the memory of his words like a blow to the gut: "One day this will save your life, Alex. Remember that. One day this will save your life."

The woman who'd been her father's companion had lived in this house after her father's death or while her father was off working. She claimed to be his wife and she had the paperwork to back it up. At the time, it'd felt like a betrayal, but then she'd been so angry about him being dead. The woman had buried Joe McBrady in a place where Alex could not visit his grave—a place where her enemies could lie in wait and control, a place her father would have hated. Alex wondered if Peter had a hand in that planning. Too late to ask him.

She rose to her feet as the air pressure around her changed, indicating that the front door of the home had been opened. Seven swordmasters, one witness, and death moved with them.

She slid the Sword of Souls into the scabbard strapped across her back. When she died, she figured the Offspring would take these relics that her father had collected. Perhaps they would lock them up in the tower of the house in Hiroo, the forbidden tower that even Sakai never entered. She'd gone into that tower and she'd read the journals the Offspring kept over centuries. Their stories were as embellished and tainted as most of their souls. So, it wasn't much of a stretch to assume they would take these weapons and claim they belonged to the holders of the Sword of Souls past. They wouldn't credit any of them to her. Perhaps they planned on extinguishing her from the records completely. Or perhaps she would be listed as one of the pretenders, a whore who'd seduced an old man for a few years of power while the real heir prepared for his rite of passage and to come of age.

She should be angry about; but, when she searched her soul, she felt nothing. The Offspring's opinion simply didn't matter much to her.

She reached behind her to the wall and touched a built-in panel. It lit up at her touch. She typed in a passcode quickly and a touch screen computer appeared. She swiped to the screen she wanted and hit one of the options.

All the lights in the house switched on.

It lit up the place like an arena—an irony Alex appreciated.

She felt the tension from the invaders. She could taste their fear in the air, like a bitter hint of coffee in the candy of anticipation. She pulled her hair back and tied it up with a blue elastic band. She leaned back against the wall, crossed her arms over her stomach and yawned.

They found the room quickly, flowing into the room like swarming black ants emerging from a hive. Three of them held pistols on her. They all wore black, even the old Asian man. Not that she had much more fashion sense: black boots, jeans, a long-sleeved heather-blue t-shirt that hung untucked with the sleeves shoved up to her elbows. Their clothing leaned towards the looser fitting workout type of clothing. The old Asian wore a business suit, his small frame and face looked tight with a haughty arrogance. The other men were all of Arab descent.

The leader wore a black *gi* and a curved mohannad sword hung in a metal sheath on his belt. He glanced around at the walls. He smiled, bright white teeth inside neatly trimmed jet black facial hair. His arms spread out. "What is this, Alexandria?" he asked. "Am I perhaps supposed to pick which one of these is the Sword of Souls?" His voice was jovial, amused, and friendly; but, none of that went to his eyes. He had the eyes of a psychopath: empty and cold and looking to devour light and life in a fevered need to just find a way to feel alive. Alex suspected her eyes were similar.

Alex shrugged. The sound of the sword's name spoken aloud made cold squeeze her spine. "If that's an option, take whichever one you want and call it what you want, then leave," she told him. Her voice was hoarse but even and steady while it danced with an accent that lilted and twanged and drawled all at once.

The man tilted his head like a dog hearing something curious. "Perhaps you just want to point out the one I should take and walk away from here alive yourself."

Alex smiled at him and stifled a yawn. "If only it were that easy," she said. "If only world peace were possible. If only we could all get along and people would stop trying to kill me."

"Is that what you think you're doing?" he asked her. Behind him the six other fighters spread out, filling up the side of the room, blocking any exit. They all had various styles of swords. Their eyes were intense and they stared at her, the tension rippling through them. "Do you think the Sword of Souls is yours so you can bring peace and tranquility to the world?"

Alex chuckled. She dropped her arms. In her head, she assigned numbers to all seven men, preparing to wipe them out of existence.

The men flinched when she dropped her arms.

She smirked in amusement at their reaction. The simple move revealed the speed of the men and their level of tension. Their twitches and their postures showed her which disciplines and which schools they'd trained in. All this information raced through her brain as she stifled another yawn. "Yes, because a blood thirsty weapon is all about bringing peace," she said sarcastically. "That's exactly what I think. Rainbows on the edge of a blade."

The old Asian guy frowned.

Alex sighed and rolled her eyes at the man. "Seriously?" she asked him in Japanese. "The Offspring thinks this is all about peace and good versus evil? You guys have really doubled down on your own propaganda."

He pointed a gnarled bony finger at her. "You are an abomination. You are a thief."

Alex arched an eyebrow at the leader of the group. "Don't the rules say something about an impartial audience?"

"I found it difficult to find someone in the Offspring who actually supports you," the man admitted. He took a few steps into the room, towards one of the display cases. He glanced into the case, then back at the wall covered in swords.

"They're assholes," Alex conceded.

The man chuckled. "A necessary evil though. They control the Sword of Soul's bloodlust." His hand traced over the top of the case. "They keep it under glass so innocents don't get hurt." He tapped the glass display with his knuckles.

"Innocents?" she asked. "Like my father?"

He sighed. "Peter killed your father."

"Under your orders."

"A tactical maneuver which he chose on his own."

328

"You needed to weaken me?" Alex asked. "You lacked the confidence that seven of you could defeat one abominable woman?"

The man shrugged. "I'm not the fool that many of the Offspring are, Alexandria Rae McBrady. You are a student of the Great One Chen Sakai. Your name has drifted through the best schools in the world. I know that you are not just a girl who seduced an old man to get some power. I know by your own right you are a phenom and a warrior with some skill. I do not think this will be over in five seconds, like my colleague from the Offspring here believes." He waved a hand at the Asian.

Alex laughed genuinely. "Wow. Thanks. What are you thinking? Ten, fifteen seconds? Maybe a whole minute?"

"The world of the Offspring will speak my name when I'm through here, Alex. I will be the one who defeated you and won the Sword back."

"Did the Offspring tell you they have a successor picked out? Did they tell you they think the True One has returned to the Earth? That if you win here today, you'll only be hanging around until they have their big plans finished and the one they've chosen turns 40? Because for some reason, they think someone has an age limit on when they can have the weapon."

"There will always be challenges," he said. "What you can't possibly understand is how the Sword of Souls has called me from the moment I could breath. It's not just a weapon. It's part of me. It's mine. I want it."

Alex arched an eyebrow at him. "If it calls to you, pick it out," she said nodding at the wall that his eyes kept drifting to. "Tell me. Which one is it?"

He turned purposefully, intending to draw Alex's attention with him.

Alex felt the first of the men move to attack. She hadn't been sure if they'd come one at a time or one by one. She couldn't remember the details of the stupid Rule of Sevens challenge. She moved quickly, instinctively, dropping down under the swing of a blade, spinning around and hooking his leg, pulling him off balance, drawing her sword, and cutting off his head as he fell backwards. The man she'd named "One" had died.

A fountain of blood sprayed into the face and chest of the man a step behind him. Alex jumped and landed a kick in the center of his chest.

Another man came at her, leaping over a display case.

Alex leaped out of the way and blocked his swing with her forearm.

The others fell in. A blur of motion and flashing swords.

Alex didn't think. There wasn't time to think. She moved, using sword and boots and fists.

She cut down the second man, but with his dying breath he tackled her.

She smashed through a glass display with dead weight on top of her. The time to get out from under his weight lost her some of her advantage. She took a punch as she stood up and stumbled backwards.

One of the others waited for her as she fell back.

In slow motion, she saw him lift his weapon—a big heavy broadsword—in anticipation of ending her life by crushing her skull. The world seemed to stop, the players around her seemed to freeze. Alex's hand tightened around the sword even as her other hand moved to meet it. Instead of trying to avoid the broadsword, she turned up the speed to move under the swing. As the blade started to fall, hers came up. She twisted and slid on her knees, under his blade and between his legs. She sliced up as her back arched and took off the man's leg.

However, she didn't stop to admire her work as her weapon twisted in the air, turned and impaled the fourth man as she rose to her feet. The fourth man managed to get his sword on her side before he died, slicing deep across the bottom rib. The edge of his weapon scraped against bone. Alex stared him in the eye and pulled the sword up through his guts.

He gasped. His weapon fell from his hands. He said something as he died, something in Arabic which Alex could not understand.

She used her boot to shove him off her weapon even as her body twisted to meet another threat. She turned to the remaining three men. The two who were the best of the lot and their leader who hadn't even drawn his weapon yet.

The leader's eyes darted at the Japanese man in the suit.

Color had drained out of the small man's face. He'd been edging out of the room.

"*STOP!*" Alex snapped at him in Japanese.

He paled and froze at her bark. His hands shook.

Alex smirked at him, then slowly turned back to the three swordsmen.

The two blocked her path to the leader.

Their dead companions gushed blood over the floor.

Alex lifted her chin at them. "Well, I'm warmed up," she said. She spit blood out of her mouth.

The two attacked with lightning speed, both of them coming from different angles, both working on getting her to twist and use her torso where she continued to bleed heavily.

Alex defended herself.

She took a kick to the side that smashed her into a display case filled with throwing stars. She grabbed a few of them and threw them at the man who charged. They imbedded themselves deep into the man's skull and heart. He felt to his knees in front of her.

"They said you were a fake," he said. He pulled the star out of his chest, blood from his heart spurted, he stared at it for a second, then collapsed.

Alex side-stepped a spiked mace swinging at her from the sixth man, who'd suddenly realized this had gotten serious. She landed a kick in the man's side and landed another one against the side of his leg.

He yelled and went down to one knee. His fist collided with her injury.

She felt ribs break--again. The chain of the mace wrapped around her ankle. The man pulled.

She fell, slipping on blood.

She started to bring the sword back, but the master swordsman, leaped on her arm and pinned it to the floor, shoving it onto a piece of glass from one of the destroyed display cases. Alex fought but watched the glass slowly go through her entire arm at the wrist, making a "T" with the scar that wrapped around her wrist from Peter's torture. Blood pumped from the wound.

He punched her in the face. And pinned her by hovering over her on all fours.

Her vision tunneled when her head hit the floor.

He smiled, bloody white teeth and punched her again.

Alex's left hand found a dagger from one of the display cases. She grabbed it and tried to stab him.

He caught the hand and used his superior strength to stab her.

Alex coughed out blood at the impact. She growled in anger and pulled the dagger out of her side. She gritted her teeth and managed to knee the guy in the groin. The shot wasn't good, but it was close enough to a vulnerable area that the man shifted. She took advantage of that shift and used all of her speed.

Suddenly, she was on top of the guy's back. In the next instant, she'd cut his throat. She reached for her weapon.

Before she could catch her breath, a garrote snapped around her neck and pulled her back, away from the Sword of Souls.

She struggled against the leader of the group as the wire dug into her throat. The fighting had left her needing more oxygen than normal and she wasn't getting any. The man avoided her boots and elbows expertly. He swung her against the wall using the garrote.

She collided with a club covered in nails that hung on the wall. She ripped herself off it, to avoid the leader's sword. She stumbled, but managed to stay on her feet as she avoided his sword.

His eyes glittered with maniacal rage. He smiled.

Alex was gasping for air. She put her hand on her side where she'd been stabbed with a dagger and felt blood bubbling out with air. Her chest hurt. Her back hurt. Her head hurt. Her throat felt like it'd been slit from the wire. Covered in blood, she recognized that most of it could very well be her own. Her limbs felt heavy with exhaustion. The injury to her wrist was making her bleed out like some suicide. Six months of torture, three months of living on the streets as a drunk had left her less than in her physical prime anyway. Her eyes darted at the Sword of Souls lying in the blood. Its blade seemed to glow with bright blue energy that throbbed in time with her thumping, racing, heart.

The Arab landed a roundhouse kick.

Alex would have gone down, but she hit another, already smashed display case. She flipped over it and hit the wall.

She slid along the wall, knocking off her father's collectible rifles and fell into the corner. Her breath came in wet gasps, each one hurting. She lifted up her hand as he slowly walked towards her.

"I will let them know that you were a worthy opponent," the Arab said. He laid his weapon down on a case and crouched down. "Where are the bombs? I want them too."

Alex, used the corner of a display case to hold herself up. A Glock 21 had been attached to the back of the case, just below her hand. "They're in the fallout shelter," she told him. "Take them. Let me live." She didn't have to fake the begging sound, her inability to breathe made it sound that way without effort or acting.

The Arab wrapped his hand around the handle of the Sword of Souls. "It's cold," he said in a surprised voice. "Gods! I can feel the power in it." His dark eyes reflected the weapon's glow which still throbbed with Alex's heartbeat.

The Arab turned from the weapon and looked at her. "I thought the power was just figurative. I had no idea," he said. He laughed. "I had no idea that something like this could even be possible."

"It will control you," the Japanese man warned. "You must fight it. We will help. First you must sever the tie with the girl."

"Fight it?" the Arab laughed. "I am going to join it. I can feel it in my bones. It wants to feed." He turned to Alex slowly.

Alex shivered. In her head, she heard a soft, malevolent chuckle. The voice in her head knew who would win. The sword wasn't craving her blood it was craving the life of the Arab. A touch of power and confidence kills. She sank to her knees. Her father would never stash an empty weapon and his weapons were kept in top condition. He'd only been dead a little more than a year. The weapon would work.

The Arab walked slowly towards her, carrying the sword. "Time to die," he said.

Alex lifted her chin. "Do it then," she managed between gasps for air and wheezing breath.

"It hates you," the Arab said, his voice filled with wonder. "It hates you so much. Because..." his voice trailed off. He tilted his head. He furrowed his brow. "It hates you because you control it," he said.

Alex saw the eyes of the Offspring observer widen in shock. She heard him gasp as she lifted the gun. She didn't bother to pull back the slide. It was a hidden weapon, placed for self-defense. Alex new her father. There would be a round in the chamber and it would be ready to go. The Glock 21, .45 caliber, with an expensive red dot optic sight. It was her father's weapon of choice. She aimed and pulled the trigger. The recoil hurt her arm and her wrist.

The Arab staggered two steps backwards. He looked at the hole in his gut. The Sword of Souls fell to the ground in front of her.

Alex aimed higher, pulled the trigger, then lifted again and fired again. One in the heart. One in the head. Her father had been a good shooting teacher. He'd made sure she could defend herself with more than just a sword.

The Sword of Souls fell to the ground in front of her.

Alex turned the gun on the Japanese man.

"No!" he said. "You can't kill the observer! That's against the rules."

"Fuck your rules," Alex replied. She pulled the trigger, killing him on the first shot.

She sighed and fell back against the display case. The gun dropped from her numb hands. She couldn't move.

"Alex!" Guang said, his face blurry in front of her.

She reached around and tried to grab his shirt with a swollen hand. "Can't—" she wheezed. "—breathe."

"I've got you," he said.

"Can't—"

"I know, Alex," he said. "We have to go. Powell and the Marines are on the way. This is going to hurt."

She felt the ground drop away. Pain shot through her ribs and her head. She screamed before she passed out.

EPILOGUE

Alexandria Rae McBrady stood in the corner of the boardroom of Nyx Enterprises with her left shoulder against the floor to ceiling glass which looked out over Tokyo. The rising morning sun was just getting high enough to reach the streets thirty floors below her spot, glittering off cars and trucks and trains and masses of people bustling to their places of work. Even up here, the place gave her a tingle of claustrophobia. She'd arrived the night before and taken public transportation from Narita to the heart of the city. She'd stayed with the tourists, resisting the urge to find a private *dojo* and work out the stiffness from 30 hours of flying commercial. Instead she'd gotten a room in a Hilton hotel and sweat out the alcohol which had gotten her through the plane trips without flashbacks.

She'd slept some. Then roamed the city. It had taken her thirty minutes to get into the building of the world's leader in security systems. Another 30 minutes to find the offices of the executives and to break into each of them. Dorije Jennings walked her through getting into the computers and within an hour he'd hacked into the entire system of Nyx Enterprises.

That had left her with 2 hours until the scheduled board meeting. Boredom set in quickly while she roamed the building, playing cat and mouse with the security guards and the systems that DJ now controlled.

The first sign of life in the boardroom came when a young woman entered. She turned on the overhead lights and did not notice Alex standing in the corner. The secretary wore a white blouse, a black pencil skirt, and shoes which were somewhere between flats and high heels. The woman turned on the coffee maker and a machine to heat water for tea. The narrow buffet table along the wall opposite the windows and to the right of the door to the offices was covered with a white cloth. The woman pushed aside the cloth and retrieved canisters of tea leaves which she set next to the gurgling machine heating water. She also put bottles of water at each chair around the large u-shaped table. Fifteen bottles of water, placed carefully next to each name placard which pointed to the inside of the "U."

Alex watched her work from her space in the shadows. She had worn clothing to get inside the building and to avoid the security cameras: black hiking boots, black cargo pants, and a dark green top with long sleeves. Despite the brightness of the room her outfit blended with the potted trees in the corner of the room with her. She didn't move and the woman didn't see her. Neither did the second woman, about the same age as the first and wearing an almost identical outfit. She carried a box to the buffet and began arranging a display of colorful sweets on a tray by the mugs and cups.

The women conferred about the way to best display the edibles, then they left.

Alex moved from her spot. She walked by the potted plants and a red enameled suit of ancient armor. She moved silently on the industrial carpet. She grabbed some food and moved back to the board table. There were three chairs at the bottom of the table with six on each arm of the "U". She took the chair in the middle of the bottom. The chairs were cushioned white leather designed for maximum comfort. She leaned back in the chair and put her feet up on the glass table.

The door opened again. This time a man in a conservative, but impeccably tailored business suit stepped in. He stopped and stared at her as two men behind him went right for the buffet while talking about baseball teams.

"Who are you?" demanded the first one in.

Alex finished the last bite of her breakfast and reached for the bottled water. She screwed open the cap.

"You can't be in here!" he barked as the others turned and gaped. He turned behind him and ordered someone to call security. "You don't know how much trouble you are in."

Alex grunted and took a gulp of water. She wiped her mouth with her sleeve.

The man marched towards her. "Get up out of that chair! This isn't America. Prison isn't nice here."

Alex watched others filter in behind him, all of them staring at her. She thought they all looked the same in their conservative, expensive business suits.

Akiko Tanaka stepped inside alone. She gaped. "What are you doing here?" she gasped.

"Do you know this woman, Ms Tanaka?" demanded an older man entering the room with a younger man on his heels. He eyed Akiko with disapproval. "Just more proof that you're not fit for your position."

Akiko's mouth moved but she didn't say anything. Her eyes darted between Alex and the older man.

Alex picked up the name placard in front of her as she took another swig from the water bottle. She glanced at the name, then back at the older man.

Akiko paled.

The older man glared. He pressed his lips together and glanced at one of the men standing around in shock. "This is a serious breach in security," he said. "Someone will pay for this."

The man by the buffet swallowed and looked a little sick.

Three security guards charged into the room.

The older man pointed at Alex, who remained in the chair with her feet up on the table.

Alex yawned and finished the water.

"Get her out of my chair and find out how she got in here and who she is," the old man ordered, pointing at her. "This is a major breach of security and someone will pay for it."

The security guards moved with well-trained synchronization, a sign that signaled danger to anyone who knew something about fighting.

Alex knew quite a bit about fighting. She felt the world slow down around her. The rush of the three men, all about her size with hard, chiseled bodies under dark suits and white shirts, turned into a movie special effect. Alex tossed the empty water bottle up in the air.

Only one of the security guards watched it, his attention drifting from the formation of their assault. The other two were well trained and kept their attention on their goal.

"Get up," one of them ordered, reaching for her as the men attempted to surround her on the chair.

Alex grabbed his outstretched hand and moved out of the chair. Her moves came with a fluidity which belied their speed. She twisted to ram her elbow into the reaching man's face. His head jerked backwards and he went down. She spun, swept the second man's feet out from under him even as he tried to set himself for a fight. She punched him hard in the temple. He crumbled to the ground beside the first man. She caught the empty water bottle and the attention of the third guard.

He swung at her, fast.

Alex blocked the swing and brought her knee into his side. She grabbed his hand, twisted it.

He fell to the ground with a grunt, his face twisted with pain as she controlled the pressure points on his arm. Still he tried to bring up his other hand and punch her exposed side.

She threw her leg in front of the punch and pounded her knee into his face.

339

He flew backwards. His head bounced off the floor. Like the other two, he lay there unconscious.

Alex didn't bother to make sure they were unconscious. She knew exactly how hard she'd hit them and how badly she'd hurt them. All of them faced time in a hospital. The last guy probably would have headaches for a very long time. The instantaneous brutality of the violence shocked some of the suits in the room. A smirk pulled across her lips as she sized up the suits.

Akiko stared, her face pale and her lips pressed together in a thin line. Her glasses magnified her eyes.

Alex stepped over the bodies and up to the old man.

"You have no idea what you have done here," the old man spat at her. "You will pay for this." He turned to Akiko. "Call—"

Alex's hand shot out like a cobra striking out at a victim. She grabbed the man's shirt and tie. Her eyes burned in fury.

He sputtered, the words lost on his lips.

"We won't be getting rescued from our own egos today," Alex said in a low, menacing voice. "I am upset that my proxy to this board is not being allowed to exercise her power as if she were me. So I decided to attend this board meeting myself. Imagine my surprise when I discover that the person pushing her out has been stealing money from the corporation, my corporation."

Color drained from his face.

Small gasps of shock drifted through the room.

One of the girls came into the boardroom. She stopped and gave a little breathless cry.

Alex shoved the older man back a few steps. She turned on one of the suits, the one the old man had threatened.

"You're head of security?" she asked.

He stiffened, lifted his chin and nodded. "*Hai.*" Beneath his suit, muscles were hard and ropey. His jaw was set.

"Tired of having your decisions second guessed and over-ridden by people who know virtually nothing about security?"

she asked. "Upset that you can't seem to hire anyone with extensive financial security experience?"

He swallowed. His eyes darted at the old man for a second, then back at Alex.

Alex arched an eyebrow at him and twitched her head to him indicating he better answer.

"Yes," he said. "I am. There is a breach in protocol for this building."

Alex smiled. "What power does your word hold on this board?"

"Hayashi-san—"

Alex waved a hand to interrupt him. "Forget about Hayashi-san. Can you work for a woman?"

He nodded. "I often collaborate with Tanaka-san on—"

"Good," Alex said. "A security expert should be high ranking in a security company." She turned to Akiko as several men came in to help the wounded. "He's your new Vice Chairman of the board."

"You can't do that," the old man growled. "The board has to vote and—"

"I am the majority stock holder in the company. Me, personally. Sakai did not put it in a trust. And despite years of you people trying to get me to sign things, it remains mine. As such, the bylaws of the corporation also clearly state that I can fire and hire and appoint from and to the board of directors at any time that I might choose. A power that Akiko Tanaka has been denied due to the inability of some to respect the rules of her proxy status." She glared at the other men in the room. "If any of the rest of you have a problem taking orders from a woman, you should resign. You should resign quickly. I'm not known for my patience."

The broken men on the ground had started to moan and wake up. Alex grinned at Akiko. "I kind of like this corporate crap. Maybe I'll stick around for the rest of the meeting."

"No!" Akiko said, a tinge of panic in her voice.

Alex arched an eyebrow.

"I mean, I'm sure you're jetlagged and hungry and have other things to do," Akiko said quickly.

Alex shrugged. "Board meetings seem more exciting than I expected."

Akiko eyed the security chief.

"Oh, I think the two of us can handle things with Tanaka-san acting as your proxy," the chief said.

Alex glared at everyone in the room to make sure that would happen. She didn't see any defiance in the group. "Okay then. If you call one of your security men to drive, I will just escort Hayashi out of the building."

The old man stiffened. "I have a driver," he said.

Alex laughed at him. "The corporation pays for your driver and your car. You no longer work for the corporation."

He paled and a shiver ran through him. He lifted his jaw and his eyes went cold and deadly. "You have made a very big mistake."

Alex rolled her eyes. She grabbed his arm and started leading him out of the room. She shot a glance at Akiko who stared at her with concern.

Hayashi pulled his arm out of her grip and straightened his suit jacket. "You will pay for this. I promise you this. Perhaps you can ruin me here, but you won't be able to damage me elsewhere."

Alex let him go, she walked beside him towards the elevator, making sure he kept moving forward. He seemed to pick up pace as if anxious to get out of the place now. Workers were beginning to show up, many of them glancing at the man they'd come to fear and the redhead with the Western features. Hayashi kept his head up and made it look as if he were going willingly. Saving face was everything for the Japanese. Alex could have humiliated him more, but she didn't feel like it. Truth was, she was hungry and she wanted to get north. She'd spent two weeks in Thailand, in the jungle recuperating, but now she needed to start getting her training back up to par. She needed to run stairs. Soon, the Offspring would be ready to attack. She'd need to be ready for them. Whatever Hayashi wanted to do, as long as he left and stopped subjugating Akiko, Alex didn't care. "And you won't be able to embezzle funds to construct an arena to plot my death any longer," Alex said. "A decade of construction, it must be quite a place."

"You are nothing but a thief. This is money I earned. Not you."

"This is money that the Offspring were supposed to protect and administrate for the weapon which cannot be named. Which is me, Hayashi. Unlike others, I don't need this money. It should be accumulating exponentially. Instead you've used it for yourself. You've forgotten the dedication of your ancestors and made it about yourself. Of course, I expect nothing less from the descendant of the man who murdered the last True One for his own personal gain. I suppose you come by your greed and your ignorance by genetic code."

"I will destroy you and reunite the weapon with its rightful owner. I will beg it for forgiveness for the errors of my ancestors. And then I will destroy Akiko Tanaka for trying to stop me from righting the universe."

The elevator doors opened. Alex grabbed his shirt and whipped him into the room.

He collided hard with the back wall of the empty elevator.

Alex followed him in to the small room.

He stared at her, eyes widening.

The doors closed behind her.

"You can't hurt me," the man said.

"I am a killer," Alex replied. "You and the rest of the Offspring should go back and read your own history. Hell, you want me to be your private assassin. Remember this. If anything happens to Akiko Tanaka, I will kill you in ways more horrific than you can imagine. I will kill your children and your wife and anyone who might even remotely carry a smidgeon of your pathetic DNA. I will wipe every trace of you off this planet. Then I will start on the rest of the Offspring and I won't stop until I've exhausted all of my rage." She took a deep, shaky breath. "And I have a lot of rage, you self-righteous prick. Centuries of anger. Generations of rage. You

343

cannot imagine what that feels like to carry around. I will be happy to expend it on your bloodline."

The elevator doors opened.

Alex turned and glared at the people waiting to get in.

They took a step back. By instinct, they all stepped aside to make a pathway.

Alex felt the cold of the weapon searing through her bones, hungry, angry, lusting for revenge and feeling the victory of its recent challenge. She stepped back and waved the older man out.

He paled. Alex followed him as he walked the gauntlet.

At the end of the gauntlet was a monk. His eyes were hard and in control.

Alex met his eyes and felt a kinship.

He gave a slight nod.

She slipped into the crowd.

The old man turned to say something to her. He blinked at the empty space behind him.

The monk approached him. "Sir, you should never look back. It is dangerous."

"This isn't over," Hayashi promised.

Guang shrugged. "That is your choice."

90235486R00189

Made in the USA
Columbia, SC
28 February 2018